Awakened Runes

The Rune Fire Cycle, Volume 1

Lance VanGundy

Published by Lance VanGundy, 2021.

AWAKENED RUNES

Second edition. December 9, 2021.

ISBN: 978-1735427256

Written by Lance VanGundy.

Table of Contents

Dedication

I imagined writing this page often over the years, mainly as a way to motivate myself to keep looking forward with "eyes to the horizon." I shall try to be brief.

First, I am a child of old school D&D, with one parent who served as the dungeon master to my small goofy troupe of friends and the other the dungeon mistress. You know the scenes from Stranger Things where the boys roll dice in a frenzied panic to see if the fireball spell works against the demigorgon? Add a forty-year-oldmenacing DM, a few more fellas, a few bowls of candy, and that was us. Mom and Dad provided a safe place to geek-out, binge on skittles, and lose ourselves to imaginary worlds of fantasy. For their inspiration, I am forever grateful.

Next, nothing good comes out of my efforts without the unconditional support from my wife of more than thirty years. You are the spark behind any of my motivations.The same can be said of our three children, all girls, all amazing in their own journeys. Yes, I know "their own" is a tautology. If that bothers you, mayhaps this is not the book for you. Thank you all for your belief, encouragement, and support.

A special thanks to my beta readers: Bill Edens, Brian Bentley, Colette Lothe, Jason VanGundy, and Madisun VanGundy. Your willingness to read and respond to my work was both a kindness and tremendous motivation. To a struggling author, it was the much needed water at the end of a long walk in the desert.

I am grateful to my patient editor, Courtney Andersson of Elevation Editorial.Thanks so much for your work on this project. I do, though, wonder if I am the first author to feel like the inventor of past perfect tense should have been, or possibly should be rightly smited? Should might yet to have had a smiting?

Thank you for the wonderful cover art Jamie Noble Frier of thenobleartist.com!

Finally, if you are taking the time to get to know Karsk and the characters that call this place home, then thank you, most of all, reader.

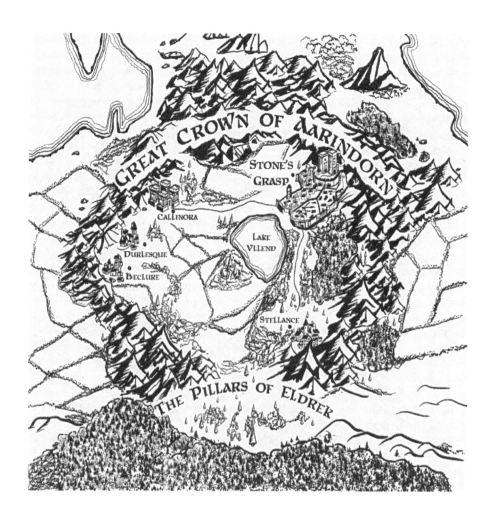

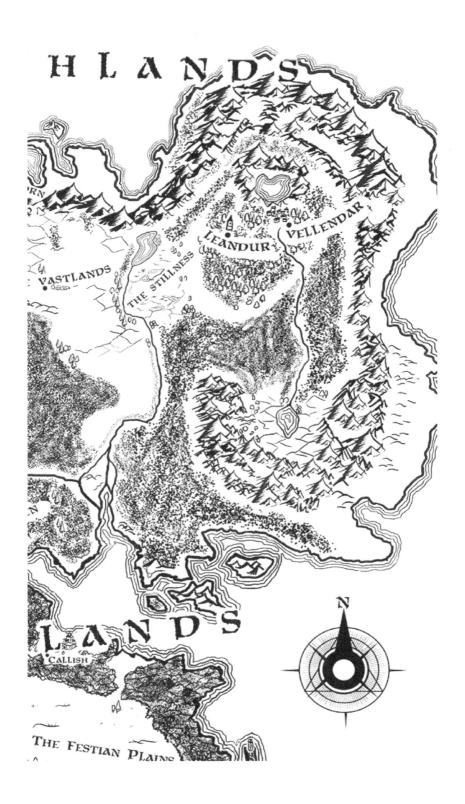

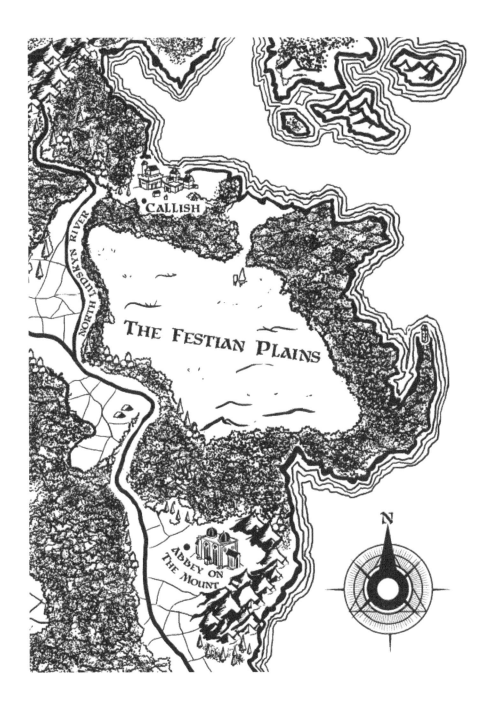

Chapter One: All Bindings Crack

Trade winds off the coast whisked sea spray up a rocky bluff and across three tents, speckling the shelters in a fine patina. Inside his tent, Bryndor Scrivson rubbed his thumb across the smooth leather of a stowed saddle, removing a thin layer of salty powder. Something about the air here made everything sticky, and the leather felt more supple. He often discovered strange things like this when he traveled with his brother and uncle in their work as cartographers.

He inhaled the aromas of the morning seascape and could not decide if the sensation was pleasant or cloying. The sea saturated everything from their clothing to their bedrolls and even made the parchment tacky.

While I would give a lot for dry clothing and a hot bowl of Aunt Ro's stew, I could probably get used to this life. At least it makes sense that everyone sees me as a stranger out here.

He sat long moments thinking about how his life might change once they finished their current project mapping the remote territories of Vendal Braveska, the king of Hammond. The contract guaranteed a wage more than double the amount of any previous expedition. With his bit of coin, he could strike out on his own. His sense of excitement about that possibility withered, however, as he thought about how to tell his uncle he planned to leave.

"Bryn, hurry up with the map!" The deep voice of his Uncle Kaellor interrupted his thoughts. Bryndor lifted the saddle to reveal several long, cylindrical leather cases. He fingered over the tubes to make sure the caps remained sealed, keeping all of their precious work protected from the elements.

With Kaellor's guidance, Bryndor and his brother had drafted some of the most accurate maps of the Southlands. In numerous expeditions over the last few years, they'd navigated the western coast of the lands south of the massive trek of the Korjinth Mountains. The outings had given the brothers a unique opportunity to combine adventure, their nimble minds, and no small amount of math in completing their projects. All the while, their uncle cultivated in them a natural education and sense of wonder about the different regions they traveled.

Bryndor retrieved the largest tubular case and a small box of writing instruments and tucked them both under his arm. After emerging from his tent, he sucked a bit of briny powder from his thumb. The crystals melted, leaving a faint mineral taste on the back of his tongue. He would definitely have to trade for some of that before heading home. The salt alone made the difference between eating to live and living to eat. He ducked into the tent where his uncle and brother knelt around a small portable table.

"Here you go, Kae." Bryndor offered the cylinder case, then plopped down beside his brother. The two shared a friendly glance, their resemblance evident as they sat side by side.

Lluthean, the younger of the two at fourteen years of age, was growing the beginnings of a scruffy beard. His nimble fingers were always busy, and lately, he'd taken to rolling a flat stone across the top of his knuckles. While both young men stared back at the world with their father's penetrating grey eyes, Lluthean favored their mother, with light brown hair and a lean frame. In particular, her nature permeated his smile and the agile way he mounted a horse—or so Kaellor always said. However, despite his supposed resemblance to their mother, Bryndor struggled to imagine a female version of his brother.

Bryndor, only two years older and broad-shouldered, puffed a breath of air at his unruly strands of dark hair that draped below his brow. He hoped his Aunt Rona would tolerate his unkempt bangs and scruffy beard; he rather liked the way the wind caught in his hair when they rode. Unfortunately, attending to their haircuts would probably be one of her first priorities when they returned home. He combed his hair back with his fingers, then withdrew several writing instruments and a compass from the delicate wooden box.

Kaellor grasped the leather cylinder and removed the lid, producing a resonant thump. Mindful of the delicate nature of their project, he unrolled a large parchment onto the table.

"Llu, the clamps if you will," said Kaellor. Lluthean moved to secure the edges of the map, his clever fingers making quick work of the stiff clasps.

"Alright. We left the port of Malvress some ten miles to the north of our current location." Kaellor indicated a point on the map north of their current position. "Measure it out in leagues and start with Malvress, Bryn."

Bryndor started to measure the map with the compass and ruler, saying his calculations out loud. "Right. Ten miles, and that makes three and a third leagues, which puts Malvress right about here." He moved to record the town, but Lluthean interrupted him with a gentle hand. Bryndor paused and looked up with a puzzled expression.

"Don't you mean five leagues?" Lluthean asked.

Bryndor considered the map a long moment, puzzling out his brother's calculation. He knew Lluthean usually had the right of things and was offering the correction without malice.

"Remember, here along the coast, with all of this irregular terrain, a league is not as far as back home," said Lluthean. He continued coaxing the stone across his knuckles, the activity drawing an unusual expression of focused intensity.

"How did I miss that?" Bryndor shook his head. "So two miles in a league, not three. Thanks, Llu."

How many other times have I made a similar mistake? If it were up to just me, our maps would have folks walking in circles.

Before drafting a permanent emblem for Malvress, Bryndor double-checked the accuracy of its location on the map. He looked to Kaellor for reassurance. His uncle winked, appearing satisfied with Bryndor's precision, but said nothing. Bryndor nodded and committed to the action.

After recording the town on the map, he sifted through several smaller parchments, reading the notes he'd made the previous day. He inscribed the map with significant points where the coastline had surrendered to rocky headlands and where the ocean currents had carved out fjords.

Eventually, he had consulted the last of his notes and looked up, breaking the silence. "There, that's the first third of our day. Who kept a record of the next leg?" he asked, holding up the writing tools.

Lluthean leaned closer to their makeshift workspace. "That would be me, royal cartographer to His Majesty King Vendal!" he announced with a dramatic flourish. Without consulting any notes, Lluthean began recording the terrain in detail where his brother had left off.

Bryndor relaxed back and shook his head in wonder as Lluthean documented his portion of their travels from memory. *Circles indeed, you are more blessed than you know, brother.*

With his contribution complete, Lluthean handed the instruments to his uncle. Kaellor pulled thick, black hair behind his ears and revealed the same grey Scrivson eyes, a strong jaw, and angular cheekbones. His bushy black beard had started to show his age with a shock of silver at the chin, and little crow's feet accentuated his eyes when he smiled, though he smiled less and less these days. He consulted his notes and updated the map to their current location.

"From here, we should make the outskirts of Hammond by tomorrow evening if we head south along the King's Road," said Kaellor. He removed the wooden clamps, rolled up the map, and replaced it in the sealed leather case.

"It's been a long couple of months away from home. Aunt Rona had to make due longer than we planned," said Bryndor. He grunted with the effort of pulling apart the stout legs supporting the table. The wood, swollen with the humid sea air, released from the fittings only after considerable effort.

"Rona's a capable woman and doubtless had no trouble managing back home in Journey's Bend. But you're right. This project carried us farther south than I intended," said Kaellor. "You've both done well. With our survey of the Southlands finally complete, we should keep busy for the next year with the reprints alone."

"Do you think we've been gone too long?" Bryndor asked. "I mean, I know people back home won't remember us, but will it affect Aunt Ro?"

"Your aunt practically raised you both. The mantle that conceals you is strong, but I don't think it's enough to erase all those years, and besides, she's too stubborn to forget you," Kaellor replied. "No, it works in a more subtle way to obscure the memories of people who meet you for short periods of time. As you practically grew up on the Tellends' farm, I don't think they will have difficulties remembering you either. But most of the others in Journey's Bend will have to get to know you all over again."

Bryndor recalled the countless times he'd befriended strangers on their travels. He often used the encounters to test the strength of the mantle. He would share stories about himself, and Lluthean would add heroic embellishments to make the stories more memorable. But in the morning, their new acquaintance never seemed to recall meeting them or hearing about their fictional adventures. The experience only created more alienation.

Lluthean, on the other hand, found endless ways to turn the anonymity to his advantage. Especially in Journey's Bend, Lluthean had become adept at learning what made someone happy and even better at finding out what motivated them to action.

While his brother seemed to enjoy their concealment, Bryndor often thought about how difficult it was to make meaningful friendships when everyone you met forgot you existed. Every time they showed up in a town, the locals looked upon them as foreigners, and it didn't help that they looked like outsiders. Their slightly taller than average height and grey eyes marked them as from the lands north of the Korjinth, and while most of the people they interacted with were polite, sometimes that's all they were.

So, more and more, he had been considering striking out on his own. He worried about leaving his aunt and uncle to make his own life, but many young men left their families around the age of seventeen, and that was only about a year away for Bryndor.

That grinded mantle gets in the way of everything.

How would he buy a plot of land if nobody could recall selling it to him? How could he settle down and make a family if no woman could remember him calling on her? How many times would he have this internal conversation? He wished he could be more like his brother.

Lluthean pocketed the stone and cocked his head to the side. "You look like you just swallowed one of Aunt Ro's medicines."

Bryndor sighed. "I was just thinking about how hard it can be to start all over again."

"There is one good thing about it, Bryn," said Lluthean. "Since nobody can remember us, we don't have to go around making up names or remembering what names we gave; isn't that right, Kevold?"

Kaellor cocked an eyebrow at his nephew but only shrugged a response. They all knew he'd chosen the rather pedestrian name "Kevold" because it afforded a degree of anonymity. He had used the name successfully for years and tied it legally to all their work.

Lluthean stood and stretched, then said through a yawn, "The sooner we start, the sooner we get to an inn with a real bed and something that passes for hot food."

Bryndor held his hand out, happy for the distraction. "Help me to my feet, and we can take down the tents." Lluthean hoisted his brother up. Over the next hour, they attended to familiar tasks: securing their maps, packing the tents, and preparing their mounts.

Bryndor saddled Kaellor's horse, then greeted his own gelding with a pat on the nose as he gazed out toward the sea. Voshna, the pale blue moon, hung low on the horizon, obscuring all but a sliver of her sister Vaeda, the red moon. Both waned in the morning light.

"Good morning, Scout," he whispered to his horse. The oldest of their mounts, Scout, was part of the family. Bryndor thought the old gelding might be the only friend outside of his immediate family who remembered him. The horse still managed to pull the wagon once a week, and Bryndor favored his steady temperament.

He placed the saddle on Scout, then secured the bindings before giving him a small apple. Usually, Scout responded with a nicker of appreciation, but today he just took the treat and turned his attention to the coast. The old horse perked his ears forward and pawed once at the ground.

"Does something about being so close to the sea make you nervous? We'll be going soon enough, and you don't have to pull the wagon today, boy," he said.

They alternated which mount pulled the small pack-wagon, and today was Lluthean's turn to guide the cargo. Bryndor walked over to the tracings and sighed when he discovered their condition. Lluthean had unharnessed Scout from the wagon the night before and left everything in a tangled mess. Bryndor tugged at the leather straps encrusted with mud.

By the Drift, Llu, when are you going to learn? It's like you tried to make a mess of things.

He took a long breath and prepared to call out for Lluthean to sort out the snarled tracings, but a rumbling cascade of boulders startled him to silence. Loud clacks of rock colliding with timber punctuated the growing thunder on the cliffside. The sounds of the avalanche lasted nearly a minute, followed by distant screams and shouts of alarm.

The three men rushed to the cliffside at the edge of their camp to look down. At the bottom of the cape, the King's Road rose just above the ocean and sat against the rocky face. They watched in disbelief as the last of a massive rockslide of timber and boulders smashed into what appeared to be a horse-drawn caravan and escort. Men screamed in alarm and agony. Several bodies lay crushed under the debris, barely visible under a rising cloud of dust.

Lluthean looked on fish-mouthed, but Bryndor looked back up the cliff face and spied a small group of men picking their way down toward the caravan. They crept with purpose and had their weapons drawn. He tapped his uncle on the shoulder and directed Kaellor's attention to the bandits.

"We have to help them," said Bryndor, his words quickened by his heartbeat.

"Grab your hunting bows; we'll have to circle around to get down there," said Kaellor. "You two ride double; there's no time to waste saddling your mount, Llu."

The boys raced to grab their weapons and followed Kaellor as he urged his mount south down the gradual slope. Once they reached the road, they turned north and began galloping toward the ambush.

Despite their urgency, the descent down to the King's Road and back north felt like it took a long time, too long. Scout panted hard from the exertion, and Bryndor tried to keep the old gelding from making abrupt turns for fear of throwing Lluthean. He wondered how his brother was managing to hold the bows and quivers and still remain on horseback.

At last, they drew up adjacent to Kaellor, who remained atop his horse as he surveyed the site of the devastation. The three watched as the cloud of dust and debris dissipated, leaving behind a bloody landscape along the base of the shaded cape. Timbers and boulders had ground up at least two men and one horse, judging by the number of exposed mangled limbs. Bryndor wrinkled his nose; already, the iron scent of blood had spoiled the sea spray.

He took in the scene and found himself uncertain of how to proceed but felt reassured by his uncle's composure. Kaellor just sat, considering and listening. Though they lived a life of some variety and adventure, they'd never experienced violence like the scene before them. Bryndor wished they had time to prepare a plan, but necessity mandated prompt action. Kaellor seemed to sense as much and gave them direction.

"Tie up Scout here and dismount. Be prepared to cover me with your bows. If you have a shot, don't hesitate. Never hesitate." Though he spoke with resolve, he turned a soft gaze on the brothers. "Better to beg forgiveness from the dead than linger as a ghost of regret above your own corpse." He edged his mount forward at a steady walk.

Bryndor dismounted and strung their bows while Lluthean tied Scout to a piece of deadfall.

"What now?" asked Lluthean with a strained whisper.

Bryndor licked salty beads from his upper lip and made a quick assessment. "I'll go up to get a better vantage point. Why don't you see if you can get around between the rubble and cliffside? Pick your way through the shadows."

Lluthean nodded once, then crept around the debris. Bryndor watched him disappear, then climbed on top of the fallen timbers and boulders. Looking down, he saw the shiny knee joint of a horse protruding from the rubble. Shredded, pink muscle and sinew surrounded the odd, rounded bone. Thick, bloody, purple ropes of bowel coiled on the ground below the bone, but the rest of the horse lay buried under rock. Bryndor's limbs quivered with an odd weak feeling, and cold sweat soaked the shirt at the small of his back. For just a moment, he felt light-headed and nearly lost his footing.

From his perch, he counted at least six dead men trapped in the rubble. Four wore chainmail and two the exquisite silks that adorned those of the court. By the insignias on their uniforms, all of them claimed affiliation to the royal house of Malvress: a silver scale set off-balance on one side by a large fish.

He eased forward onto a larger boulder and discovered three more dead. However, these bodies were not crushed by the debris. Marked by their camouflaged garb, these belonged to the bandit party. Blood congealed like dark purple pudding on the corpses from a variety of wounds.

His mouth watered, and he swallowed back a wave of nausea before drawing a deep breath to steady his nerve. The fight must have been terrible. One man looked to have bled out from a wound that had removed most of his left arm. Another's face was caved in on the right, and his left eye bulged out unnaturally. Another lay with his head set at an unnatural angle, a garish slash deep into the side of his neck, nearly decapitating the corpse. Two had gaping belly wounds, and the fetid stink of blood and excrement hung heavy in the air. *By all the darkness in the Drift, the ride down here took a long time.*

At the thought, he lifted his attention from the butchery. *Where did you go, brother?*

He knew Lluthean was working his way around the backside of the debris but couldn't see him just now. Bryndor redirected his attention to the careful progress of his uncle.

Kaellor directed his gelding around a boulder and discovered a lone man sitting with his back to one of the fallen timbers. He wore a polished breastplate and the crest of Malvress. The knight panted with shallow breaths, and an unnatural whistling wheeze escaped from some wound under his chest piece. Rivulets of dark blood trickled from the wounds visible on his legs and from others under his breastplate. The crimson streams mixed with the blood spilled from the bandits, four of whose corpses lay at his feet. The man turned even more pale and sweaty at Kaellor's approach.

"Please," he rasped. "I'm done. But Lesand, she yet lives, and there are still a few more. Please, for Malvress." The knight coughed a pink, foamy material from his mouth, and his eyes fluttered closed. He twitched unnaturally for several seconds.

Kaellor turned and made eye contact with Bryndor, still hidden on top of the boulder. He nodded once, then drew Bryndor's attention to the carriage, which sat lopsided at the side of the road. The front wheel had been shattered by stones from the avalanche, and three of the bandits stood with casual arrogance outside the carriage. A young woman screamed from just inside the doorway to the carriage, and a middle-aged thug dressed in worn brown leathers stumbled back a few steps after she kicked him in the face. The man grunted but smiled, unharmed.

"I see the filly's got some spunk! Good, I like a fighter!" He grinned and produced a long curved knife.

The other thugs chuckled, and one responded, "Be sure you leave something for us, Elcid!"

Kaellor cleared his throat. "I don't think the lady prefers your company."

The men turned to glare at Kaellor. "Where did you come from?" asked the one named Elcid as he held forth the menacing knife. The bandit appeared to be in his fourth decade, older than Kaellor, with unkempt, straggly grey hair matted by too many nights without a bath. Even at this distance, Bryndor nearly gagged at the stink of dirty feet mixed with a sickeningly sweet odor of sweat and lust. Two of the others held similar weapons, and one brandished a short sword.

Elcid seemed to consider Kaellor, who sat relaxed and confident astride the gelding but wore none of the fancy clothing common among the noble classes. "You're no royal!" he spat accusingly, then smiled as if the pronouncement alone released him from any consequence. His beady, nervous eyes scanned their surroundings.

Bryndor crouched low behind the debris and cursed inwardly at the heavy thrum of blood in his ears. His hands trembled so much he had difficulty nocking an arrow to the bow. To occupy his mind and settle his nerve, he carried out a deliberate mental assessment of the brutes.

Elcid held a crude knife. Neither his dirt-stained clothes nor his blade showed any blood. He appeared to have avoided all of the direct violence of the initial attack. *The man must only be an opportunist.*

Bryndor thought he likely survived off the leftovers and that his companions must have carried out most of the hostilities. A small pot belly draped over his trousers, but he had thin arms and a ruddy nose. *So he spends too much time at the bottle as well.* Under Kaellor's silent, unyielding scrutiny, the thug fingered his knife nervously.

Two of the others looked not much older than Bryndor. They shifted their weight from side to side and kept looking back to Elcid. The last thug looked to be in his prime and had a few scars on his muscled arms. This man wielded a bloodstained short sword that reflected the sunlight from its decorative hilt.

He must have pulled that from one of the escorts. That's too fine a weapon for any in this lot; still four on three, though. Lutney favor the odds.

"You, you better get now," said Elcid. He took a nervous step with his knife held forward. "You got no business here, and we're taking what's ours!"

"Be that as it may, I have to wonder," Kaellor replied, "what tragedy befell you to make you murder all these men and defile a noblewoman? You lose a wife? Children? You'll pardon me, but none of you really have the look of the marrying type."

Clearly confused by the turn of the conversation, the thugs looked first at Kaellor and then to Elcid in confusion. The grimy man screwed up his face and answered, "Look, I ain't never been tied to no woman and certainly don't suffer no bastards runnin' 'round my feet! None that I know of."

"I thought you said you were only taking what was taken from you. If you lost no woman and no children, then again, I ask what? What was taken from you that gives you just cause to act this way?" Kaellor challenged.

Bryndor watched his uncle use the momentary distraction of the conversation to slide his hand back against his saddle, reaching for a dagger. He knew Kaellor kept the weapon secreted there but had never seen him reach for it in all their travels.

"That's it!" The ruffian slammed the door to the carriage shut and strode forward, brandishing his blade. "You trying to talk me to death? Be on your way, or we'll send you to Mogdure!"

Kaellor sighed. "I would advise you against invoking the god of death unless you plan to greet him in the Drift yourself."

Elcid seemed once again bewildered by Kaellor's calm banter. Even the man wielding the sword lowered his weapon and turned to Elcid for direction. The grimy leader seemed to assess their options for a moment, then screwed up his face in anger. "Get him!"

Everything happened all at once, but Bryndor kept his eye trained on Elcid. The leader stepped forward as the other three fanned out to circle Kaellor. A quick nicker from Kaellor directed his gelding to retreat a few steps, creating a bit more distance between him and the bandits.

As the thug with the sword strode forward, Kaellor flowed off the saddle with a lithe economy of motion. Once on the ground, he picked up a fistful of sand and tossed it at the man with the sword. The bandit grunted in surprise and staggered back with a wild swing of the weapon while rubbing at his eyes. Kaellor swept in low and thrust the knife up into the man's chest. The thug grunted and dropped the short sword before crumpling to the ground.

Kaellor grabbed the sword just as the two younger men lurched forward into the melee. Kaellor shifted to his right, then cleaved the short sword into the shoulder and neck of the thug on that side. The man fell back, grabbing at the sword. Without pause, his uncle turned and threw his dagger at the last young man. The blade embedded into his chest, and the bandit stared dumbly at the weapon as he dropped to his knees.

From somewhere to the right, one of Lluthean's arrows skittered harmlessly to the ground. Elcid had raised his knife and was prepared to join the fight, but upon seeing the arrow, he turned and ran toward Lluthean. His brother just stood there, casual as a house cat out for a stroll on the King's Road.

Bryndor felt his body move as if by instinct. A small part of his awareness screamed from a corner of his mind. *Is this really happening? Grind me straight to the Drift! Llu, what are you doing?*

Bryndor rose and balanced his feet on the boulder, drew a deep breath, focused on Elcid's back just between the shoulder blades, pulled the bowstring to his jaw, and in a fluid motion, released the arrow. He watched the shaft streak with an odd, slow purpose through the air.

The grimy man's steps halted when the soft twang from Bryndor's bow was followed by the eruption of an arrow from his chest. He fingered the bloodied tip of the barb in confusion, then turned to observe Bryndor standing on top of the large boulder.

Bryndor stared at the man down another arrow shaft.

When did I notch another arrow?

He waited to see if the man would take a step.

How many arrows does it take to bring a man down?

He released a second arrow, and it sunk deep into the man's belly. The thug curled forward, then slumped to the ground, gasping with labored wheezing.

Bryndor looked to his uncle for direction. Kaellor took a moment to survey the surroundings. The muscled bandit twitched on his back in death. The two younger thugs stared with dead eyes at the sky. Bright red stains blossomed from the killing wounds on all three corpses. The fresh stink of excrement lingered in the air.

"A bad end for bad men," said Kaellor, as he retrieved his knife.

Kaellor approached Elcid. The thug kneeled on the sand and struggled to reach his blade, which lay just beyond his reach. Kaellor bent down and placed the handle of the knife in the thug's hand. The man grimaced with each shallow breath, and bright red bubbles frothed around the arrow exiting his chest. Pink and purple spongy lung tissue hung from the menacing barbs. Kaellor leaned in close, enduring the peppery stink.

"Though you likely deserve it, no man should suffer long in agony. I can help you or leave you to your misery. It's your choice," said Kaellor.

Defeated and panting in splinted breaths, the man nodded.

"Alright, then, are you ready?"

"Do it!" the man growled.

Without a word, Kaellor wrapped his hands around the bandit's, holding him fast to the handle of the blade. He plunged the rusty knife hilt-deep into the left side of Elcid's chest. The weapon entered with a crack, splitting a rib. The bandit grunted with wide-eyed surprise.

"It still takes a moment," said Kaellor in answer to the man's pleading silent question. After several seconds, the thug relaxed his grip, and his agony ceased.

Kaellor reached down and grabbed a handful of sand and the petals of a small pink wildflower. He rubbed his hands together vigorously to remove the lingering taint of the thug's odor, then stood and waved his nephews over toward the broken carriage.

Lluthean gawked at the corpse of the last bandit. Bryndor thought it strange how fast all the color had drained from Elcid's ruddy complexion. Though his eyes held no expression, his jaw muscles still moved as if the body was trying to draw breath.

"Is that normal? Is he dead?" Bryndor asked cautiously.

"He's well on his way. You did well; are you alright?" Kaellor asked softly.

Bryndor only shrugged and nodded, staring at the bloodied meat still clinging to the protruding barb. His arms felt suddenly very heavy. He became aware once again of his tunic sticking to the small of his back where an unnatural sweat gathered.

"Do they always smell that bad?" Lluthean asked, holding his nose.

"That's not death on the man; he simply stinks," Kaellor replied plainly.

Bryndor reached down to retrieve the errant arrow Lluthean had released. He considered the initial volley and wondered if his brother had lost his nerve. Lluthean was usually the better marksman with the bow. "Your aim seemed a little low, Llu?"

"After hanging onto you and the bows all the way here, my arms cramped up. I wasn't certain I could make any shot, especially with all those moving targets. So I thought to at least get his attention. He's kind of a gangly fellow." Lluthean smiled and placed the arrow back in his quiver. "So I thought to get him to turn a bit and give you a broad target. Besides, if I missed wide, I might have hit Kae. Where you stood, the shot was better."

"The task is well begun, but not finished. Let's see to any survivors." Kaellor approached the carriage.

Kaellor cleared his throat. "You can come out now; it's safe. You will come to no harm."

A long moment of silence passed, so Kaellor stepped forward and tapped on the door. "My nephews and I travel to Hammond. Your escort is dead, and the King's Road has proved a dangerous place. Why don't you come on out, and we can see you safely on."

The carriage door creaked open, and a brown-eyed adolescent girl with dark skin stepped into the light but remained hesitant at the threshold. She twirled a nervous finger through black wavy hair, and the breeze caught at the hem of her delicate silken gown. "You will not hurt me?" she asked with a quivering lip.

Bryndor stared, shocked. He looked back at the corpse of the man named Elcid with renewed disgust. Then he wondered who might require such a large escort.

Kaellor took a knee, then spoke, "No child, we only came to help. I'm sorry for your loss. Is there anyone else with you?"

The girl nodded. "Yes, but I fear they are all dead. That man, the one you shot, he choked my governess blue, and now she's dead." The girl's gaze lingered on the bloodied rubble. "Did none of them survive, not even my guardian, Lord Krestus?"

Kaellor sighed. "If Krestus wore a breastplate, then he died fighting to protect you, child, but not before he dispatched four of them."

"Then, I really am the only one?" she whimpered as tears pooled in her eyes.

"Yes, I'm afraid so," Kaellor replied. "My name is Kevold, and these are my nephews, Bryndor and Lluthean. We are surveying the King's Road for King Vendal and travel to Hammond. What's your name, child?"

The question gave the girl cause to attempt to regain her composure. She inhaled, stifling a sob. After a few moments, she wiped away her tears and stood taller in the threshold of the carriage. "I know who you are, my lord. You met my father only a few days back. My name is Lesand, youngest daughter of Duke Leland Braveska in Malvress and niece to His Majesty Vendal Braveska, high king of Hammond. I'm to spend summer at court and attend my aunt, the Queen Shellend Braveska."

"Your father is Duke Leland?" Bryndor asked, now appreciating her resemblance to the younger brother of King Vendal.

"The king and queen will doubtless be concerned for your safety," said Kaellor. "Why don't you come along with us, and we'll see you safely to your uncle?"

Lesand burst into tears, scurried over to Kaellor, and buried her face in his side. He endured her embrace with awkward silence for a few moments before patting her on the back. They all remained still until her sobs eased.

"Bryn, why don't you and Llu retrieve our things and our wagon. I'll stay here with Lesand until you return," said Kaellor.

Happy to leave the carnage behind, Bryndor mounted Scout and pulled Lluthean up behind him. They allowed the old gelding to return to camp at an easy pace. He felt exhausted and shivered as the breeze caught at his sweat-soaked clothing. He rolled his shoulders, trying to release the sense of fatigue. Behind him, Lluthean repeatedly flipped a small, flat stone in the air with his thumb. As Scout stumbled on the uneven ground, the rock arced close to Bryndor's cheek, but his brother snatched it from the air.

Bryndor readjusted his balance in the saddle and secured his bow across his lap. "You took quite a chance down there, trusting me with that shot," he said.

"I don't know that I had much of a choice. I spoke true when I said my arms were cramped," said Lluthean in between flips. "But I think I just knew you would manage it. You always manage things when it comes right down to it. You always do what needs . . . doing, you know? I guess I figured it would be like that, and I was right." Lluthean jabbed Bryndor's ribs lightly, giving emphasis to his declaration and causing Bryndor to chuckle.

"Still, what were you going to do if I missed?" Bryndor asked. "Run away?"

"Well," said Lluthean, "I only have to run faster than you. So yes, running could work, I suppose. I didn't really have time to think about it. And thanks to you and Kae, I didn't have to." Lluthean flipped the stone a few more times, then stopped his repetitive game. "I've never seen him move like that. Kae, I mean."

Bryndor nodded, chewing on his lower lip. "Me either. Sometimes it's better to be lucky than good, but Kae never relies on luck."

"He moved so fast. First one, then the other," said Lluthean. "It was like he had the whole thing planned out ahead of time, but that doesn't make sense."

"Sometimes things just have a way of working out, I guess," said Bryndor.

"What was it like, Bryn? Shooting a man?" asked Lluthean.

They rode in silence for several minutes while Bryndor considered the question. "I don't know. I mean, one moment, all I could think of was how shaky my hands felt. I've never felt my heart pound that way. But then the next moment, it looked like you could be in danger, so I made it all stop."

"Made what stop?" Lluthean asked.

"All of it. The sweats, my racing heart, my hands. I just let it all go. Before I knew it, I had drawn and released. And that was that."

Lluthean resumed his game of flipping the rock into the air. "We have to come up with a better story than that before we get home. You make it all sound pretty plain."

Leave it to his brother to lift the conversation from a dark place. He loved him for that most of the time. "I don't know that anyone will care to listen to the adventures of two relative strangers back home. But if it comes up, I'll try to recount how brave you were to draw that bandit's attention," Bryndor said.

"And maybe don't forget the bit about the king's niece. Everyone loves a story where commoners rescue the nobility!" Lluthean flipped the stone once more, but this time Bryndor swatted it away, sending it skittering back down the trail.

"You're hopeless, Llu," he said. *And we are not just commoners, but nobody else knows that.*

"You're supposed to catch the stone then flick it again. Like this," said Lluthean. He flipped another rock up into the air and snatched it back. "Anyway, if you let me do the telling, I wager I could score a round of free drinks!"

"That's if Aunt Rona will even let us go to the tavern again," said Bryndor.

They reached the campsite, and Lluthean hopped down. He led his gelding over to the front of their wagon and retrieved the knotted tracings. He held the tangled mess for a moment and shared a look with Bryndor, who only arched an eyebrow in an expression of, "Don't look at me!"

They spent the next half hour in companionable silence as Lluthean worked to untangle the mud-crusted leather bindings. Bryndor double-checked the placement of their belongings on the wagon, but his mind kept wandering. The late morning sun was warming their coastal camp, and short purple wildflowers carpeted the ridge. A magnificent hawk soared at the edge of the bluff, where the cliff dropped off to the King's Road.

Normally, Bryndor could lose himself in that kind of beauty. But he returned again and again to the moment he stood on the boulder. He couldn't seem to dismiss the lingering taint of excrement and blood from his awareness. He kept reliving the simple act of drawing his bow, aiming, the vibration of the bowstring and the slow, deliberate path of the arrow . . . then the abrupt way the man had lurched in surprise when the arrow struck.

Chapter Two: A Girl and a Sword

Kaellor watched his nephews depart back to their camp. He gave Lesand time to regain her composure, all the while wishing that he was the one retrieving their gear. The last time he'd comforted an emotional child felt like years ago, and this situation frayed his patience.

He had intended to give her more time, but she seemed to regain her composure after a few minutes and started to look around the site of the ambush. *These bandits were rather brazen to attack anyone on the road so close to the city gates of Hammond.* "Have you met any others on your journey from Malvress?"

"No, my lord," the girl answered. "We passed some people making their way to the market close to Malvress, but in the last part of the day, only those men and you crossed our path."

That was at least possibly some good news. With a little luck, they could be away from the area before any opportunists arrived. "I don't have the tools to bury the dead, but I'm going to see if I can retrieve any of their belongings to return to their families. You should probably stay here in the carriage, Lesand."

"I go with you, my lord." Lesand turned and closed the carriage door softly. "Besides, I don't think I can sit next to Millisand." Kaellor cocked an eyebrow in puzzled question. "My governess."

Of course. He stroked the silver chin hairs in his beard and reflected on the girl's situation. *You shouldn't have to see this, little one, it will age you more than you deserve, but that arrow is already in flight.* He knew from prior experience that seeing the dead often gave one a sense of closure; when that finality was left to the imagination, one could think up any number of horrors far worse than the truth.

"Come along then, let's see what we can salvage for their families." He stepped forward, and they explored the site of the devastation. He was able to remove small personal trinkets, a few rings, and several swords. They set anything of value next to the carriage.

Finally, they approached the body of Krestus. The young knight had put up quite a struggle; managing to dispatch four of the bandits was no simple task. Kaellor felt more than a little kinship with the man and had to admire his commitment to duty. *You did well, my friend.*

Without further delay, he dragged the fallen knight clear of the blood-soaked ground and made quick work unclasping his breastplate. The metal peeled away from his torso with a sucking noise, congealed in place by blood. A small dirk protruded from his lower ribs on the left, the hilt only just visible. He removed the man's bloody gauntlets next, found two family rings, and placed them in a small pouch.

Lesand looked at her guardian for long moments while Kaellor carried the breastplate over to the carriage. He returned to find her staring at the knight's pale corpse.

"Lesand, maybe you should wait over here by the carriage," said Kaellor.

The girl pulled her eyes away from her guardian and pointed to his side. " None of the things you recovered hold any value compared to his sword. He was never without it." She tiptoed around pools of blood to retrieve a longsword, then handed the sword to Kaellor.

He started to place the weapon with the other equipment, then paused as he considered the sword. The short sword he'd briefly held earlier was a reasonable weapon, but nothing like this. The sharp and well-oiled blade had been crafted from a strange dark metal. *Curious. I've never seen a weapon of such make.*

The blade balanced perfectly with the hilt, allowing either a single or double hand grip. The crossguards each housed a large gem: one purple and the other an exotic smoky onyx. In the pommel, the same gemstones wove around each other.

He stood and, without thinking, stroked the weapon smoothly through several stances. He stopped, surprised that he still remembered all the complex motions. He retrieved a piece of cloth from the rubble and used it to clean the blade, then worked to remove the bloodstains from his hands.

"You know the dance?" Lesand asked.

"The dance? You mean the sword?"

"Krestus called it the dance and would practice just like that every morning and night. You move as he did," Lesand answered.

He gently placed the blade beside the small pile of other belongings. "It was in another life, long ago. But yes, once I knew the dance."

"You and your nephews, you're not from the Southlands, are you?" she said, making it a statement more than a question.

"No, we are not, but for all practical purposes, we might as well be. The boys have lived pretty much their whole lives below the Korjinth." He scratched at the underside of his beard with the top of his hand. Something about the girl's observation nibbled at the fringe of his thoughts. "What gave us away?"

The girl busied herself with braiding her hair back over her ears. "You're taller than most, and you don't tan like a man from the Southlands. But mostly, nobody here has grey eyes."

Kaellor palmed the beard along his jaw. *Thank the Giver this one's not in league with the abrogators.*

Eventually, Bryndor and Lluthean returned with the small wagon. At Kaellor's instruction, they gathered up the small pile of personal possessions and packed them alongside their own belongings. Kaellor had planned to ride his mount but sensed Lesand's unease at being separated from him. With a sigh tempered by understanding, he forced himself to admit that the girl had been through enough for one day. He decided to drive the wagon and keep Lesand at his side, where she seemed most comfortable. They got on the road to Hammond and left the carnage behind.

They traveled at a steady pace, and by midafternoon crossed paths with a small group of mounted knights patrolling the road. After a brief conversation, Kaellor informed the company about the attack. A young knight inspected Kaellor and his nephews and appeared dubious.

"If it would please His Majesty's niece, we will assume responsibility for her transport." The knight held out a gloved hand.

Kaellor recalled his earlier conversation with Lesand. In this part of the world, they did have the look of foreigners. He made a quick assessment of the company. *Six mounted knights with fresh horses. It's not really possible to gauge their capabilities, but they are well-armored. It would serve no purpose to provoke the company. But how to proceed?*

Before Kaellor could offer a reply, Lesand stood in the wagon. "His Majesty's niece has a name and a voice, and she would not be pleased to finish the journey on horseback. I owe my life to Kevold and his nephews, which is more than I can say for my fallen countrymen who were killed riding not more than a few hours back on the King's Road. The road your company is no doubt charged with protecting. So if it is my safety that concerns you, then you may escort us to Hammond." She sat back down, wrapped one hand around Kaellor's arm, and gazed straight ahead.

Kaellor looked down at the girl. *This one's made of more metal than I gave her credit for.*

The young knight sat a moment registering her statement, then slumped his shoulders in acceptance of the truth of her words. He directed a few of his men to take up the rear, and they turned to escort the group. As the wagon lurched ahead, Kaellor leaned down to whisper, "Remind me never to get on your bad side." He winked, and Lesand flashed a weary smile.

Under escort, they traveled through the outer gates, bypassing the routine inspections of the guard. By sunset, they arrived at the gatehouse of the castle. Shadows danced in the torchlight, and Hammond, the city proper, stirred with activity even at the late hour.

Though most shops had closed for the day, sounds of merriment echoed into the streets from taverns standing on every block. Amber light spilled out from the establishments, most of which stood open to the air this time of year, taking advantage of the seasonal trade winds. The aromas of evening cookfires mingled with sweet tobacco, beer, fish, and occasionally the rank odor of too many unwashed people. The complex smells wafted through the air and took Kaellor back to another city in another life. He dismissed the memory before it had the chance to distract him.

The young knight from their escort approached on foot. "My Lady Lesand, why don't you accompany me inside, and we'll announce your arrival to His Majesty, King Vendal?"

"I appreciate the escort," said Lesand, "but this man has business with the king. I will enter with Kevold and company and none other." She made a pretense of dusting off her clothing and dismissed the young knight. He sighed and turned back to the gatehouse.

After an exchange of words, the sturdy gate lifted, and they were granted entrance to the inner bailey. The expansive castle grounds spread out beyond the torchlight, and they waited in silence for several minutes in front of a well-manicured garden of low hedges that circled a central fountain. Eventually, large double doors swung open, spilling more light across the courtyard.

A group of servants and a few royal guards approached. The latter wore ceremonial silver scale mail over their chest, with the crest of Hammond decorating the shoulders. Amber torchlight flickered over their curved swords. The group surrounded Kaellor and Lesand on the wagon and Lluthean and Bryndor, who rode just behind.

Knowing the customs from their previous visit, they all remained calm, hands visible on their reins. Kaellor glanced back, happy to see that even Lluthean was minding his restless fingers. Finally, the king approached with his wife. The royal couple walked with a small entourage of royal handmaidens and manservants.

"Kevold of Riverton and company." King Vendal's rich voice filled the courtyard. Six decades had colored his curly hair and beard a silvery-white, in stark contrast to his dark brown skin. Dressed in flowing dark purple robes, he moved with a slow grace matched by a deep, resonant voice. He addressed them in a relaxed, natural cadence. "I understand you bear more than just a survey of the kingdom, but a cargo far more precious to me."

Queen Shelland wore flowing ivory robes and a calm expression. She swept kinky locks of silver hair back over her shoulder to reveal gentle eyes, then opened her arms in a warm gesture, welcoming Lesand.

The girl turned a grateful expression to Kaellor as if waiting for something. He kept his eyes trained on Vendal but dipped his head to the side. "You're safe here, Lesand. Don't keep the queen waiting."

Lesand hugged him with a fierce strength for several seconds, then scurried down from the wagon and ran to the queen's waiting embrace. Queen Shelland wiped trail dust from her face, then ushered the girl inside the castle. Kaellor felt the muscles between his shoulders relax as he watched her depart.

The king snapped his fingers, and the servants approached the wagon and mounts. "I cannot repay the debt but would start to show my gratitude by offering you lodging here in the castle. I shall have your things delivered to your rooms. I see that you have hired some help on your journey."

Kaellor hopped off the wagon and bowed. "Your Majesty, these are my nephews. I would trust none other with the opportunity you laid before us. This is Bryndor and Lluthean." The brothers dismounted in turn and bowed in formal greeting.

"I seem to recall you accepted the contract in the company of two others but can't at the moment place their faces," said the old king. His brow wrinkled in concentration.

"You are correct, Your Majesty. There was always a plan to have my nephews finish this survey with me. I think you will find their skill unmatched." Kaellor observed the king with a wary eye, but the monarch accepted his explanation without suspicion. Vendal directed the servants to begin unloading the items in the wagon.

"A moment, Your Majesty," Kaellor interrupted. "We retrieved several items of personal significance from the deceased from your niece's caravan. I could not attend to their bodies and did not want others to loot their corpses." Kaellor directed one of the servants to a large bundle at the back of the wagon.

"You are ever thoughtful, my friend," King Vendal commented. "Come, the hour is late. I would share wine with you and learn more of your story, but please indulge an old man. I should like to spend what little of this day is left with my niece."

"Your offer for lodging exceeds anything we expected, Your Majesty. It would be our pleasure to present you with the survey at your convenience." Kaellor bowed his head politely.

"It's settled then," said Vendal with a warm smile. "Rest yourselves inside, and we shall discuss the matter further in the morning."

Royal servants attended to the mounts and ushered Kaellor and the brothers to their suite. They were escorted up a winding set of steps to an elevated walkway on the inner side of the castle gardens. At the northwest corner of the castle, another set of steps led up to their rooms.

Standing under the portico, they looked out across the harbor. Voshna, the blue moon, perched full and high in the night sky, dwarfing her sister Vaeda, who remained a small red ember in the distance. Where the waves crested, they took on a light blue hue. A servant unlocked large double doors and ushered them into a grand suite.

Somehow, the staff had already delivered their belongings. Their numerous delicate leather tubes containing the surveys and maps lay stacked neatly in a corner. Three sets of formal clothing rested on three separate beds. Stairs descended into an enormous bath, from which steam arose. A dining table adorned with assorted pastries, bread, and a steaming platter of fish and lobster awaited their arrival.

Lluthean set down his bags and stretched. "There's not a lass in sight, but I don't think we can beat the accommodations."

"Indeed, sometimes the Giver gives," Kaellor said, invoking the old phrase as he surveyed the suite. "We could not afford such luxury, but let's not forget we have a map to complete. Vendal is generous—but he is also demanding and deserves a finished product."

"I have my notes from the first part of the day in my saddlebags." Bryndor searched their belongings and sighed. "They've kept my saddlebags with the mounts. Should I try to get them?"

"Llu, do you think you can manage without any notes?" Kaellor asked.

"It might cost you a portion of lobster, but yes," Lluthean answered with a wink, "I think I can manage."

"Fair payment for fair service rendered," Kaellor replied. The three sat down and enjoyed a lavish meal of warm bread, baked fish, lobster in a cream sauce, and a delicate dessert wine that left a lingering hint of berry.

Bryndor hunched forward in a chair and kept swirling the last bit of wine in his glass. He gazed into the burgundy vortex. "I didn't hesitate," he mumbled, more as an observation of his actions than any intent to initiate a conversation.

Kaellor eyed his nephew. "You did not. You did what was needed. Does that bother you?"

Bryndor shrugged. "I feel like it should, like I should feel different. But under the circumstances, I don't, and . . ."

"And perhaps that very thing bothers you?" Kaellor answered for his nephew. "Good. It should tickle at the edges of your conscience a little. Killing a man, even one as dark as that bastard, should always give you some pause. Whether you realize it or not, taking a life changes you. Committing to the action is one thing. Reflecting on the outcome is inevitable but necessary among good-hearted men." Kaellor swallowed the last of his portion of the dessert wine.

Bryndor considered the words for a few moments. "It was a just death?"

"I daresay Lesand, and her family, find it a just death," Kaellor suggested. "And so do I," he finished without allowing Bryndor the chance to question himself further.

"It didn't make me feel powerful," said Bryndor. "I thought maybe it would."

Kaellor sighed, then forced a smile to offer reassurance. *How will this day change you, Bryn? I can't think of you as a boy any longer. Your burdens are already greater than anyone knows. By the Giver, how are you even supposed to make your way in the world with that cursed mantle? Sometimes I wonder if my brother was right to invoke the concealment and send us away.*

He wanted to give his nephew a measure of peace tempered by honesty, so he considered his next words carefully. "The truth is, we are connected to everyone we encounter in this life. You will, in some small way, always be connected to the life you take from another. And I would argue that your ability to feel that makes you a better man."

Bryndor listened intently and seemed to mull the matter over in his mind a bit longer. Servants returned to clear the dining table, and the three finished the last leg of the map of the King's Road to Hammond. Bryndor appeared happy for the distraction, even though Lluthean completed most of the work. Once they finished the master, they crafted a replica to carry home. Finally, they retired for the evening.

In the morning, they gathered in an anteroom before Vendal's grand library. A few other dignitaries sat on benches in the large round room. Kaellor disliked confinement in such spaces. There were never enough exits, and this deep into the castle, it was difficult to control any of the variables.

Two guards in the room, two more outside the door, two windows, but far too high to jump out if things go awry. If a fight breaks out, that small set of fire-irons could be used as a last resort.

He tugged hard at the silver hairs of his beard, frustrated that his thoughts assumed the worst. *All these years of hiding have really taken a toll. There is no danger here. Finish the business, settle the contract, and depart amicably.*

He dismissed his sense of unease, then contacted the attendant. They waited while the official notified the king. After several minutes, Lluthean sat down on a bench and pulled a loop of twine from his pocket. He nimbly threaded his fingers into a geometric design, eventually holding the pattern out in invitation for Bryndor in a game of cat's cradle. Bryndor obliged by placing a finger into one of the spaces in an attempt to find the one that might trip the noose.

Kaellor watched them for a moment, then turned to take a seat but came up awkwardly nose to nose with a man dressed in stiff white attire. His doublet, pressed crisp at the edges, was tucked into his spotless white pants, and a luxurious white cape was slung over his padded shoulders. He even wore white gloves. A gold forearm bracer served as the only interruption to the strange dress. Some type of oil slicked back his dark hair, and the grooming of his beard and mustache created the appearance of thin, angular lines over chubby cheeks. The man took a step back and tipped his head. "Apologies," said the stranger.

Kaellor squashed any rancor. *This fop could be an important official of the court.* "No need, I'm sure my clumsy feet got the worst of me," he said.

The man bowed politely again, then stepped forward, extending the forearm with the gold bracer. "My name's Gavid. Archon Gavid Strictor. I represent the Immaculine."

Kaellor clasped the man's forearm in the traditional Southland style. The bracer felt oddly cold, even through his shirt sleeve. Gavid held the embrace overlong.

"I am Kevold of Riverton, and these are my nephews Bryndor and Lluthean." He paused, considering the man's purpose. He'd obviously wanted to make an introduction, and he held himself with great confidence. "Forgive me, did you say the Immaculine? I'm not sure I'm familiar with all of the royal families here in Hammond."

Gavid walked over to Lluthean and Bryndor and offered a formal greeting and forearm shake to each. His odd manner of introduction seemed to take longer than one would expect, but none of the other nobles paid the man any attention. Something about the man's demeanor changed after he completed what appeared to be more of an assessment than an actual greeting. Gavid leaned against the wall and released a natural smile.

"The Immaculine are not part of the local aristocracy. My home, and that of my superiors, is far to the southeast in Caskayah. I'm here to begin diplomatic relations with the king."

Kaellor raised his eyebrows. "You've likely traveled as far as we have. Isn't that past Grenn?"

"Indeed it is," said Gavid, "but most of the locals here haven't even heard of that kingdom." Gavid considered them further, taking note of the large map case. "You three are the surveyors? The whole city is talking about you this morning; how you rescued the king's niece, drove off a score of brigands, and mapped the province all at the same time. The Immaculine could use good men like you."

"We just happened upon Lesand at the right time," said Kaellor. "I'm afraid any heroic tales were just that."

"Really? The tavern talk did seem a bit embellished." Gavid ran gloved fingers along his mustache. "But that really does make more sense. I mean, how would a simple mapmaker and his nephews manage such a task?" He laughed at his own jest. Kaellor understood the insult in his words but didn't care to reveal his awareness to the strange man. *This fella makes my teeth ache.*

"So, the Immaculine sounds regal. Do you represent the ruling family in Caskayah, then?" he asked.

"The Immaculine are sponsored by the Caskayan Church. Under Exemplar Gre'Kanth, we thrive. In his light, we shine that we might see the foul shadows cast by those tainted by the twin moons."

Kaellor mastered his frustration, the conversation already overlong for his preference. Instead of growling at Gavid, he decided to present the man with the appearance of a simpleton. "Huh?"

Gavid sighed. "It's all part of our higher teaching, but then I shouldn't be surprised if nobody in these parts is familiar with the tenets. All in good time, though, all in good time."

"Master Kevold and company, His Majesty will see you now," announced the attendant.

Kaellor sighed inwardly with relief. "Well, excuse me, we don't want to keep His Majesty waiting. It was a true pleasure to meet you, sir, that is, Archon Strictor. Good luck with your dealings with the king." He bowed, and Gavid tilted his head in return.

The oily man called after him as he entered the library, "Do think about my offer. We really could find a valuable place for you in the light of the Exemplar."

Vendal turned to welcome them as the attendant led them into the library. Kaellor set the large map case down on a table and glanced back through the doors at the strange man in the white suit. "Your Majesty, a friend of yours?" he asked.

The old king spied Strictor before the doors closed, then sighed with an expression of distaste. "The Immaculine are zealots from Caskayah. Somehow they obtained a foothold there. My understanding is that they already have an enclave in Grenn. That archon, as he calls himself, has been petitioning an audience with me for two weeks now. I thought he would have given up, but he persuaded one of my sons, who in turn convinced me to spare him some time. But enough of that. Please, let's see your final work."

Kaellor unrolled the large map onto the table. He stepped to the side, allowing columns of light to filter through the stained glass to illuminate their finished product. The king studied the map for long moments, appreciating the details of the surrounding mountain range, the valleys in between, and several of the smaller towns and villages under his domain. He then traced the path from Malvress to Hammond along the King's Road.

"I've always wondered about placing the road so close to the sea. At the time of its construction, we chose the scenic and far cheaper path. I never imagined bandits would dare strike so close to our front gates, but I now understand how this stretch makes any caravan quite vulnerable."

Vendal pushed back from the table and regarded Kaellor and his nephews through bushy, white eyebrows. "Your reputation appears well-founded, Kevold of Riverton. I thank you not only for the diligent accuracy of your map but also for the census information you collected from the different parts of the kingdom. To see it all displayed so artfully before me gives an old king cause to take stock in his accomplishments."

"I'm glad the work meets your satisfaction, Your Majesty," Kaellor replied. Something seemed oddly reserved about the old king's demeanor. *Does he intend to alter the contract?*

"When we agreed upon this undertaking, you mentioned my kingdom was a good distance from your home. Might you be so good as to educate me where it is that you call home?" Vendal asked.

Kaellor relaxed and dismissed his unease. He unrolled the map to its full breadth and placed a finger far to the north, where the Shelwyn River emerged from the southern edge of the Korjinth Mountain range and carved through vast tracks of forest. The Shelwyn turned a serpentine path, then meandered south, flowing through the entirety of the Southlands.

"This is our base of operations, though we actually live a little to the north and west in a smaller village, where the Shelwyn turns back on itself; here, at Journey's Bend."

The king considered the distance. "You have wandered a long way from your home in Borsec's kingdom. I made such a trek in my youth for a diplomatic meeting with my father. We ventured to the very foothills of the Korjinth, but those days are long behind me. How is old King Borsec these days?"

Kaellor rubbed at his chin hairs. "Word has it he is well. We don't really travel in the same circles as His Majesty," said Kaellor.

Vendal sat back in an oversized chair and waved for one of the servants to approach. "Well, you certainly did not travel all this way to listen to the rambling of an old man longing for days gone by. Lest we delay your departure any longer, for your trouble then, as we agreed."

Servants brought forth a small iron lockbox and opened the lid to reveal it packed with silver scales and gold fins, the currency of the region. Kaellor considered the sum for an unusually long moment. The last time he'd looked upon so much gold, he'd had no reason to consider its value. Now, the amount before him nearly left him speechless. "Your Majesty, there must be some misunderstanding. This is far more than we agreed on."

Vendal held up his hand. "It's only a fraction of the value of the real treasure you delivered to me, my friend. Lesand is the youngest child of my youngest brother. As we have been separated by years and distance, Leland and I have never been very close. Her safe arrival here marks a turning in our relationship, and one I have longed for. But none of that would be possible were it not for your timely, and dare I say heroic, intervention." Vendal turned. "And I'm not the only one who feels that way."

The door to the library opened, and Lesand rushed forward to embrace Kaellor, who stood adjacent to the large table. She hugged him around the waist with exuberance, then stepped back to stand near the king. She whispered with a twinkle and smile, "Now, Uncle?"

Vendal's smile indicated he enjoyed her term of endearment instead of a stiff, formal title more than a little. "Yes, Lesand. I think now is the right time."

Lesand disappeared through the doorway, only to return a moment later, holding a longsword protected by an ornate sheath with an attached shoulder harness inlaid with silver gilding. She cradled the weapon in her forearms, approached with a confidence beyond her youth, then presented it to Kaellor.

"Kevold of Riverton," said Lesand, "with the grace offered me by His Majesty King Vendal Braveska of Hammond, first of his name, I present to you a token of my sincere gratitude. This weapon was given to Krestus by my father, Duke Leland Braveska, that it might allow him to serve the realm. The blade has been in our family for generations. Crafted in a Logrend forge, it is of rare make. The weapon was used against our people in the Insurgent's War and secured after our victory over the Logrend Empire. Long may it serve you and remind you of our gratitude."

She looked sidelong at the king, seeking his approval. Vendal winked at Lesand, who exhaled a breath. She had clearly invested significant effort into learning the speech.

Kaellor dropped to a knee to receive the weapon. He pulled the longsword only a few inches from its sheath, recalling the feeling of the blade from the prior day. He had no practical use for the sword but could not deny the honor such a gift bestowed. "Lesand, it's more than I . . . I can't accept this. You shine too much honor on me this day. It really should remain with your family. Your Majesty, it's too much, I think."

Vendal replied in a mischievous tone, "Are you trying to tell me that the value of my niece is not worth at least ten times these rewards?"

"Your Majesty, you know that is not my intent." After a quick read of the room, he realized there was no graceful way to decline the gift. He stifled any further argument and nodded.

"Lesand Braveska, most honored and noble daughter to Leland Braveska and niece to His Majesty, King Vendal Braveska, I am humbled, and I thank you for your gift. I shall keep it safe all my days, that it might allow me to protect the realm and remind me of our friendship."

Lesand beamed with approval. She leaned in and whispered, "Just be sure to take it out to dance once in a while."

A half-smile finally tickled at his beard, and Kaellor replied, "I'll try."

Lesand turned back to the doorway and nodded at two manservants, who approached the brothers. Each servant held a bow and quiver and presented them for inspection. "Bryndor and Lluthean," said Lesand, "for your service in assisting your uncle Kevold, we present you with two other Logrend artifacts."

She leaned in closer to say softly, "I don't have anything quite like the sword, but King Vendal thought you might appreciate these."

The unstrung bows appeared shorter than the longbows common in Riverton, and the weapons appeared to be crafted more for artful presentation than utility. The polished, dark amber grip curved to fit naturally into the palm, but the tapered ends curved back, making the bows appear warped.

"Logrend recurves," explained the king. "My second son returned a few years ago from a trading expedition and told me these are superior to your longbows. You will notice that the bows are crafted from an exotic type of wood and that the limbs curve back. I can't say that I understand the mechanics at all, but I am told it makes for a slightly easier draw. At the same time, the arrow is delivered with much more speed and, believe it or not, can outdistance your longbows. My sons find these ideal on horseback or when hunting in the brush, but I must warn you not to overdraw the bowstring. Such an action apparently causes the string to strike your forearm."

The old king held up a finger to make his point. "My son learned this lesson the hard way and flayed the muscle from his arm; he gave the surgeons quite a task that day. This risk is assuaged not only by the weapon's performance, but there is also something about the way the Logrend fashion their bows that makes them resistant to the ravages of time and use."

Lluthean admired the gift and offered his sincere thanks, but Bryndor looked like he might throw up. Kaellor wondered if some bit of the rich food the night before wasn't agreeing with him, or perhaps the gift was only a reminder of the prior day's events. Bryndor's pallor lasted only a moment and was replaced by a deep flushing of his cheeks. Eventually, he seemed to fully recover and also expressed his thanks.

They spent the next hour in polite conversation. While Lluthean did his part, Bryndor remained unusually silent as they packed their belongings. The older youth remained withdrawn until they were several minutes down the road outside of Hammond, then pulled their small wagon to the roadside.

"You feel alright, Bryn?" asked Kaellor. "You don't seem yourself this morning."

"Did either of you notice anything odd about all of that back there?" asked Bryndor. "Anything at all strike you as strange?"

"I'm not sure what you're getting at," said Kaellor. "Strange how?"

"With Lesand," Bryndor said, drawing out her name for emphasis. "The girl?"

Kaellor thought back over the morning's events but couldn't rightly think of anything she did that was off-putting. He glanced to Lluthean, who only shrugged.

"Let me ask you both this," said Bryndor. "When was the last time a relative stranger ever remembered us? When was the last time anyone ever called me by my name in the morning?"

Long moments of silence passed, and Kaellor felt his jaw slack in genuine surprise. *How did I miss it? I must have been too preoccupied with minding all the rules of courtly etiquette.* "It was this morning," he stated. "She did remember you."

"Exactly! Thank you! What does it mean?" asked Bryndor.

Kaellor's mind worked through several possibilities. *If that girl remembered them, it could mean any number of things. Could it be that her near-death circumstances were enough to override the mantle? Or is the binding, after all these years, weakening?*

He knew he would not find the answers right away and pulled his hand across his jawline as if he could remove his unease. "We can't be certain. It could be something unique about Lesand, or it could be related to a flaw in your mantle. Let's not take any chances. Until we get home, you're Kemp and Firth, the sons of Kevold. We avoid travel with anyone else. No inns, no taverns. We need to get home and fast."

Kaellor waited for his nephews to acknowledge his instructions, but both seemed bewildered by the revelation. "Boys, tell me you understand."

Both nodded, and Bryndor said, "I'm Kemp, and he's Firth, your sons. No small talk."

"No inns, avoid others, make for home straight away," Lluthean finished with a vacant expression.

Kaellor directed his mount to return to the road. Their journey home had just become much more complicated.

Chapter Three: Lluthean's Luck

Their travel north to Journey's Bend took much less time without the tedious work of surveying the region. Still, Lluthean felt restless and bored. He tried to engage Kaellor in conversation, but his uncle seemed to prefer riding in companionable silence until they gathered around the camp in the evening. Bryndor seemed even more distant and moody. Something definitely had the both of them preoccupied, though he didn't know why exactly. He hoped that they could talk about everything that had happened in Hammond, and soon.

If their concealment was lifted, then perhaps he could finally make headway with Sadeen Tunkle. Under the influence of his binding, he'd had to start a new friendship with her all over again every time they returned home.

On the other hand, if the binding persisted, he was more than happy to turn the anonymity to his favor. He was old enough now to go to the tavern alone. He had, on more than one occasion, used his familiarity with the regulars to give him an edge in card games. In addition, he understood when to leave the game with his winnings and which regulars would allow him to depart peacefully.

Never take too much. Lose now and again. That way, the regular patrons won't shun an outsider on general principle. Oh, what I would give for a card game tonight.

When the sun dropped low in the sky, Kaellor pulled their wagon under a stout billow tree with plenty of shade overlooking a gentle bend of the Shelwyn. The trees grew thick along the riverbanks closer to home and were a good marker of progress on their journey, as they were following the river north and usually camped along the banks. The timing of their stop could not have been better, at least according to the rumbling of his stomach.

He walked his mount to the water's edge, then began attending to the mundane tasks of setting up camp. He set out three fishing lines and staked them deep into the ground, started a small cookfire, then groomed his mount. Once Kaellor and Bryndor erected the tents, they set about making a stew from leftover bacon fat and a potato.

As the stew simmered, he checked the fishing lines and found the first two dangling slack in the water, but the third one was pulled tight enough that the stout bit of dowel he'd used to anchor the line quivered. He deftly snatched the line just as it threatened to pull loose from the ground and was immediately rewarded by the thrumming vibration of a fish - by the feel of it, a very large fish.

With tedious focus, he rolled the line back on the dowel, careful not to place too much tension on the line and occasionally letting the dowel unroll. His forearm muscles burned in achy protest, and he was wondering how long he would have to play out the fish when Bryndor startled him.

"Kae says soup's on, but you know his cooking," said Bryndor.

"Smells better than it tastes?" Lluthean grunted. "With a little luck, we might enjoy something better tonight."

Bryndor crouched down to watch in anticipation. "I would ask if you need any help, but . . ." Bryndor stood with excitement as a large, yellow fish emerged from the murky depths. It floundered with fatigue, then made one last attempt to evade capture and fluttered back into the dark waters.

Lluthean allowed the dowel to unroll again, then began the arduous task of rolling the line back in. The thrumming vibrations of the fish dissipated, and his forearms threatened to cramp. He slowly walked back up the bank and held his breath, fearing the line might break. He was rewarded as the flat, yellow head of a giant catfish broke the water, followed by two, then three feet of glorious fish. The sun reflected off the creature's iridescent gold and yellow scales. Long tentacle-like whiskers ended near a fat belly, which merged into a thick tail.

He watched Bryndor wrestle the catch safely onto the bank, then fell back, panting. The ground pressed his damp shirt against his back, and he realized for the first time that his hair had matted to his forehead.

"I can't believe it. Look at that," said Bryndor. "The hook was barely set, but the line got tangled around its gill. One roll the wrong way, and all that would have been for nothing!"

Lluthean propped himself up. "Sometimes Lutney favors the bold," he said, repeating the old expression of the rectors.

"And sometimes you make your own luck, brother," Bryndor finished. They retrieved the lines and made quick work of the catfish, spearing it in hunks over the fire. Bryndor spiced the fish with a pinch of Hammondian salt.

The sun waned as they finished what was possibly the best meal Lluthean had enjoyed since leaving the coastal region of the Kingdom of Hammond. Kaellor retrieved a small flask from the pack-wagon and passed it around as they relaxed for the evening.

"Malvressian honey-cut," Kaellor said as he handed Lluthean the flask, "but have a care, it's for sipping." He offered the advice a moment too late, as Lluthean had already tipped the vessel back and received a large gulp. The liquid hit the back of his throat and seemed to both incinerate and evaporate all at once. The fumes carried into his lungs, and he couldn't help but break out into a fit of tear-filled coughing. He barely managed to hand the flask to Bryndor, who sniffed it dubiously.

After several minutes of coughing and sputtering, he wiped tears from his face and looked up with a watery grin. "Honey-cut, you say?" His voice was raspy from the effects of the liquid fire, but the pain had dissipated and left him with a warm feeling in his belly.

Kaellor shook his head in an "I told you so" expression. "If you take just a sip, it warms you and leaves a lingering hint of honey on your tongue. Give it a try, Bryn."

Bryndor took a tiny cautious sip, blew the fumes out, then smacked his tongue on the roof of his mouth a few times. "Humph . . . after the burn, there is a hint of honey."

Sitting around the campfire, Lluthean ran his fingers through the long grasses and found two rounded seeds that had fallen from the nearby billow tree. The flat, dark seed pods, each the size of a small skipping stone, always reminded him of home. He often kept one in his pocket. As long as one kept a billow seed dry, it lasted for years, at least as far as he knew.

Back home, they often used the pods as fishing bobbers. But once exposed to water, the pod would swell and crack, and eventually, the seed would pop open and release a delicate white fluff that billowed out into the wind.

He flicked the pair of pods into the air in practiced repetition and, on occasion, would toss one into a high arc, then attempt to alter its trajectory by hitting it with the other. It took a few attempts, but he finally got it and recalled the last time he'd sat on their front porch playing the same fidgety game.

"What do you think the chances are that people will remember us, Kae?" he asked.

Kaellor took a small sip of the honey-cut and stoppered the flask, replaced it in his travel pack, and pulled at his silver-streaked beard. "Who can say, but I imagine we'll learn the way of things pretty fast."

"I, for one, would be just fine to have the binding lifted," Bryndor said. "We could finally be like everyone else. We could finally get from one day to the next without starting all over. We could be remembered."

"We've been hidden for what, twelve years? Do you think it even really matters to anyone anymore?" Lluthean asked.

"It matters," said Kaellor.

Lluthean waited for more, but his uncle just stared with a distant expression into the small campfire. Fragments of stories popped into Lluthean's mind, and he reviewed what little he knew of their history. Over the years, Kaellor had remained tight-lipped, but he'd occasionally allowed a few pieces of their past to float to the surface. From what Lluthean understood, he and his brother were born into royalty, of all things. His parents once ruled a kingdom far to the north, but twelve years ago, they had faced a rebellion at the hands of a usurper.

He didn't understand more than those loose concepts; Kaellor was always so close-mouthed about the whole affair. His uncle often redirected inquiries about their past with something like, "What matters is your life here and now, not what was." What he did know was that in the end, his parents used some type of ritual to hide his and Bryndor's identities.

The mantle, Kaellor called it, kept anyone from remembering them unless they spent a significant period of continuous time with them. The Usurper's supporters, the abrogators, would otherwise surely hunt them down. Tasked with their safety, Kaellor had brought them into the Southlands, below the Korjinth range. Lluthean's parents had asked him to raise them in relative anonymity.

He'd taken a wife, Rona, though the couple had always seemed more like brother and sister. They had separate bedrooms and treated each other with deference more than passion, but together, they had made a living at the outskirts of Journey's Bend.

"Why would anyone bother to come looking for us?" said Lluthean. He waited, but his uncle remained transfixed on the flames. The only sound came from the occasional popping of embers and the bubbling whisper of the Shelwyn.

Bryndor finally broke the silence. "Does Aunt Rona know everything about our past? Because if she does, isn't it time for us to hear everything too? I mean, it's our past, Kae, and—"

"Yes," Kaellor interrupted softly, "that story is long overdue."

Lluthean was so surprised that he allowed the billow tree seeds to drop to the ground. He shared a look with Bryndor, who sat mouth agape with his eyebrows arched and the whites of his eyes luminous in the light of the campfire.

"Really?" Lluthean asked.

Kaellor lifted his gaze from the campfire. "Yes, it's time. I should have told you everything a few years ago. I just didn't want it to change you, and it will change you." He looked at each of them for a few long moments. "I need time to think about how to tell it all to you."

In unison, the brothers bemoaned the delay, "Aww, Kae!"

"I promise, everything," he said. "I'll tell you everything when we get home." He held up a hand, and Lluthean knew he would brook no arguments. Just like that, Lluthean's hope for something entertaining this evening was dashed away.

"Boys, it's a story that will carry us deep into the night, and I'm tired. It needs a proper telling, and I promise to give it to you when we get back," said Kaellor.

Bryndor looked like he was going to press for more but then seemed mollified. "If you promise, Kae, we can wait."

Chapter Four: In Dreams, We Remember

K aellor stirred in his sleep, pulled through waves of memories, both heartwarming and melancholy. He peered up through the darkness from the lowest recesses of Stone's Grasp, the castle that towered over the capital city of the same name in Aarindorn. Intermittent scintillating lights flickered along the veining in the stones, a reflection of the wards repelling the attacks of the Usurper. The collision of channeled currents of nadir against the zenith-powered wards caused a deep rumble that reverberated down to even his shadowed alcove.

He ran a finger over the veining just as a bright flash from the castle defenses erupted in the dark. Like a discharge of lightning, the sudden flash left him momentarily blinded. Sterile, galvanic vapors cut through the musty smell of the castle depths. The air felt oddly crisp and dry.

Yesterday's binding ritual had left him unable to appreciate the buzzing tingle usually created when zenith streaked along the castle defenses. With his ability to channel zenith stifled, he'd lost all awareness of the creative force.

Just another strange deficit to get used to. How do the ungifted ever make their way in the world? How will I?

His brother, King Japheth Baellentrell, had struggled in the previous weeks to convince Kaellor to commit to the plan of binding his gift. Japheth had made the bold proposal to enable Kaellor to flee with his nephews and live, hidden, beyond the grasp of the Usurper. The king had even thought they could return once it was safe.

Kaellor's ability to channel zenith had connected him, grounded him, and fortified him. With his gift, he felt rooted within the community of Aarindorn, and through the manipulation of zenith, he'd found purpose, a way to make a difference. But that connection was also an anchor, a link through which Tarkannen and his abrogators could track Kaellor and his nephews.

Short conversations became heated debates, and Kaellor had offered any number of plausible alternatives. Send an ungifted away with the boys. Ask another to commit to the ritual. Kaellor's place was at Stone's Grasp, fighting alongside his brother. He would join the struggle or die trying.

Further complicating Kaellor's decision was the knowledge that the binding ritual demanded the same sacrifice from another person. The only way he could surrender his gift was through the unnatural process of stripping it away from another willing participant. Something about the act of removing another person's control of zenith was at once both intimate and deviant. The only way to accomplish the task was to make one's self equally vulnerable to the process.

So, two gifted were needed to enter the sacred contract, and the only person he trusted with such a sacrifice was his betrothed. But how could he make such a request of the woman he loved more than the kingdom itself? He couldn't. It was an ask far greater than he dared.

In the end, it was his betrothed who convinced him. Her unconditional acceptance and pure grace broke through his angry defenses. She melted his resolve, stilled his mind, and gave him focus enough to listen to the words of their trusted friend, Councilor Therek Lefledge.

Therek had, in a rare foretelling, predicted the rise of a strange dark moon and an end to their bloodline if Kaellor stayed. If he joined the battle, only ruin and destruction would result. And so, Kaellor had acquiesced and surrendered his gift in the binding ritual.

So much changed in that one day. They called the process a binding, a voluntary release. But it felt more like a smothering at first. The process leeched something out of him, stealing at first his breath, then his vigor, and for a time, even his will.

In the first hours after the loss, all he could do was collapse into a chair and simply recover. Profound, suffocating exhaustion eventually became severe fatigue. Everything ached, from the joints in his toes to the smallest muscles in his face. It was like the worst part of the fevered flux he'd suffered in his youth, and he remembered thinking they should have given it a name more befitting the process. Binding didn't begin to describe the sense of unfathomable loss, of having some part of yourself siphoned away.

And now, bereft of his connection, he felt . . . hollow? *Is that the feeling?* Hollow was definitely part of it. Hollow and blunted. It felt like reaching for a glass of juice but instead drinking water. The sensation of liquid was there, but none of the delicious tanginess that made the juice . . . juice. That was a little how he felt now, and his inability to sense the thrill of zenith pulsing through the castle wards only reminded him of the loss.

Better to think on the solution and not the problem. He sighed and tried to make himself think of anything other than his awareness of being incomplete.

He peered up again through the dark center of the massive spiral staircase and strained to spy any motion in the shadows. A groan of stone on stone echoed from far above, followed by a dim, flickering light. That must be them; only he and Japheth knew of the ancient passage.

Moving with alacrity, his brother, King Japheth, and Nebrine, the Queen Mother, descended the steps. They bore two precious bundles. The toddlers slept despite the thundering onslaught. The king and queen held hands, forming a link that bathed them in a faint silhouette of blue light, just enough to navigate the ancient stairs. They picked their way down the spiral steps as the booming thunderstrikes continued to reverberate through the castle.

Once they reached the bottom, Nebrine found an old sconce with a candle in it. She loosed her hand from her husband's and reached forward. A delicate rune on her wrist flickered with light as she channeled zenith. A small spark jumped from her hand, igniting the sconce. Amber light illuminated the circular room and the several dark passages that descended in different directions.

"Kaellor? Kaellor!" Japheth searched the dark corridors in earnest.

Kaellor drew back his hood, stepped out from the shadowed alcove, and approached the couple. "I'm here, Japh." He spoke in a raspy, weary voice that was accompanied by darkened circles beneath his grey eyes. His face looked naked without the runes of enlightenment, which had, just a day ago, adorned Kaellor's cheeks. Though his voice trembled with fatigue, his hands did not as he reached to clasp the forearm of his brother. Japheth pushed back the sleeve on his brother's forearm to reveal smooth, pale skin where the runes of balance and judgment had once lain.

Japheth's forearms remained covered in silver and gold runes. The complex symbols wove intricate patterns from his hands to his torso, coalescing in a central braid across his chest. Kaellor had never realized until this moment how much the veining of his brother's runes accentuated his appearance. They silhouetted his cheekbones and made his penetrating azure gaze all the more potent. Other runes defined his musculature at every curve and angle.

As the brothers regarded one another, a vibration of thunder rumbled again through the castle. The runes along the king's arms flickered in concert with the stone veining as defensive wards reflected the nadir from the abrogators above. With little regard for the assault, Japheth studied Kaellor. "You look tired, Kae; are you well enough for the journey?" Genuine concern flavored his tone.

"I'll manage. I must if we are to have a chance," said Kaellor. The king only nodded in understanding at his brother. "I'll admit the binding takes a bit more out of you than I anticipated."

"It stole the very light from your eyes. Did it hurt much?" asked Nebrine. "I mean, will it hurt them?" She nodded at her bundled children.

"The ritual itself was painless. After has been difficult, but I don't think they will feel the loss as I did. Time will tell, but I suspect they will be fine. Are you certain you can complete the binding for them? It's never been done like that before."

Japheth grasped the back of Kaellor's neck, his hand both rough and warm. The king stared long into his brother's eyes. "Have faith, Kae. We researched the mantle thoroughly, and it's exactly the kind of sacrifice needed to empower our trap for Tarkannen."

Another rumble vibrated through the castle, followed by a cascade of zenith across Japheth's runes. Kaellor nodded. "We must be away. You need to craft the mantle quickly," said Kaellor.

Nebrine nodded her understanding, then unwrapped the bundles and placed them tenderly in Japheth's arms. She shrugged back the arms on her silken robes, revealing delicate hands laced with silver and gold runes. As she faced her husband with her hands outstretched, palms up, she asked, "Are you ready, my love?"

The king inhaled a deep breath, then offered a weary smile in agreement before tossing the two bundles into the air. The toddlers rose up several feet, then hovered between them.

"Baellentrell balladure!" they said in unison as they began channeling currents of zenith. Blue ribbons of creative power coalesced and filled the chamber. Shaping the force to the limits of their gift, the king and queen drew more and more zenith, condensing the energy to their will.

They funneled the power into a cyclone of blue light that cradled the hovering bundles. Flickering silver and gold lights emanated from the runes pulsing across their arms. The energies mingled in the vortex of power and wove around the Baellentrell children.

The couple then joined hands, forming a circle. A soft humming murmur emitted from within the center of the vortex. As the vibration intensified, the gold and silver runes emitted an intense white light. Then, in a flash, the light discharged out in a brilliant sphere and conducted into the veining of the castle stones.

In the wake of the eruption, a deep, inky blackness enshrouded the couple. Swirls of subtractive nadir, harnessed only for the completion of the ritual, undulated around them and formed a liquid cyclone. The vortex absorbed sound and light. Nebrine gasped as her very breath was siphoned into the center of the twisting mass. Japheth locked his eyes to hers and tightened his grip on her hands.

Kaellor watched, all too familiar with the suffocating feeling the binding left. He shivered in revulsion at the memory. The inky cyclone towed the king and queen to its center. He knew this was the most challenging part. His binding had left him gasping for breath and shivering. He couldn't imagine what sacrifice would be required to impart the binding and mantles of obscurity to his nephews.

Nebrine and Japheth stood, unyielding. For a moment, all light and sound left the chamber. Then, like the remnant of a distant thunderstorm, a reverberant lone pulse of energy thundered, and the currents of zenith and nadir dispersed. Slowly, the sleeping toddlers descended, and Kaellor stepped forward to swaddle them in blankets.

Japheth and Nebrine staggered to support each other under the wave of fatigue that the ritual had thrust upon them. They held each other for a few long moments, each panting and shivering.

The temperature of the cavern plummeted, and the musty cavern smell dissipated. There was, Kaellor noticed, simply no smell at all now. Through the vapors of his breath, Kaellor thought his brother's complexion looked blue, like that of a man who had nearly drowned. Gone were the runes that had adorned his face, and his once brilliant azure gaze now stared back with a cold, grey purpose.

"Go swiftly, Kaellor. The Giver protect you," said the queen through labored breaths. She gathered her robes tightly around her and turned grey eyes to the stairs. Though bereft of her runes, she still looked determined. Nebrine Baellentrell, Queen Mother of Aarindorn, blinked away a tear and ascended without further words.

Kaellor looked down at the bundled children in his arms. They were cold but breathing and still quiet. *Isn't she going to say goodbye? This is all happening too fast.*

He regarded Japheth through tear-brimmed eyes. His brother offered only a soft smile. "We said our goodbyes; needs must, brother. And there really is no more time. You must be away when we meet Tarkannen."

As if to reinforce his words, the foundations of the castle rumbled and shook dust loose from the ceiling high above the spiraled staircase. This time, the veins of the castle remained dormant. The king blessed each of his sons with a kiss on the forehead.

"You have my love, my thanks, and my trust. You have my everything," said Japheth. Kaellor nodded and watched his brother ascend the spiral stairs.

Japheth stopped part of the way up and called down, "Remember to keep to the Southlands, brother; it'd be hard to find a wolvryn in those parts!"

"What do you mean?" asked Kaellor.

"I know you don't believe, but humor me. No wolvryn, no prophecy. Now go!" The king's voice echoed down the shaft as Kaellor Baellentrell swiftly descended a damp, secret corridor and spirited his two charges away.

Outside of Stone's Grasp, he waited for his betrothed to join him. After tense moments of hiding in the shadows, he watched her approach along the outer walls of the castle. But in a terrible twist of misfortune, the abrogator Tarkannen chose that moment to unleash a destructive blow on the unprotected walls.

Kaellor stood helpless as the walls collapsed and buried his beloved. He lost track of how long he stood there, rooted in place. Eventually, the dust cleared. He wanted to confirm whether or not she lived, but the mass and sheer volume of the debris convinced him of the reality of her death. The longer he remained, the more difficult his escape with the heirs. So, he fled into the night.

Kaellor stirred in his sleep as the images replayed over and over again.

JAPHETH SHOULDERED open a heavy door and stole a moment to recover. He locked his knees and set his feet against one side of the door frame, allowing his back to rest opposite. The ascent back through Stone's Grasp was pressing his stamina more than a little, and the binding ritual had already left him utterly spent.

Nebrine climbed the last few steps to join him, but instead of taking time to rest, she peered past him through the doorway and down the corridor. Her face held only a vacant expression as she panted and stared into the shadows. "By the Giver, Japheth, what have we unleashed?"

The king lifted his head to peer down the hallway. At the far end lay the mangled remains of three castle staff. The entrails of at least one had spilled onto the floor, slimy and wet. Japheth unlocked his knees, ignoring a wave of light-headedness, and staggered down the corridor. He stepped lightly around the bodies, each bent at the neck or torso in unnatural angles. The walls, splattered with blood, framed the macabre scene. The metallic tinge of blood mixed with excrement hung in the air.

Vibrations from an explosion unleashed by the abrogators shuddered through the foundation. "Come on; he's likely made it to the sanctum by now."

They raced across a large receiving room with vaulted ceilings. Members of the royal guard too numerous to count lay in clustered formations, many still holding their weapons. Japheth dropped to a knee and turned the body of one of them over. The smell of charred flesh rose from the young man's corpse. A dark hole with seared edges was burrowed clean into his chest.

"This looks like a wound from rune fire," said Japheth, puzzled by the discovery.

"We knew Tarkannen recruited some of the gifted to his cause. Rune fire or nadir burn; it's a puzzle for others to sort out later," said the queen.

They continued toward the inner sanctum, passing halls and corridors strewn with the wreckage of the abrogators' assault. More than once, Japheth slipped in boots slicked with the blood of the dead. In the great hall, the bodies of guards mingled with the remnants of castle staff and even their children. Some bodies lay in piles, and others rested where the abrogator horde had speared them down as they tried to escape.

As the couple finally approached the inner sanctum, they found the once-grand stained-glass double doors shattered into pieces. The doorway opened to reveal a massive circular hall, in the center of which rested a reflecting pool. Behind the pool stood a twenty-foot-tall statue of Eldrek Baellentrell, the first king of Aarindorn and the first to sit on the throne at Stone's Grasp.

The first king's statue held both arms outstretched, welcoming the future with palms up and eyes to the horizon. His chiseled arms, ringed with intricate runes of gold and silver, held a hawk in one hand and a winged dragon in the other. The statue stood on a large marble dais, and at its foot stood the Usurper, Tarkannen. The tall, brawny man wore a dark hooded cloak. He stood before the statue tracing the runes down its legs.

"I forgot how detailed the runes of the first king were." The abrogator's voice echoed in the great chamber. He continued inspecting the statue, seemingly oblivious to the arrival of the royal couple. "Really though. . . I'm now left to wonder if Eldrek actually carried these in life or if the artisans embellished their appearance for the sake of posterity."

Japheth stepped through the threshold with Nebrine at his side. "Tarkannen! You shame the Lellendule name and defile the empire! By the Giver, I'll cleanse the palace of your stain!"

The figure turned a slow circle to face them. His entire appearance was otherworldly. Intricate designs covered the flesh of the once mortal man. These sigils, however, writhed like iridescent black snakes under the surface of his skin. The arcane symbols covered even his face and bald head, leaving only his eyes to glow with a sickly jaundiced hue.

"So it's true," said Nebrine with an astonished voice. "You've fully embraced the path of the abrogator."

Tarkannen held up a hand to deflect her recrimination. "It didn't have to be this way, you know. All you had to do was grant me access to the deepening well. That was all I needed. All this death could have been avoided."

Japheth shook his head in disbelief. "You can't truly think we would ever provide an abomination such as you access to the very source of our power."

Tarkannen looked down at the sigils on his forearms, considering Japheth's words. "Small minds can only fathom small things. So be it," he sighed. The abrogator then cocked his head to the side, inspecting Japheth and Nebrine. "Dark is the hour, and darker still your gaze. You've lost your runing, my king," he said in a sibilant voice. "And Nebrine, did you think you could hide the heirs from me so easily? I sensed the binding the moment it was cast. You can't touch a sliver of nadir and not expect me to sense it. Tell me you two weren't foolish enough to place the concealment yourselves only to come straight here?"

"I am not your king, and your time is at an end, abrogator!" Japheth strode into the hall and swallowed back a wave of revulsion as he realized that his boots, sticky with the blood of innocents, left tracks on the floor. A sickly, musky odor drew his attention to the shadowed edges of the hall, where he saw the abrogator's horde.

In the perimeter of the sanctum stood Tarkannen's minions. Grotvonen, the small, hairy, humanoid creatures summoned from deep underground, clustered in groups. They chattered with what sounded like anticipation. Most stood on two legs, but a few crouched on all four as if prepared to bound forward in attack. Interspersed with the grotvonen mingled a few umbral. These latter dark creatures looked humanoid but were cast of oily shadow and lacked distinct eyes and noses. Summoned from the Drift, they responded to the power of nadir. Only an abrogator could command them with any authority.

The horde remained shrouded in the shadows of the sanctum, but their strange clattering teeth and guttural voices echoed in the great chamber. Japheth muscled down the cold fear settling in the pit of his stomach. He glanced at Nebrine, who nodded once. *I know what we came here to do, so let's be about it.* He took her hand and stepped forward.

"Think you my equal, son of Baellentrell? Even with the full moon of Baellen, you could never channel enough zenith to best me. I am that which withers and destroys. I am a return of the balance that was lost. I am nadir incarnate!"

"No, Tarkannen, I cannot best you, nor has that ever been my way. But some lessons are never learned the easy way." Japheth and Nebrine stopped in the center of the room, facing the enormous statue of Eldrek. Without a word, both held their arms out, palms up. Japheth looked to his wife, and they shared in that moment an understanding of their love and desperate commitment.

"What? How? You are bound!" the abrogator hissed. "Take them!" he yelled, and in the same instant, channeled coils of nadir.

The Usurper held his arms out, and the sigils on his flesh writhed in agitation. Surging forward from his palms, malevolent ink-black cords of nadir arced toward the king and queen. The sanctum dimmed to shadows under the oppressive release of pure nadir, and the hordes lumbered forward from the dark recesses of the hall brandishing bloodstained weapons.

The power of the Usurper rocked through the great hall and descended on the king and queen. "Eyes to the horizon, love," said Japheth. Nebrine and Japheth stood, awaiting the expected rush of death as black tentacles snaked forward to envelop them.

In the moment between heartbeats, the trap released. The statue of Eldrek crackled. Ancient magic danced across the runes of the statue with lightning ferocity. Streaks of zenith, as intense as the sun, burst forth from the figure of Eldrek and engulfed the room. The blinding radiance seared across the grotvonen and umbral, instantly petrifying the masses into garish poses with expressions of anger and pain. The frozen horde lingered a moment, then crumbled to ash on the sanctum floor.

"No! You'll ruin us all! This can not be!" Tarkannen turned his hands inward and pulled the currents of nadir back into himself. Oily coils of power speared through his torso, and the writhing mass of black tentacles tangled into a dense knot. He evaporated into a smoky vortex, leaving the great hall with a lingering scream of agony.

The haze of ash lingered in the air, eventually drifting to rest on the sanctum floor. Where the king and queen previously stood, two flawless statues remained, arms outstretched, palms up, eyes to the horizon.

Chapter Five: The Regent of Aarindorn

Therek Lefledge hunched over a large table in a private library on the fifth floor of Stone's Grasp. As the regent of Aarindorn, he often used the suite to conduct strategy meetings, review missives, and attend to the daily business of running the kingdom. This day, he was sifting through several reports spread across the oversized workspace. His lanky arms ranged over the table from one pile of papers to another, and his long, nimble fingers divided the significant from the mundane.

The early morning sun broke through the window and reflected off a mirror, casting light across his back and filtering through his arched, white eyebrows to cast a strange pattern on the table before him. He tried to press down the unruly brows, to no avail. He would have to see the court barber soon, but such matters could always wait. For now, he concerned himself with the daily memos.

The healers of Callinora had provided him with lists of roots and herbs needed to treat the infirmed. He planned to supply these from the duchies along the east side of the kingdom. In addition, the Geddins, Halbreks, and one of the Endule families had all made overtures for social outings.

Those decisions could wait. More importantly, a scholar in Callinora had reported with alarm that the number of new gifted in the kingdom continued to dwindle. *I'll have to take that up with one of the elders there.*

And finally, Stellance, a duchy in the south of the kingdom, had made yet another request to send a trade envoy to the Borderlands. *That at least merits consideration.*

Therek glanced at a map underneath a plate of glass on the table. The kingdom of Aarindorn lay along the northern edge of the lands north of the Korjinth Mountains. Protected by the Great Crown, a smaller mountain range, the kingdom remained accessible only by passage through the Twin Pillars of Eldrek at the southern edge of the range.

Stellance lay at the southernmost edge of the kingdom. Despite their relative isolation, the Stellancians had cast their lot with the loyalists during the Abrogator's War. As such, they had suffered terrible losses when the abrogator's horde invaded. Led by umbral, the throng of grotvonen and grondle had decimated the city at the entrance to the kingdom.

Years ago, Stellance had prospered from the ores and minerals mined from the Great Crown, but after the war, the scattered hordes of grotvonen retreated into the deep caverns. Stellancians had been forced to abandoned most of the mines, even collapsing tunnels to seal away the last remnants of the Usurper's forces. Since then, the duchy's wealth came mainly from the vineyards, which produced wine, and the potent distillate, resco. The latter could serve as antiseptic or spirit. *How did that old phrase go? Something like, "One splash kills the rot; two makes you brave, three grants a dreamless sleep, and four grants the grave."*

In the last three seasons, Stellancians had harvested bumper crops from the vineyards and distilled the excess wine into resco. Casks of the potent spirit crammed the cellars in Stellance. He sighed. *If I owned that much resco, I too would look to export the stuff.*

But so much had changed after the war. The kingdom had adopted an isolationist position and allowed the dense alpine forest to flourish between the Pillars of Eldrek. The borders remained closed to trade. *But if the Stellancians are ready for change, then perhaps others are too.*

The notion unsettled him more than a little. Therek held the regency under the firm belief that a Baellentrell heir would one day return to sit the throne and return Aarindorn to prosperity and stability. *I saw something of that in our future, didn't I?*

Now, he couldn't be sure if it was an actual vision or just the dwindling hope of a man straining under the weight of an office he had never desired. *If I'm uncomfortable with opening the borders to trade, then that makes me an isolationist too. When did that happen?*

A soft knock on the door interrupted his thoughts. One tap, pause, then two quick taps. "Come in, Chancle," he said.

Chancle Lellendule always used the same knock. *Always reliable, that one.* He wore a crisp blue uniform that matched with the blue moon of Baellen, and his close-cropped, dark brown hair was trimmed in the current fashion, above the ears. A well-manicured beard finished his seasonal look and reflected his attention to detail. The middle-aged man entered the library after greeting Therek with his familiar soft smile. His blue oval eyes were turned down at the edges and always made Therek feel like his friend empathized with his struggles. *And who better to act as my vice regent these days?*

Chancle closed the door but held his hands behind his back, obscuring something. "Good morning, Regent," said Chancle.

Therek frowned. "You haven't called me regent behind closed doors in a long time."

"Yes, well, you appeared to be engaged in something . . . regenty, my friend."

"Regenty . . . yes, I suppose that does describe most of my mornings of late. Let's sit a bit and discuss your meetings." Therek paused and inhaled, searching the aromas in the air. "Is that by chance a crownberry muffin hiding behind your back?"

Chancle grinned widely and approached, revealing a plate of plump muffins packed with the dark blue berries. "From the first harvest this summer. The highlands are flush with them. I know we have to tackle serious issues today, but thought first, maybe a little indulgence?"

"You know me all too well, my friend," said Therek. His wispy white eyebrows turned up with his smile. They sat in comfortable chairs at a window overlooking all of Stone's Grasp and affording a view of Lake Ullend. The castle, with its massive white stone parapets and towers, cantilevered directly out of the Great Crown.

Stone's Grasp was not a formal keep, but rather a sprawling collection of connected buildings that erupted from the base of the mountains and descended in several tiers from bailey to bailey. At the bottom, a stretch of forest extended to the curtain wall and surrounded an expansive manicured green.

Quarried white stone from the Great Crown had been used to create all of the castle structures. The process of quarrying and polishing the stonework left a visible veining of silver and, in some places, gold. Instead of creating areas of weakness, the veining melded the stones in place, defying conventional logic. The unusual properties allowed the behemoth structure its precarious perch.

None of the grandeur of Stone's Grasp or the surrounding city of the same name entered Therek's mind. He was instead enthralled with the simplicity of the crownberry muffin. He took generous bites, allowing the purple-red fruit to pop at the sides of his tongue. The mixture of the tart berry tempered by the sweetness of the muffin made him temporarily forget his earlier concerns.

Funny how food does that: eases the mind and triggers memories of childhood. "So then, now that you have plied me with sweets, let's have it. How was your meeting with the noble families?"

Chancle nodded. "Your suspicions were correct. There is a fair amount of uncertainty. Several houses voice concern with the kingdom's immediate and long-term future."

The ephemeral concerns of the nobles could mean anything but most likely have to do with another marriage proposal. Karragin would squash any notions; she really is her mother's daughter. What was I thinking when I forwarded that invitation from the Geddins? She would unman that boy before the main course. And Nolan, he's far too young. Therek waited for his friend to continue.

"Many feel that it's time to clear a road through the Pillars of Eldrek and open trade to the south. There are merits to the proposal, but it would require a certain amount of finesse with the Lentrell's and others who favor an isolationist strategy."

"The old wounds are healing, perhaps more than we both realized. I just received a similar request from merchants in Stellance, of all places. That duchy suffered more than most, and if they are prepared to open trade, then it's likely others are as well."

"It's a reflection of your leadership, I think," said Chancle. "You've given us stability and growth at a time when the kingdom threatened to tear itself apart. If people can look past those dark times to a brighter future, it speaks well of you."

"But I suspect not well enough; you mentioned concerns voiced over our long-term future?"

Chancle pulled his gaze away from the window. "Do you want the eloquent explanation or the plain truth?"

Therek replied by raising one of his wispy eyebrows as if to say, "What do you think, my friend?"

"Yes, of course, the plain truth it is." Chancle swallowed, exhibiting more than a little discomfort. "There is a feeling held by many that it is time for Aarindorn to abandon the old rules governing the succession of the kingdom and turn to something that embraces the future."

"You're talking about abandoning a process that built our kingdom, that both sustains and strengthens our people. Does your brother share this view?"

"Hestian remains loyal to the old ways. Understand, my old friend, *we* are not talking about any of this," said Chancle, "but others are. And their words are not just whispered as impolite dinner conversation anymore, but spoken loudly at gatherings for all to debate."

Therek thought back to a vision he'd endured years ago, before the Abrogator's War. The complex images had warned him about parts of an impending attack and allowed King Japheth and Queen Nebrine to prepare for the eventual struggle. He'd been so overwhelmed in the moment of receiving the prophecy that he fell into the waters of Lake Ullend and nearly drowned. The incident had left him with an incomplete recollection of the last part of the vision, but he was sure he'd seen Aarindorn rising from the ashes of war with a child of the blue moon leading the kingdom to prosperity.

Didn't that mean a Baellentrell? Historically, the Baellentrell bloodline rules when the blue moon of Baellen dominates the night sky, as it will do for another seventy years.

"Do you believe me, Chancle? Do you think I would cling to hope where none exists?" Therek asked.

"I want to believe you, but you have to admit, with no sign of anyone in the Baellentrell bloodline for over what, twelve years? It makes sense that we should at least consider how we might govern ourselves if an heir never returns. Nobody can imagine the kingdom in a regency until the turning of the moons, and the notion of a Lellendule assuming the throne at this time is unthinkable."

"Some wounds require greater time to heal," said Therek.

"Well, yes, there is the obvious fact that the Usurper was a Lellendule," said Chancle. He looked like he'd just swallowed the bitter part of a turnip. "But even if you set that aside, a Lellendule would never inherit the full measure of the gift while the red moon wanes. You put that together with Tarkannen's treachery, his use of abrogation, and—"

"And the Assembly would never even consider a Lellendule," Therek finished the obvious conclusion.

Not that I was thinking of you or Hestian, but you, my friend, know the nobles, and your brother has command experience. You both have served the kingdom honorably these past years.

"So, what do they propose in place of the office I hold?" he asked.

"There are several possible paths forward," said Chancle. "Their most reasonable submission endorses you remaining in your position of leadership, but not as a regent. Regent indicates only a temporary position and undermines our collective need to move the kingdom forward."

Kingdom. Does that word even apply to Aarindorn anymore? What would we call ourselves then, a city-state? Grand duchy? No. Those sound too fractionated, and though we are a divided people, that's precisely the thing we need to overcome if Aarindorn is to thrive in the future. Republic? Country?

Therek rubbed his temples in frustration. *This office has been more trouble than I ever imagined it could be all those years ago. These political games are exhausting.*

He approached the map of the kingdom on the high table and surveyed the duchies in the west: Callinora, Dulesque, and Beclure. The scholars of Callinora usually abstained from political discourse. Dulesque and Beclure had sided with the Usurper in the war. The postwar reparations had weakened the two duchies, but the restitution arrangements ended two years ago. Though the ruling families of those duchies sat as quiet participants at assembly, too much of the flavor of the conversation tasted like something served at Dulescan court.

"How much time do you think we have before this debate is pushed before the Assembly?" Therek asked.

Chancle rubbed a thumb across a hangnail, frowning. "A year, I would think, which gives you the chance to engage most of the ruling families at the Harvestmoon assembly. You have the lesser houses of Endule and Lentrell in full support, but garnering the support of the nobles from the western duchies will require some investment."

Therek considered how he might best address some of the unrest. Perhaps an envoy could be sent, now that the roads favored travel. A diplomatic mission could travel south toward Dulesque and contact several minor duchies on the way. As he traced a possible path, the rune on his chest, his arca prime, tingled, and he was overcome with a surge of vertigo.

Sensing the release of his gift, he grasped the edges of the great table and felt his awareness tumble into the map. The terrain of local rolling hills and meadows undulated, rising from the table. *No, not rising. I'm falling into the map!*

The Great Crown's white peaks erupted from the table. His stomach lurched, and he endured the sensation of falling. He descended through the clouds ringing the summit of the mountain range; his nose even stung from the chill of the brisk mountain air. Then he caught an updraft that warmed his wings and slowed his descent down the mountainside. *Wait, wings? By the Giver, I'm a hawk? That's never happened in a vision before, but it does explain the odd sense of floating.*

He hovered above the kingdom momentarily, then was propelled to the south. The images rolled under him with nauseating intensity. Stellance, then the peaks of the Pillars, broke into view, but only briefly. Then he was speeding across the alpine forest to the plains beyond. Villages, towns, and cities unknown to him rushed past. The vision carried him up and over the massive, impassable peaks of the Korjinth Mountains, where the frigid gusts threatened to overwhelm his senses.

At the summit, storms erupted around him as thick ribbons of zenith collided with black tendrils of nadir. Vast, wild currents of the two forces gathered across the peaks of the Korjinth range and thrashed about with savage intensity, eventually exploding with showers of light. Where they collided, strange keening wails shredded the still air, and sterile vapors overwhelmed his senses.

He broke through the tempest to a view of the mountainous horizon. The moons of Baellen and Lellen dominated the sky. He glanced down to see a verdant valley below before plunging through the clouds and descending into darkness on the south side of the mountain range. Tracks of untamed forest passed below him, and then the images drew to a halt.

He gasped as the sudden deceleration stole his breath. Scintillating lights danced at the periphery of his vision. *Focus, stay awake. You will not miss the end this time!*

He had a vague awareness of returning to his body, of being on his hands and knees and retching with violent dry heaves. His head and face felt swollen as if he'd hung upside down, and his lungs burned. Enthralled in the grip of his gift, he couldn't seem to make his chest muscles relax.

He grounded his awareness in the vision. Delicate purple wildflowers sprang up between his fingers. His stomach cramped, and prickly tingling rushed into his hands and feet. He clenched his fists, tearing the stems of several flowers loose, then gritted his teeth and forced himself onto his back. Just as the edges of his vision dimmed, his stomach relaxed, and he gasped a breath of sweet air.

He lay on his back for several minutes, allowing his strength to return and the tingly sensation to recede. Finally, Therek staggered to his feet. He pocketed one of the flowers, then considered his surroundings. He stood at the edge of a small pasture adjacent to a dwelling with a covered porch. He could smell horses, and a chorus of frogs accompanied the whisper of a nearby river. *Where, by the Giver, am I? The architecture of this home is not of the Northlands.*

The home, crafted from thick timbers on a base of fieldstone, pitched an unusually steep roof. *The last orange blush of the sunset is to the west, so the silhouette of the Korjinth must be to the north.*

The clouds parted, and a brilliant shaft of blue light radiated from the moon of Baellen. It fell upon the house, where a woman rocked in a chair on the porch. Not knowing how long the vision would last, he loped up to the porch with a gait that defied his years. The woman had no awareness of him. She wore a plain dress and worked a needlepoint, crafting what appeared to be the outline of mountains over a compass rose.

He started to enter the dwelling in search of some clue that would identify who the woman was or where the house was. As he crossed the threshold, his arca prime pulsed once with a paralyzing thump. Stinging pain lanced from his chest and into his neck and chin, then down his arms and legs. All at once, searing pain and then momentary blackness overwhelmed him.

Something cold and firm pressed against his left cheek and ribs. His breath felt labored, uncomfortable under his weight. The sensation grounded him, and he opened his eyes to find himself sprawled over the glass-topped table in the library. He pulled in deep, reassuring breaths and felt the recession of the tremendous pressure in his head. Chancle guided him to one of the oversized chairs, then joined him.

"Where did you go this time, my friend?" asked Chancle.

Therek grasped the arms of the chair and curled his toes in his boots. His toes and fingers still tingled with prickly numbness. He sighed. The last time his gift had channeled so much zenith, it was weeks before he returned to feeling normal. "How long has it been since I sent someone scouting for any sign of the heir?"

"It was three, perhaps four years ago, I believe?" said Chancle in a questioning tone that indicated he was searching his memory. "Yes, it was one of the Lentrell boys. Gerrik or Herrik, something like that. He was a proficient tracker and skilled in woodcraft."

"He was the fifth child of Aarindorn I sent beyond the Pillars, and none have returned; we have not even received a message indicating their success or lack thereof." Therek tapped the tingly tips of his fingers together, trying to dissipate the numb feeling. "I told myself I would not send anyone else out into the world without knowing at least where I should send them."

Therek reached into a side pocket of his robe and withdrew the strange wildflower. The delicate, green stem was adorned at the base by long, thin, recurved leaves. The stem bent under the weight of a cluster of pitcher-shaped, deep purple flowers that emitted a sweet scent. "And by the Giver, now at least I have some idea."

"That's wonderful news, and the timing couldn't be better! Tell me how I can be of assistance," said Chancle.

"Can you organize a trade expedition to the Borderlands? Coordinate it with the merchants in Stellance; they are eager for expansion to the south. If I understand the vision correctly, we need to reopen the road through the Pillars of Eldrek as soon as possible." He scribbled several orders on fine parchment and handed the document to Chancle.

After inspecting the requisition, Chancle folded the paper into a breast pocket. "I will see to it at once. Is there anything else I can do this morning?"

"Send word to your brother that his budget estimate for the needs of the military this next year is overdue. Hestian hates that part of the job, but unless he wants to explain to his soldiers why they have to forage for their own food, he needs to get it done. See to those details, and I will take care of the rest."

Therek watched his friend depart. Who could he call upon for a mission with such gravity and risk? Five times, he'd sent capable people beyond the Pillars, and he felt the absence of each one of them. None of the families in Aarindorn would suffer the loss of a favored son or daughter lightly, and such sacrifices were felt all the more in the years after the Abrogator's War. Five families had already watched their loved one depart, never to return, and five families now cast dubious glances at the regent and whispered to those who would listen that his judgment was tainted. The mission had become known as Therek's folly and, in some corners of Aarindorn, used as a euphemism for something doomed to fail.

Can I really blame them? He understood their grief all too well. But he also bore the weight of the kingdom, and now he had some idea where to send them. And he knew who to send. *He will be my faint flicker of light at the end of this very long, dark tunnel.*

Chapter Six: Karragin the Outrider

Karragin Lefledge woke with the first morning's light and rubbed at the runes on her left forearm. The delicate silver veining interlaced with gold spirals in an intricate pattern from her wrist to elbow. The entire rune flickered briefly and tingled with a mild burning sensation, like brushing against nettles. She lay still and searched the images in her sleepy mind, trying to recall something solid. Rarely did her lesser gift of foretelling leave her with clear ideas. More often, she felt like she was trying to grab images made of smoke, there one moment and fading the next.

The incomplete premonition had been frustrating her for three days, and with a sigh, she sat up and pulled errant strands of slate and silver hair back into a topknot. She sucked in her upturned upper lip and ran her tongue across the groove of an old scar on the right side as she tried to recall what her gift might be telling her from that place between sleep and waking.

Something like thundering hooves, or maybe stampeding cattle in the grasslands? She felt a sense of urgency like she needed to investigate the plains south of Aarindorn. *But investigate what? Cattle? Come on. Clear the mind, Karra, be open to the gift, focus your zenith. It's no different than your ability to commune with animals.*

Except that it was different and very elusive. Why did the Giver bother to impart the talent of foresight if she couldn't call upon the skill at will? She sighed in frustration. On the nightstand adjacent to her bed, she leafed through a small journal. She kept it there as an attempt to record something of her talent while first waking. The trick had proved useful about once or twice a year. A search of the journal revealed nothing new.

She made water in the chamber pot then began her daily routine of stretches and calisthenics. Sometimes the mundane repetition helped her to remain clear-minded, so she started with push-ups.

Her morning would be filled soon enough with sidestepping social interactions with minor nobles. She didn't trust most of them. Since her father's appointment to regent some twelve years ago, she'd avoided several betrothals and false friendships, all aimed at currying favor with her family. Fortunately, her father possessed an uncanny knack for reading people and had never pressured her to engage meaningfully with anyone of dubious motives.

Lately, however, he seemed tired, or at least preoccupied. His usual hawkish demeanor had softened under the chronic stress of the position, and just last week, he'd mentioned that she should consider an invitation to dine with the Geddins. Marsona Geddins was perhaps twelve and already preoccupied with boys; far too young, and they had nothing in common. If the girl's habits were any indication, her runes involved flowers and drawing. She hadn't even sat through the Rite of Revealing to determine her arca prime. *It will probably be something shallow, like eyelash fluttering.*

No, they had nothing in common, which meant the invitation's purpose was a formal introduction to Marsona's older brother, Ashrof. He was nice enough on the eyes, she supposed: tall, broad shoulders, pretty good on horseback, though he was lousy with the bow. All that paled in light of the spineless way he followed the other nobles at court. He was a year older, perhaps eighteen, and had completed the Rite. *What was his main talent, though, distance measurement or something? He could be pretty handy on a survey, but why did the Giver gift anyone that skill? Silliness, really.*

The muscles in her chest burned in protest, and she realized she'd lost count of her push-ups. She vacated all the jumbled, superficial concerns in her mind and focused inward, then pushed herself to activate her arca prime and imagined the runes across her chest flaring to life.

Channeling the zenith came easy; forcing it to conform to the confines of her runes proved more difficult. She had labored for years to gain some semblance of control of her lesser rune of premonition, and her morning already proved how frustrating that endeavor had been. The process felt more fluid when she created a need, so she held herself in a plank position for several minutes and occasionally repeated a deliberately slow push-up. Her arms, shoulders, chest, and core burned, but still, she held the pose. Sweat gathered on her brow, but she controlled her breathing and pushed her body further. Her torso trembled. She gritted her teeth, determined to force zenith through her greater gift.

She balanced all her weight onto her hands and slowly drew both feet forward. Just when she thought a foot would drop to the ground, she found it. A spark flared from a deep place in her center, and zenith infused her body. The arcane force streamed along her runes and coalesced over the intricate symbol on her chest, where it pulsed and tingled. The surge of her gift was painful at first, especially over her nipples, but just for an instant. Then the cold sting became a throbbing pleasure that infiltrated her core and suffused all of her muscles with unnatural vigor.

She pushed and then pulled herself into a handstand, pivoted on one hand, then sprang herself to a standing position. Her control remained, and she pulled in more zenith. Her body vibrated with the strength she commanded.

She hurried to a series of rounded boulders in the corner of her room. She hadn't tried to lift the third boulder in the line yet; its top reached above her knees. *Nothing to be gained by staring at it.*

With an economy of motion, she squatted down, embraced the cold stone, and deftly hoisted it up above her shoulder. She took a few steps in a circle and prepared to return the stone in place when her thoughts were interrupted by a knock on her door.

Her concentration faltered, and she was forced to drop the stone rather unceremoniously. She danced back out of the way as the boulder landed on the stone floor with a resonant crack. She eyed the damage. *Nothing a good mason can't fix.*

"Karra? Karragin, open the door! Is everything alright?" The tenor and pitch of her father's voice made him sound nervous. *Father is never nervous.*

She opened the door. "Good morning, Father," she said with mild irritation as her grasp on the gift faded. Her strength receded to normal, and all her muscles began aching. Therek Lefledge, regent of Aarindorn, stooped in the doorway.

Her father cut a lean, angular silhouette and stood a head above others in any crowd. Her deceased mother used to joke that he was never born but hatched from a crane. Certainly, the builders of Stone's Grasp never imagined the passages and doors would need to accommodate someone with her father's stature.

He tilted his head under the stone header and peered at her through thick, long, silver eyebrows. The way his eyebrows swept up toward his temples always made him appear somewhat feral, and they reminded Karragin of the pointed ears of the silver mountain lynx. She knew all too well the sharp mind underneath.

He looked past her into her room, utilitarian as it was, to investigate the cause of the noise. She twisted and bent, stretching sore muscles as she waited for him to complete his inspection.

"Are those atlas stones? How ever did you convince Captain Oren to bring them here?" he asked.

"None of the militia have touched them for years. He was happy for the space. Getting them here was more difficult than convincing him to part with them."

"Being on the first floor of the upper bailey has its advantages, I suppose," he said. "Might I come in?" Karragin motioned for her father to enter. Just three sweeping, long strides placed him deep into the room. He turned to sit on one of the atlas stones. She remained standing, which allowed them to make level eye contact. "Tell me then, how is your control? Can you summon your gifts at will?"

"Depends on which one you mean," she said. "I've been empathic with animals for as long as I can remember. Yet, I've had this for years, and I'm no closer to controlling it today than I was six years ago." She indicated the runic veining of premonition on her left forearm. "It's easier lately to engage my arca prime, my strength, but I only completed the ritual last year."

Therek nodded to her with what seemed to be a father's understanding. "When your own father can't provoke his arca prime at will, why are you surprised?"

Everyone in Aarindorn knew of Therek's rare ability: premonition. Though his visions of prophecy revealed important truths, he had little to no control over how the gift manifested. Once, a vision overwhelmed him, and he fell off a boat into Lake Ullend and nearly drowned. When he recovered, he predicted the return of the abrogator Tarkannen, the Usurper. His foretelling allowed the Baellentrells to prepare their defenses, but to Therek's endless lament, his understanding of the future was incomplete.

His visions had never revealed how many noble houses would side with Tarkannen or how civil war and the subsequent recovery would set the kingdom back for nearly a decade. Most tragically, he never foresaw the death of his wife, who'd fallen under an umbral blade when Tarkannen's minions attacked Stone's Grasp.

He seemed to look through her, wrestling with those distant memories even now. *Where did you go this time, Father, and how long will you stay there? After Mother's death, you were always so distracted. How did you carry on? I become frustrated by the limitations of my own premonitions; I can't imagine how angry I would be to learn so much but still be blinded to so much more. The Giver can be a tricky bitch.*

She reached out to touch his hand, returning him to the conversation. He smiled softly in thanks for the way she grounded him back in the room, back in the present. "You haven't asked me about your brother's revealing. Aren't you curious?"

Surprise flickered across her porcelain face. *That's right! Nolan did start the ritual, but he just began last night, and most trials take days. Why didn't I think of it this morning? It's this damn minor gift of foresight. It has distracted me every morning this week.* She rubbed a thumb across the rune on her forearm.

"You're either really excited or possibly angry his Rite of Revealing only lasted a day. By your expression, I can't tell. Nolan may have your mother's hair, but you definitely inherited her uncanny ability to restrict emotion."

"Are you trying to say I've got Mother's resting asshole gaze, Father?" she spoke the words with perfect indifference. "Nolan says that's why you spelled my name with an *R-A-G* in the middle. The common spelling has it different."

Therek arched one of his angular eyebrows. "Karra, you know I never thought of your mother that way. She was one of the only people I could never read. I suppose that's what drew me to her in the first place."

"What do you mean?" she asked.

"Imagine how boring life would be if you always knew everything your partner was feeling. No spontaneity, no surprise. That was the life I faced after my gifts matured—until I met your mother." The beginnings of a smile creased the wrinkles at the edges of his eyes.

"I see," she said. "And you have the same trouble reading me?"

He nodded. "Sometimes . . . most of the time, yes. It's why I check on you more than Nolan. Your brother wears his emotion so plainly the Giver and the whole world can see them. Don't ever let that boy play king's gambit. He would lose everything in the first hand. But you... I can't usually tell what sways you."

She searched his eyes, waiting. *You really can't tell what I'm thinking? The Giver's tits Father, tell me about Nolan's gift already!*

She felt the expression with passion, but her face, she realized, remained still. She glanced at a small wall mirror. *Taker's abyss, I do have resting asshole gaze!* She lifted her eyebrows in an uncharacteristic expression of surprise.

"So I check in, Karra. I want you to be happy, and most days, unless you indulge me, I can't tell."

"I would be very happy if you could tell me about Nolan, Father. Is he well? He didn't fail, did he? His trial was so short."

His eyes twinkled with a hint of mischief. "I think your brother should like to tell you himself. Get yourself sorted out and come join us for breakfast."

She washed her face, tightened her topknot, and donned her Outrider uniform. She then inspected her profile. Leather reinforced the joints of the midnight blue pants and tunic. She liked the flexibility afforded by the cut and the way the heavier material blunted the silhouette of her breasts but accentuated her shoulders. Silver threaded embroidery adorned the high neck and shoulders and indicated her station as a seasoned member of the elite group. The front panels of the tunic crossed before tucking under a belt.

Those invited to join the Outriders enjoyed significant prestige but endured arduous training. Only one in five finished. She'd climbed to her position as second in her quad a year ago. A branch of the Aarindorn military, Outriders combined expertise in woodcraft, reconnaissance, infiltration, and espionage. Their training exercises focused on mastering the latest weaponry and survival in harsh elements.

Most Outrider candidates managed to complete the trials involving the secretive infiltration of a guild or duchy. Far more struggled with the rigorous survival training required. As she walked to the dining hall, she wondered about the usefulness of the skillset since the kingdom had settled rather amiably into peace since the Abrogator's War twelve years ago.

She found her brother sitting at a long table in a common dining hall surrounded by several other tenders, first-year initiates in Outrider training. Instead of the midnight blue, they each wore simple tunics of tan and green.

Nolan's wide-mouthed grin beamed through the unkempt, thick cinnamon curls that tumbled down over his eyes. Karragin approached just as one of the tenders giggled, slapping Nolan on the shoulder. "Well, that seals it. There's no way they can send you to Callinora now! What use would a scout be to a bunch of healers?"

Scout, he says? Sometimes the Giver gives, but that would be a true blessing.

While a good medic was an absolute requirement in every quad, they were commonplace. But someone gifted with scouting—actually inheriting that arca prime—was rare. As she approached, his comrades deferentially parted. She straddled the bench he sat on, facing him.

"Morning, Karra." He beamed a toothy grin, but she just stared plain-faced. Nolan recovered and sat up stiffly. "I mean, sir, good morning, sir!"

She held his attention for several seconds. *If I do have a resting asshole gaze, then I may as well use it to good purpose once in a while.*

After a few seconds, though, she couldn't help herself and felt the edges of her mouth soften in a smile. They touched foreheads, and she whispered, "I'm so happy for you, brother."

She leaned back and tried to peer inside his tunic. The rumpled green and tan panels flopped together in an untidy manner, and she could only make out the top edge of the rune upon his chest. She pinched a corner of the neckline between two slender fingers. "May I see?"

He turned to face her and nodded, his toothy grin returning. She separated his tunic to reveal delicate silver and gold runes. The pattern started low over his sternum, and the intertwined symbols spiraled over each breast then gathered tightly in the center before delicately receding at his shoulders. Some trick of the light made the central braid appear to shift. For just a moment, two feral eyes peered from deep in the tangled veining. She pulled the crossed panels of his tunic crisply back and ran her hands across his shoulders, smoothing out a few wrinkles.

"What do you think?" he asked.

"It's not what I think that matters," she said. "What do you think?"

"I've spent a lot of time working with these," he said, pointing to the runes on his forearms. "I thought for sure I was Callinora bound, you know, another medic. Not that there's anything wrong with being a healer. But I think this finally puts me out of the alchemists' guild."

"You say that like it's a bad thing, and I know you haven't been content working there." She paused, thinking of the right words. "But at least you learned something of your gifts. This definitely changes things, though." She tapped on his chest, emphasizing the words.

"I haven't really had time to get used to it, but it's good, right?"

"None of the Giver's gifts are good, and none are bad; they are what we make them," she repeated the old expression. "This will make you invaluable to the Outriders, though, so try not to grind the whole thing up, will you?" She sat back and regarded him. *My brother, our first true scout in years. He's going to be alright, Mother.*

He nodded, and thick curls of hair jumbled back over his eyes.

She stood. "And Nolan, either pull that mop of hair back or cut it—we can't have the kingdom's newest scout blinded by his own sloppiness." Without waiting for his response, she grabbed an apple from the table and tousled his hair once for good measure.

She turned to find her father. He sat sipping on hot tea at a larger table reserved for positions of authority. Next to him sat two senior members of the Outriders, Wardens Reddevek and Elbiona. She approached, saluted her superiors, and nodded to her father.

"Karragin, Reddevek, and I were just discussing Nolan's gift. What do you think?" asked Therek.

"He will be a definite asset to the Outriders if he successfully completes his training," she said. "He will have to make some adjustments. He was prepared to travel to Callinora for training in the healing arts."

Therek nodded once. "He is not the only one of my children who will have to make adjustments this day."

Her expression remained placid, but her mind raced with possibilities. *Father, you never drop hints lightly. What adjustments will I have to make? I'm only second in the quad. A solid position, but nothing guarantees my status there. None of us hold rank beyond that. Just last week, I did turn down an invitation to transfer into the city watch under Captain Oren. But he doesn't have the authority to mandate a transfer. This better not have anything to do with that spineless Ashrof Geddins.*

Each warden commanded twenty-five quads, and Elbiona stood in Karragin's chain of command. Karragin considered her a good leader, crafty when it came to strategy contests, a quick thinker, and an excellent communicator. Years ago, she and Reddevek ran in one of the few quads known to have made a ranging deep into the Borderlands south of Aarindorn. Their mission had incurred serious risk, as it was back when grotvonen and grondle still plagued the countryside in large numbers. Elbiona swept errant strands of grey hair behind her ears and pierced Karragin with her steely pale blue eyes. "Karragin, do you know Alvric Endule?"

"Yes, sir. Alvric is prime in his quad under Warden Reddevek."

"Not anymore. Overwarden Kaldera granted his transfer into the city watch, leaving that quad without a prime. Reddevek's ranks are thin. You'll be taking lead of the quad." She paused for Karragin's benefit, then continued. "I hate losing one of my finest, but I told Reddevek you were the most capable, and I think you're ready. I expect you to make me proud, Rider."

"Yes, sir!" Karragin bowed her head and held her hands thumb to thumb and finger to finger in the formal circle of unity. She stood, regarding Reddevek, who hunkered broad shoulders over a plate and used a bit of bread to soak up the last bit of runny egg yolk before licking his thick fingers.

Unkempt locks of long brown hair draped over the high collar of his crisp Outrider attire. His entire appearance drew to mind a feral creature barely contained within the confines of the uniform. A deep furrowed scar traveled across his bearded right cheek before disappearing into his hairline, but it was those silver-blue eyes that unnerved her more than anything else.

His left eye looked directly at her, but his right eye was set slightly to the right. She felt like at least part of his concentration was looking past her to something she couldn't see. *Dammit to the Drift! Which eye am I supposed to concentrate on? Can he tell that I can't tell?*

She kept switching from his left to his right eye and back. He tilted his head, and for the first time in a very long time, Karragin felt her face flush with heat. *He can tell!*

She made herself focus on his left eye. *Definitely the left, that was the one looking directly at me. Or was it the right? Oh, grind me sideways!*

"Your quad is still down a rider," Reddevek said, his deep voice carrying across the hall. "The fourth broke his leg in a fall last week. You have Velda and Berling, and you'll need to pick your fourth from this year's tenders." The resonance of his voice quieted the idle chatter of the initiates, who turned to observe the exchange.

Karragin calculated the strengths of the Endule cousins, Velda and Berling. Velda seemed like a strong rider, and she'd even won last year's archery competition. Berling was a capable healer from one of the duchies southwest of Callinora. *Dulesque, maybe?* "I'm to choose from the current tenders, sir?"

"Is that a problem, Rider?" he growled, then drained the last of a tankard and wiped his beard on his sleeve.

By Baellen's blue moon, who drinks ale this early in the day?

Elbiona turned to her colleague, and a hint of irritation tempered her usually calm voice as she said, "It's time for the tenders to start ranging with the quads, but this year's class is larger than usual. We can't have more than one tender per quad; it's too much to manage. We don't think it's wise to break up an experienced quad to add to yours. So you will have to—"

"Nolan, then." She realized a second too late that she'd interrupted her superior. "My apologies, sir. I choose Nolan."

Reddevek looked at her in that strange way, still making her feel like he was inspecting something to her side. She fought the intense desire to look over her shoulder. She knew the selection of her brother might seem like nepotism, but Nolan would pass or fail on his own merits. Reddevek carefully measured all of his tenders, and his quads endured the highest attrition rate of all the Outriders. She chose him anyway because, of all the initiates, none demonstrated a talent as valuable as Nolan's. He would whine about the fact that she'd doomed him to a quad governed by the one warden most likely to drop him from the training, but she could deal with that easily enough.

Reddevek seemed like he was going to argue the choice. Instead, he shrugged indifference. "You're prime now." He stood up and looked past her at Nolan, who withered on the bench. "Welcome to the Redd Riders."

Nolan lifted an empty glass of juice in a hollow salute. Several classmates slapped him on the shoulder in praise, but Nolan looked like he'd just wandered into the stables to muck out the stalls and discovered that all the shovels were broken. She planned to find him later and explain her choice. For now, she needed to find Velda and Berling.

"Lefledge." The low rumble of Reddevek's voice cut through the clamor of the tenders.

"Yes, sir?"

Reddevek cast a sidelong glance at Elbiona and Therek. "Pull that brother of yours from his class and gather your quad. I'm sending all quads in the Redd Riders on a ranging in two days. The quartermaster will expect you within two hours. Gather what you need for an expedition to the Borderlands."

Chapter Seven: Karragin's Quad

K arragin awoke before the other members of her quad with unusual stiffness in her hips and low back. She blamed her sore muscles on the long days of riding, but if she were honest, something else had disturbed her normally restful sleep. Her quad was ranging south through the kingdom with the rest of the Redd Riders. This day, however, her company planned to break off from the others, leaving her in sole command of the quad for the first time. The anticipation of the moment weighed on her more than she realized.

Reddevek had set a hard pace for the Outriders, and now they were in the alpine forests between the Pillars of Eldrek. Though the Pillars stood over a mile apart, the massive columns of natural stone dominated the skyline. Occasionally, sunlight glimmered off a vein of silver in the cliffside, reflecting on the ground in a prism of color. Oblivious to the natural beauty, she threw herself into her morning calisthenics.

Several times, she forced her body to the point of achy fatigue and that place where she could easily engage her arca prime, her strength. But this morning, she chose not to. Instead, she found an odd peace in the struggle of grinding out one more push-up, three more squats, five more up-downs, and seven more crunches.

She thought about repeating her circuit once more, then stopped to consider the day before her. They had a lot to accomplish today, and if she continued like this, her stamina would be tested. She still felt a strange desire to push through one more round.

A deep voice interrupted her thoughts. Warden Reddevek led his mount, an Aarindin, around a copse of evergreens. His jet-black gelding stood taller than most and exemplified the breed standard: sleek jet-black coat, muscled graceful limbs, a flowing mane with a long neck, and a well-chiseled head. The mounts, prized for their stamina and speed, performed well under the stress of combat and had proven remarkably surefooted. The Balladuren family raised the stock exclusively for the Aarindorn military and Outriders.

"The morning's gettin' on; shouldn't your quad be as well?" he asked.

Taker's saggy balls! Snap out of it, Karra; you didn't even hear him approach! She stood at attention. The cold morning air chilled her now that she wasn't exerting herself, and her sweaty undershirt clung uncomfortably to her chest. For the first time in years, she felt self-conscious. She was thankful Reddevek had spoken to her in his odd way, looking out across the southern valley and not directly at her.

"Yes, sir. I was just about to rouse them," she said.

He stared off to the horizon for a few long, silent moments. The morning breeze gusted, and his hair temporarily fluttered back, revealing the edge of a silvery scar. From his right cheek, the old wound ran into his scalp and clipped off the top edge of his ear. *Wolfespark.* The nickname came unbidden to her awareness. She heard once that he'd earned the nickname slaying the last of the wolvryn in the time before the Abrogator's War.

"I'm told you're an empath . . . with animals. Is that true?" he asked.

She wasn't surprised that he knew of her talent, but she was by the direct way he asked. It was considered rude in polite society. "Yes. It was my first gift."

"So you've had a chance to hone your skill. Good." He turned to address her directly. "Tell me about this mount then. Is he sound?"

Karragin was struggling again to pick out which of Reddevek's wandering eyes she should focus on, so she was happy for the distraction and stepped forward. The gelding paid her little attention as she stroked under his mane. It took only a moment to awaken her empathic gift and link it to the mount. Tingly vibrations of zenith cascaded from the complex right forearm rune up to her shoulder and fused into her center. The Aarindin turned to her with a nicker.

He is proud, this one, and holds himself aloof, expecting something. What are you expecting, my friend? You seem uneasy. She searched through the shallow, superficial memories of the horse. He was new to Reddevek, and his prior owner was gentle and had spoiled him with an apple every morning.

With nausea-provoking vertigo, the images abruptly swirled. The horse began controlling the exchange of information and broke into her thoughts with an almost accusatory tone. "*You are like a filly that can't wait to run the meadow.*"

She'd forgotten that when she linked empathically to animals with higher intelligence, they could learn something of her mindset as well.

"*I suppose in some ways I am.*" She stared deep into his eyes; his ebony pupils were barely discernible in the center of the black orbs that looked back at her. "*What's your name?*"

"*Zippy. But he has yet to call me that. He took me from my herd.*"

She nodded in understanding. "*Zippy, this rider you carry, he is great in my herd. It's an honor to bear him across the land. Are you up to the task?*" She struggled to convey the context of honor to the horse and brought forth images of the stallion and lead mare of the herd. Eventually, she sensed he understood her intent.

"*Can you be my rider?*"

"*No, Zippy. I walk a different trail.*" There was a long pause, and she wondered if the horse had severed their connection. Upon searching further, she understood that Zippy was actually considering her question.

Eventually, he responded. "*I will carry him. He wants you to be the lead mare and not the filly.*"

Karragin struggled to connect the meaning of the images Zippy sent her. "*I don't understand.*"

"*Be the lead mare. Lead my brothers and sister, and I will do as you ask.*" Zippy looked over to the four Aarindin used by Karragin's quad. Three geldings and a young mare stood stoically, watching the interaction. Zippy stood slightly taller and more muscled than any of them. She began to release her connection to the Aarindin, but the lingering sentiment echoed in her mind. *Be the lead mare, not the filly.*

"I will try." She released her command of the gift, and the tingling of the rune on her forearm subsided. She dropped her hand and looked to Reddevek, settling comfortably on his right eye.

"Well? Learn anything useful?" asked the warden.

Karragin nodded. "If I may ask, sir, why did you choose this particular Aarindin? You only recently pulled him from the herd."

"One of the Balladuren boys, Willard, handpicked him. Told me he was smart and had better stamina than most."

"They were right, at least about Zippy being smarter than most. I don't often have animals, even Aarindin, engage in a dialogue. But he did," she said. "I think he was even trying to negotiate with me. Most times, I only get a sense of their temperament or emotion. But we had, well, a conversation."

Reddevek grunted either in surprise or contemplation. She couldn't be sure. "What did he say?" asked the warden.

"He will perform well for you. But you need to show him the kindness and respect to which he is accustomed if you want his best." She walked over to a satchel tied high in a tree, lowered the pack, and began rummaging through the last of her quad's rations. She tossed a small apple to the commander.

"One of the Balladurens favored him with a treat most mornings and always addressed him by his name," she explained.

Reddevek sighed, nodding understanding. "The treat I can understand, but that name . . . I can't explain why, but it's like shaving against the grain."

She didn't think her feral commander shaved very often and nearly blurted the words out loud. *Filters Karra, filters.*

"It's what Zippy knows," she explained. "Also, he seemed concerned for the other Aarindin in my group. I'm not sure why. They are herd animals, but his concern seemed odd." She sucked on her upper lip, reviewing the conversation. "We have an understanding. I tried to convey the importance of your mission. He will perform well for you. But if you want his best, you should maintain his routine as much as possible. So a treat in the morning and address him by his name . . . sir."

Reddevek offered the small apple on his palm, and Zippy accepted the treat, then swished his tail and nickered. It didn't take an empath to see the value of Karragin's advice.

"Do you have any questions about your orders?" he asked.

"No, sir, we're ready."

"A warden's counsel then, since you helped me with Zippy." He acted like the words left a bad taste in his mouth. "You're not prime of this quad because you're the regent's daughter. It's like Elbiona said, you're ready. Sometimes a new prime will be challenged, but Velda and Berling are experienced enough to know better. So don't get in your own way. Just lead, and you'll be fine."

She nodded, unsure of how to respond. "Thank you, sir."

"And one other thing. I need you to test your tender's gifts. We need to know if he has the stuff of a real scout. It's one thing to have a gift and another to know how to use it."

Reddevek turned and mounted his Aarindin with an agility that defied his bulky shoulders. He leaned forward and said in a soft voice, "Come on, Zippy, let's go." They trotted to the edge of camp and disappeared around a copse of pine.

Karragin inhaled and finally noticed the crisp alpine aroma in the morning air. She donned fresh riding fatigues, packed up her tent and belongings, adjusted a thin saber at her side, and directed her attention to her quad.

Velda and Berling rose and, after storing their gear, joined her around the remnants of their small campfire. Nolan's tent and belongings remained undisturbed. She stepped over and grasped his bedroll, the foot just protruding from his tent.

Brother, you're not making a great impression. She gave a gentle tug to see if he would wake. Sensing no motion, she adjusted her grip and searched inward for her gift. Her ability to engage her unnatural strength had improved in the last few weeks. Before, the triggering of her gift had required anger or need, but lately, she found channeling zenith into her arca prime more natural. After only a minute of concentration, the familiar invigoration of her power infused her core and spread to her arms and legs.

The ache in her lower back dissolved, replaced by unbridled raw strength. She twisted her wrists, and Nolan's bedroll slid unceremoniously out of his tent with him on it.

He awoke sleepily, lying on his back with his unkempt cinnamon curls covering his eyes. He stretched his arms overhead and arched his back with an uncontrolled yawn, then struggled to a sitting position. "Good morning," he mumbled.

"Is that how you address your prime, Tender?" she asked.

Nolan sighed but scrambled to his feet in attention. She waited for his response, but all she heard was a snicker from Velda. The archer fingered over the unique purple fletching of an arrow, then pointed it at Nolan's groin and said, "Some parts of him are more awake than others."

Nolan's cheeks flushed red, but he remained still. Karragin glanced down, puzzled by Velda's observation, then realized the source of her brother's chagrin.

"Indeed," she replied. "At ease, Tender. Get yourself sorted out." He disappeared behind brush and undergrowth to relieve himself.

Velda sat with Berling, and they parceled out the last of the rations they'd obtained from the quartermaster. With dark brown hair cropped short and unusually burly shoulders, she almost appeared more masculine than Berling. The best female archers either bound their breasts or naturally had small ones. The latter was the case for Velda. What she lacked in femininity, she more than made up for in simple, deadly skill. *I wonder what other skills she commands? That is something I should have discerned by now, right? It's considered rude to just ask someone about their gifts; how did Reddevek get away with it?*

Berling offered a portion of salted pork and dried fruit to Karragin. He had all the look of a Dulescan highborn: thin sharp nose, thick curled black hair, and an exaggerated upper lip that drooped down, making him almost appear to have an underbite. "Thanks," she replied and took a seat next to him.

"That tender's shaft rivals the ones in my quiver," said Velda.

Initiates wore the title tender until they completed their first ranging. The practice carried over from times when the Outriders encountered higher attrition rates. It felt a little odd not to be able to use Nolan's first name, but it also afforded a sense of professional distance.

In their first few days out, Karragin's initial instinct was to mother Nolan, offering guidance and teaching him the lessons she had already learned. She quickly recognized that her behavior gave the appearance of favoritism. By not addressing him by his first name, she maintained a formal distance.

"You shouldn't tease a man for something natural, something . . . the Giver bestowed," said Berling.

"Not teasing, just pointing out the obvious," said Velda with a sly grin. She looked at Karragin, who took the opportunity to stifle the conversation with her perfect resting asshole gaze. *By the Giver, what makes Velda think I would want to talk about my brother's morning wood?*

The archer finally sensed as much and cleared her throat. "I meant no offense, bad form there. It won't happen again."

Karragin waved a hand, indicating the conversation held little meaning. Sexual relations between Outriders were commonplace as long as they didn't affect one's ability to carry out their duties. Besides, from what Karragin had gleaned, Velda preferred to keep company with other women. Nolan returned and accepted his portion of breakfast from Berling and plopped down beside them.

"Be sure to savor that, Tender—it's the last of the salted pork," said Berling.

Nolan ripped a piece of the dried meat with his teeth and spent the next few minutes chewing. After he swallowed what appeared to be a less than appealing morsel, he grimaced and washed down the breakfast with a long pull from a waterskin. "I don't mean to sound ungrateful, but I think I would rather take my chances foraging."

"Like it or not, you'll get the chance to do just that," said Karragin. "Our orders are simple. All of the quads are fanning out to explore the Borderlands. We are to head directly south, make contact with any towns or villages, and gauge their interest in further discussions for trade. We have the Aarindin and should cover a lot of ground. Seven days out and seven days back. We rendezvous back here in the forest between the Pillars. Berling and Nol—tender, you are to take samples and record any new plants of note, but be on the lookout for darksun and blue-trumpet."

Berling nodded. "You know those, Tender?" he asked.

Nolan pulled his unruly curls back into a topknot. "Darksun is the deep purple flowering plant with a central purple ball; it grows in full sun and is used to combat flux. Blue-trumpet grows in vines along tree trunks and can be steeped for a tea that aids breathing."

Berling's plump upper lip turned in a smile. "The Giver finally saw fit to place me in a quad with someone who appreciates the finer aspects of botany? It's about time."

"Until just recently, I thought I was bound for Callinora, so I studied a little," said Nolan.

"I already considered myself in good company, but now I really like the way things are shaping up. The flux this winter was rough, and our supplies of darksun and trumpet are low. We can always use another pair of eyes to search," said the healer.

Karragin continued, "All of us will be accountable for foraging along the way. If we encounter any groups, I'll take point. Velda remains hidden to allow her to utilize her skill with the bow in case we encounter any trouble. Any questions?"

"Quad formation or free-ranging?" asked Velda.

"Free-ranging with overlapping contact every two hours. Velda and I will range to the farthest east and west. Berling and Nolan, you two in the center on a more direct southern course. Gather at midday and one hour before dusk. We're not likely to encounter anyone so close to the border the first few days, but if that happens, find me if possible," said Karragin.

She waited for any other questions, and sensing none, stood to mount her Aarindin. The Outriders traveled without saddles, training the Aarindin in stealth. She issued a sharp hand gesture, and the Aarindin lowered its belly to the ground. She rewarded his obedience with a bit of apple, then easily mounted. She clicked her tongue twice, and the horse rose to a standing position. "Alright then, eyes to the horizon."

The others followed her lead, packing their belongings on their mounts. Within the hour, they had left the cover of the alpine forest and ranged into the Borderlands. The highlands of the Great Crown slowly receded to rolling hills adorned with emerald green scrub and wildflowers.

Karragin directed her mount to the southwest and lost sight of Nolan and Berling after only a few minutes. She allowed her Aarindin to pick its way down to the plains following game trails. On the way, she discovered two clusters of darksun. Near midday, she crested a tall hill to obtain a better vantage point. She spied Berling and made her way to him as he filled a pouch with herbs. Together they made their way to Nolan, who accompanied Velda.

Berling nodded to the others. "Any luck?" he asked as he twirled the stem of a darksun blossom between his fingers.

Velda shrugged indifference, but Nolan lifted the flap of a satchel crammed full with darksun and even a few blue-trumpets.

Berling hurried over to pat the satchel, surprised at how full the pack seemed to be. He whistled low in appreciation. "You filled that already? By the Giver, that's nuts, Tender!"

Nolan grinned and readjusted his hair into a tidy topknot. "Thanks. I expect we'll need to dry them this evening. The darksun was easy enough to find, but there aren't enough trees to support the climbing trumpet vines out here." He waved a hand across the rolling hills. Tall grasslands spread to the horizon.

They shared a ration of nuts, cheese, and berries, then dispersed, ranging further south. Once separated from the others, Karragin found her thoughts wandering. She considered Nolan's early success and was surprised by how relieved she felt that he'd already proven his value.

Something about ranging through the Borderlands made her feel free. The simple act of being the first in a decade to explore the region, coupled with the chance to leave all the political games behind, allowed her thoughts to wander uninhibited. The realization struck her as odd. *How did I ever come to feel trapped? I wonder if Father feels that way every day?*

She allowed the concern to dissipate and tried to focus on searching for darksun as she journeyed further south. Out of boredom or curiosity, she engaged her empathic gift to link with her Aarindin. The familiar tingly sensation rippled along her arm and blossomed as a warm sensation across her torso. She felt a link form with the horse, who nickered as he picked his way along a game trail. *"Do you know who made this trail?"*

"Yes." The Aarindin responded by sniffing at small hoofprints in the soil. An image of a vestek, an elusive deer of the plains, sifted through the horse's awareness.

She tried to ask other questions but found her mount either not as intelligent or not as engaged as Zippy. She discerned that her horse had no formal name and that he remained content in their journey across the plains, but getting him to participate in anything more meaningful proved difficult. More than once, he stopped abruptly on the trail as if to consider her probing. Images of nibbling on seed heads from the grasslands, a stream, and more vestek drifted in and out of his mind. Eventually, she concluded that the horse struggled with more complex thoughts and contented herself just to gauge his mood.

One hour before dusk, they gathered for camp along a small stream that ran between two hills. Berling pitched the tents while Nolan set a small fire and stirred a pot of broth and potatoes. Velda skinned two rabbits and placed them over a makeshift spit. Karragin attended to the Aarindin, using her gift to make a quick assessment of the mounts. By the time she joined them at the fire, the aroma of Nolan's stew made her stomach gurgle loud enough for everyone to take notice.

Berling smiled and inhaled deeply. "If this tastes half as good as it smells, I can safely say our tender here has secured his place in the Outriders." Karragin arched an eyebrow in question. "When was the last time I ever whipped up something that smelled this good?"

Karragin shrugged. Her ascension to prime had occurred less than two weeks ago, so she didn't feel like she had much experience to render judgment on Berling's capabilities as a cook.

"Never," said Velda, interrupting her thoughts.

"Exactly," said Berling. He withdrew a wooden spoon from the pot, sipped at the broth, and moaned before pointing at Nolan. "Oh . . . by the Giver, that's sweet tuber and what, wild leeks? You found both of these, Tender?"

"I got lucky." Nolan shrugged and finished bundling the last bit of darksun, then looked to Karragin out of the corner of his eye. She subtly nodded her approval, and he flushed slightly before smiling a toothy grin.

They shared the meal, and Karragin took the opportunity to walk the hillside along the camp perimeter. She returned to find Nolan giggling at something Velda had said. It warmed her to see him fitting in so well. *Not bad for the first day out.*

The next several days unfolded in a similar peaceful fashion. The rolling plains provided an abundance of foraged food and herbs, all readily procured by Nolan. They each contributed small game. Karragin even stumbled across several large duck eggs to add to the fare. All in all, their week of exploration unfolded smoothly.

On their fifth day out, they met at midday—everyone except Nolan. Just when she started to feel concerned, he crested a small hill leading his Aarindin on foot. He staggered ahead, focused on something unseen on the ground. Velda stood next to her mount, adjusting a small pack and checking its contents. "Someone needs to teach the tender not to use so much of his gift so far from home," she said. "He looks spent, and the day's only half gone."

Nolan walked forward, shoulders slumped and preoccupied with studying something on the ground. Karragin spied a twinkle of scintillating light cascade over the top of his arca prime. She approached with concern, but not for the reasons Velda suggested.

Nolan knew full well the dangers of drawing upon his gift so far from home. One of the first lessons taught to all those inheriting runes of power from the Giver was the Law of Connected Strength: any gift bestowed by the Giver finds strength only by its connection to other gifted. Violating the Law of Connected Strength was possible but came at a price.

Channeling zenith, then shaping it to one's will, took a toll. Somehow, the proximity to other gifted minimized the price. But when channeled in isolation, the action siphoned one's own essence. Outriders learned of the dangers of the practice early in their training, but by the way Nolan was staggering along, he'd ignored this rule for far too long.

You know this brother, so the question is, why did you do it?

"You found something. What is it?" she asked.

Nolan walked past her as if in a trance, crested a small hill, and prepared to descend to the south. Karragin grabbed the reins of his mount and gently slapped him across the cheek. The gesture brought him back to full awareness. He looked around, showing the first signs of recognition.

"Thanks," he said, appearing relieved.

Karragin offered him a waterskin, and he pulled a long draw. "Permission to sit, sir?" he asked.

"Yes, Nolan, what is it, why did you—explain yourself, Tender." She issued the command with a soft tone flavored with genuine concern.

"I'm not sure, but it's not anything I've seen before. And it's big," he replied. "About two hours ago, I came across tracks I've never seen before."

"You lost yourself to the gift for the sake of curiosity?" Berling interrupted.

"Maybe at first," Nolan admitted. "But there's something very wrong about whatever made the tracks. It has four legs and is hoofed, maybe like a moose, but bigger, and with something sharp, like a clawed hoof. Its scat didn't have any sign of grass in it, and I found the carcass of a vestek, a fresh kill."

Berling interrupted him. "So you're saying you got all worked up over hoofprints and poop?"

Nolan looked a little chagrined and pulled at the seed pods of the long grasses. "No, I'm saying whatever made the tracks is a predator. It's big, fast enough to fell a vestek, eats meat, and roams in a pack. Before I released my gift, I was tracking them there, to that." Nolan pointed to a small plume of smoke rising on the southern horizon.

They each stared for a few long moments. Eventually, the wind dissipated enough of the gathered smoke to reveal the outlines of a few small wooden structures.

"Looks like a village," Velda guessed.

"Or maybe a farmstead," said Karragin. "Tender, the tracks you followed, they continue south?"

Nolan nodded.

"How many sets? Any guess on their number?" Karragin asked.

"At least eight, maybe a few more," said Nolan.

Karragin ran the tip of her tongue over the scar on her lip, considering their options. The whole reason for being out here was to gather information. She considered ordering a retreat back to the north. That would be the safest course of action, but something more than curiosity told her they should investigate the fire and find out more about Nolan's discovery.

"Making that village or whatever it is should take us about two hours with reconnaissance," said Karragin. "We'll rest here a bit longer, then ride out in quad formation. I'll take point. Nolan and Berling flank, and Velda rear. We came out here to scout, to learn something from anyone who lives here in the Borderlands. Let's just hope we arrive before our first contact is reduced to ashes."

Chapter Eight: Trouble in the Borderlands

Nolan watched his sister walk back and forth across the crest of the hill to their south. She wasn't pacing; that was something he might do. No, Karragin sauntered through the tall grasses, allowing her hands to brush the green seed heads. Velda and Berling stood by their Aarindin in quiet conversation. Sensing nobody would really care if he stole a moment, he allowed himself to flop back, flattening out a silhouette in the tall grasses.

His body felt so heavy that he plunged into a half-sleep. Whenever he hovered in that space between sleep and wakefulness, he lost the ability to tell which leg crossed the other or which hand folded over the other. It was like his awareness didn't care where his body lay. He was holding himself poised to tip over completely into sleep when a hand rocked his shoulder.

"Tender, time to get moving," said Berling.

Nolan sat up feeling worse than before. The tired muscles across his shoulders threatened to cramp, and he considered engaging his gift to draw in more zenith but knew the short-term gain would only make recovery worse. Berling offered him a small canteen, and he took a drink.

Leave it to a Dulescan to carry a fancy canteen.

The water had a refreshing taste and smelled faintly of something like anise. He swallowed two large gulps. "Is there bandle root in here? I'll never make it the rest of the day!"

"By the Giver, no," replied Berling. "But you are clever to notice. No, the anise taste is from its cousin, vivith."

Nolan felt his face flush and stood up, alarmed. "You gave me vivith?"

"Relax tender, it's not what you think," Berling said, placing a reassuring hand on his shoulder. The medic sniffed through his long nose, inhaling the fragrance of a small white flower. "Vivith, the drug, is nasty stuff. But you can take the petals of the wild version," he said while crushing the petals between forefinger and thumb. "Much less potent. Make a weak tea and dilute it into a canteen, one part to ten. Lets you stay alert all day without all the nasty effects."

Nolan sniffed the canteen cautiously, replaced the stopper, and handed it back to Berling. "Oh. Thanks, I guess."

Berling winked. "You looked like you could use a little boost. I've used this to get me by on long rangings. Have a care, though. The stuff gives you dry mouth, so be sure to drink plain water the rest of the day and not more of this." He slipped the small canteen inside the fold of his tunic.

Nolan wandered over to his Aarindin. The horse sat with its belly to the ground, allowing him to swing up a lazy leg. Without waiting for a command, the Aarindin stood and trotted into place along the left flank. Karragin led them at point. Berling rode along the right flank and Velda somewhere at their rear.

They made steady progress south over the next two hours, and the remnants of a small village emerged with more definition through the smoke. The fieldstone foundations of several small homes and what was likely a barn remained, along with smoldering timbers. The light morning wind had weakened, allowing the thick clouds of smoke to eddy on the ground, obscuring further surveillance without getting closer.

Nolan felt like the scene before him should pique his interest at least a little. Instead, an odd numbness settled over his mind, and he found himself reciting lessons from the alchemists' guild.

Nettle tea will make you pee: crush six dried leaves, steep, and wee. He smiled sheepishly, always fond of that particular one.

Weeping bark for aches and pains, bear-claw leaf for more of the same. The rhythmic rocking of Nolan's mount stopped, but only a dim peripheral part of his awareness registered the change.

Gellseed root and blackberry tincture: control diarrhea and tighten up the sphincter!

He snorted out loud at that one. It was his own limerick and was frowned upon by the master of the alchemists' guild. *I wonder how old Gwillion is doing. The poor man got himself addicted to vivith and had to leave the guild just as I was getting ready to sit for my Rite of Revealing.*

Nolan's limbs felt heavy, and he clacked his front teeth together. They felt numb. He giggled again and tried to make his lips speak. To himself, he mumbled, "Rebleeding . . . revleading . . . revealing!"

He pointed a clumsy finger into the air, proud of the simple accomplishment of speech. The awkward gesture threw him off-balance, and he slid to the ground with no more control than a sack of grain. His Aarindin whinnied and snorted, but Nolan couldn't seem to care.

He felt himself being turned to his back, and Berling's pointy nose came into view.

"Shay Bervling," he slurred, "you made a mish . . . a mishtake. Mashter Gwillion shmelled like pi . . . pine . . ." He struggled to lift his lower lip to his teeth. "Vidith . . . vilith smellsh like pine, not anish . . . you ga me bandle. Why did you do?"

"Yes, you're right, Tender," Berling responded in a whisper. "It's better this way. No pain, don't you see? If Velda had her way, you and your sister would . . . Well, let's just say my way allows for a much more pleasant exit."

Nolan sensed the medic pat him on the cheek but couldn't feel his face anymore. Berling propped something under his head and situated his arms at his side, and Nolan had completely lost the ability to resist. He'd felt tired before; now, he couldn't even seem to marshal the will to make his limbs move. He watched as his sister approached and tried to mumble a warning, but even blinking was difficult, and his eyes brimmed with tears.

Karragin walked over, a small furrow creasing her normally placid expression. She leaned forward with her hands on her knees as she waited for Berling to complete his assessment. The medic gave the appearance of probing Nolan's torso and limbs, then looked up.

"I should have paid more attention. I didn't realize how tired he was. He fell, and I think he struck his head." Berling spoke the words with a perfect look of grief.

Karragin approached, weaving through the tall grasses. She dropped to a knee with an expression Nolan had never seen before. Her eyes were fixed on something distant, and her mouth parted as if to say something, only she just looked ahead. Nolan struggled through sleepy confusion to understand what was happening. *What is going on? Why would Berling give me bandle root? What does he mean, exit? Karra, why don't you say something? Taker's balls, did Berling give you bandle root too?*

He blinked once; hot tears streaked down his neck. He struggled to speak, but all he could manage was an unintelligible moan. From the periphery of his vision, faint, iridescent light flickered across part of the rune along Karragin's left forearm. As her rune of premonition faded, she dove forward. Nolan felt her weight against his legs, followed by the sound of an arrow thwack and a curse. Berling looked down at the shaft embedded in his chest. The arrow must have protruded through to his back, as the purple fletching was resting flush against his outer tunic.

The Dulescan coughed once and grunted. "Grind me with a sharp stick." He sputtered bright red blood, then slumped backward.

Karragin rose to her feet with her saber drawn and crouched in a defensive stance. Through the tall grasses, Nolan couldn't see who had shot Berling. *But Velda's the only one I've ever seen carry those.*

"Velda!" Karragin growled with a feral edge in her voice. "Drop your bow, and I'll let you live to explain yourself to the warden. Don't you do it, or I swear I'll send you to the Drift!"

The soft twang of a bowstring interrupted Karragin's order, and Nolan felt something thud into his outer thigh. Looking down, he could just make out the purple feathered tip of another arrow. The numbing effect of the bandle root waned, and he sensed a slight burning pain along his outer leg. Karragin sprang forward and beyond his view. He heard the whinny of an Aarindin and a few grunts, then silence.

A gentle breeze rustled across the plains. Nolan strained to hear any sign of the confrontation. His addled mind struggled to both remain calm and understand what was happening. Berling had given him bandle root and made a cryptic comment, then Velda shot him with an arrow meant for Karra?

Is that what happened?

He glanced at Berling's corpse. The medic lay next to him on his back with his knees buckled unnaturally under him. Still, Nolan's mind struggled to understand why the medic had acted so strangely. Long moments passed without answers. He looked at his wounded leg. Dark blood oozed out around the shaft of the arrow and was saturating his uniform.

The sounds of someone crawling through the grass interrupted his thoughts, and Karragin's face popped into view. She placed a finger to her lips to garner his silence. She spoke in soft tones while tending to his leg.

"If I'm right, Berling gave you bandle root tincture, so this shouldn't hurt much." Without waiting for Nolan's reply, she grasped the arrow shaft, and with a swift jerk, withdrew the arrow. From over her shoulder, she grabbed Berling's satchel. She applied firm pressure on the wound with one hand. With her free hand, she rummaged through the medic's pack, all the while scanning their surroundings.

"I need your expertise, Nolan. I don't know which herbs disinfect the wound or what to pack into it to stop your bleeding. Can you speak yet?"

The burning in his leg became an ache, and he sensed the ability to move his shoulder muscles a little, but everything else remained numb. A moan was all he could produce.

"Never mind, blink once for yes, twice for no," said Karragin. Still scanning their surroundings, she held up several envelopes. The first one revealed delicate yellow flowers.

He struggled to focus his thoughts. *Kaliphora, good for vomiting.*

He blinked twice. She lifted another filled with a tea and held a pinch of it up for him.

I'm not sure; hold it to my nose. He raised an eyebrow and sniffed. She held the tea close for him to inhale. *Ground heh-gava, good for a cough.* He blinked twice.

Karragin upended the medic's bag and sprawled the contents onto the ground in frustration. She held up several more packets in rapid succession, each inappropriate to treat a wound. He blinked twice each time.

"Did that Dulescan dickhead bring anything of use! What about this?" Karragin held up a blue bottle filled with a viscous oily substance. She unstoppered the cork with her teeth and spat it out, then held the bottle close to his nose.

Embertang. Why did it have to be that? Soldiers faint from wounds treated with that!

He sighed and gave a slow blink one time. Karragin wiped her mouth across her sleeve. "Are you sure? Just a splash of that stuff from the cork, and my face is on fire!" she said with teeth clenched and tears rolling down her cheeks. He blinked slowly once again.

Without warning, she ripped his pants apart, exposing the wound, then splashed half of the contents of the oily tincture into the gash along his outer thigh. There was only a deep, achy warm feeling for the first few moments, but instead of waning, the burning sensation cut through the haze of bandle root with searing pain. Nolan looked down, expecting to see a hot iron brand or smoking flesh.

She wrapped a linen dressing around his thigh, and he thought it must be trapping in the heat, for the pain only intensified. He struggled to reach down to the wound but couldn't make his arms work right. He imagined red embers searing into his thighbone. The pain caused him to recall an apprentice at the alchemists' guild who broke a beaker of caustic acid. The substance had melted the flesh on his hand in moments.

His mind raced to retreat from the absolute agony. But somehow, the bandle root prevented him from collapsing, and long minutes passed in which he imagined the inferno inside his leg smoldering to the lesser pain of embers. As the burning agony diminished, a breeze chilled him through his sweat-soaked tender's uniform. He rose to his elbows but had little time to thank his sister.

Velda stood from a dense thicket of grasses and knocked an arrow. "That was not a very nice trick with the horse, making him buck me like that."

Karragin reached for her sword, but the archer fired and redrew her bow with stunning alacrity. The shaft landed right where Karragin's hand would have been if she'd grasped the hilt.

"Why are you doing this?" Karragin shouted.

"We have a saying in Beclure: the only good Baellentrell is a dead one," Velda yelled back. "But I've got four arrows in my quiver, and I think we should have a little fun first."

"You know well and good, I'm not a royal."

"Maybe not, but your family holds the seat of power in their stead. Losing two of you on a ranging is rare but not unheard of. Don't worry. I'll come up with a hero's tale for your father."

Karragin stood up and stuck out her chin. "I see. Well, go on then!"

A gust of wind raced across the plains, and Karragin gestured in frustration, scattering the rest of the embertang as she did. Droplets of the balm sprayed across the short distance between the two Outriders and traveled downwind. Velda squinted in pain and jumped back, trying to loose an arrow at the same time. The purple fletching vibrated against Karragin's boot, but the shaft embedded into the ground. A sound like a wounded alley cat rose from Velda, who rolled in agony while scratching at her eyes.

Karragin watched the Outrider writhe, then retrieved her sword. Still howling with unintelligible feral growls, the archer managed to fire another arrow, which flew disturbingly close to Nolan—so close that Karragin took up a defensive posture.

Velda struggled to nock another arrow to the bow, all the while screaming both in anger and agony. She staggered, loosed another arrow, then dropped a hand to swipe at her eyes. She nocked another arrow, and her venom organized into words. "My eyes, you bitch! Oh, the Giver make it stop! I swear I'll send you straight to the Taker!"

Hurled from beyond the hillside, something twirling and glinting arced toward the archer. Her threats ended as a hand axe embedded itself into the side of her skull. Velda crumpled to the ground, silenced.

From the south, approaching from the smoldering ruins, Reddevek strode forward. He considered the scene before him with a detached demeanor, then walked around the area covered by the embertang. "Neat trick; I'll have to remember that one. How's your brother?"

Nolan's bewilderment was surpassed by the utter look of bafflement on Karragin's face. She sheathed her weapon and stood with her mouth slightly agape. Reddevek retrieved his throwing axe with no more concern than if he had thrown it into a tree trunk. He cleaned the weapon, then knelt to inspect Nolan's wound. Satisfied with the dressing, he pulled off Nolan's boot and pinched the toes on the injured leg.

"Can you feel that?" Reddevek asked.

Nolan grunted an affirmation.

"Good, the foot has good color. Try to wiggle your toes," the warden directed.

The foot? You mean my foot?

Nolan made an effort to wiggle his toes, but all he could manage was a jerk of his ankle. Reddevek then pulled down at the skin under Nolan's eyes and searched. Nolan felt oddly reassured by the dispassionate inspection.

"Your field dressing should hold. His pupils are still constricted. Bandle root?" asked the warden.

Karragin shrugged. "I think so, but I'm not sure. Something. Berling slipped him something. Nolan, was it bandle root?"

Nolan blinked slowly once in response.

"He thinks it was bandle root," said Karragin.

"In my experience, he won't be fit to ride until tomorrow. I'll stay with you until then. Come morning, I want you to return to Stone's Grasp. You can regroup with the rest of the riders; there aren't any others like these two. But I need you to carry a message to the regent," said Reddevek.

Karragin sucked at the scar of her upper lip and glanced down at Nolan. "You knew about Velda and Berling? Why didn't you say something? They nearly killed us." She spoke the words without anger, presenting the warden with her placid expression.

Nolan tried to grunt a giggle, knowing all too well the seething anger building up under her stoic countenance. A subtle grunt was all that escaped his lips.

Reddevek scratched at his unkempt beard and finger-combed thick locks of hair behind his ears. The gesture uncovered the scar on his right cheek and temple. *There is something primal about this man.*

But instead of a feral rebuke, Reddevek offered soft words. "I didn't know they might try something like assassinating the regent's children. But I was aware of their heritage. They're both of Endule descent. They both come from families with a certain . . . history. We hoped that by spending time with you two, they could learn to see past the fog of their anger."

"We?" asked Karragin.

"Your father suggested the arrangement. He hoped it could be the start of rebuilding a sense of solidarity. But neither of us imagined this," said Reddevek.

He stood and whistled. A moment later, Zippy trotted over a hill and nuzzled under Reddevek's arm. The warden retrieved a small apple and rewarded the Aarindin. "When you return to your father, I need you to convey something more than just the treachery here."

"Alright, what is it?" asked Karragin.

"You were making for that village to the south, the one with all the smoke?" asked the warden. Karragin nodded once. "Don't bother. It was overrun by grondle."

Reddevek reached into one of his packs for a parcel swathed in burlap. He unwrapped the item to produce a strange curved horn. It looked similar to a bull's horn but much larger and curved into a crescent. The tan base tapered to a blood-splattered, pointed tip. "You're too young to have seen these firsthand, but do you know about them?" he asked.

Karragin nodded. "I read about them in books on the Abrogator's War. Tarkannen summoned them from the Drift and used them as shock troops in his assault on Aarindorn. Part man, part bull, and capable of incurring great physical trauma before falling. They use crude battle tactics but possess otherworldy stamina," she recited.

"Books have most of it right," said Reddevek, "but what they leave out is that they don't have much more intelligence than a well-trained dog. Also, if you ever run across one, remember their weakness is their man parts, their torso. That, and their nature."

"You mean their balls?" she asked.

Karragin stared at him with that vacant expression that made it impossible for anyone to know what she was thinking. Reddevek continued his explanation, "No. Well, yes, that might work, but that's not what I mean. Most areas of their bodies are impervious to normal attacks. The only easy way to fell one is to concentrate your attacks on the parts that resemble a man. As for their nature, they're crude and bestial. They always go for blood and always charge into a melee without thinking. That makes it easy to lure them and pick a battle that suits your strength."

"Why?" Karragin interrupted. "Why would we run into grondle? They were hunted to the Drift years ago."

"That's a question for someone like your father," said Reddevek. "I fought them in the war and never imagined I would see one again. I counted a crush of ten this morning. This horn came off of one that was wounded in a scrap over meat. The crush left it behind, and I dispatched it before the others took notice. Take the horn back as proof."

"What are you going to do?" she asked.

Reddevek gazed back to the smoldering ruins. "I have to find the rest of the quads, send them back before anyone runs into the grondle, then finish a task your father laid before me," he said.

"We could help you gather the others; Nolan tracked the grondle here from a day's ride away. His gift, it's the real thing," she said. Nolan felt his cheeks warm despite his fatigue.

"I don't doubt that, but I need you to get word of everything that happened today to the regent, and as soon as possible," he said. "Now, let's get that tender up on his mount. Double up and ride behind him. We don't need to move fast, but we have to get away from this bloodshed. It will draw the crush by nightfall."

"Should we do something with their bodies?" asked Karragin.

"There's no help for it. We don't have the time," said Reddevek. "You ready?" he asked Nolan, who nodded slightly. Nolan felt his body being lifted but still couldn't manage to make his hands or feet work right. The warden grunted with the exertion of lifting his flaccid weight.

"Let me, sir. It's one of the things I'm good at," said Karragin.

She waited for the warden to nod his consent, then took a moment to engage her gift. A current of blue zenith played across the arca prime, just visible at the neckline of her tunic. With ease, she hoisted Nolan over her shoulder and strode over to her Aarindin. With a hand gesture, she directed the mount to kneel. The sleek horse lowered its belly to the ground, and she placed Nolan on its back, then adjusted herself behind him. She managed to remain balanced as the Aarindin rose to its feet in silence.

Reddevek gathered up Berling and Velda's mounts and tethered them to Zippy. They rode north at a fast walk. An hour after sunset, they made camp along a steep bank carved out by a small stream. The effects of the bandle root had dissipated more, and Nolan found he could dismount and walk on his own. Though he stumbled like a drunkard, he was able to get to a small bush to relieve himself. As he did, he wondered how awkward it might have been had the bandle root lasted longer. *Thank the Giver for small miracles.*

They slept restlessly that night, and Reddevek kept watch. The next morning, without any idle banter, the warden gathered his belongings and mounted Zippy.

Karragin approached before he left and patted the Aarindin, who released a soft, guttural nicker of pleasure. "Zippy says he likes you. You don't talk too much, and you didn't make him approach the feared ones," she said. Reddevek raised an eyebrow in question. "I think he means the grondle. He can smell them. They scare him."

"That makes sense, I suppose," said Reddevek. "Tender, you get your legs back?"

Nolan stood up, testing the sensation of his muscles. He stomped his feet, noting the lingering tingle and numbness in his toes but none of the other effects from the prior day. "Yes, sir, thank you, sir!"

"Good, ride out soon and keep north. Tell the regent about the treason of Berling and Velda, all of it. Including how they both died. He'll understand. Then tell him about the grondle and how a crush of ten slaughtered a village of over a hundred," said Reddevek.

"I will," said Karragin. "We have the horn packed. Is there anything else, sir?"

Reddevek eyed the terrain to the south. "One more thing. Tell Warden Elbiona I need her to assume command of my quads until I return. She won't be surprised, but you might want her along when you tell your father about the grondle. She's one of the few Outriders with firsthand experience with them."

"Eyes to the horizon then, sir, and safe journey," said Karragin.

Reddevek inhaled a deep breath and gazed south across the horizon. "Yup . . . eyes to the horizon indeed," said the warden. Without another word, he directed Zippy south and disappeared among the hilled grasslands.

Chapter Nine: Laryn Among the Cloudwalkers

Laryn Lellendule emerged from her hut and stretched before pulling her dark brown hair into a casual bun and tucking the stem of a white flower behind her ear. The blossom complemented the lone, thick shock of white hair that framed her face. She cultivated the flowers from a fragrant shrub in a small garden next to her hut and loved the way its delicate fragrance reminded her of a similar flower from her home in Aarindorn. On occasion, she steeped the leaves into a tea that invigorated one's spirit. Alternatively, one could place a few leaves between cheek and gum and enjoy a more subtle effect for hours.

She plucked a few of the leaves for just this purpose and made her way down a path paved with rounded stones. Clouded mists eddied in lazy swirls and draped the ground with morning dew in the Valley of the Cloud Walkers. The mists parted to reveal the common grounds and the gathering house, where stout columns crafted from local timbers supported an arched thatch roof. The expansive single-story structure sheltered the tribe when they gathered to share meals and socialize.

In the winter, the Damadibo erected walls reinforced with hide and thatch. This time of year, though, the central hearth warmed the gathering house more than enough to maintain an open-air feel.

As Laryn entered, several villagers sitting at long tables greeted her with kind smiles. The Cloud Walkers differed from Laryn in many ways. Most were no taller than four feet, and all wore body paints of intricate designs. Tiny dots arranged in swirling patterns adorned their wide cheekbones and accentuated their dark olive skin. She loved the way sunlight silhouetted their muscled forms and revealed gold undertones in their complexions. Sitting next to them, she always felt rather plain.

She regularly felt humbled by their generosity, their kindness, and the way they could say so much with so few words. She'd come to the valley five years ago at the urging of the regent in Aarindorn. He'd glimpsed in a vision that her path forward lay within their domain. So, with a heart for adventure, she had traveled to the strange land and lived among the Cloud Walkers.

Isolated from the rest of the world by the massive Korjinth Mountains, the Damadibo, or Cloud Walkers as they called themselves, lived relatively idyllic lives. And thankfully, the villagers had welcomed Laryn like a long-lost sister. She regarded her new family with deep affection. As she'd never borne children of her own, she found significant meaning in time spent with the children here. They often asked her to tell stories or play games and treated her like a treasured aunt.

She had learned their customs and mastered their silent finger language of signing. To repay their kindness, she became a student of herb gathering and often ventured high into the mountains to collect rare herbs.

She collected a bowl for breakfast and loaded it with her favorite fruit, kevash. The kevash trees dropped their round fruit in crops all year. She removed the bright green, pitted peel to reveal wedges of dark red fruit. Without care for the seeds, she bit deeply into one of the wedges. The fleshy pulp burst to release tangy, sweet juices. The first morning's bite always danced upon her tongue and awoke her senses as if she were tasting it for the first time.

She released a familiar moan of pleasure and sat next to Ellisina, a young girl who loved to play hide-in-the-clouds. The child turned with a feline growl and revealed a complex pattern of gold and brown spots on her face that resembled the markings of a jungle cat. Her mother made the face paint from local fruits, and the staining would last for weeks.

Locks of brown and black hair, commonplace among the Damadibo, played across Ellisina's full cheekbones. When the girl smiled, her amber eyes twinkled, and all of Laryn's lingering somber thoughts vanished in the light of her pure exuberance.

Ellisina purred and pretended to wipe a paw across her nose. The girl held out her hand, expecting a small morsel of fruit. Laryn found the request too charming to deny and rewarded her with a generous wedge of kevash.

"Many blessings, my Laryn, honor to you," Ellisina signed. She gave Laryn a full toothy grin speckled with the red, fleshy fruit.

Laryn giggled, then used nimble fingers to gesture back, *"Many blessings and honor to you, little kitten. Is your grandfather about?"*

Ellisina's smile abruptly twisted into a suspicious scowl. She interrupted the relative silence with her boisterous retort, "Is today going to be your day, my Laryn?" Her use of the pronoun to claim Laryn as hers further reflected her fear that some force of the world might one day take Laryn away from the valley.

"The knowing of that is not to my knowing," said Laryn with a soft voice. She tapped the girl on the nose with a reassuring smile.

"As long as today is not your day, then he's just left for the spirit house. If you hurry, you can catch him," said Ellisina.

"Thank you, little one," Laryn signed. She rose and hurried out of the gathering house, mindful to collect the last of her kevash. She walked along a stone path around the edge of the village, soft ferns brushing against her ankles with each step. The fronds stretched out through the moisture-laden clouds that meandered across the ground in the morning hours.

She passed several villagers and shared the traditional greeting. Without words, each person touched their heart, then their forehead with the fingertips of one hand. The gesture served to communicate that in their heart and mind, they felt the other.

Cloud and mist wafted before her as she strode up to the front steps of the spirit house. She pushed past the low-hanging broad leaves from a nearby kevash tree already picked clean of its delicious fruit. With disappointment, she found the front doors closed. *I'm too late. He already entered.*

To Laryn's understanding, no one but the village elders ever entered the spirit house. She stood on the bottom step and used a toe to trace imaginary patterns on the ground. Her mind wandered. She could always assist some of the villagers harvesting in the lower valley. She sucked on another wedge of kevash and considered her options.

The Cloud Walkers lived in peace and tranquility, but sometimes the slow pace made her feel restless. With one hand on her hip, she rocked side to side. She thought perhaps she could find some solace running the wolvryn with Mahkeel, the wolvryn handler.

An old man rounded the corner from behind the spirit house. As he approached, iridescent blue butterflies hovered around him. One rested on his palm. With delicate grace, he stepped forward and bowed his head to Laryn, then touched his heart and forehead. *"Many blessings, Laryn, honor to you,"* gestured the elder.

Laryn smiled at the unexpected meeting, then replied, *"Many blessings to you, Elder Miljin, honor to you."*

"Tell me, child. Have you come to trade the last of your kevash fruit for one of my butterflies? I do not part with them easily, but for you and a bit of kevash, I could be persuaded." The old man's dark brown eyes twinkled with mischief. His cheeks, silhouetted with a swirling pattern of red and purple dots, only magnified his cherubic nature. *Ellisina definitely inherited her mirth from you.*

Laryn playfully responded, "Why you know that I have indeed!" She handed him the remaining wedges of the succulent, red fruit. Elder Miljin smiled and accepted the trade.

"Off you go, Sheshla," said the elder. With a wave of his hand, the butterfly on his palm took flight and rested on the white flower tucked into her hair.

The old man turned to walk up the stairs into the spirit house. Laryn called after him, "Elder Miljin, please. Is my finding day close?"

The elder turned around to face Laryn. Two steps up, he now stood face to face with her. His warm eyes gazed upon her bright face. The thick shock of white hair dangled across her eyes. With gentle fingers, he tucked the hair back behind her ear.

He paused before answering the question Laryn had asked every week since arriving with the Cloud Walkers. Instead of his usual reply, he lifted her chin with his tiny hand and said, "I sense that your spirit is restless, my dear. Your finding day is not this day. But that day, I am happy to say, is very close."

He tapped her nose the same way she had with Ellisina. "I need to consult the spirits, dear one, but you should come back to me here when the blue moon swells in the night sky. It will make its greatest journey across that night, before the death of summer."

He looked to one of the butterflies hovering about his shoulder. "Do you agree, my winged friend?" The iridescent butterfly on Laryn's shoulder took flight in response and circled Laryn's head.

"Yes, be here then, my child. That night we shall start you on the path to your finding."

Laryn felt like a little girl who had just received a surprise Harvestday gift. She embraced the elder in a hug and bounded off down the trail. Her feet felt lighter than at any point in the last year. She returned to the gathering house. If she had only the summer left among the Damadibo, she would spend it with people she loved. Suddenly a game of hide-in-the-clouds sounded like the perfect way to spend the morning. Ellisina and several other adolescents beamed at the invitation to play the game.

When Laryn had first arrived among the Cloud Walkers, she was always the person most easily captured and the worst person to be it. In one game, the children had evaded her for hours until she begrudgingly gave up. With time though, she had learned how to fold into the mists.

The skill eluded her for the first few years. Then one day, a child fell from a kevash tree. Before she realized it, she had scooped the boy into her arms and felt herself sliding through the misted valley up to the gathering house, where she tended his injuries with the help of his mother. From that day forward, folding into the mists seemed so natural.

She suspected the skill employed zenith. Elder Miljin explained that the mists acted like receptacles, storing excess zenith and trapping it in the valley. He also believed that, because of their elevation and proximity to the moons, the currents of zenith penetrated everything with exceptional strength. She remained puzzled, though, at her ability to tap into even a trickle of power, especially so far from home.

After four rounds of hide-in-the-clouds, she left the children with a smile on her face. She spent the afternoon visiting with friends in the gathering house, then assisted a group of men and women with preparing the evening meal of fish and sweet bread.

Knowing that she had only weeks left, she took in the moments with renewed appreciation. She loved the simple way the community worked together to prepare the food, set the gathering house tables, and socialize.

Following the evening meal, she folded into a small cloud bank and felt herself slide through the cool mists. Once, twice, and a third time, she emerged from the clouds. Each time, she traveled farther southwest until finally, she arrived at the end of the valley.

A mixture of tall grasslands and dense stands of trees covered the foothills leading up into the mountain range. As they were in the prime of the growing season, vegetation covered the region in a lush carpet. She climbed a small boulder to obtain a better vantage point above the meadow. The sunset warmed the stone as she sat, admiring the view.

A male Cloud Walker stepped through the grasses. *"Many blessings and honor to your house, Laryn,"* signed Mahkeel.

She eyed the wolvryn handler. At first glance, he appeared average among the tribe. Closer inspection revealed intricate, spiral markings adorning his proud cheekbones and arms. The outline of a dark wolf stained his bare chest, and he carried a small spear and wore soft leather breeches. An enormous charcoal-colored wolvryn with a silvered muzzle sat next to him.

Using the hand language, she replied, *"You startled me! Many blessings to you, and honor to your house, Mahkeel. And good evening, Ghetti."* She smiled at the wolvryn, who wagged her tail.

The majesty of the matriarch of the pack had always fascinated Laryn. She stared for long moments into the amber eyes of the wolvryn. A distant relative to the common mountain wolf, the wolvryn rivaled the Aarindin both in size and intelligence. Ghetti stood as tall as a small horse but moved with a lithe grace uncommon for creatures of such girth.

The wind blew across the creature's flank, allowing the late-day sun to filter through her undercoat. Her fur rippled like a midnight blue wave. The wolvryn sniffed at the air, then gazed off to the sunset.

As a child, Laryn had seen the creatures hunted to extinction in Aarindorn. Discovering not just one but an entire pack among the Damadibo had brought her significant joy. *And what do your bright eyes see in me, Ghetti?*

Mahkeel interrupted her thoughts using the hand language. *"Much time has passed since you last visited. What brings you to this part of our valley?"* He climbed onto the boulder and sat down next to Laryn. Ghetti seemed content to lay down, matting a bed of the softer sedge grass.

Our valley. Every day, someone surprised Laryn. Mahkeel used a distinctive turn of the thumb and finger to include her in the ownership of the valley. The specific use of the simple word meant he viewed her as one of their own, not separate or different, but the same. The inclusion was so unlike the home from which she traveled. "I have not seen the wolvryn run in a long time," she said.

Mahkeel sat in companionable silence. A gust of wind whipped across the meadow, creating undulating waves of green and yellow. After a few long moments, he turned and smiled at Laryn. "Your finding day must be near! You needed to see them once more?"

"You are the clever one, Mahkeel. I see why the elders made you the handler," she replied. *"And you are right. I would like to see them again. I need to make a memory,"* she signed.

She inhaled, savoring the faint, delicate fragrance of the wildflowers of the meadow. "Tell me, has the pack grown much this season? There were no pups last year."

"There are a few this season, and they are strong. Do you remember Hillen's female wolvryn, the large black one? When he passed from the accident this spring, she became feral. I think it was the grief," Mahkeel said softly, his eyes distant with memories of his friend. "Anyway, when she left, she was pregnant with at least two pups, but I have not seen her for months. I keep hoping to find her with one of her pups, but I fear I will only find her bones at this point. Only the spirits know. Maybe she slipped through the mists and left our valley; it happens sometimes."

Laryn recalled the young Cloud Walker. Hillen was a strong man, quick to smile, and he had a good heart. He'd been helping a neighbor repair a thatch roof after a spring storm and fell while weaving reeds into place, incurring fatal injuries. His female wolvryn had shadowed him most of the day. When the young man died, the lonely animal became aggressive and distant. Mahkeel had brought her back to the pack to try to rehabilitate her.

"Tell me again why the longstriders do not run with the wolvryn," signed Mahkeel. Longstrider was the term used by the Cloud Walkers to describe outsiders. Laryn thought it referred to their collective inability to fold into the clouds.

She thought back to her youth. In her eighteenth year, she'd bonded with a small male wolvryn. The two were inseparable. The next spring, a small group of men with hearts full of fear had killed the creature. Though her recollection of the men's justification had faded, she could still recall her heartbreak when her friend died. She inhaled deeply to disperse the subtle ache that had settled into her chest.

"It's complicated," she said. "There was a time when many longstriders ran with the wolvryn."

"Maybe they just need to come visit us." He signed the phrase with humorous exaggeration, slapping his chest to emphasize the last part. Mahkeel then smiled and stood up on the boulder. He whistled to Ghetti, who perked her ears and rose to her full height.

"Call them, Ghetti?" he signed. The wolvryn stretched lazily, then walked around the boulder. Laryn reached out and ran her fingers through the thick mane and scratched behind her ears. Ghetti craned her neck toward the meadow and released a long howl across the valley. The melancholy song started low and throaty, and Laryn could feel it vibrate in her core. The howl crescendoed to a lingering call of longing. In moments, the echoes of similar cries answered her summons. Ghetti waited a few moments, then repeated the howl.

Over the next several minutes, low-pitched howls and higher-pitched yips filled the meadow. A pack of twelve wolvryn bounded across the foothills toward the meadow where Laryn and the handler stood. The creatures approached their matriarch with tails wagging and offered affection to Ghetti.

Laryn marveled at the collective splendor of the creatures. Despite their girth, they loped around the boulder with agile grace.

"Would you like to see a calling, Laryn? Just after sunset, when there is still light, but not too bright, is the best time to see," Mahkeel said in an excited tone that indicated his own desire to commence the ritual.

"I would love nothing more. Are there enough here?" Laryn signed.

"I think so. It's always better when there are more, but we have been practicing," he signed.

Mahkeel untangled a small leather cord with a piece of fluted bone attached to one end. He began to swing the bone flute overhead. A low, droning buzz echoed over the grassland. The wolvryn, previously milling about the boulder, each stopped and released overlapping resonant howls. Mahkeel continued the steady circular twirling, and the pack continued to overlap their howls.

The wolvryn song blended into a melancholy call of yearning. After several minutes of the song, a warm breeze circled the entire group, drawing leaves and flower petals into a small whirlwind. As the orange and pink haze of the sunset streaked across the valley, wispy images appeared to hover around the pack.

Laryn gasped in delight as a myriad of spirits danced around the boulder. Silver and white apparitions of Cloud Walker ancestors mingled about the circle. The sunset outlined their translucent wispy forms, with highlights giving them radiant silhouettes of red and orange. The spirits of long-deceased wolvryn, deer, small game, and even birds intertwined as the howls of the pack lingered.

At the height of the wolvryn song, the spirit of a wizened woman approached Laryn. Her soft face exuded kindness and warmth as she drifted closer. The ghostly figure bowed, then placed a delicate hand on Laryn's chest. Though she felt nothing, the gentleness of the gesture moved Laryn to tears.

The apparition then turned and blew a kiss to the southern horizon before rejoining the soft dance of the spirits. Finally, Mahkeel slowed the spinning wind flute, and the wolvryn allowed their song to fade. The dancing apparitions receded with the sunset, and the swirling, gentle column of air dissipated.

"Thank you, Ghetti," she signed. Laryn's eyes brimmed with tears. She hopped down and embraced the female wolvryn.

"Now, that was special," said Mahkeel. "Never before has an ancestor blown to me a kiss! Very special indeed!"

Folding into the clouds, Mahkeel and Laryn slipped to the village with warm hearts and a story for the night. Laryn pondered the encounter with the elder spirit and its timing with her anticipated finding day. She retired to bed, restless with thoughts about the future.

Chapter Ten: Haircuts and History Lessons

The aroma of savory meat on a cookfire wafted across a field as Lluthean rode his mount north around the outskirts of Journey's Bend. He suspected that the pit master at the Bashing Ram, a local tavern, was busying himself with turning the spit. The entire trip home, they had avoided encounters with other travelers, and as they approached Journey's Bend, the fatigue of their journey, coupled with a gnawing hunger, drove them to take a direct path home.

Finally, he rode along a familiar ivy-covered stone wall. The stone barrier stood only four or five feet tall, but flowering ivy added another foot in most places. His aunt had planted the fragrant flowering vines years ago and used the leaves in her favorite tea. His view of their home remained partly obstructed until he passed the stone wall and turned onto their small yard.

Two goats kept the yard somewhat tame, though clusters of fragrant purple wildflowers grew near the buildings. The goats mewed a welcome, and Lluthean's gelding quickened its pace upon realizing their long journey was nearing its end.

Stacked stone walls covered with more ivy framed the window of the single-story ranch home. The faint aroma of a cooking fire wafted from the single chimney, and a familiar round face appeared in the window. Aunt Rona's stoic expression brightened when she met his gaze. She nodded once and seemed to inhale deeply, then released a soft smile.

She left the window and reappeared on the front porch. In the late afternoon sun, she folded her hands under a sage-colored apron and leaned against one of the two timber columns supporting the roof over the front entry. Bryndor rounded the edge of the stone wall leading Scout by the reins as she spoke.

"I hope your uncle looks better than your mounts there," she said.

"They managed pretty well, but it might be the last time Scout pulls the wagon," said Lluthean.

"I figured as much," said Rona. She strode forward and tucked a few errant strands of grey hair under a simple cloth bonnet. She stroked the muzzle and forehead of his gelding. "Well, hop down, and let's have a look at you."

Lluthean dismounted and offered himself for inspection. Though he'd outgrown her over a year ago, she still commanded his attention. She grabbed his jaw and ran a thumb along the scruff of a thin beard. Next, she tucked his unruly bangs back behind his ears. He grinned under the scrutiny and tried to maintain her eye contact, but she turned his chin side to side. He leaned in for a hug, but she held him at arm's length.

"The sun bleached your hair but hasn't done a thing for the trail dust. How long has it been since you boys used an inn with a proper bath?" she asked.

"Well, that's a bit of a story. We didn't stop at any taverns or inns on the return trip," said Lluthean.

Bryndor walked Scout across the yard and stood next to Lluthean. "My turn?" he asked with a wide grin.

Before she could respond, Kaellor pulled up in their small wagon.

Rona made a pretense of being disappointed for a moment. Her eyes, turned down and soft at the edges, made a scowl appear unnatural on her kind face. She folded her hands under her arms, withholding any welcoming hugs.

"Mother Maedra, forgive me; I can barely stand not to hug you all, but you need baths worse than anyone I've run across in ages. Stable the horses, and I'll grab soap and a brush. The river runs warm enough this time of year. See to removing whatever that smell is that followed you here, and I'll see to supper."

Lluthean sniffed under his arm and recoiled back in surprise. *Mogdure's bunghole, is that me? How did I ever get used to that?*

"I see what you mean, but just for the record, some of us argued to stay at an inn," he said defensively.

She raised an eyebrow in a show of disbelief and kept her arms folded. "Well, the only help for it now is a good soak. Get yourselves sorted out; then, we can catch up."

Lluthean started a mock protest, but his uncle cut him off. "Your aunt is right," said Kaellor. "I've been eating your trail dust for the better part of the day, and we could all use a good soak."

He surveyed the yard and their home. A neat garden with tidy rows of climbing vines occupied the west side of the yard. A grey and black striped cat wandered over and entangled itself between Rona's legs. Its loud purrs accompanied its serpentine dance as it circled first around one leg and then another.

"We were gone longer than I planned, but I see you managed pretty well, Ro," said Kaellor. "And we have a cat?"

She reached down and scratched the cat along its spine, causing it to arch in eager anticipation. "I call him Rings," said Rona. "He's a good mouser and keeps the rabbits away from the garden."

Rona seemed preoccupied and fidgety. Sensing she was about ready to cave to maternal instinct, Lluthean held his arms wide and tried to corral her into an embrace. She sidestepped and wrinkled her nose. "Go, before I change my mind. Be quick to the river so we can have a proper reunion."

"Ahh, you're no fun, Aunt Ro," Lluthean quipped.

"Fun's got nothing to do with that terrible smell you dragged into our yard. Now off with you," she said, folding her arms under her apron. He recognized the posture.

Lluthean sighed, defeated, then led his mount to the small stable. They made quick work of stabling the horses and unloading the travel gear from the wagon. A short walk down a trail through thin timber brought them to the banks of the Shelwyn. The river meandered along a gentle bend near their home.

Lluthean threw his dirty clothes over a familiar tree, then grabbed a rope he and Bryndor had secured a few years ago. He leaned back, testing the rope, then swung in a lazy arc over the river. He released the line and flipped once into the cool waters.

He turned to watch Bryndor employ the same technique, shouting a whoop, though he landed with an unorthodox splash on his side. Kaellor waded into the waters, shaking his head at them both. After more than one round of lathered brushing, they were finally presentable. They returned home as the sun set.

The aroma of stew and bread filled the central room inside their home. Rona stood with her back to them, attending to the last details of a platter of cheese. Four doors exited the far side of the room to each of their sleeping quarters. On the wall opposite the hearth sat three desks adorned with writing instruments.

Lluthean set his pack down on his desk chair and grabbed a mug filled with a few pencils and writing tools. Oil lamps over the desks reflected light off a polished metal sheet on the wall and bathed the room in a soft yellow glow. He turned over the mug and removed three billow tree seeds he'd left there for safekeeping. He began the effortless juggling of the seed pods, then moved to stand near Kaellor and his brother.

Rona set a generous table with fresh bread, a thick stew, and a platter of soft cheese. Once done, she tucked errant wispy hair under her bonnet and resumed her businesslike inspection of their appearance. With clever hands, Lluthean picked the seed pods from their flight and pocketed them to stand at attention. He noticed even Kaellor stood quietly, awaiting her inspection.

She walked around the table and drew close to each of them, appraising the cleanliness of their hands, checking for dirt behind their ears, and even giving each one a sniff test. As the last to suffer the inspection, Lluthean held his breath with feigned anxiety. After a long moment, he gasped then cocked an eyebrow in question.

Rona stepped back and nodded her approval, and they all rushed in to give her an exuberant, albeit clumsy, group hug.

"Now that's a proper welcome home! By the All-Mother, did I ever miss you all. Come sit down and let's hear all about it!" she said.

After a long embrace, they sat down at the table. Rona offered a short prayer to honor the All-Mother and the other six gods, then ladled out the stew. Lluthean spread some of the soft yellow cheese onto a hunk of bread. The buttery silk was slightly sour at first, then a wave of herb and garlic played across the back of his tongue. He swallowed, and his stomach immediately growled for more.

"Whoa. Where did you come by this?" he asked, stabbing a knife into the hunk of cheese for a generous helping.

"While you were gone, I managed to learn a few things," said Rona. She watched as they each helped themselves to the meal. "It's spiced goat cheese."

"It's spiced-amazing-goodness!" Lluthean barely mumbled the words through another mouthful.

Bryndor dunked a hunk of bread into the stew and sampled the broth. He released a growl of pleasure. "Ahh, it's good to be home, Aunt Ro."

"Indeed it is," said Kaellor. He raised a mug of water in salute. "What's the latest news in the Bend?"

"Well, let's see. There's not much to tell, really. There's a new rector in town teaching the kids about the seven gods and whatnot. Three or four new homesteads sprouted up on the southeast part of town, not far from the Tellends. But all that can wait. Tell me about your adventures," she said.

Lluthean took the lead describing their journey south and the villages and kingdoms they had traversed, then rushed to describe their experiences in the Kingdom of Hammond. He ended with their realization that the king's niece seemed unaffected by their concealment. "And once we realized that she remembered us . . ."

"She remembered you," Rona interrupted. "Your faces, your names, what? What did she remember?"

"The girl had no trouble recalling their names and the circumstances under which they met the day before," Kaellor confirmed.

Rona sat quietly, contemplating the revelation. Lluthean used the break in the conversation to fill his bowl with another helping of stew. "So, that's why you avoided the inns on the way home," she surmised. Some of the ruddy color drained from her cheeks as she thought more about the news. "Well . . . what now?"

Kaellor shrugged. "First, I think we will have to see if their mantle remains. The only folks in the Bend who should remember them are the Tellends since they grew up with Harland." He pointed a spoon at Lluthean and Bryndor.

"We could make a trip to town tomorrow for supplies and try the same script, introduce them as our nephews visiting for the summer. If we get the same blind acceptance of the cover story, I imagine the mantle holds."

"And if it doesn't, what then?" she asked.

Kaellor sighed, but Lluthean spoke before he could respond. "If it doesn't, then I'm finally going to court Sadeen Tunkle right and proper!"

"That poor girl won't know what hit her," Rona uttered. "You know everything about her, and she likely can't recall a thing about you. I've half a mind to warn her mother."

"Half's better than all, I suppose," said Lluthean. Rona looked at him with a puzzled expression, then chuckled and blew across a hot spoon of stew, finally understanding his jest.

After the meal, Rona produced a set of shears and an old sheet she used for a drape. She pointed at a chair and arched an eyebrow. Bryndor peered at her through strands of unruly dark hair, then smiled. "I thought I might make it at least a few days before you took me to task," he said.

"Just because you're the first doesn't mean you look more shabby," she said.

He smiled and took a seat. She draped the sheet around his shoulders and produced a comb to manage the project ahead of her. As she began the subtle art of clipping, they continued sharing stories of their adventures.

After they disclosed most highlights of their trip, Kaellor stood and disappeared into his sleeping quarters. He returned a few minutes later with a leather cylinder map case and a heavy iron lockbox. Before either brother had time to ask any questions, Kaellor scratched the back of his head and addressed them both.

"Boys," he said with a sigh. "On the road, I promised you the story of your past. I don't know what tomorrow will bring, whether your mantle will continue or not. But it's time you learn the why and how of it all."

Lluthean watched his uncle curiously. Typically, Kaellor was a calm river—steady, predictable. Lluthean recalled a time when he and Bryndor were practicing with the bow. Lluthean had caught an arrow through the outside of his thigh. Though a minor wound, Bryndor believed he'd dealt his brother a mortal blow. Lluthean remembered limping inside to find his uncle, who had calmly investigated the injury and tended the wound with little surprise or worry.

Now he fidgeted with the dirty plates and moved about the table uneasily. He grabbed their mugs and dropped one to the floor, splashing water in the process. When he sat down, he gazed ahead, eyes unfocused, attentive to a distant memory. Lluthean stifled an urge to play with the billow seeds in his pocket. Whatever Kaellor was about to reveal, he meant to hear it all. Their uncle was not given to small drama.

"Alright." Kaellor sighed. "It's time you both learned the whole truth about our heritage. Goodness, where to begin?" he mumbled.

Rona peered from behind Bryndor and winked. "Just start at the beginning. Tell it as you told me," she said.

Kaellor nodded. "You both know some of the story about our arrival at Journey's Bend. I've done my best to raise you both, with no small help from your aunt. For my part, I've enjoyed the life we live here. But as we move forward tonight, I apologize for the secrets I've kept these long years."

Kaellor pulled on the silver streak at the center of his beard and looked the brothers each in the eye. Lluthean thought he looked like he was about to tell them they descended from something in the Drift.

Kaellor continued, "You know that your parents crafted the concealment to protect you. The need for this anonymity is surely still present. Understanding why they made such a sacrifice . . . it's a long story."

He looked pointedly at Lluthean, who had just started to tap his fingers on the table. "I mean a really long story. So sit back and just listen. Hear the whole thing. Then you can begin to understand that we have some tough choices ahead."

Kaellor paused, considering how to proceed. "To begin, our true last name is not Scrivson. When we arrived at Journey's Bend, I chose the name, knowing it would befit the role of a cartographer and his family."

Kaellor's eyes focused again on some internal, distant memory. "Bryn, your birth name is Bryndorllean Baellentrell. You are the highborn son of the ruling Baellentrell family in our homeland far to the north, Aarindorn."

Lluthean guffawed and could not help himself. "Bryndorllean." He spoke the name with exaggerated aplomb. "It sounds a bit flowery, like something you would use to fragrance linens with." Lluthean slapped the table at his joke.

Kaellor seemed to anticipate the jibe, cocked an eyebrow, and shot him a glance. "And Llu, or rather Llutheandellen Baellentrell, you are the second prince in the royal family. Your father, Japheth, was my brother, and we are the last of a royal bloodline. Our family ruled in peace in Aarindorn, and your parents were beloved not only to each other but to our people."

Given the straightforward tone in their uncle's voice, neither brother chose to interrupt the revelations. Kaellor hoisted open the iron lockbox and removed three ornate necklaces. Each piece of jewelry consisted of interwoven veins of silver and gold, and their delicate chains looped through a palm-sized circular hoop.

Kaellor slid one of the necklaces across the table for Lluthean to study. Lluthean inspected the artifact carefully. The craftsmanship was far beyond anything he had seen from the gilders anywhere in the Southlands. Silver and gold dragons formed the circular pendant. The tails of the creatures intertwined, and their heads met at the apex, with their serpentine bodies creating the hoop's edge. Each dragon appeared to support the other, and each clutched a gemstone. One held a red sapphire, or possibly a ruby, and the other a gemstone of deep blue. Lluthean immediately surmised the worth of the heirloom was more than the family business would bring about in several years.

"These represent the two houses or families of power in Aarindorn," said Kaellor as he traced the dragons upon the pendant. "Our family, the Baellentrells, and the other, the Lellendules, have shared rule in Aarindorn for centuries. When I last left Aarindorn, your father and mother sat on the throne. Thirty-one years ago, in 1600 PC, at the shifting of the dominance of the moons from red to blue, the rulership of Aarindorn transferred from the Lellendule family to ours." He pointed to the two separate gemstones in the pendants.

Kaellor picked up the long leather map case. A weathered patina and layer of dust indicated that it had rested undisturbed for years. Beyond this, nothing made it appear noteworthy. He removed the wax-sealed cap. The container opened with a pop that sounded like the uncorking of a bottle of ale. He gently withdrew a rolled parchment stored in the container, then unrolled the ancient paper on the kitchen table and used mugs to hold down the corners of a large map.

Lluthean struggled to stifle several questions. *Why did we have to leave? Can we go back? Should we go back? If we don't go back, why don't we sell these artifacts and live a life of ease?*

Feeling restless, he gathered the three billow seed pods and rolled them around in circles in the palm of one hand. Their soft rattle eased his mind as he pondered the significance of his uncle's words.

Kaellor tapped a portion of the map below the Korjinth Mountains. "We live here in Journey's Bend, part of the Southlands," he explained. "This is all of the world you have ever known and is only a fraction of the continent of Karsk."

Lluthean leaned forward, noting that the region of the Southlands appeared on the map as a vast wild continent. This older map showed none of the details the three of them had recorded in their work in the last few years. Even more strange, the Southlands appeared much smaller than he ever imagined. Separated by the Korjinth Mountains, the landmass to the north dwarfed the region to the south.

Kaellor traced his finger in a slow, winding path to the northern reaches of the map. "But we once lived here in Aarindorn," he said. "Miles beyond the Moorlok Wood, beyond the peaks of the Korjinth range. Past all these kingdoms. Here," he indicated, tapping on the ancient parchment.

The seed pods dropped to the table, failing to hold Lluthean's interest. He stood and leaned over the map for a better inspection. The detailed portion of the map, the Northlands, revealed a massive continent with kingdoms and regions he had never heard of before. He whistled long and low in astonishment.

"When you were a toddler, Llu, our kingdom found itself at the heart of a struggle against Tarkannen Lellendule. Having embraced the path of the abrogator, he sought to overthrow our family and claim Aarindorn.

Civil war divided the kingdom. About twelve years ago, the Usurper, Tarkannen, battled his way to the heart of our home in the capital city, Stone's Grasp. There was a great struggle, but your parents arrived prepared. They were students of foretellings and prophecy. Using power granted only to those in our bloodline, they banished Tarkannen. But to overcome his strength, your parents had to sacrifice everything. They gave their very life force to the power of the enchantment, as they knew only that level of commitment might generate a binding strong enough for the task."

Kaellor continued, "Along with all of this, they feared Tarkannen's allies would seek vengeance on our family. In an attempt to shield you from that danger, they bound all traces of the gifts our bloodline bestows upon you to hide you from the detection of the abrogators. The mantle they crafted shielded even your very names from any who might seek to track you down. Your mother and father charged me with your care and sent me away with all of their hopes and fears. They assumed that with all traces of your identities masked, we would live undetected and in peace. But as Lesand demonstrated in Hammond, some part of your mantle, perhaps even all of it, has faded."

Lluthean sat back, taking in the gravity of his uncle's story. He glanced at Bryndor, who sat stoically enduring the haircut. Eventually, his restless nature got the better of him. "Kae, what was the war all about? Why did Tarkannen oppose our parents?"

Kaellor sat back in his chair and tapped his fingers together. "In Aarindorn, the ruling family in power alternates every century from one of the two high bloodlines, Baellentrell and Lellendule. When the red moon, known here as Vaeda, dominates the sky, the Lellendules rule. When Voshna dominates the skies, as now, Baellentrells assume the throne.

"At the turn of the century, Tarkannen was the highborn Lellendule. Simple bad timing interrupted his opportunity to rule the kingdom. In 1600, in accordance with the laws and traditions in Aarindorn, the governance of the kingdom switched to our family before Tarkannen took the throne. The transfer of the crown was peaceful at first. But Tarkannen left shortly after, only to return in 1619 at the head of a dark army. War broke out and consumed the entire kingdom."

"If it was a civil war, does that mean at least part of Aarindorn threw in with this usurper?" Lluthean asked.

"Yes, I'm afraid so," said Kaellor. "Tarkannen was the first abrogator in sixteen hundred years. Our people were ill-prepared for his power to destroy, to incite fear, and to divide. Some flocked to his banner out of fear. The worst swore blood oaths to him, lusting for the same power he wielded. In the end, the pressure to assault the throne influenced about a third of the population of Aarindorn."

"So, abrogators are real?" Lluthean asked. "I thought they were just things of legend."

"If that were true, we would still live in Aarindorn," Kaellor replied.

Lluthean rolled a seed pod under the palm of his hand. "What exactly is an abrogator?"

Kaellor flared his eyes and, for a moment, looked like an exasperated schoolteacher. "So, there aren't any kingdoms like Aarindorn in the Southlands. Have you ever wondered how a rector in the Southlands can petition the gods for small boons? What is it that enables them to heal the sick or conjure rain for a dry crop?"

Lluthean looked at Bryndor, and both shrugged. Bryndor finally spoke up. "You never really made us think the rectors of the seven gods were very important. We never made pilgrimage like so many others."

Kaellor nodded. "Fair enough. For now, let's talk more about how a rector's power works. We'll save the religious scholarship for another time." He looked sidelong at Rona, who nodded her agreement as she clipped away.

"In every living thing exists a current of zenith. It's the essence that connects us and sustains us. I think rectors can tap into small amounts of zenith and shape the world when their gods favor their prayers. But in Aarindorn, most of our people carry within them something special—a gift, if you will.

"For some, this gift enables them to carry out simple tasks, like discern whether or not a plant needs water. Others can heal disease, and some use their gift to craft works of art. The gift runs in most of us, but in the Baellentrells and Lellendules," he explained, tapping the pendant, "the gift is much more. In our bloodlines, the gift enables power beyond anything you have seen. We are trusted with the ability to defend our people and, if needed, even strike down our enemies. We accomplish these tasks by channeling zenith, the essence of all life.

"Your original question, Llu, pertained to abrogators. Tarkannen abandoned his gift. When he returned to Aarindorn, he wielded nadir. Nadir is the opposite of zenith. Where zenith grows and propagates, nadir reduces and destroys. The currents of zenith run naturally through this world. Somehow, nadir leeches in from the Drift. To my loose understanding, the two balance each other. An abrogator is someone who has surrendered all ability to channel zenith and instead employs nadir."

They sat in silence for a few moments until Lluthean asked, "If Tarkannen became an abrogator, why did he even bother returning to Aarindorn?"

"Who can really say?" replied Kaellor. "I suspect a small part of it was out of anger for missing his chance to be king. Your parents thought his motives were far more sinister. They learned that Tarkannen abandoned our ways and tainted himself with the nadir. Somehow, they also knew that he believed that one of you two held the key to stopping him. In his madness, he believed he had to eliminate all members of our bloodline.

"Your parents knew they might be able to banish Tarkannen, but the exact outcome was uncertain. They also realized they could not destroy him outright, and so they sought a stalemate. They sought to hide you and banish him. They accomplished this in the ritual that bound your gift and forged your mantle."

Lluthean finger-combed his bangs back out of his eyes and frowned under a new realization. "What about you, Kae? Can you use zenith?"

Kaellor sighed and seemed to struggle to condense a complicated answer into a simple explanation. "My gift was lost a long time ago in a very complicated string of events. But the simple fact is, the abrogators can trace the Baellentrell gift. So to remain hidden, I and another bound our gifts.

"Normally, the creation of a mantle or a binding requires sacrifice from another. Two people together can establish a binding for one another. However, in ways I don't completely understand, your ability to channel zenith was concealed by your parents. But I wonder now if they knew how long the binding would last."

Lluthean studied his uncle, who was rubbing a thumb over one of the dragon pendants and focusing on something distant. He turned from his uncle to make eye contact with Rona. She spied him from behind Bryndor's ear but kept quietly clipping. "What about you, Aunt Ro?" he asked.

She leaned back, inspecting Bryndor's new trim, then frowned once and made another small clip above his ear. "My parents migrated from a backwater village to Riverton when I was a girl. But that's another long story, most of which you already know. I'm not from the Northlands. I'm thankful for a strong back and these two hands, and I don't need anything more from the All-Mother or the other gods," she said.

Lluthean's mind raced with so many other questions. He turned to Bryndor, who remained in his chair, listening. Lluthean tossed a seed pod at his brother's chest. It bounced off and rattled on the table. "How can you just sit there? I have a hundred other questions!"

Bryndor looked at Rona, who nodded once that she was done before removing the drape and allowing the errant hair to spill to the floor. She waved Lluthean over for his turn in the chair. Bryndor took a seat at the table and inspected one of the elaborate pendants. He seemed surprised by the weight of the jewelry. Finally, he looked up.

"Alright. Kae, I still don't quite understand why you were sent away, or why we were bound, as you say. I mean, we have a great life here, but it's a far cry from the lot of a prince," said Bryndor. "If our parents banished this Tarkannen, why not just return?"

"Several reasons," said Kaellor. "First, we knew that Tarkannen had recruited other abrogators, but how many and in which duchies we could never be sure. Some of them might even still live in Aarindorn."

Kaellor stood and withdrew to his bedroom again. He returned a moment later with a package wrapped in fine linen. Unwrapping the parcel revealed a thin, leatherbound book.

"This text, *The Book of Seven Prophets*, is an example of what I'm trying to explain," he said, tapping the spine of the book. "This was written by scholars or madmen centuries ago in Aarindorn. There are some passages in here that speak to the possibility that one of you might inherit the power to thwart a resurgence of the abrogators. I can't begin to explain the extent of what that means here at our humble kitchen table in the Southlands."

Kaellor paused again, trying to find the right words. "Remember what I said. Just because the Usurper was banished does not mean he was necessarily defeated. Your parents became convinced he could one day return and would seek revenge upon any Baellentrells left behind, namely us. In part, that's why you were secreted away with me to the Southlands and why we live here in this quiet place in the world."

"You make it sound like our binding, and the Usurper's banishment are all wrapped up in the same package," said Bryndor.

"I regret that I didn't study and search for answers like your parents," he said. "So I don't have all of the answers, but I think you are correct. And I fear that if your bindings are failing, then there is cause to believe the banishment might also be failing."

"Where exactly did Tarkannen go when he was banished?" Lluthean asked. An exasperated sigh from Rona interrupted his question. She swiveled his head back to a neutral position. He strained to make eye contact out of the corner of his vision.

"That's a good question. I don't know," said Kaellor.

"You're telling them all of the scary parts," said Rona. "Tell them more about Aarindorn."

Kaellor nodded in agreement and smiled. "Aarindorn is a beautiful place. Good and decent people live there. Much of our culture centers around the changing dominance of the moons. Every century, when the moons exchange position in the sky, one looms larger, brighter. In Aarindorn, we call the red moon 'of Lellen' and the blue one 'of Baellen.' Since the blue moon dominates the night sky in our family's reign, different shades of blue accent our family crest and banners.

"Stone's Grasp, the capital city, is named for the ancient castle that cleaves into the mountains. It is a city more grand than any we have encountered in our travels. It sits above a clear glacier-fed lake and rises in tiers up to the mountains that surround it. There are gardens and pools and actual tracts of forest within its walls. The markets dwarf even the ones in Hammond. Your father and I got into our fair share of trouble in those busy streets." He grinned at the recollection.

"There was also always a palpable awareness of the responsibility of nobility. Unlike some of the greedy nobles in the Southlands, the Aarindorian notion of nobility is not a lofty selfish privilege but rather a shared mantle of responsibility. The ability to channel zenith is tempered by the strength of all Aarindorians who support it. While we might command unusual gifts, it's our connection to Aarindorn that strengthens those abilities."

He continued, "As the moons traded position in the sky, our family's ability to tap zenith strengthened. My grandparents spoke of sensing the change throughout their lives. Your great grandfather, Bierden, never sat the throne but was one of the last able to channel enough zenith to command rune fire. In battle, he commanded massive, thunderous gouts of blue flame. Every time he released his fury, the skies splintered with thunder. But his ability to marshal enough zenith to carry out such a feat did not occur until perhaps five years after his son sat the throne. Had he not died before the Abrogator's War, I suspect your parents would have made different plans."

"What about your mother and father then, our grandparents?" asked Bryndor.

"My father, Kaellex, sat the throne for about ten years, then abdicated, as did his father before him. Neither man could stand all the politics of the throne but chose instead to serve the kingdom in other ways. The Giver provided him with subtle but meaningful ways to shape zenith. He was capable of foretelling weather and, on occasion, major events that affected the kingdom. My mother, Phethnem, was a healer and continued to work in the royal sanatorium right up to the war."

Lluthean twisted his neck, spilling errant hairs to the floor. Rona sighed and swiveled him back in place, but he pressed on. "So, let me get this straight," he said. "Is Bryn next in line for the Aarindorian throne, or you?" He cast a sidelong glance to his brother, who seemed unconcerned by the revelation.

"Well, your father was the oldest, and Bryn is his eldest son, and so the general rules of Aarindorian succession place him as the heir. Besides, I had more than enough to account for as a prince." Kaellor cocked an eyebrow and smiled.

"Still, prince of a country, and you left all of that behind. It's a lot to get your head around," Lluthean noted.

Kaellor waved off Lluthean's statement. "At the time, your parents believed that the only safe way to raise you both was away from Aarindorn and with the full measure of our Baellentrell gift hidden. Tarkannen and his minions have ways of finding us if we employ our gift. Frankly, at the time, I was honored to be so trusted by my brother and didn't fully realize the implications of leaving home until much later."

They sat long moments until Bryndor interrupted the silence. "Kae, you speak of the Giver while Aunt Ro praises the All-Mother, but I get the feeling these are not the same?"

"No, they are not," said Kaellor. "In the Southlands, people worship gods unknown in the north. In the north, the Giver is thought to be the source of all zenith and the one who bestows our unique channeling abilities, while the Taker resides in the Drift and wields nadir."

They sat around the table in a strange silence, the snipping of Rona's scissors the only sound for several minutes. Kaellor's words gave even Lluthean too much to ponder. *So, who is right? Do we curse Lutney or the Taker for a bad hand at cards? Do I praise Maedra or the Giver when things go right?* He tapped a rhythm on his knees under the sheet.

Bryndor broke the silence. "Kae, why couldn't you tell us all of this before?"

"There are lots of reasons," Kaellor said with a plain expression. He pushed out his lower lip. "And in hindsight, none of them are very good. I suppose, at first, it was easier to keep our secret if there was nothing for you to divulge accidentally. But in recent years, I thought to spare you any regret."

"I don't follow," said Bryndor.

"Well . . . growing up is tough enough without always wondering what if," he said.

Lluthean did not understand his uncle's answer, but his excitement overshadowed any confusion. "Where does this all leave us now?" he asked.

"I don't know that much has changed, except that we need to see if anyone in the Bend remembers you with more than a passing notion," said Kaellor. "Our good fortune in Hammond means we don't need to take any risky expeditions. If you're willing, we can make a pretty good living crafting reprints of our survey of the Southlands."

"That beats trail food and sleeping on a bedroll," said Lluthean.

Bryndor rolled his burly shoulders, then stretched overhead with a yawn. "Permission to be excused?"

Kaellor and Rona nodded, and he retreated to his room. Rona removed the sheet, dismissing Lluthean. "You're as done as you'll ever be. I would trim that scruff if I thought you could hold still long enough."

Lluthean stood and brushed off a few random hairs, then rubbed the scruff at his chin with the back of his hand, mimicking Kaellor. He dropped his voice low, sounding not unlike his uncle. "I don't know. I think it makes me look . . . princely."

Rona shook her head with mock chagrin. "You're handsome enough, but that beard needs a few more years to fill out. Leave it on, and I'll shave it in your sleep. Now off to bed!"

Lluthean flicked a billow seed into the air. "Well, the younger prince still has lots of questions," he said.

"And that's why I never shared any of this before," said Kaellor with a half-smile. "Save your questions for later? It's my turn in the chair, and I need a good night of sleep more than your brother."

"Alright, later then," said Lluthean. He stepped back from the table. "Need help with the dishes?"

"I think your uncle and I can manage," said Rona.

Lluthean wandered over to the small window overlooking their front yard. The blue moon appeared large on the horizon, and the red moon waned small and distant.

"The moon of Baellen," he said, trying the phrase out for the first time. "It's got a nice ring." He sauntered back to his room and spent the night dreaming about magical powers and the princes who might wield them.

Chapter Eleven: To Tame a Feral Wolvryn

After dinner, Kaellor sat in companionable silence as Rona trimmed his hair and the most unmanageable parts of his beard. He thought over the night's conversation. Part of him felt relieved like a burden had slid away, but another part of him worried about the binding and what the morning would bring. His shoulders tightened, and he inhaled a deep breath to force the muscles to relax. *No sense worrying about things I can't change.*

Neither spoke until she finished clipping. He stood, then stepped lightly over the pile of accumulated hair. "Better?" he asked.

She inspected her work. "It will have to do, I suppose. I left you more length than the boys; apparently, it is the custom of the distinguished in Riverton these days."

He arched an eyebrow. "Distinguished? I suppose I need all the help I can get when it comes to haggling with the money changers. Thanks, Ro, let me get this." He reached for a broom, but she pulled it from his grasp. "I'll see to this mess if you get the dishes."

"Deal." He nodded and got to work. After stacking the last of the dishes, he gazed out the window across their small yard. Rings hopped up onto their wagon, and Kac noticed a dark groove along one of the front wagon wheels. *I'm surprised we didn't have to make repairs before we got back.*

Rona finished her task and came to dry dishes next to him. She peered out the window, curious about the object of his attention. "Miss that old wagon seat already?"

Kaellor arched an eyebrow and released a chuckle. He rubbed at the small of his back. "Not at all. My sore back would do well to never sit in it again. I was just thinking how lucky we were to make it home with that damaged wheel."

They finished the dishes, then sat together on the front porch and shared a pot of tea. He clutched his cup in both hands and savored the fruity aroma. Tonight she'd brewed his favorite, a mild tea with dried apple. Stirred with a stick of cinnamon, the brew served as the perfect end to a long day. Rona did always brew the most amazing combinations: strong, stout blends to wake you up and smoother blends to send you to sleep.

The aromas always made him recall the first time she'd poured the tea. When he first arrived at Journey's Bend, he rented a room at the Tellends, farmers on the south side of town. After a few months, he realized that rearing two boys and making a living were not things he could accomplish on his own. Markum and Emile Tellend couldn't help him; they had enough to do with their own son and the daily tasks of managing a farm. As the coin he arrived with dwindled, he had struggled to determine how to establish his own home.

He grew up learning how to politic with aristocrats and was schooled in geography, history, mathematics, and local economics. Once he sat through his Rite of Revealing, his arca prime had revealed itself as the guardian symbol. From that moment, his training began in earnest. Military tactics, swordplay, and strategy became part of his daily diet. But none of that had prepared him for the challenges of raising his nephews.

Emile Tellend realized as much early on and invited Rona to sit with Kaellor to discuss a potential arrangement. Rona's parents had died in an outbreak of flux earlier in the spring, and she needed a way to make a living. Somehow, Emile knew both of them needed a partner without all the romantic attachments. Someone to share the work and responsibility with, and also for the security. And so they had formed a partnership at the Tellend dining table over hot apple tea stirred with cinnamon sticks.

"Where did you drift off to, Kae?" Rona asked.

He lifted his gaze from the steam above the cup. "Every time you make this tea, I'm taken back to the very first time we met at the Tellends."

"That was a good day," she replied. Her plump, rosy cheeks framed a gentle smile.

"It was the start of making all of this possible, and them," he said, gesturing at the doors to the nephews' rooms. "I never could have managed without you."

"We do make a fine team, I think." She sipped at her tea.

"Ro, we started all of this out of necessity and grew into a family. Do you ever think about what you might want to do once Lluthean is old enough to leave? I mean, you could do anything." He asked the question with a sly crook to his eyebrow.

Rona appeared taken aback by the question and set down her teacup to consider him formally. Her cheeks colored, and she spoke with a flat tone. "I am not certain what you are trying to say, Kae, so perhaps you should just say it."

Kaellor stood up and quickstepped just inside the front door to the small pile of their gear. He found the iron lockbox from King Vendal. "Do you trust me?" he asked from where he stood.

She considered him with a cool expression, appearing unsure of his strange behavior. After a pause, she nodded once.

"Good, then close your eyes," he said. Rona closed her eyes. He hoisted up the box with a grunt, then gently placed it on her lap. She startled at the weight and opened her eyes.

"What's this?" she asked.

"When the boys and I rescued the king's niece, Lesand, you didn't think he would let us leave without a proper reward, did you?"

"No, but you said he gifted you with a sword and two bows," she replied.

"Yes, I did say that. What we failed to mention to you was this." He opened the lockbox to reveal the silver and gold coins from Hammond. Rona's mouth remained open only for the moment it took him to collect some of the coins and rain them back into the box. She considered the treasure before her with wordless amazement. With trembling hands, she gathered some of the coins.

"They have an odd make," she said.

"In Hammond, everything revolves around the sea. They worship Foden above all others. They call the gold pieces fins, and the silver scales," he explained.

She placed the coins back into the box and looked at him with a shake of her head. Her silence left him puzzled. "Well, what do you think?" he asked.

"I think we don't need to bother with a broken wheel when we can buy a whole new wagon."

"Wagon? Ro, this is enough for us to buy an entire estate in Riverton, and then some," he said.

She didn't answer for a long moment. "You know, I don't think I could really be happier than I am right here. It's a grand thought, Kae, but all our friends are here. Imagine though, what we could do for the boys or this town with that kind of wealth," she said.

Kaellor felt a subtle tension between his shoulders relax. He realized he'd been feeling a little anxious over the thought that she might want to move to an estate in Riverton. He winked at her.

"I was hoping you would say something like that. So, tomorrow, I plan to ride back to Riverton and open accounts at the king's bank. One for each of the boys, one for us, and one that, well, we can decide what to do with it later."

She smiled and nodded. They sat in agreeable silence for several minutes.

"Kae, why didn't you tell them everything? You started with that book of prophecy, but you never really got into the darker parts of it," she said.

Kaellor sighed. "I know. I can't explain it. I prepared for that conversation for a long time. But I realized as I was sharing everything that maybe I should have been telling them these things all along, years ago, teaching them their heritage."

He blew across his tea, considering everything. "And I think I was surprised that I had to work to recall some of the details." He paused for a sip. "My mind wanders back to Aarindorn all the time, at least I thought it did. But in telling the story out loud, I realized how unfamiliar it all felt. I had to search my mind for some of the details to answer their questions. It made me feel like we are about as far removed from Aarindorn as we can be."

"And just at the time you figured that out, their mantle might be fraying," she said for him. She tilted her head and turned her soft eyes to him. Talking to her was always like talking to a wise friend. "What do you think about that?"

"Like most things in life, it's a mixed blessing," said Kaellor. "I can tell Bryn is restless to strike out on his own, and the Giver knows he's got every right to. He's always struggled with being anonymous to everyone but family. Lluthean is . . ."

"Lluthean is Lluthean," she said. "I expect he'll need to learn how to interact with people without the advantage of already knowing their reactions in a card game. He'll adjust. But that's not what I mean, Kae."

Rona never invested herself in small drama. The fact that she had redirected the conversation back to the mantle meant she understood the possible dangers. *No sense avoiding the truth with her.*

"It's a concern. We do need to see how folks in the Bend react to them. If their identities are unmasked, it could mean that a layer of their binding has lifted. But I think as long as their access to zenith is restricted, they will be safe from anyone affiliated with the abrogators."

"Zenith," she said the word slowly as if tasting how it felt in her mouth. "I can't say I understand any of it. Do you think the prophecies in that book of yours are about the boys?" she asked.

"My brother did," said Kaellor, "and he was a student of such things. Part of me thinks it's possible. There is greatness in each of them. But the price, the risk, it's far too high. If I have to choose between steering them to a secure, boring life versus one in which one of them has to die, then it's an easy choice."

They sat for a few long moments in silence before Rona finished his thought, "But you can't make that choice for them, can you?"

Kaellor felt a sting in his eyes and a tingle in his nose but held back any further swell of emotion. "No, I can't. They would never forgive me once they learned the truth. One thing about Baellentrell men, sometimes you just have to get out of their way and let them make their own choices. Anything else is like trying to control the path of a river or tame a feral wolvryn."

She arched an eyebrow in question. "That sounds like something from your book. Why don't you tell me more? Maybe it will ease your mind to remember."

He smiled, recalling his father speak the same phrase. "Wolvryn were majestic beasts. No, that's not the right word. Creatures?" He pulled at the silver part of his bearded chin.

How to explain?

"The closest thing they might resemble are wolves only, not just wolves. They were much broader in the hips and shoulders, and the large ones rivaled a small horse. Occasionally, a pup would wander down from the mountains surrounding Stone's Grasp. People would compete for the pup's attention, and eventually, the wolvryn might take a liking to one person, and that was that. They would be inseparable. There was something intelligent in their eyes, and we used to say zenith ran thick in their blood, but I never really knew what that meant."

"Is it wolvryn or wolvryns?" she asked.

"Both," said Kaellor. "The same word applies whether we're talking about one or several."

"You never had a wolvryn of your own then?" she asked.

"A full-grown wolvryn was more animal than my mother would have allowed in the castle. She was a lovely woman, but she didn't really like animals. Besides, if a person separated from their wolvryn for too long, the creature became feral. It usually only happened when someone died, but with all of my commitments, it would have been difficult to manage. If one did go feral, the poor creature had to be hunted down. Once feral, they became unpredictable and just as likely to take human life as that of anything else."

"And so the phrase 'tame a feral wolvryn' came about?" she asked.

"So the story goes." He pulled a long sip of the tea, then realized with regret that he'd neared the end of his cup.

"You haven't shared stories from your home in a long time," said Rona. "I like hearing them. Do you ever think of returning?"

Kaellor sat back, considering her question. He peered through the door into the common room of their home, and his eyes ran along a vertical beam, part of the doorframe. It was notched with the heights and years of his nephews. A different beam over the hearth wore a blackened scar, a remnant from a grease fire caused when he and the boys had tried to surprise Rona with dinner on her birthday and nearly burned the house down. "I suppose I think about it, but not with any serious intention. We do have a good life here, good memories, and there's no guarantee that it's safe for the boys to return."

"What if they . . ." She paused. "What if, after hearing everything, they want to take their inheritance and go back. What then?"

"I'm not sure. Someday soon, they are going to have to make their own choices, but only after they understand the danger," he said.

"Someday soon?" she asked.

"Yes," he said. "Let's get through the next few days first, and then I will finish telling them everything."

He stood and kissed the top of her head, then lifted the lockbox. They retired inside. After securing the door, he picked up the artifacts from the table. Rona placed their cups near the sink, then made her way to her room. She stopped at her bedroom door. "The house felt empty, Kae. It's good to have you all back. Good night."

He looked up after gently rolling the ancient map into the case. "It's good to be back, Ro. Good night."

Chapter Twelve: Abrogators Visit the Abbey

Lanterns flickered in the arched windows of the Abbey on the Mount, welcoming travelers on spiritual pilgrimage to the seven gods. Through a thin haze of rain, the light cast a vague outline of the front portico and arched front door. Volencia stopped her horse next to her partner, Mallic. They surveyed the structure.

From beneath a hooded robe, Mallic growled, "You're certain this is the place? We've already lost weeks since the sounding."

She sighed inwardly. Mallic had become more and more impatient as their journey continued. Sometimes she felt like the mother of a shortsighted five-year-old.

"Do you see any other keeps, or for that matter, any other buildings around?" she snapped the response in irritation with clipped words. "And stop reminding me of the time—I am quite aware of it, Mallic."

She took a breath to consider their approach. *How does he always manage to sour my mood? Our exile together is like too much time and old milk.*

She shook off her irritation and tried to continue in softer tones. "We need to appear common. Dismiss the dome."

"Fine, but as soon as we're done, I plan to reinstate it. I don't care how we look; I detest riding wet." With a dismissive flip of his hand, Mallic released his command of nadir, allowing the barrier to dissipate. Cold rain saturated his dry robes, which clung to his bony frame. In the poor light, his silhouette resembled that of a much older, frail man.

He sighed as rivulets of rain ran across his flawless, angular cheeks and thin, pointy nose. Both horses shifted their weight in discomfort and pawed the ground in soft protest at feeling the rainfall for the first time.

The pair sat in the darkness, out of range of the abbey lanterns. Once Volencia was satisfied that they were appropriately soaked, she eased her mount forward.

"Wait a moment," said Mallic. "If we're going to play this your way."

He dismounted without further explanation, then pointed a finger at his horse's hind leg. His wrist extended beyond the cuff of his sleeve and revealed a fine iridescent black sigil over pale skin. The symbol looked like a decorative vein on his forearm until it pulsed and writhed.

"Maladictor," he murmured.

The familiar invocation they used to give focus to their intent was accompanied by the feeling of a subtle vacuum of nadir drawn into action. Unseen in the rainy night, an inky black shard darted from his finger into the horse's hind flank. The animal grunted at the surprising flash of pain and shuffled a clumsy step to the side.

"Let's go then." He led his mount forward by the reins. The horse limped along behind him.

They marched under the portico, and Mallic grasped the knocker. He rapped on the door several times. Long minutes passed with no response. He rapped the knocker again, several times and with more force. A shadow crossed the thin shaft of light under the door, indicating that someone had finally responded. They waited, and the figure on the other side of the door offered no greeting, so Mallic lightly rapped on the door once more.

"Hold a moment; I'm looking for the right key!" a man's muffled voice responded. A loud clunk of metal engaging the lock echoed once, then the voice spoke again. "Umm, who is it? If I might ask?"

Even through the door, Volencia could tell that suspicion flavored the abbot's tone. She watched as Mallic bent his neck to the side, a sure signal that he'd exhausted his limited patience. She placed a calming hand on his shoulder. He turned with a grimace and glared at her for a few seconds, but she just stared back intently, then nodded at the door.

Eventually, he just shook his head and responded in a light tone, "Please, sir, my wife and I, we've traveled so far, and my horse is lame. We need shelter and can pay."

The heavy door opened, spilling light across the portico. "Far be it for a humble abbot to deny anyone their chance to pay homage to the Seven," said the abbot.

He filled the doorway, his rotund girth silhouetted in simple brown robes. He inspected the pair for a few moments. "Your horse favors that hind leg, sir. Perhaps in the light of Drexn, we can beseech Maedra to heal the poor creature."

The rector arched his eyebrows and waited for a response. Volencia cleared her throat and said, "If you could beseech the goddess of nature to favor us, we would truly be grateful. Praise the Seven."

The abbot nodded at her formal response. "Come in then, and let's have a look. I gather you're a long way from home. Callish?"

"Yes, my lord, you have our thanks. You have a keen eye to recognize a Callashite from so far away. How could you tell?" asked Mallic.

"Your clothing mostly; the stitching is unique to Callashites, but you both have the accent as well. It warms my ears; it does! I haven't had a good conversation with anyone from Callish in months."

Volencia stepped inside the entry hall and looked at her face in a small mirror on the wall. Thick strands of short, wet black hair matted to her forehead, but her porcelain cheeks remained unblemished.

Pink, full lips traveled unnaturally wide across her face such that when she angled her head to the side, she could always view a part of her smile. A lover joked once that she had a smile like a fish. She'd rewarded him with a wet kiss, then removed his eyes and carved off his lips to guarantee that hers were the last he would ever see or kiss.

She dismissed the memory and lingered a moment, gazing into her own black eyes. *How long has it been since I saw myself in a mirror?*

She realized she had half-expected to see faint purple or red irises looking back. That was how her eyes had always looked as a child. So much time had passed since she'd looked at herself in a mirror that sometimes she forgot the change. *Small price to pay to access nadir.*

After making a pretense of adjusting her hair, she wrung out the hem of a rain-soaked sleeve. The zigzag white and black stitching at her wrist did provide a clear indication of their home in Callish. *This rector is perceptive.*

"My name is Mallic, Mallic Shawlin, and this is my wife, Volencia. We only have need of shelter from the rain and stabling for our mounts. We can pay for your hospitality."

Volencia appraised Mallic's acting. Usually, when he spoke, he tilted his head back in a way that allowed him to look at someone down the length of his nose. Most found the posture disconcerting. For the moment, he kept his head down and his tone respectful.

The rector seemed to finally be put at ease by Mallic's appearance and offer of coin, and he smiled in return. "My name is Homnibus, and welcome to the Abbey on the Mount. May the blessings of the Seven be upon you."

How interesting it is that you distrust us from the other side of the door, and yet to your face, you are so easily beguiled into seeing what you expect.

The notion made the edges of her wide mouth start to curve up in a smirk, but she resisted, keeping her mind on the task at hand. The pudgy man ushered the couple through the humble entrance hall to a larger round room. Seven curved benches ringed the room. Above each bench, an elaborate portrait of one of the seven gods hung in an alcove: Drexn, god of light; Maedra, goddess of nature; the twins, Voshna the blue and Vaeda the red; Foden, god of the seas and wind; Lutney, the trickster; and Mogdure, god of death. At the apex of the room, an image of the All-Mother Malldra hung above them all.

Lanterns set in seven windows illuminated the otherwise sparsely decorated room. "If you will wait here, I'll see to your horses, and we can find you adequate accommodations, I'm sure."

Homnibus leaned over a railing to yell up a set of curved stairs, "Timson! Timson, come down. We have two visitors whose horses need stabling!"

From the top of the stairs, a teenage lad in nightclothes appeared. His hair defied gravity at odd angles, and a pillow crease across his cheek bore witness to the late hour. With glossy eyes, he descended the stairs and pulled on a weathered overcoat. He slogged in silence out the front entry without making eye contact and led the horses away to the stable.

As the entry door closed, Mallic turned to the abbot. "Do you get many guests this time of year, Master Homnibus?"

"I'm no man's master, my lord. Just Homnibus, or rector if you prefer. Aye, this is a slow time, but you are welcome all the same. Most folks make pilgrimage in spring to allow plenty of time to return home for Harvestmoon celebrations. It's good to have someone to talk to other than Timson for a change," Homnibus replied.

"Surely, it's not just the two of you?" asked Volencia.

"Oh, no." The man chuckled and led the couple through the circular room and down a side hallway. "There are six other abbots here in service this time of year, but they have taken oaths of silence. So if it's conversation you're after, well, it's just Timson and me."

Volencia schemed. *Seven abbots and a boy. If this is the resting place of the blood pool, we should have no trouble at all once we find it.*

She glanced to Mallic. His expression indicated he'd arrived at the same conclusion.

Homnibus led the couple into an empty dining hall. "If you would forgive me, I'll see to your room upstairs. Preparations should only take a moment," he muttered. Mallic offered a sardonic smile, and the portly man disappeared through a door on the opposite side of the room.

Mallic removed his outer riding cloak and placed it over the back of a chair. He walked the perimeter of the room, rubbing at his rain-soaked sleeves, then blew warmth into cupped hands and whispered, "The pool has to be in the foundation level somewhere. We need to get to it before I catch my death from the chill."

"I know, but unless you've become clairvoyant, we have to continue the show a bit longer," replied Volencia. "Once we get to the pool, we can deal with any number of these rectors. Their command of zenith has always been weak, even in this shrine. But we might still need their help to gain access."

Besides, while I don't believe in their gods, I don't care to linger overlong in one of their holy places. I wonder what it would take to provoke one of them to appear? Are they even real enough to actually do so?

Mallic interrupted her thoughts. "You do love the game, don't you? All these charades when we could simply bend him to our will." He scowled in mock exhaustion.

"Where is the sport in that, my dear?" Volencia purred. "The game is so much more interesting when the prey becomes entangled in my web. Savoring the surprise is like foreplay."

Mallic snorted. "While I can't entirely disagree, I would rather take this Homnibus, slice off one of his fat arms, then use it to whip him to take us where we need to go."

In his irritation, Mallic failed to notice Homnibus, who had reappeared in the doorway, holding a tray of bread and cheese. The abbot stood awkwardly, trying to melt back into the corridor. The surprised look on his face indicated he'd heard too much.

Before Homnibus could react, Volencia channeled nadir. Her instant connection to the dark power vibrated a thrill of pleasure along the black sigils adorning her forearm. She gave the nadir focus and definition, then sent it forward to lash the abbot in place. Oily black vines erupted from the floor and snaked around his ankles.

Homnibus struggled to free his legs and dropped the tray of food. He lifted his robes to view the black shackles, then sucked in his breath. "Abrogator?" he said, a high tenor of disbelief flavoring his voice.

"Drexn, lord of light, and Maedra, mother of nature, bring your power to dwell here and protect me!" The rector gathered a sphere of pale blue light in quivering hands. The zenith coalesced as thin wisps and swirled between his fingers. He attempted to hurtle the conjured globe forward, but it dissipated as it left his hands. A gentle breeze wafted across the room as the only indication of his command of the power.

With casual disregard, Mallic strode to the whimpering abbot, who was scratching and pulling at the black tethers. Volencia watched as he mumbled a prayer, and tendrils of blue zenith slid under one of the shackles and popped it open.

Volencia flicked her wrist, engaging another binding of nadir. The thrill of shaping the dark substance tingled down her arm and settled as a burning vibration in her hands. Before Homnibus could finish his second evocation, she lashed the shackle back around his leg, but this time clamped it tight enough to provoke pain.

The rector gasped in wide-eyed fear and surprise. "Leave me be! Get out, go away!" he cried.

"My dear Homnibus. That is no way to treat a guest." Mallic clipped his words short and married the aggressive speech with a feral grin. "Now listen closely, and no one need be harmed. We've traveled a long distance and have need of an ancient circular pool. We know it is in the lowest levels of the abbey. It may resemble a shallow well. Do you know of this item?"

Homnibus continued to struggle and didn't seem to register Mallic's question. "Get out! Please just leave, take what you want, but go away!"

Mallic sneered and rolled up his sleeves to reveal wiry, pale arms decorated with thin, black, and elaborate sigils. With a lunge, Mallic appeared to throw his hands forward. At the same time, he invoked his word of wrath, "Maladictor!" This time, his intent erupted as black, smoky wisps that surged forth from the sigils on his forearms and leeched into the abbot's chest.

Homnibus craned his neck in agony so intense he couldn't even scream; he just arched and writhed uncontrollably. The torment appeared extreme and lasted several minutes.

Volencia knew the technique well. With the right invasion of nadir tendrils, one could disrupt the flow of blood to different parts of the body. The resulting pain became truly excruciating. Yet, if performed correctly, no actual damage occurred. In this fashion, the torture could last for days.

She became concerned that Mallic would overreach. The rector was an unfit, older man; any longer and he would be useless. Just as she was about to say something, Mallic released the man from the torture, and Homnibus slid to the floor, panting. He looked up with tear-streaked cheeks and continued to whimper. Bloodstained snot ran out from his nose and onto his chin.

"I trust I have your attention then," said Mallic. "Now, you will lead us down to the room with the circular pool without further delay. Unless you need more incentive?"

Volencia released the shackles, and Homnibus nodded in agreement. He rolled to his hands and knees, then staggered to his feet. "It's this way," he stammered.

He grabbed a small candle lamp, then led Volencia and Mallic to the back of the abbey, passing what appeared to be a sanctuary and other smaller chambers of worship. At the end of the hall rested a heavy door reinforced with iron bindings.

Homnibus retrieved a large key ring from an oversized pocket in his robes. He counted past several, then selected a weathered rusty key. With tremulous hands, he rattled the key into the lock; the lock springs emitted a wrenching screech that echoed in the empty hall. The door eventually relaxed open.

Beyond, a short landing preceded a large spiral staircase, and the abbot led the couple downward. At three places, the descent was interrupted by corridors, but Homnibus paid these no attention. As the three descended, the air became cool and heavy. Time dusted the steps, and the musty aroma of mold revealed that no one else had traveled this deep into the abbey in years.

Finally, the spiral stairs ended in a hallway. "It's the second one on the right. That double door opens into a larger room with your well, my lord," Homnibus said, his voice trembling.

Volencia held a hand forward. "Continue on then."

She knew full well that ancient dwellings of power often carried certain protections and barriers. If any such protections needed a trigger, the abbot would suffice just fine. Following Homnibus at a distance, they turned into a dark vaulted room. Crude stone benches melded with the floor and ringed a circular object. In the center sat what appeared to be a four-foot-wide circular well. The edges of the well, crafted of stone, rose three feet from the floor.

"Take your lamp, Homnibus, and look inside there. Tell me what you see," she directed.

Homnibus rose to his tiptoes and shone the light into the well from as far away as possible. Eventually, he stepped closer to peer into the water. "Why it's, it's not a well at all." Homnibus looked relieved.

He likely thought we were going to toss him into an abyss.

"The bottom is flush with the floor here," he said, tapping his foot against the base of the circular structure.

"Thank you, Homnibus. It is as I thought," said Volencia. "Hold the lamp so we can inspect the well."

They all leaned in to examine the inner wall of the pool. The flickering light revealed a series of carvings of feral beasts with oversized claws and fangs feasting on dismembered and disemboweled bodies. Some creatures ran on four legs, others had wings, and some had multiple heads or beaks instead of noses. Depictions of people wailing in agony interspersed the otherworldly creatures. The dancing light of the flickering candle lamp and the tremor in the abbot's hands combined to make the carvings seem to shift and weave.

The images left a look of utter bewilderment on the rector's face. "Such terrible things . . . who would ever make this?"

"Thank you, Homnibus," Volencia said, smiling in satisfaction. "You've brought us to an ancient blood pool. Tell me, do you know how the blood pool functions?"

Homnibus swallowed, obviously afraid to disappoint the couple. "No, my, my lady. I'm sorry."

"Well, allow us to show you," she hissed.

The abrogator turned to face the double doors and clapped her hands. Black ribbons of nadir erupted from her palms, and the very atmosphere of the room was siphoned into the dark currents. The doors slammed shut, and the candle lantern flickered out, leaving the room pitch-black. In the darkness, she slashed across the room with a tentacle of nadir until she found the rector cowering near the blood pool. She coiled the nadir around his midsection, forcing the air from his lungs.

Mallic invoked a small focus of nadir, then said, "Shethes." A faint green aura appeared above the blood pool. Homnibus also floated above the pool, suspended by Volencia's tentacle of nadir. His face purpled and contorted in pain.

Mallic extended his hands beyond his robes. The nadir marks undulated under the surface of his flesh like thin rivulets of oil, then snaked forward, and more jet-black cords entwined themselves around the rector's torso.

Slowly and with deliberate care, Volencia turned her hands in a corkscrew. Mallic deftly wrung his in the opposite direction. The black tendrils of nadir responded by wrenching the old man and tearing him in half at the abdomen. They suspended the husks of his corpse above the blood pool and milked his fluids into the basin. After depleting his corpse of all fluids, the abrogators discarded the halves of Homnibus and approached.

Standing on opposite sides of the pool, they prepared to summon their master from the Drift. Volencia felt a thrill in her chest. After years of planning, they now stood poised to take the first steps toward releasing him. She squashed the excitement and anticipation she felt. Their channeling required perfect execution.

"Wait," she said. "There must be complete commitment. If one of us falters even a moment, we will fail, and something darker than Tarkannen will emerge through the portal."

Instead of responding with a snide remark, Mallic only offered the firm directive, "Steel your nerve, then."

In unison, Mallic and Volencia held their arms forward, palms down, and allowed small currents of their oily power to seep forth. The thin streams merged over the pool and began to swirl. Gradually, they channeled more and more nadir into the summoning. The streams slowly twisted into a black vortex, gathering speed and breadth. They labored to balance the tendrils of nadir with flawless precision.

Together, they directed the onyx cyclone into the blood pool. The dark liquid, all that remained of the rector's life force, swirled in a helix for several seconds. A miasma of shadow and smoke roiled across the surface of the pool, then shifted into a silver, mercurial, oily liquid.

"Now!" Volencia signaled, and they stopped funneling nadir into the pool.

The mercurial pool swelled to the rim of the well and became still. Occasional slicks of color and wisps of blackness twisted in eddies on the surface. Several moments passed, and at last, the surface rippled. A voice that sounded like granite sliding on granite grated forth from the pool. "Name the contender!"

"Tarkannen Lellendule," they said in unison.

"The contender is named," the voice growled.

The pool remained still, but occasional ribbons of color and wisps of complete blackness eddied against the silver surface. "Now we wait to see if he can prevail," said Mallic as he sat on one of the stone benches.

Volencia did smirk this time. *We shall not have to wait long. Master will prevail. I am sure of it.*

She sat opposite her peer. Long moments passed, and then the surface of the pool began churning with violent currents of color and shadow. Small torrents of smoke and vapor skittered across the surface, filling the chamber with a stench reminiscent of decaying flesh.

A humanoid head and then torso pushed its way to the surface of the pool. The creature thrashed about in a struggle to push through the mercurial substance, but after several seconds, seemed resigned to its captivity and became still.

Its form became more distinct, revealing the features of a naked, large, and well-muscled man, like a statue dipped in hot silvery wax. Ripples of oily, otherworldly liquid swirled across the figure.

Volencia considered erecting a barrier, but then the apparition turned and opened its eyes to gaze upon them. A familiar malevolent orange and yellow glow outlined the man's eyes.

"Stay your might, my dear. I cannot leave the pool; not yet, anyway. I may only use the portal to communicate from this place," the shade of Tarkannen explained.

"Master, I am pleased to hear your voice all the same," answered Volencia with sincere deference.

"Tell me, how much time has elapsed since my banishment?" asked Tarkannen.

"Roughly twelve years, my lord," answered Mallic.

Tarkannen contemplated the answer. "Just more than a decade. I thought the strength of the banishment might last longer. But it is no matter. What news have you for me of the world?"

"The sounding occurred two weeks ago this night, my lord. We sought you through this portal, believing that perhaps your bindings were loosed," said Mallic.

"Have you any idea which child carries the mark? I know they have not claimed the full measure of their power, but what can you tell me?" asked the apparition.

Neither Volencia nor Mallic cared to present their master with news of failure, so they both remained silent. "You hesitate, so I assume then you have not discerned these things. Your lack of success is disappointing," said Tarkannen.

"My lord," Mallic implored, "I assure you, we have exhausted all measures in the search for those brats and their cursed uncle, but until two weeks ago, they remained shielded to our detection attempts."

"And what of the banishment? Have you been at least able to discern anything more from the library at Callinora?" Tarkannen pressed.

"Master," Volencia said in a pleading voice, "nearly all of the Lellendules were jailed or driven off after your banishment. The regent in Aarindorn is a Baellentrell sympathizer. We have had to resort to less accurate means to discern how we might ensure your rebirth."

"I assumed as much," murmured the shade. Something unseen drew Tarkannen's attention down into the oily pool. He frowned, and his eyes flared a deeper yellow and orange as he gazed back through the portal. "I have little time remaining here, but I can sense that the banishment weakens. When it unravels, we will seek that which eluded me previously."

"How can we assist you further?" Mallic asked.

"Seek to destroy the Baellentrell heirs. They yet live, and in their demise is our sovereignty, I am certain of it. For now, this is all the power I can pull through this gate."

He plunged a fist through the mercurial veil, and a muscled forearm densely covered with black sigils emerged. He tossed three black, walnut-sized spheres to the ground, then withdrew his arm back beyond the veil.

Volencia bent to scoop up the objects. They oscillated in random movements, and to her surprise, each sphere weighed a few pounds. She looked to the shade in question.

Tarkannen answered her look. "Shadow chasers. They run the shadows and can find prey from miles away. Monitor the sounding. It will ring once another layer of the binding deteriorates. When that happens, release the chasers into the night. They have the sense of the shackles that hold me here. That should be enough to leash them to any Baellentrell channeling zenith."

The surface of the blood pool rocked with a powerful wave, causing the shade to scowl. "Go, and do not fail me, or I shall make your welcome to this place most memorable. We shall meet again!"

Without waiting for a reply, Tarkannen splashed, formless, back into the blood pool. Flares of lightning skittered across the oily surface, and the head of a reptilian creature erupted from the portal. A thick neck gave rise to a broad head ringed with several sets of beady black eyes. Its dark scales glistened in the lamplight as the beast flicked a tongue out as if tasting the air. It made a frantic effort to grasp the sides of the blood pool with curved claws. The walls of the pool fractured under the stress.

Before either Mallic or Volencia reacted, onyx tentacles jetted forth from beyond the portal and strangled the beast. The creature opened its mouth, but no sound came forth as Tarkannen towed it back to the depths. Once it submerged, the surface became placid. The mercurial color faded to a thick paste of congealed blood, which leaked out across the floor.

Chapter Thirteen: The Giver's Peace

Karragin's stomach growled. Her mount turned and flapped its lips with a short puff. She smiled and dismissed her link to the Aarindin; she'd meant to check if the horses needed a rest but, in her fatigue, forgot that sometimes the communication traveled both ways.

She and Nolan led the mounts abandoned by the traitors, Velda and Berling. Having extra horses allowed them to press hard on the return to Stone's Grasp, and the Aarindin's stamina had fared better than her hunger.

The aromas of cookfires from a small village outside of Stone's Grasp triggered a long gurgle from her stomach. In their hasty return home, they'd exhausted their trail rations. A routine return trip allowed time for hunting, but they'd sacrificed foraging for speed.

"Ugh," Nolan groaned. "I can't stop thinking about that patch of wild berries we found two days back. Now it's stew, bread . . ." He inhaled at the same aromas that teased her appetite. "Oh man, bacon? I seriously smell bacon! That's just mean. Bacon is breakfast food! Who cooks bacon in the evening?"

He leaned forward, grasping at his empty belly with exaggerated drama. That he suffered more than she did help to ease her discomfort. She felt her lip turn in a slight smile. On the first day of their return journey, they'd ridden mostly in agreeable silence. Nolan's near-death experience had made her question her decision to bring him into her quad, and on the ride, she had wrestled with a number of "what if's." *What if he did die? What if it was my fault? What would Father do?*

Yet, as they rode, Nolan's carefree nature had diminished her anxiety. Even when it was just the two of them, he deferred to her judgment and the command structure, and his ability to find mirth in the mundane became infectious. Something about the way he looked at the world eroded her hard edges.

Oh my brother, you alone give me cause to smile some days.

"If we press on, we can fill our bellies tonight and still have time for a full report to Father," she said.

"I don't suppose the Aarindin need a break?" he asked hopefully.

"No, but I did check. Let's ride. Once inside the gates, it will take us nearly an hour this time of day to pass through the lower commons," she said.

Nolan puffed out his lips in resignation. "Yes, but once inside the curtain wall, we have to climb all four lower tiers to reach Father. That will take another hour at least!"

"How's the leg then?" she asked, trying to change the subject.

Nolan rubbed at the wound along his outer thigh. "It's better every day, but we've been riding for the better part of a week. I haven't had to test it out much," he said.

"Tell you what," she said. "Once we make the curtain wall, the master of the green will be none too happy to see four Aarindin trodding across his garden. You settle the Aarindin in the royal stables then fetch a bite to eat. I'll make straightaway to Father."

"Really? Karra, that's generous, but no," Nolan replied. "I'm not a tender anymore, so I suppose I shouldn't act like it."

Good choice, brother.

"Suit yourself." She clicked her tongue, and the Aarindin picked up their pace. The main road skirted around Lake Ullend, and the sun hung low on the horizon, reflecting off the calm waters as an orange beacon. She shielded her eyes and gazed up at the capital city.

A massive wall ringed the city, which rose in tiers from the lower districts to the castle itself. Blue pennons flapped in the wind on top of pinnacled towers scattered along the city walls and farther up around the curtain wall of the castle. The highest levels of Stone's Grasp appeared to protrude directly out of the Great Crown Mountains. She squinted and thought she could just make out the speck of one of the windows to her father's study. *We still have a long blade to oil.*

The roads, cast from nothing more than compacted soil and loose rock, made for a dusty end to their long ride. Eventually, loose-fit pavers outlined by stubbly grasses marked their approach home around the lake. Within shouting distance of the outer gates, they had to slow to a walk. An unusual number of people were meandering in and out of the gates on business. Vendors pulled empty wagons home, and others still sought entrance to the city at the late hour. Merchants walked alongside carts partially filled with geese or chickens. Others herded lambs, goats, and oxen back and forth. All of them added to the congestion.

They stood bottlenecked in the crowd for several minutes. Karragin stood in her saddle to see if the gate to the east appeared less congested, but an even longer line of people stood there. She sucked on the scar of her upper lip in frustration.

A voice yelled out, "Make way, make way for the Outriders!" A guard at the gate waved them on.

Nolan turned in curiosity. "That's us, brother. Let's go." She directed her Aarindin forward.

The crowd moved to the side, allowing them to pass. Thick, white stone walls housed a gate wide enough to accommodate wagons and tall enough to ride on horseback. As Karragin rode through, she shivered a little at the abrupt temperature change in the shade. She nodded her appreciation to the guard, a middle-aged man dressed in a tailored blue tunic over a chainmail shirt. Judging by the deep tan of his hands and face, his post must always be on the southern gate. His dark skin accentuated his lively blue eyes, which were so common among the gifted.

"Your quad appears a little thin, Prime. Did you find trouble, or did trouble find you?" the guard asked.

"Nothing we couldn't manage," she responded coolly.

"At least you got your tender back. Congratulations, lad! The Redd Riders could surely use you," the guard said with a casual smile.

"Thanks!" Nolan flushed awkwardly.

Karragin studied the guard. His recognition of their position could be innocent. Nolan did wear the green uniform of a tender, but the man seemed to know a few too many details. He seemed too familiar. After an awkward pause, the guard bowed his head with a sigh.

"I did it again, didn't I?" he said sheepishly. Karragin knew if she remained quiescent, most people would fill the space with conversation and information. In moments, the guard proved her correct.

"My apologies. Name's Griggs," the man explained. "I sift people. I can remember. It's my talent and why they keep me at the gates. I remember your quad riding out weeks ago with the Redd Riders. But don't think anything of it. I can recall nearly anyone passing through in the last month."

Karragin nodded her understanding and did feel a bit more relaxed, though she resisted the urge to introduce herself. She didn't want the man to know any more about her identity than he already did.

"I don't recall so many people milling about the gates before. What gives rise to all this activity?" she asked.

"The Regent Lefledge decided to allow trade into the Borderlands. He's opening up the old roads through the Pillars of Eldrek. Some of these folks are excited about the opportunity to work. Others are looking to be a part of something new. Some talk about striking it rich with a caravan, and I hear tell of Stellancian merchants looking to broker all sorts of deals." Griggs spat over the side of the wall into a stream and waved an ox-pulled wagon past the gatehouse. "Others just fear what an open border will bring."

She considered his words with mixed emotions. Being a member of the Outriders afforded her freedom and escape, but the world had seemingly changed much in such a short time. Moreover, it had changed without her. The thought preoccupied her as they began the winding ascent through the commons.

At first, the aromas of tavern fair permeated the air: ale, bread, stews, and too many savory meats roasting on spits. The next several blocks of the district housed an open market. Vendors tried to hawk the last of their inventory of vegetables, fruit, fish, and a few thinning spits of roasted meat, probably goat. Others sold flowers, textiles, or leather goods. She marched her Aarindin around the perimeter of the market to the next block, which housed a variety of formal storefronts.

A blacksmith stood outside on the small boardwalk before his shop. He used water from a rain barrel to wash away soot from his face and forearms. His neighbor, an artisan of leather goods, made small talk while cleaning his hand tools. Nolan waved and received nods in return as they passed.

The next store offered tobacco, and still another storefront tea and baking spices. She had to admit that something about the rich smell of leather and tobacco was comforting, even if she found the habit of smoking off-putting.

They passed by a large cistern surrounded by grassy hills with fragrant wildflowers. Several locals, mostly women and children, relaxed on the green space that marked the end of the markets. In the late-day sun, several people splashed knee-high in the waters.

They continued along the road and left the park behind. A few more blocks in, the fetid odors of a residential quarter assailed her senses. *How did I forget that in such a short time?*

She wrinkled her nose and spurred her Aarindin to trot past the worst parts of the lower commons. The road climbed along the outer wall and eventually rose high enough to allow a faint breeze to pass. She inhaled, savoring the lingering hint of mountain pine, and continued.

The city used no formal wells and relied on a clever aqueduct system. A canal fed from mountain springs and glacier melt supplied water to different conduits. These, in turn, utilized gravity and spread downward throughout the city before continuing to Lake Ullend. One of the channels ran along the inside of the outer wall. She reached out a hand and scooped up several mouthfuls. The glacier-fed waters numbed her fingers but invigorated her mood.

The path wound up through wooded hills to a larger square cistern surrounded by shade trees and ivy-covered pergolas. More locals relaxed in the shade and cooled off in the glacier-fed waters.

They turned down a broad street and passed several residential quarters, where the houses were stacked two or three stories tall. Crafted from milled timber, she felt like the structures hunkered over the streets at unnatural angles. The tightly packed housing cast dark shadows despite the ample evening light.

They passed a group of boys in dirt-stained clothing harrying a leather ball. The game came to an abrupt halt as they ogled Karragin and the remnants of her quad.

Eventually, the pair turned onto a wider street. The central avenue ascended the last distance to the formal outer curtain wall of the castle. The road, crafted of tightly fitted pavers, provided a seamless approach. A central green space with a cistern divided the road.

Only the wealthy occupied dwellings in this district. Ornate gates identified individual properties and revealed one- or two-story homes crafted from the stone of the Great Crown. Occasional streaks of pale blue light pulsed along the silver and gold veining as the moon of Baellen peeked above the horizon.

At last, they reached the gatehouse to the curtain wall. Karragin retrieved their saddlebags and left the Aarindin with a servant tasked to take the mounts to the royal stables. They stepped inside the gatehouse to register with the guard there.

"I see an Outrider in a tender's uniform!" The resonant, vaguely familiar voice filled the small guardhouse. Karragin squinted as her eyes adjusted to the interior.

They approached the counter, and Nolan expressed the surprise she felt when they saw who had spoken. "Master Benyon? What are you doing pulling guard duty?"

Benyon Garr stood more stout than the average man and managed to fill up a room more than most. Furrowed lines creased his forehead, and a frizzy tan beard fanned out from a gap-toothed smile. Sharp eyes twinkled from under saggy lids. His brown beard had paled to a faded yellow at the edges, and Karragin realized she had not crossed paths with her mentor in a long time.

Benyon tongued the gap between his teeth, considering Nolan's question. "Well, they were shorthanded, and an old man's got to find things to keep busy."

"Yes, but surely you're overqualified. I mean, there must be others?" Nolan asked, puzzled.

"Now, don't you worry about how I spend my time, lad. When there are more gifted that need training, I'll be available easy enough. Until then, name and date, please." He smiled and turned a ledger around to face her.

While she penned her name, he whistled, and two servants arrived from a back room. The servants, two boys, gathered the saddlebags with instructions to deposit them in Karragin's rooms. Karragin retrieved the burlap sack holding the grondle horn and slung it over her shoulder.

"Should I send a runner to notify your father then?" asked their old mentor.

"No. We will attend him directly, but thank you," she replied.

He nodded with the same toothy grin. "You be sure to let me know if you care to spar sometime. I haven't had a good muddle in an age."

His words provoked a rare smile from Karragin. She recalled all too easily the lethal skill Benyon employed in his sparring. *Your idea of a muddle makes an angry street fight seem like innocent child's play.*

"You are about the only person in Stone's Grasp I might decline. I learned my lesson more than once in your training hall," she said.

They shared one last smile before she opened the door to exit onto the expansive green. While the perimeter of the space appeared manicured to perfection, different footpaths led around and through the wooded hills.

As evening approached, small lanterns along the inner curtain wall began to glow with a blue nimbus. They also marked the different footpaths that disappeared into the forested park. Karragin knew little about the crafting of the arcane lanterns, though she understood that gifted artisans had managed to harness zenith in tight clusters and that the lanterns illuminated only at night. The crafters had exhausted the materials to create the invaluable lamps before the turning of the moons. To her knowledge, none existed outside of Stone's Grasp.

They crossed the green to a ramp that served as a wide rampart around the lowest level of Stone's Grasp. Over the next half hour, they walked up the different tiers. The higher they climbed, the more Nolan limped, but he continued without a grumble. His pace slowed each time they crossed a smaller green. Finally, they reached the top levels, where the castle cantilevered out from the mountainside.

They walked through familiar restricted corridors to their father's private library. He sat in a chair overlooking the city while sifting through a few papers. As they approached, he stood with more than a little surprise.

"Well, don't just stand there, give an old man a hug!" he said.

After embracing them, he took a step back to inspect his children. "You were not due back for another week or so." He tilted his head and angled his eyebrows, giving him the familiar look of a cat on the prowl for the truth. "What happened?"

"You can stop trying to read us, Father. We're not kids anymore," said Karragin. "Let's sit. Nolan and I have a lot to explain."

Therek looked first at Karragin, then Nolan. He must have sensed something in their weary and travel-stained appearance. "A moment then. Here, sit down." He pulled three chairs together around a small corner table in the library. He stepped out into the hallway and returned with a pitcher and a set of mugs. Nolan drained one mug and poured another.

"That's . . . really good!" Nolan smacked his tongue then gulped another mug. Karragin sipped on hers but had to agree that the drink was more refreshing than the plain water.

"It's got muddled crown berries and some local herb, lemongrass, I think. Cook brought me a sample a few days ago," Therek explained. "But if you think it's that good, you must have pressed hard to get here. The question is, why? Why does my son walk with a limp, and why have you both returned so early?"

Karragin had mentally rehearsed the report she intended to give her father several times on the way home. Without her realizing it, she'd used the mental task to fortify her inner defenses. She'd organized the events by day and location and had assessed significant findings beyond just the betrayal of her quad and the presence of the grondle. However, now that she sat before her father in the security of their home, she felt a crack in those defenses.

She had little awareness that the barrier existed. It served to wall off that dark place she'd created after her mother died. It was the deep recess that stored all of her anger, loss, and fear. By keeping the worst of those demons secluded, she didn't have to manage them. But when she thought about how close she had come to losing Nolan, her brother with the sloppy ginger hair and that grin that ran from ear to floppy ear, something in her resolve fractured. She struggled to organize anything meaningful.

So instead, she blurted out the only thing that came to mind. "Why didn't you warn us about Berling, about Velda? Nolan, he almost died, but you could have warned us."

Therek sat back in his chair as if slapped to sobriety. He looked at Nolan, who stared without words into the bottom of his empty mug. "Oh, Karra. I'm so sorry. I thought . . ."

He paused and withdrew into his thoughts a long moment. "When I was young, shared struggles fostered strong friendships. I thought if they spent time in the field with you both, that a friendship would develop. I hoped that any comradery the four of you built could spark similar feelings in Dulesque or Beclure."

"Reddevek said as much," she replied.

"Where is the warden now?" Therek asked.

"He rode south; after I mean. First, he intervened with the grondle, and then everything happened all at once." The words spilled from her like water threatening to burst a dam. "My premonition flared with zenith, then Velda shot Berling with an arrow meant for Nolan, and—"

Her father placed a warm hand over her own, stopping her mid-sentence. "Don't be alarmed, my dear. I can see the stress upon you. I'm going to use a small bit of my gift to give you focus, alright?"

She nodded once. Part of her wanted to break down, to unleash her pent-up emotions, but a more substantial piece of her didn't want to feel them. She knew one of her father's talents enabled another to maintain focus. She welcomed the chance to slip away from her inner turmoil.

From the edge of her vision, she saw the delicate runes along his forearm pulse with iridescent, blue light. Just like that, the crack in her wall sealed up. A sense of organized calm settled across her mind, and she presented the report she'd rehearsed earlier.

She described their findings in the Borderlands, including the different plants and herbs Nolan discovered as they ranged. Her summary culminated with a matter-of-fact description of Berling's betrayal, then death, how her gift of premonition saved her, and eventually, Velda's death at the hands of Reddevek.

She recruited Nolan to describe his findings in tracking the crush of grondle. While he filled in some of the details, she produced the horn, though she knew her father required no such proof to discern the truth in their report. He reached out, appearing intrigued by the trophy.

Therek listened without interruption until they finished, and his eyes appeared glossy. He inhaled a deep breath, and for a moment, revealed the burden of his regency. Then he exhaled, and all vigor returned.

"Well, I, for one, am glad that you had each other," he said. "I can't think that any of the other riders would have prevailed under such circumstances. I will need to meet with Chancle and a few others to discuss how to proceed. You need to debrief with Warden Elbiona tomorrow. However, I have a request of you both."

He tilted his head forward and filtered his gaze through his wispy eyebrows. "Aarindorn balances on the edge of a cliff. Our future winds a precarious path. The high houses of Aarindorn bicker about my regency. Some even desire that we abandon the regency and seek a more permanent solution."

He reviewed some of the details of Chancle's counsel regarding a departure from the monarchy. "I have reason to believe Aarindorn will only prosper under the return of a Baellentrell to the throne. We have to hold the kingdom together until that day. However, your news could tear apart the frayed rope that holds us together. So, in that light, I need you to keep Velda and Berling's betrayal a secret."

Karragin felt heat rise from her neck to her cheeks, and a prickly feeling burst from her chest and cascaded across her shoulders. A strange desire to immerse herself in zenith, engage her strength, and smash something filled her mind. After a moment, she mastered her anger. Her inner storm cooled further when Nolan placed a hand on her shoulder.

"Karra, Father is right," he said. "Velda and Berling came from strong houses in their duchies, Endule duchies. I believe Father. So, for now, at least, we can do this. For the good of Aarindorn."

She thought about the consequences as her father had laid them out. "What about Warden Elbiona? Shouldn't she at least be made aware? Perhaps she could manage to prevent similar risky groupings."

"I don't think that's a good idea just yet," Therek answered. "Holding a secret is like storing too much wine in a skin. Telling one person amounts to poking a tiny hole. You can usually keep a finger over that one hole. But when two or three holes develop, the integrity of the skin is compromised. We three are enough for now, and if we commit to absolute secrecy and seal it up in our mind, then we are far less likely to divulge the secret until its proper time."

Her father always presented solid arguments, but she wondered how many wineskins he now held his fingers to after all his years as the regent. She eventually nodded her agreement.

"Their families will want an explanation. What should we tell them?" she asked.

Therek watched his daughter long moments, then finally patted a hand on the grondle horn. "Tell them that they died trying to save villagers from the crush of grondle. That news will temper their grief."

They agreed on the details of the cover story before excusing themselves to the kitchen. On their way through the restricted corridors, she ruminated on the fact that people might remember the traitors as martyrs, or worse, heroes. The injustice of it all left her feeling tense.

She watched Nolan slide down a short banister, hollering, "Whoop!" He landed with a clumsy stagger favoring his sore leg but turned to grin back at her with a look of expectation. His mirth dissipated the last of her venom, and she gave in. With a dexterous hop, she landed rump-to-rail and slid down the banister, following his lead.

Before he turned down another hallway, she grabbed him by the shoulder. "Wait," she said. "I don't get it. Why was it so easy for you?"

Nolan lifted his eyebrows. "Why was what so easy?"

"Berling and Velda. I was ready to insist that they and their families be held accountable to the truth. You were the one on the cusp of death, and yet you agreed with Father so readily," she explained.

He looked back up the steps in thought. "Do you ever think about how different our lives would be if he weren't the regent? I don't remember the last time he laughed or the last time we shared a simple meal without him being preoccupied with some important decision for the kingdom." He drew his gaze back to her. "It wasn't easy, Karra. I did it for Father as much as anything else. If holding this secret lightens his burden, if I make it more likely that he can stop being the regent and just be Father again, then I'll gladly do it."

She swallowed at a thick feeling in her throat and sniffed back the stinging beginning of a tear. "Agreed. Now, let's see what leftovers we can pilfer."

His expression beamed at the suggestion, and he turned to continue toward the kitchen. *When did you get so smart, brother, and how did I not see it? The Giver grant me the same noble peace if I ever see a highborn from Beclure.*

Chapter Fourteen: A Warden on the Move

Reddevek wrinkled his nose as the reek of stale fish and offal mixed with the throng of people assailed his senses. Though he felt relief at stepping off the ship and onto solid ground, the stink of Callish, the port city, left him on edge.

He paid the boatswain a few coins for passage and waited for a deckhand to deliver Zippy from the hold. When the Aarindin emerged at the top of the gangplank, Reddevek sensed the horse disdained their new surroundings as much as he did. Zippy's eyes bulged white, and he pulled back at the lead rope attached to his halter. The deckhand raised a switch to strike the horse's flank.

"Don't hit my horse," Reddevek growled. He quickstepped up the gangplank to wrestle the switch away from the deckhand, then took charge of the lead rope. "I'll take it from here."

"Suit yourself, but getting them onto dry land can be a trick," said the man.

Reddevek glared at the deckhand and resisted the urge to use the switch on the man. Instead, he tossed the switch overboard, then gave Zippy a three-day-old apple. He spoke in soft tones at the Aarindin's ear. "We're not in Aarindorn anymore, Zip. Karragin gave me the idea that you're smarter than most of your kind. I don't know if you can understand me, but we need to get off this ship and onto dry land. The sooner we take that first step, the sooner we can leave the stink of this place behind. So, what do you say?"

The warden stroked the horse's neck and jaw. Zippy turned a dark orb to him for a moment, then swished his tail and nudged against Reddevek's shoulder. Without further coaxing, the Aarindin stepped onto the broad plank. Despite the odd bounce of the timber ramp, they made a steady descent.

Reddevek led Zippy along a wide boardwalk, following carts of freight. A ramp ascended from the boardwalk to a wide road that ran alongside a district comprised mainly of warehouses. The cobblestone street branched in three directions. He needed to travel south and west.

The southernmost road disappeared into a rather seedy-looking neighborhood. Taverns and brothels lined the first block of the street. Zippy whinnied low and guttural, a sound of unease.

"I don't intend to waste any of my time or coin there, Zip. I'm just not sure which way is the fastest way," he said.

Reddevek spied a boy loitering under the awning of a portside tavern. He looked no older than eleven or twelve, and Reddevek waved the youth over. "Boy, you know the city?" The boy strode forward with a casual swagger unusual for one so young. He wore threadbare clothing, and the pants, too short by far, revealed dirt-stained ankles. His sunken cheeks indicated a malnourished state, and drab strands of honey-colored hair sprouted from under a grey cap.

"Maybe. What's it to you?" he asked.

"You look like you could use a meal, a bath, and some new clothes. I don't care how you spend the coin, but I can pay you one copper for showing me the most direct way out of town."

The boy looked at Zippy. "I never seen a horse so fine as yours, and you have a funny way of talking. You're not from Callish, are you?"

Reddevek cocked his head to the side and turned his peculiar gaze on the youth. He let it linger there, knowing it tended to unsettle people. "Would I be asking for directions if I was?" he said more than asked.

"I suppose not," the boy replied, then looked to his feet. "I can get you to the south gates, but it's slow going with a horse. Lots of turns that way, and the warrens is tight quarters. A bit longer around will take you to the west gates. That's the road you want if you plan on keeping - is it a him or her?"

"Him. Zippy's a him," Reddevek answered.

At the horse's name, the youth arched his eyebrows. "His name's Zippy? What kind of name is that for a horse?"

"I don't know. You would have to ask the man who named him," said Reddevek. "So, do we have a deal?"

"Three coppers and I get to ride the horse along the way," said the boy.

The warden grunted in amusement. *This one's got some stones.* "Two. Half now and half later. You can ride, but I hold the reins."

The boy stepped forward then seemed to consider his words. "Foden's teeth, mister, what do you think I would do with a horse?"

"Who is Foden?" Reddevek asked.

"You really are a long ways from home. Foden, god of the seas, everyone knows that." He held out a dirt-smudged hand. "Alright, two. Half now?"

Reddevek placed a copper piece in his hand. "Want a hand up?"

"Sure," the boy said, revealing a toothy grin.

Reddevek reached down and lifted the lad onto Zippy's back. He weighed even less than Reddevek imagined. *I've seen more meat on a butcher's apron.*

The boy settled in between the travel bags that straddled the mount. His brown eyes looked around with curiosity. "Where's your saddle, mister?" he asked.

"We don't use saddles much where I come from," he answered. "Which way?"

The boy pointed down the street to the west. "If we go this way for a bit, then we can turn south down Porter's Alley and make straightaway to the west gate."

Reddevek led them to the west, following the boy's directions. "So what do I call you?" the warden asked.

There was a long pause. Reddevek glanced back, wondering if the lad had heard the question. The youth cocked his head at an angle before answering, "Ranika, or Nika if you like. That's what my friends call me."

Reddevek didn't miss a step and returned his gaze forward. "Why didn't you tell me you were a girl?"

"Because most people who would proposition a girl are either really creepy or really weird. I get more honest business if folks think I'm a boy," she said.

"No offense, but you don't look like you've had much business at all," said Reddevek. "What sort of work can you even get here?"

"You're not the first stranger to need directions. Then there's all sorts of work for a courier or a porter. If I take you to a whorehouse, I get a small cut. I could take you to a nice whorehouse. Not like the cheap ones portside. There's fancy ones where the ladies smell like, well, ladies. And I know the best places to eat or grab a drink. There's always someone comin' or goin' who needs that kind of information. Like you!"

Curiosity tickled at the back of Reddevek's mind. What would happen to this girl once she stopped looking like a boy and more like a woman? He pushed the thought out of his mind and focused on his mission.

Nika interrupted his thoughts. "What do they call you?" she asked.

"That depends on who they are," he replied.

She sighed. "Fine then, what do I call you?" she asked.

"Red, you can just call me Red." He didn't offer up more conversation. He'd already revealed more than he thought might be wise in a strange city.

They walked in a westerly direction, turning sometimes south and eventually onto a broad, paved street that stretched west over a bridge. They crossed a small river leading to the sea and eventually left the worst of the portside smells behind. The road wound through whole neighborhoods, some residential, others a mixture of artisans and shops. About an hour later, the western gates came into view.

"Alright, I can take it from here, Nika. Let's get you down." He held his hands up.

"We aren't at the gates yet, are you sure?" she asked.

"I can see the steady traffic of wagons back and forth through the gate. You've done enough." He helped her down. She reached up and patted the horse on the neck. "Thanks, Zippy."

He gave her the other copper piece. He considered giving her a generous tip. *The Giver knows she could use a hand up, but I don't want her remembering me any more than she already does.*

He gave her a polite nod and turned to the gate. Some small part of his awareness cast a disparaging judgment, and the coins in his purse felt heavy. With a sigh of self-recrimination, he retrieved two more copper pieces and turned.

"Nika," he said. The girl looked back over her shoulder. A glint of surprise brightened her eyes. She caught the two coppers as he flipped them through the air, smiled her thanks, and disappeared into the crowd without a word.

Reddevek turned back toward the city gate and rested a hand on his hip, where something felt strange. He looked down to discover an empty leather sheath, which used to house a long hunting knife. A ruby-colored gemstone rested in the hilt of the blade, but he thought grime and debris had obscured its appearance enough to make the weapon appear utilitarian.

He searched the crowd for any sign of the waif but knew she would have disappeared into the warrens of the city. *And I don't have time to go down that rabbit hole. She's got a good eye and a light touch; I'll give her that. The sooner we're away from all these people, the better.*

He double-checked the security of his other valuables. Once satisfied, he led Zippy behind a steady flow of wagons out a well-traveled road to the west. The sun began to set over the edge of a massive mountain range on the horizon. Zippy nickered as if in answer to his thoughts.

"That's where we are heading, Zip, but we'll skirt to the south. We don't have much to go on, but we might get lucky."

Within an hour of sunset, he wandered away from the random traffic of the road. They passed several small caravans pulled into tight circles to camp for the night, but he never considered approaching one. He didn't like the idea of gambling on the goodwill of strangers and knew he would travel faster alone. They moved a good distance from any other travelers before finding a secluded copse of trees by which to settle in for the night.

The next morning, he opened a small leatherbound journal. All the pages sat blank except for one with a drawing of a compass rose. Therek had said the symbol might assist his search for the heirs. He turned the page to inspect the wildflower from Therek's vision, where it lay pressed flat between the pages. Now desiccated, the pitcher-shaped flower's deep purple hues had muted to a dark black, but the sweet fragrance lingered on the pages. He studied the way the recurved leaves alternated about the stalk.

Years ago, as a tender, he had often employed his gift to search out herbs, but so much time had passed since then that the particular skill had withered from disuse. *How did I filter the patterns back then?*

He thought long moments about how to utilize his skill. Over the years, he'd honed his gift to follow the alterations in zenith left by living creatures. Channeling zenith with that specific intent had become second nature. *That's not going to work on a stationary plant.*

Wasting his stamina by channeling zenith so far from home seemed pointless, but he needed to start practicing how to filter his gift. He held the wildflower with reverence, then took a knee. He slowed his breathing and found his focus, allowing the ambient sounds and smells of the roadside to slide away from his awareness. He fixed the wildflower in his mind, then summoned zenith. The current suffused across the rune upon his chest and tingled with a vibration that pulsed out into the rest of his body.

Once he felt intimately aware of his connection to the ground, he opened his eyes. The silhouettes of birds, a martin, and a family of rabbits manifested in his awareness. Their faint blue outlines appeared to him even through the dense foliage and underbrush. He labored to alter his filter.

Finally, he forced his gift to assess the wildflower. Tendrils of zenith ran through the stem and up through the flower petals. The dried plant began to vibrate under his scrutiny and crumbled to dust, but not before he committed the pattern of its make to memory. Every living thing carried with it a resonance and a design. Even in its desiccated state, the wildflower was able to reveal the secrets of its unique identity to him.

He cast the pattern of the wildflower out across the hillside and compared it to the hundreds of plants and shrubs in the vicinity. He didn't expect to find a match here but felt confident that he would be able to reproduce the surveillance going forward.

He felt the ground shift and tilt. A trickle of sweat ran across his temple. He released his command of zenith and realized for the first time the labor of his breathing. He chided himself for not being more mindful of the toll of channeling for so long and in such isolation.

He remained in the kneeled position for a few long moments, allowing his strength to return. He clicked his tongue, and Zippy approached. The Aarindin lowered its belly to the ground beside him.

"Sorry, Zip, that took more out of me than I planned." Reddevek stood, hoisted a leg over the horse's back, then clicked his tongue again. Zippy rose easily. They sauntered back to the road and continued southwest. Reddevek brushed his hands together, removing the last of the dried wildflower debris from his fingers.

Over the next week, he made steady progress along the southern face of the Korjinth Mountains. The grasslands and sagebrush outside the coast blended to foothills and enormous tracks of evergreen forest. Usually, he enjoyed this kind of isolation, but in the last two days, he had found himself attentive to an unsettled feeling. Try as he might, he couldn't dismiss the feeling that someone was following him. As he rounded a dense cluster of trees along a game trail, the feeling washed over him once again, stronger than ever before.

The calls of birds and chirps of pine martens and squirrels always quieted in his vicinity. After he passed, they returned to their normal social activity, but recently it felt like their chatter remained stifled longer than usual. He rubbed at the hairs standing up on the back of his neck and decided to backtrack with Zippy.

They trotted back up the game trail and climbed a ridge to a small cave along the southern mountain slope. From the vantage point, he surveyed the valley to the east and west. He picketed Zippy behind a stand of pine trees and crouched in the shadows of boulders and deadfall.

Once or twice an hour, he tapped into zenith to cast a net of his awareness across the valley. For several hours, he inspected the silhouettes of animals common enough in the forest. As the afternoon wore on, he became frustrated.

What are you doing? Everything here is just as it should be. The only thing that doesn't belong is you. And here you sit, lost to the regent's folly.

Reddevek growled to dismiss his suspicion and doubt. He walked out of the cave and mounted Zippy, then continued. He leaned forward to address the Aarindin. "We've been out here alone too long, Zip. So let's see if we can do something about that."

He clicked three times, and Zippy trotted back down the game trail to the west. Reddevek tried to leave his feelings of unease behind, but they followed him deeper into the wilds of the Southlands.

Chapter Fifteen: Into the Bend

Bryndor awoke with a smile on his face and rubbed his feet back and forth against familiar soft sheets. His pillow released a faint smell of lavender, one of Rona's many unique, thoughtful touches. His old wool-stuffed mattress formed to the shape of his back, reminding him that he was finally home. He stretched and wandered out of his bedroom just in time to see Kaellor ride out on one of the geldings.

"You're up early, Bryn. Fancy some tea or something to eat?" Rona stood in the kitchen and poured hot water into a teacup.

He rubbed at his eyes. "Tea, please, the stout stuff. I need something to pick me up." He grabbed a small bit of cheese and a hunk of bread. "Where is Kae off to?"

"He's gone to deposit that small fortune you boys brought back from Hammond. He wanted to open accounts for you both at the king's bank in Riverton, then hoped to be back by supper," she said.

He walked out to the front porch sipping at his tea. Rona's farm cat weaved in between his legs, then busied itself pouncing on a cricket. Rona joined him for a time, and they sat in companionable stillness, watching the goats nibble at the edges of the yard.

"What are you figuring to do with your first day back?" she asked.

Bryndor sipped at his tea and thought. The last few months had allowed for some adventure, but mostly the work gave structure to his days. The routine of setting and breaking camp, crafting their maps, and caring for the horses had occupied most of his time.

"I suppose I should set the horses to graze. Beyond that, I hadn't thought too much about it."

"Don't bother with the horses. Kae already beat you to it before he left."

He nodded, feeling at peace. He rather enjoyed not having to busy his mind with plans and details just yet. "I think I might work on redrafting some of our maps. I'm better at that sort of thing if it's fresh. I still don't know how Lluthean manages it from memory."

He made his way to their workspace. A long desk partitioned into three areas ran the entire length of the wall. Thin plates of hammered tin mounted on the wall reflected the sunlight and allowed for proper illumination in the daytime.

He pulled back his chair and situated his tools and utensils, then retrieved a random map from its tube and pinned it to a corkboard to use as a template. It was their rendering of Hammond and the surrounding country. He started a new sketch, recreating the outline of the western coast. This first part always took the longest. He divided the new map into square grids and carefully transposed each small section.

A few hours later, he leaned back and relaxed his achy shoulder muscles. He began again and placed the symbols for Malvress and Hammond, then worked on the King's Road. His hand stopped when he crossed the low-lying portion where they had met Lesand. He paused and thought over that day. Though only a few weeks had passed, the events felt like they had occurred ages ago.

He set down his writing tools and stared at the original template, feeling restless for the first time that morning. He remembered the confrontation with the bandits, the way the bow had vibrated in his left hand, and the ease with which he'd loosed one arrow and then two. His memory of the sound of the shaft striking, like a pitchfork stabbing into wet hay, gave him goosebumps. He thought about the way Kaellor had dispatched the others with almost casual grace. *I've been so wrapped up in my own thoughts I never really asked him more about how he managed that.*

Lluthean pulled his chair out and sat down next to him. "At it already?" he asked.

Bryndor shrugged and fingered his writing tools. "I was just trying to keep myself busy until you crawled out of bed, sleepyhead."

Lluthean wolfed down a bit of bread, dusted the crumbs from his hands, then upended a cup with a few writing tools. While Bryndor labored with original-size copies, Lluthean would reproduce miniature versions of the maps onto costly vellum sheets edged with tin snips. These miniature duplicates could sell for more than the bulky, full-size maps to the travelers at the Riverton markets.

In preparation, Lluthean removed the other original templates and pieced them together on the corkboard. He sat back, inspecting the entirety of the Southlands. After long moments, he hunched over his smaller map, then began to work as well.

They continued in silence for another hour until Lluthean leaned back with a sigh of what sounded like disgust. "Well, brother, you got farther than I did," he said.

Bryndor looked over to inspect Lluthean's work area. Where Bryndor kept things tidy and orderly, Lluthean's workspace looked as if someone left the front door open and a summer wind had stirred the materials haphazardly. Sitting on top of the disarray rested a large piece of high-quality vellum. The page remained blank except for a single *N* marked at the top of the paper.

"I don't think I can sit here much longer, and Kae won't be home until suppertime," said Bryndor. "The market could be fun. Want to run into town for a bit?"

Lluthean grinned, appearing relieved that Bryndor needed a distraction as much as he did.

"Let's check with Aunt Ro and see if she needs anything," said Bryndor.

They found Rona on the front porch rocking casually. "You lasted longer than I thought you would," she said. "How about you hitch the wagon up, and we ride into the Bend for the afternoon market? I need a few things, and we can see if anyone remembers the troublemakers from the north side of town."

A few minutes later, they bounced along a well-worn riverside path that angled off to the west. They left the banks of the Shelwyn, meandering over hills, then finally crossed a small bridge over a stream into town. Journey's Bend sat several miles north of Riverton. Under the direction of Margrave Rolsh, Riverton thrived on commerce and trade, while a smaller population of artisans, craftsmen, and farmers who enjoyed the challenge of carving out a living in a more rustic setting composed the community of Journey's Bend.

Once they arrived, Bryndor tied up their wagon, and the small group began walking toward the town square. There seemed to be an unusually busy gathering of people. The population of Journey's Bend numbered less than five hundred, and it appeared that every last person was mingling through the market square.

They walked across a small green at the edge of the central bazaar. Rector Tomlek sat among a group of children reviewing the day's lessons. The thin man wore unassuming plain brown robes and handed out small bits of dried fruit to hold the children's attention. His message carried across the green.

"So tell me now, who is the sun-father?" asked the rector.

"Drexn," the children responded.

"And who are the sisters that lull Drexn to sleep at night?"

"Vaeda and Voshna!" the children chimed back.

"Which sister dominates the night skies?"

"Voshna, the blue," they said.

"Very good!" The rector looked up with a polite smile as Bryndor passed. "And who is the god of the wind and seas?"

"Foden!" echoed the chorus of children.

"And the mother of nature and all new life?" asked the rector.

"Maedra!" shouted the children.

"And who is her opposite?"

An odd pause in the almost chant-like quality of the lesson occurred. Eventually, a few brave children evoked the dark god's name, "Mogdure." For the first time, their answers lacked the coordinated choral response.

"Yes, and you are wise to be fearful of the god of decay," said the rector. "Now, we are almost done. Who is the trickster?"

"Lutney!" they cried with giggles and a return to the exuberant answers.

"And finally, who is the All-Mother, the one who sacrificed everything to birth the gods?" asked the rector.

"Malldra!" Bryndor could still hear the children's response as the trio entered the busy commotion of people milling about the bazaar. While he was more than familiar with the teachings, he felt a mild tension in his shoulder relax as they left the rector behind. After the previous discussions with his uncle, something about the way the rector carried on with conviction felt disingenuous to him.

Nobody knows the gods or what happens when you die, but rectors always speak as if they know with absolute certainty. Something about that felt wrong to him. He let the feeling go and drew his attention to the central square of Journey's Bend.

Several single-story storefronts comprised the square. A boardwalk ran along the timber buildings, but most of the activity occurred in the bazaar. Rows and rows of vendors hawked their goods in stalls under rudimentary wooden lean-tos. The aromas of cooked bread, smoked meats, and savory stews drew his attention.

They passed by a few small stands where traders sold fruits and vegetables. Rona led them, winding and turning, through the bazaar. She meandered past the first few rows of vendors, eventually stopping at a small stand where two women sold an assortment of baked goods. Sadeen Tunkle and her mother, Ellicent, ran the stall. The two looked past Rona to her escorts.

Ellicent smiled with no sense of recognition, but Sadeen locked eyes with Lluthean, and her cheeks flushed. She led Lluthean in age a year, and the two had shared more than a few conversations in the past, but due to the mantle, the girl never remembered him the next day.

Sadeen had blossomed, both in her figure and her bravery, in the last year. She brushed a long, sandy brown lock of hair from her face and smiled, inviting the boys to approach.

"Good afternoon, Rona," greeted Ellicent. "I see you keep new company."

Rona turned to introduce them both. "This is my nephew—"

Sadeen interrupted her mid-sentence. "That's Lluthean and Bryndor, Mother. The Scrivson brothers, Rona's nephews. Don't you remember? They were last here around the Harvestmoon, I think."

Bryndor felt unprepared. A warm, prickly heat crawled up his neck and into his cheeks. He arched an eyebrow and looked sidelong to Lluthean, who merely smiled back at the two women behind the stand. Rona seemed caught off guard and unsure how to proceed.

Lluthean stepped forward without hesitation. "So nice to see you both again. We only just returned with our uncle. The Bend appears to have prospered in our absence."

Ellicent frowned for a long moment considering his words. Eventually, a small flicker of recognition played across her face. "Yes, I vaguely recall—the Scrivson brothers. Yes, I think I do remember. Where have you been all spring?" she asked as the brothers eyed their products.

"Our uncle contracted us on a job in the south, and we got back yesterday," Lluthean said politely.

Bryndor observed his brother's artful exchange, then eyed a large crowd gathering at the outskirts of the bazaar.

"More of that mapmaking?" Sadeen asked. "The roads between here and Riverton aren't big enough for the two of you?"

"It's plenty big enough, but we have to go where the work is, and sometimes that means south," said Lluthean.

He fingered a heavy loaf of bread, then handed it to Bryndor. It felt dense. They both inhaled the rich aromas of sage and fennel and something else.

"Mead? You wasted good mead in this bread?" Lluthean blurted with surprise and curiosity.

Sadeen snatched the loaf from him with a playful smirk on her face. "It's not waste if it adds flavor, but yes, it's made with mead."

She replaced the dense bread on the counter. "Beer-sausage bread. But it might be a bit pricey, and you shouldn't finger the goods unless, that is, you aim to make a purchase?" She leaned in, propping herself forward over the counter.

Does she know we can see her cleavage? She must know.

He made eye contact with Rona, who, in turn, just watched the interaction. She seemed to be studying the conversation more than participating in it.

Lluthean politely kept his gaze locked on the young woman's brown eyes instead of her low-cut blouse. He also leaned forward, appearing to take her wager. "How much?" he asked.

"Two copper nugs," Sadeen replied with a challenge as if to call his bluff.

Lluthean reached into his pocket and retrieved a silver mark, which more than doubled the price. Typically they would not spend so much on ordinary food, but the windfall from Hammond did afford a small indulgence. Bryndor had a feeling his brother had anticipated this interaction the entire way home. *You do love to make an impression, brother.*

Sadeen reached forward, taking the silver mark uncertainly and regarding the brothers with surprise and renewed appreciation. They were, after all, unusual among the local people. In the Southlands, most people had brown eyes and a darker complexion. Kaellor and his nephews also stood taller than most in Journey's Bend, and all three had the unusual slate grey eyes of a Northlander. Though they were polite enough, most of the people of the Bend had never considered them anything more than an oddity.

This morning's interactions already stood to make more of an impression than Bryndor would have liked. He thought Rona might feel the same by the slightly pale color in her cheeks and her restrained, aloof manner. Sadeen wrapped the bread in cheesecloth and reached into a pocket of her apron to provide Lluthean with change.

Lluthean held up a hand. "If it tastes as good as it smells, then I'll wager it's fair payment for goods provided."

Sadeen smiled and nodded her appreciation, but her mother interrupted their dialogue. "Tunkles don't fancy beholding to anyone. Come back in a few days, and we'll have two more. Then we are square."

"You are too kind." Lluthean nodded.

Bryndor recognized the abrupt change in Ellicent's tone; it reflected the same stubborn pride that all the people of the Bend displayed. It also brought an awkward end to the conversation.

Rona stepped forward, appearing to regain her composure. "Ellicent, what draws so many people to the Bend today? I don't think I've ever seen so many at once outside of Harvestmoon celebrations."

"Rona, you need to come to market more often," said Ellicent.

Bryndor's gaze lingered on a group of mostly men gathering before Constable Whirik's small jail. "I wondered the same thing. What brings everyone out in such numbers?"

"You boys have been away a while," Ellicent replied. "The men gather to discuss possible patrols to combat all of the attacks these past few weeks."

"What attacks? From who?" Bryndor asked.

"Not who, but what," Sadeen answered.

Her expression revealed suspicion. She leaned forward again as if to reveal a valuable secret. "Some say it's the wrath of Mogdure. Some say it's a return of the untamed. Others say some great predator stalks out of the Moorlok. Whatever it is, nearly every other night for the last few weeks, some farmer has reported missing livestock. Three nights back, Lemm Sogle went missing, but he's always been fond of the drink. I think it's the untamed, myself."

Bryndor looked to Rona, and they shared an uneasy moment of silence. She began to step away, motioning for them to do the same.

"Good day to you, Ellicent," she muttered.

Lluthean raised the loaf of bread. "Thanks for the information and the goods. A fine day to you, Sadeen, Mrs. Tunkle."

He followed Bryndor and Rona, and they walked back through the bazaar until they found an empty lean-to. The color returned to Rona's face, but Bryndor could tell by the way she glanced around that she felt unnerved.

"What is it, Aunt Ro?" Bryndor asked.

She inhaled a deep breath and forced a smile onto her face. "I wasn't prepared for anyone to actually remember you. I was hoping we would have more time, is all. I suppose it's nothing we can't all get used to, though."

She looked out across the bazaar for a long moment. "I have a few more things on my list and need to check in with Emile Tellend. She's selling tea and cheese for me. Nobody's paying any special attention to you both, so I suppose it's safe for you to wander about a bit. Be sure to use your real names. Sadeen is not likely to be the only one who can remember you. It won't do trying to change that now."

"Meet back at the wagon in an hour then?" asked Bryndor.

Rona nodded. "Lluthean, dear, do try not to make any more memorable impressions if you can." She waited for his acknowledgment, then turned and walked out of the lean-to. In moments, she melted into the crowd.

"Shall we see what all the fuss is about?" asked Bryndor.

"I think that will keep me in Ro's good graces," Lluthean replied.

The brothers walked over to the crowd of men gathered before the constable's offices. Standing at the back of the group stood Markum Tellend and his son Harland. The old farmer turned and gave Bryndor a firm bear hug. The squat, burly man was well-tanned from hours of work outdoors, and a generous smile erupted on his sun-lined face.

"Bryndor, my boy, I wondered if we might see you fellas today. Welcome back! Where's your uncle? That rascal owes me some stories," said Markum.

"Thanks, Markum, Harland," Bryndor greeted their only genuine friends in Journey's Bend.

Harland was an only child and a few years older than Bryndor. The three of them had grown up together and spent a good portion of their childhood on the Tellend farm. "It's good to be home. Kae had business in Riverton but should be back tonight."

"Well, you two are just in time. Have you caught up on any of the local news? Whirik's supposed to announce a reward he's secured for anyone who can bring an end to the attacks these last weeks," Markum explained.

"What do you know about these attacks exactly?" Bryndor pressed. "Sadeen Tunkle mentioned something about missing livestock. But she also believes the untamed are responsible."

"Watch yourself around her. That girl has too much sass between her ears," said Harland.

"She sounds like exactly the kind of girl I need to get to know better," said Lluthean with a grin. "Besides, anyone who can make this can't be all bad." He unrolled the loaf of bread for Harland's inspection.

Markum chuckled. "The untamed, huh? Some nursemaid's stories never completely die. I don't imagine anything as strange as men raised by wolves. Of course, I never put much stock in those stories anyway."

The old farmer scratched at the stubble on his cheek. "About three weeks ago, farmers started discovering the corpses of mangled livestock. Most of the culling occurred among the farmsteads north of town, the ones that push up against the Moorlok Wood. I don't think any of us got too concerned in the first week. A man's got to expect some trouble from wild animals now and then. But as the weeks went by, seemed like a bloodied carcass turned up every few days. Goats, a pig or two, more sheep than we're sure of, and most recently a cow."

"Has your farm been affected?" Bryndor asked.

"No, but we're on the south side of town," Markum explained.

Harland stifled a yawn, and Bryndor noticed dark circles under his eyes. "Are you well, Harland? You look ragged."

Harland stretched beefy arms overhead and scratched his hairy belly. He took after his father, and few men in the crowd were as broad-shouldered as the pair. "I've been taking turns watching over the livestock at night. Last night was my watch."

"So, what do you imagine has caused all the trouble?" Lluthean asked.

"My guess is some predator, or maybe a pack that found easier prey than in the Moorlok," Markum offered. "But the whole thing has folks scared to venture out at night."

Constable Lawn Whirik stepped forward onto the boardwalk of the town stockade to address the group. The grey-bearded official wore a red doublet tucked neatly under a navy topcoat. He carried an air of authority, though Bryndor couldn't recall a time when anyone had ever tested the limits of his dedication to the office. Given the man's lean frame, he imagined Whirik would have a difficult time apprehending anyone truly given to violence and considered it a blessing he'd never had to take such action. Whirik raised his hands to gain their attention, and the crowd quieted.

"Alright, men, thanks for coming on short notice. As you are all aware, we suspect some beast has been emerging from the depths of the Moorlok Wood, usually at night." Whirik cleared his throat and continued, "Last week, Lemm Sogle went missing. He's skilled in woodcraft, so we didn't think much of it at first, but two days ago, we found his body."

At the constable's revelation, the crowd quieted. "What happened to him, Lawn?" a man from the crowd interrupted.

"We aren't rightly sure," Lawn answered. "It's no secret that Sogle favored the drink. We found what's left of him in the Moorlok northeast of town, but animals had already scavenged his body. We can't tell what injuries happened before or after his death." The constable paused, allowing for any other questions. Most in the crowd just murmured at the news.

"Margrave Rolsh in Riverton has empowered me to place a bounty. I'm prepared to offer five gold crowns to anyone who can provide irrefutable proof that they brought about an end to whoever or whatever plagues the farmsteads."

At the mention of such a generous reward, men gathered in small clusters. Bryndor watched as they peeled away. Some seemed to take an interest in the reward. Others shook their heads in resignation, wanting no part in the danger. Most began drafting plans for small patrols and even discussed camping in the Moorlok.

Bryndor wondered at first why the whole town didn't just band together to share the burden of patrolling the farmsteads. However, when he thought more about the independent nature of the folks of the Bend, he wasn't surprised. Most of the families here had chosen to live in a place where they provided for themselves and didn't expect someone else to solve their problems. Whirik likely understood more than most the difficulties in forcing them to do anything.

The men clustered into several family groups. Standing nearby, Bruug, Rusn, and Heff Hawklin surrounded their father. The Hawklin boys were of a similar age to Bryndor. The long-hooked nose they'd inherited from their father, Gruus, made them easy to recognize. The family lived on a farmstead on the northwest side of town. Gruus turned to regard Markum and Harland. He made eye contact with Bryndor and Lluthean but only grunted as if to say, "Hello."

"Markum, you or Harland want to join us?" Gruus asked out of the side of his mouth. Bryndor always thought the man seemed like he was trying to conceal his speech, except he knew all the Hawklins always spoke in such a peculiar manner. "We figure a group of five, we could split the reward even. What do you say?"

Markum placed a hand on Bryndor's shoulder in reply. "Harland and I have our hands full watching over our farm, Gruus, but you'll not find any more capable than these lads."

Gruus considered the recommendation but extended no further offer. Instead, he shrugged. "If you change your mind, we plan to set out on patrol from my place at sunset." He turned and pushed one of his sons without waiting for further suggestions.

Markum sighed. "I'm sorry, boys. I should have known better than to expect the likes of a Hawklin to welcome you along. They're a closed and superstitious lot. And your, eh, unique way of escaping the recollection of most likely doesn't help much."

Bryndor leaned in close. "About that, it seems that folks actually can remember us now."

"You don't say," replied Markum with eyebrows raised. "When did that happen exactly?"

"Several weeks ago, we think," said Bryndor. "Kae's not sure why or what it all means, but a few people today already remembered us, sort of."

"So will you be using your real names?" asked the old farmer.

Bryndor shaded the sun from his eyes with a hand and considered the question. "Let's refer to our uncle as Kevold if you don't mind, but it's already a bit late for Llu and me to take new names."

"Alright, Kevold it is. We're in strange times, we are," said Markum. As the crowd dispersed, he picked up a large sack at his feet and hoisted it over his shoulder, preparing for the walk home. "Bring Kevold by soon for a visit. Emile would love to see you all."

"We will." Bryndor waved.

Bryndor and Lluthean turned to make their way through the thinning crowd. As they rounded a vacant lean-to, Bruug Hawklin and his two brothers wandered past. Bruug sidestepped into Lluthean, shouldering him. Ever light on his feet, Lluthean quickstepped back, but he fumbled with the loaf of bread, bobbing it back and forth in his hands. Just as he regained control of the parcel, Bruug flapped a hand, causing Lluthean to drop the loaf to the ground.

Lluthean bent down and dusted off the bread, then looked up at Bruug in confusion. The young man stood taller than Lluthean and leaned over him with a dark expression.

"Sorry, friend. You're new here, so I'll let this slide this time. But you need to watch where you're going," said Bruug.

Lluthean stood up but just stepped back without saying more. Heat flared up the back of Bryndor's neck, and before he had time to consider his actions, he stepped forward, meeting Bruug nose to nose. "You did that on purpose, Hawklin, so you must have something to say. Unless you need one of your brothers to speak for you, I suggest you say it."

Bruug clenched his fists and stared back a few moments. His brothers, Rusn and Heff, positioned themselves around Bryndor. The hook-nosed bully had just inhaled to respond when Rona's voice cut in. "Bryndor, Lluthean, I need your help to pack up the goods from today's market."

The Hawklin brothers all turned to look at Rona, who carried on without regard to the brewing confrontation. "A fine afternoon to you, Bruug Hawklin. Do tell your dear mother I said hello and that I'll have her herbal tea delivered tomorrow. It's the one to ease her back pain," said Rona.

Bruug seemed deflated by her words but still muttered low, so only Bryndor could hear, "That bounty's ours. We don't need no outsiders mucking things up." He stepped away with an insincere smile. "You fellas have a fine afternoon." He inclined his head. "Miss Rona."

The Hawklin brothers departed, and Rona led them back to their wagon. Once there, she turned. "How exactly was that keeping a low profile?"

Bryndor's legs felt like jelly as the tension of the confrontation dissipated. He replayed the encounter in his mind, frustrated that things had escalated so quickly. "It's my fault, Aunt Ro. Bruug seemed like he was itching for a fight with Llu, and before I knew it I—"

"It's not your fault, Bryn. It's mine," said Lluthean. He looked up with an odd twinkle in his grey eyes. "He doesn't likely remember, but I've taken more coin from Bruug in cards than anyone else in the Bend. The thing is, I've seen him threaten other fellas when he lost at cards, and he's predictable. If the winner leaves amicably with their take, he never follows through. But I saw a few other men stand up to Bruug's challenge. They each ended up facing all three Hawklins at once, and none of them got the better end of that."

"That's why you didn't say anything." Bryndor sighed. "I should have followed your lead."

Rona nodded with a knowing expression. "I can't say I'm surprised you took a Hawklin in cards, but just how many times are we talking about?"

Lluthean began to respond, but Rona cut him off. "Never mind! On second thought, I don't really want to know. Whether he remembers those losses or not, he's also fond of the Tunkle girl. I don't imagine that seeing you walk around with that expensive loaf of bread she baked made him feel very friendly."

"How did you learn all of that so fast?" Lluthean asked.

She smiled and arched an eyebrow. "Don't you let my plain clothes fool you, Llutheandellen. A person can learn a lot at the bazaar if she only listens. Come on then, let's get home before any more trouble finds you."

They returned home, allowing Scout a leisurely walk in the late afternoon sun. Bryndor remained unusually quiet, his mind preoccupied. He had dismissed the constable's proposal until Bruug made his threats. Now, thoughts of an expedition into the Moorlok consumed his attention.

He and Lluthean had developed significant hunting and woodcraft skills on their journeys with Kaellor. From what he assessed of the men gathered before the constable, he and his brother might have the best chance of finding a predator. *And if we succeed, people will know about it, and they will remember.*

That thought alone dissipated any doubt about whether they should take up the adventure. Once they arrived home, he led Scout to the small barn. He worked to remove the tracings, then he and Lluthean curried and brushed down the horse in silence. The whole time, he considered different scenarios and made a mental list of some of the equipment they might need.

Lluthean stabled the other gelding for the evening, then interrupted his concentration. "Are you alright, Bryn? You've been quiet the whole way home."

"Just thinking, that's all," he answered.

"Thanks for stepping in with Bruug the way you did," said Lluthean.

Bryndor smiled but felt sheepish. "You had that entire situation well in hand. I was only going to make it worse. I don't know what came over me, but when I saw him treat you that way, I just saw red."

"I know. I started to get that same feeling right before Ro showed up," said Lluthean. "I think we could have taken them, but I didn't want to risk damaging the goods."

He winked, then tore off a generous hunk of the beer-sausage bread and handed over the rest. They sat on hay bales sharing the savory loaf as the sun crept toward the horizon. Bryndor groaned with genuine pleasure upon tasting the rich interplay of mead-sweetened bread coupled with fennel and salty sausage.

"You chose wisely," said Bryndor with a mouthful.

"You mean Sadeen or the bread?" asked Lluthean.

"Both, I think. If she can cook like this, she's worth every ounce of trouble," he said.

"I know, right?" Lluthean exclaimed. "Now, if I could just get Aunt Ro to see it."

"Good luck with that." Bryndor giggled as he wolfed down another mouthful.

"So I guess it's not really if we go, but when," said Lluthean. "I know you too well, brother, and I'll wager Bruug pulled the wrong string. Tell me you haven't already thought of at least two separate plans of action to earn the constable's reward."

Bryndor smiled. Lluthean did indeed know him too well. He was not even weighing the risks or benefits anymore. He'd made his decision the moment Bruug Hawklin challenged him to stay out of it.

"It's not the reward," he said. "It's just that . . . before our concealment lifted, I felt like we were missing out. I didn't know how either of us was ever going to make a life for ourselves. And the truth is, I don't know if I can see myself copying maps the rest of my life. Most men my age have moved out, married, or started their own life by now. You know what I mean?"

Lluthean chuckled. "Don't tell me you've forgotten the stale bread for breakfast, sleeping on hard ground, or the incessant company of biters?"

Bryndor recalled the swarms of biting insects along the southwest coast and how many times he'd awoken with welts in unsavory places after answering the call of nature at night.

"No, I didn't forget. I don't think I can ever forget the biters. But on the road, it didn't matter that nobody knew us, because we were strangers. However, we've come home, and we're still strangers, outsiders. This hunt could be the thing that lets us make a name for ourselves."

Lluthean nodded in agreement. "I go where you go."

"You're in?" Bryndor asked, knowing full well the answer.

Lluthean nodded. "Of course! Now tell me about your first plan."

He finger-combed at the strands of hair above his ears. "Well, the way I see it, we need to visit some of the places where the attacks occurred to get a sense of what happened exactly."

Bryndor continued to work through the details of his proposal. Lluthean listened, and together they contrived a plan to sneak out in the early mornings or late afternoons. They finalized their plan just as Kaellor rode into the barn.

"Just in time, Kae," said Bryndor with a welcoming smile.

Kaellor dismounted and retrieved his saddlebag. "It's been a long day, boys. Curry him and see to his grain. I'll make it up to you next time."

"No trouble, Kae," said Lluthean. He began to uncinch the straps and looked up. Kaellor stood still, frowning at him. "What is it?"

"Nothing," said Kaellor with a puzzled expression. "I just expected more complaining, I think."

Lluthean shrugged. "You had a longer day than we did, and besides, you have to try this!" He handed over the loaf of bread.

Kaellor lifted the loaf up and down, assessing its weight, then drew in a deep breath. "I believe I will." He tore off a mouthful of the bread and chewed for a few moments before lifting his eyebrows in appreciation.

"If this is a bribe in compensation for some mischief you two got into today, consider the debt paid," said Kaellor. "I'll see you inside." They watched him retire to the house and made fast work of brushing the gelding.

"Alright, now quick, tell me about plan number two," said Lluthean.

Chapter Sixteen: Laryn in the High Places

Laryn sat on the front step to her hut in the late afternoon sun, weaving a thin bracelet from fibers stained purple and orange. She intended to give the trinket to Ellisina. As her fingers entwined the fibers in the intricate pattern, her mind wandered back over the day's events. The memories gave her a sense of peace but also unrest.

She wondered how that might change once she reached her finding day. When she had first arrived in the Valley of the Cloud Walkers, she expected to discover the next step in her journey immediately. Several months later, she began to learn the patience of the Damadibo as she labored to learn their spoken language. Fortunately, a significant part of communication between the Cloud Walkers relied less on speech and more on gestures and facial expressions. On more than one occasion, laughter interrupted otherwise silent interactions.

Her earnest desire to befriend the children led to her next lesson in patience. It took several mothers a good portion of the first year to trust leaving their children in her care. Eventually, her persistence wore down their suspicion and resolve. The day she found herself leading the children on a nature walk without any other adults in her company, she realized they had all come to see her as one of the Damadibo.

Over the years, a patient disposition afforded her the chance to learn their knowledge of medicinal herbs. She became so skilled in their application that the Cloud Walkers now relied on her ability to locate and collect all manner of healing plants. They had anointed only her and a few others as herb gatherers, and she had embraced their trust and learned how to foray high into the mountain passes to find the rarest of medicinal herbs.

Mountain survival skills, herbology, and all of the cultural lore required to interact with the Damadibo meaningfully—she accumulated all of this knowledge over time. But none of it had upended her understanding of the world like their ability to channel nadir. In Laryn's world, only the abrogators tapped the dark force, but the elders and healers among the Cloud Walkers utilized nadir to accomplish tasks from the mundane to the miraculous.

She had once watched a group of elders perform a ritual that allowed them to cast a fine mesh of nadir across a field to first remove stones and then remove unwanted weeds. Then another group swept in behind them, utilizing zenith to stimulate and fortify the crop.

She did not think they tapped nadir very often, but their use of the substance always benefitted their people. Earlier in the week, a group of healers spent three full days in communion with the spirits. At the end of the third day, they emerged from the spirit house and somehow used nadir to dissolve and remove a large tumor from the abdomen of a middle-aged man. Laryn had borne witness to similar miracles by the healers at Callinora, but they employed zenith and coaxed the body to heal itself. This latter process took much longer and involved weeks or months of pain. The application of nadir had removed the man's tumor in only a few hours and seemed to cause him no pain at all.

She was wrestling with the contradiction between her experiences when Elder Miljin appeared from under the broad leaf of a kevash tree. With gestures as much as words, he pulled her from troubling thoughts.

"What troubles you, daughter?" he asked. *"The deep furrow of your brow tells me you think overly hard."*

She looked up, somewhat relieved at the timing of his question. She gestured back, *"I was thinking."* She paused, then sighed. "I was thinking about how the Damadibo can channel zenith and at other times, nadir. I wonder, how did this come to be?"

The elder smiled back at her. He folded his hands in his lap, a signal that he intended to engage her in her style of conversation. "You have raised this question before. While I have no explanation except to say that we are as we are, perhaps the question you should ask is, how did the people from your home lose the ability to channel both?"

She tilted her head in acknowledgment of the statement. "Outside this valley, the only people to channel nadir are the abrogators."

Elder Miljin nodded with a serious expression. "The ancestors revealed as much to me. From what I have learned, these abrogators crave power. They tap nadir to satisfy the darkest of motives. But among the Damadibo, nadir and zenith are each used for the benefit of all."

"Do you think our intentions shape the way nadir is used? Or does nadir blacken the heart of those who channel it?" she asked.

"None among us has ever channeled the amount of nadir you speak of, so who can say for sure?" he answered. "I have only tapped nadir twice in my life. I found it no more substantial than a wispy thread, like grabbing bubbles that rise through water. In contrast, the currents of zenith are easy to command. I did not sense good or evil in the act of channeling either force. But it is fair to say that I have not shaped much nadir in my life. Perhaps we should ask the ancestors your questions."

"If you do learn anything, I should like to hear it," she said.

Elder Miljin tilted his head, indicating he would be all too happy to share anything he gleaned from the spirits. "I sought you out this afternoon to tell you about the preparations we need to make for your finding day."

Laryn set the bracelet to the side. His announcement dissolved all her earlier thoughts, and she gazed at him wide-eyed. After a few moments of silence, she sighed, then smiled. "Elder, you know by now that I come from an impatient people."

Elder Miljin paused only a moment longer then nodded. "My apologies. Today is a poor time to teach the wisdom of patience, and that is a lesson you learned long ago, my child. The ancestors revealed to me this morning that we need to perform a ritual to breach the mountain barrier. Only through this process can you take the next steps on your journey."

She listened with full attention. "I understand. What must I do?"

"To answer that, you need to learn a lesson." He leaned back against the trunk of a leafy tree and scratched his back. "Do you know how old the mountain valley is?"

Laryn frowned at the unexpected question, then shrugged her shoulders, indicating her ignorance.

Elder Miljin signed, *"The teacher requires a place to sit."* He climbed up the tree and settled into a comfortable fork in the branches four feet up. His feet swung in lazy alternating circles as he continued, "These mountains erupted from the very sundering of the world. Those outside the valley mark the event over sixteen hundred years ago."

"You're talking about the story of Broga, the mountain god, and how he lost his heart to Maeleen," she said, "and when she broke his heart, his center, our valley was created."

"You and I are beyond this fable," he gestured, then waited for her to understand. *"We should speak as those who have more understanding, not as children."*

A sobering feeling dashed away all other thoughts. "Oh, you're talking about the Cataclysm," she said. "In my homeland, the events are poorly understood. No solid records date back to those times."

He nodded in understanding. "The rending of the world was the result of the Great War. My knowledge of those times is also limited, but through the spirits, I have learned some truths. There was a time when the currents of zenith and nadir existed in a balance. The people in those times became divided. There were those who devoted their study to nadir and others who sought enlightenment only through zenith.

"Over time, the two sides drew into conflict. Those who specialized in nadir began to grow in strength and eventually upset the balance. The Great War broke out. The final battle of that terrible time occurred somewhere here in our valley. In the end, those involved in the conflict were all destroyed when the armies who employed zenith raised mountains from deep underground, and the forces using nadir sunk the valley. Their struggle divided the entirety of Karsk in two."

Laryn turned her head to the side in a gesture of slight question and squinted with subtle disbelief. "You're saying that there were whole armies using nadir and zenith, and that the Great War led to the creation of our valley?"

"Not just armies, whole nations," Elder Miljin explained. "The number of people drawn into the conflict was more than all the blades of grass in the valley, more than the stars in the sky. And so, the release of power was equally catastrophic."

They sat long moments in silence. Laryn knew he expected her to glean something meaningful from this lesson. "I trust your words, Elder. But I admit, without your unique connection to the ancestors, I don't think I can appreciate the scale of what you are describing."

He nodded with a knowing smile. "The lesson is just beginning. The mountains are only a small part of the barrier around our valley. In the high places where the mists are thin, there is a different barrier. In those places, the currents of zenith and nadir still war as violent storms."

He placed his palms together and undulated his hands through the air. "Before the Great War, zenith and nadir flowed together." He separated his hands and then smashed them together, tangling his fingers. "Ever since then, the two currents run in opposition, and they create a barrier that can only be pierced in a ritual sponsored by the ancestors."

She considered his words for a few long moments. "When you brought me to the valley, did you use this ritual?"

He tilted his head in affirmation. "And now we get to the heart of the lesson for today. Your next steps forward must be outside the valley, but the only way to accomplish this is in a ritual sponsored by the spirits. They can open a way forward, but to do so requires samples of two rare items found only very close to the barrier. One is an ancient plant called Broga's beard. It grows among the rocks in the high places and feeds only on zenith. The other is more difficult. Roaming near the barrier is the black clouded leopard, a creature of nadir. The ritual requires a flower from the plant and a few hairs from the leopard."

Laryn reviewed the task the elder had described. She knew that expeditions to the peaks held significant risk and danger. Once, in a game of hide-in-the-clouds, she'd accidentally arrived much farther up the Korjinth than she intended. The thin air had made her feel light-headed and oddly euphoric with the simple struggle to breathe. Whenever she journeyed up the mountain to collect rare herbs, she always went prepared and usually had a guide.

"Why do I get the feeling that this flower only blooms in the summer?" she asked.

Elder Miljin once again tilted his head in affirmation. "And only under the full moon, which is this week."

"How young were you when you made the trip to collect the plant?" she asked.

He wagged a finger at her in appreciation. "I was only a little younger than you."

"This is why you made me an herb gatherer, isn't it? How long have you known that I would have to make this journey?"

"Until today, I had only my suspicions. I knew the steps I had to take to open a way for you to enter the valley. So it seemed only logical that you would need to accomplish the same task." While he smiled, his eyes appeared sad. *"I hoped that you would not have to. It's a dangerous journey,"* he signed.

She tilted her head in understanding, then gestured, *"You honor me, wise one. I am humbled. When should I leave?"*

The old man wrinkled his face in an uncharacteristic expression of chagrin. "The spirits say that today is the safest chance. In the high places, the weather can turn without warning, but these next two days, there is a chance to slide through the clouds. If you leave today, you would have perhaps two nights under the full moon in which to find what you seek."

Laryn set her mind to the task instead of fretting about the fact that she would embark with little preparation. She thought for a while, then gestured to the elder, *"I'm no hunter. Neither are you. How did you catch the leopard?"*

He pulled out a sprig of dreamsong. She knew the herb from home as bandle root. He held out the plant, expecting her to piece together the answer. She took the plant from his hand and fingered the thick, brown taproot.

"I'm supposed to feed it bandle root?" she spoke the question in confusion.

"Last week, I had a few of the boys catch three valley rats," he said.

Laryn knew the animals, though she thought the term "rat" was understated. In the valley, the rodents resembled small beavers and spent half their time in the streams. When they ventured too close to the village, they dug tunnels that damaged cultivated fields. On occasion, a family of them spoiled an otherwise pristine water source. She knew the village elders rewarded youths who trapped any of the animals who wandered too close. Once released into the southwestern portion of the valley, they seldom caused further trouble.

She stared at her feet, drawing a design in the dirt as she considered the pieces of the puzzle. After a few minutes, she looked up. "Will the valley rats eat bandle root? I wouldn't have thought that they'd consider that food."

Elder Miljin slapped his hands together once with obvious joy that she'd put the pieces together. "They will when they are hungry enough. And these haven't eaten anything for two days." He hopped down from his tree perch with a nimble grace that defied his age. "You haven't made an ascent into the high places alone before. We have a few things to prepare and review. Do you remember how to make nonlethal snares?"

She signed her response, masking her apprehension. *"Yes, I remember. So I am to make this trip alone?"*

"Yes, daughter, the spirits say it must be so, or you will fail." He tried to conceal his concern with a soft smile. *"Come, there is much to prepare."*

Within the hour, she met him in the gathering house with her travel pack. She had made similar journeys several times with other herb gatherers, so she kept most of the items she required for a safe trip readily available. She entered the gathering house to find Ellisina feeding the valley rats bandle root through wicker cages.

She placed the friendship bracelet on the girl's wrist. *"They look hungry, be sure to feed them a lot!"* Laryn signed.

Ellisina nodded back. *"Thank you, my Laryn! Grandfather is over there waiting."*

Laryn set her pack down and approached Elder Miljin. He welcomed her to sit and dine. In traditional fashion, they ate in relative silence. When she polished off the last of her portion of a meat pie stuffed with sausage, onion, and tubers, he moved to place more on her plate, but she waved him away, saying, "I'll never fold into the clouds if I eat another bite!"

Ellisina crawled onto her grandfather's lap to nibble at the scraps on his plate. He finger-combed her brown and black locks, then began an intricate braid. "I have a few words for you, Laryn. You travel alone, mainly because the clouded leopard is very shy. The spirits think that if more than one person wanders into their territory, they will hide." He lifted a small book from the bench and turned it for her inspection.

"Open to the page I marked. That is my drawing of Broga's beard," he explained.

She opened the page to inspect the image. Delicate lines recorded a strange plant with odd spikey leaves that curled back on themselves amidst a tangle of fleshy, tan roots. The tips of the leaves darkened from a pale green to a red hue. A small, feathery red flower blossomed at its center like a tuft of hair.

"They grow on rocks or suspended over deadfall. The ones you find should have a blue tint instead of the red."

Laryn arched an eyebrow, then gestured, *"Why?"*

"Because in my travels, the red moon lit the night sky. The plant feeds on zenith, and so it should taper into a shade of blue or purple." As he continued braiding Ellisina's hair, the girl pulled away playfully. His fingers lost purchase, allowing the tight braid to unravel. "Do you want me to braid your hair like your grandmother or not, little one?"

Ellisina looked back with a mischievous smirk then nodded once. "Well then, sit still, child."

Laryn giggled at them both as Elder Miljin nodded and began the task of gathering up the separate locks of hair again. "Wait, if the red moon was the . . . just how old are you?"

"Too old to go back up the mountain," he replied. "Now, you need to go soon. The bandle root will keep the rats asleep for only a night, but that should give you enough time to fold into the mists and set your snares. Make a base camp right at the point where you find the mists thinning. Then hike up a good part of the night. You'll want to set the snares in the highest places you can find. But don't delay. The currents of nadir and zenith collide to random effect so close to the barrier. Find a place, set the snares, then return. If you linger long enough to hear the death sighs, you place yourself in danger."

"What are the death sighs?" she asked.

"The sounds whispered across the mountains when currents of zenith and nadir destroy each other. If you hear this, be fast about your work," said the elder.

"What happens if I stay too long?" she asked.

"When I was young, an herb gatherer lingered while listening to the death sighs," he explained. "She returned and told us about the entrancing sounds, but even I could see she was altered. Within two days, she developed a strange withering sickness. Dark markings spread across her skin like the webbing of a spider. The elders in that time said that the currents of zenith and nadir had spread their conflict inside of her. She perished within the week."

She nodded in understanding, then stood. She looked about to sign something, but her mentor shook his head, then gestured, *Don't doubt yourself. The spirits chose you for this journey, and I believe in you.*

She took a few moments to pack up some food, then donned heavy winter gear, meticulously layering hides treated to repel water and retain warmth. Finally, she hoisted her travel pack and placed the three rats into one wicker cage. With her live bait stored, the cage weighed more than she'd expected. She tried carrying the burden in one arm but eventually lashed it around her pack straps, letting it hang before her chest. She wrinkled her nose at their musky odor. One more look over her shoulder saw Elder Miljin wink at her with a twinkle.

She left without a further word. A few minutes later, she walked into a dense cloudbank at the edge of the village. She focused on her destination and felt herself slide up and into the mists. The first slide placed her well above the village. She looked down at the few twinkling torches. From her vantage point, they looked like fireflies.

She walked around and sometimes up the mountainside for the next half hour, looking for another cluster of clouds dense enough to allow her to slide. When she found one, she surrendered to the mists and felt herself slide up again. The next cloud bank appeared after only a five-minute walk, but before she folded into the mists, she sensed the thinning air. Within ten steps, her breath became labored, and she paused; her head felt like it was swimming in the mists. She grounded herself by stamping her feet. Loose shale scattered underfoot. After another moment, she began progressing to the next stand of clouds.

She anticipated reaching the next cloudbank within five minutes, but in the thinning air, the short trek felt more like a long journey. For the last time, she slid into the clouds. They deposited her high on a ridge. She double-checked her mittens and pulled a cover over her face, but a peculiar tingling sensation still overtook her fingers. Her head felt even more strange, and her breathing came labored. Slowly, one plodding step at a time, she walked along the ridge.

In the distance, the barren rock of the summit crested. Directly above the summit, blue and red ribbons of fractionated zenith undulated in random swirls. The currents of zenith appeared to twist and bend around an inky black countercurrent of nadir. Where the forces directly collided, dazzling sparks showered into the night sky.

Fatigue threatened to overwhelm her, but she continued plodding along. Her shoulder muscles ached so much she couldn't hold her head up any longer and stared at her feet. A brilliant burst of light erupted overhead, and she heard a rasping sound. It reminded her of pulling a rake through coarse sand. The air smelled galvanic and sterile. In a few moments, the sensations dissipated, replaced by the labor of her breathing and the tingling sensation in her hands.

Laryn knew that if anyone spent too much time in the high places, their lungs could fill with water. She used to know why that strange thing happened but just now found it difficult to organize her thoughts.

Need to get off this ridge.

Feeling anxious about further delays, she dropped to her knees and pulled out her equipment. In moments, she had a small spike pounded into the rocky terrain. She removed a thick twine woven from the stringy fibers of a flowering vine. Many animals could gnaw through the noose in time, but a bitter resin permeated this particular vine. She hoped that it would delay her quarry long enough for the bandle root to take effect. After laying the snare, she sacrificed one of the sleeping valley rats, taking care to splash some of its blood on the ground.

Laryn looked at the corpse of the creature with regret but didn't allow herself to linger. She picked everything up and walked on, but exhaustion threatened to overwhelm her. *Just keep walking, one step at a time. Rest when you get to forty.*

She began counting her steps. At forty paces, she dropped to both knees and allowed herself to recover. She might have felt exhilarated at the strange rapidity of her breathing or her thrumming pulse rate, except she intuitively understood the danger of remaining too long in the thin air. Several minutes passed, and she regained control of her breathing. She staggered upright and continued the arduous task. She carried on in the darkness, wondering if she had the stamina to place the last two snares.

Chapter Seventeen: The Ride to Beclure

Nolan spooned up the last of a thick stew over lunch and listened to his sister deliver their story to Warden Elbiona. They sat together, separated from others in the dining hall. The warden listened with calm detachment.

"By the fifth day out, we had yet to encounter anyone or anything along the Borderlands. So we continued in free-range formation to cover more ground. I found Berling's body first, what was left of him," said Karragin. "I don't think he ever had a chance."

"It looked like he was harvesting darksun," Nolan added.

Karragin nodded her agreement. "A short time later, we discovered Velda's corpse closer to the ruins of the village. She emptied her quiver, but it wasn't until Warden Reddevek approached that we learned what happened to her." Karragin continued the cover story, describing how Reddevek had managed to dispatch a grondle wounded by Velda. She displayed the grondle horn and finished with Reddevek's request for Elbiona to manage his Outriders in his absence.

After Karragin finished her report, Elbiona sat quietly, sipping at her tea. The warden kept her black and grey hair cropped short, and after a few moments, she sat back and rubbed the palm of her hand over the stubbled undercut at the back of her neck.

Nolan did not have enough experience with the warden to know if her pause indicated doubt or belief. From what he knew, Elbiona had risen through the ranks because of her gift with the bow and her shrewd nature. She squinted as if considering Karragin's report. After a few awkward moments in which he began to feel uneasy, she relaxed into a smile. But the smile didn't really reach her eyes.

"I understand you managed to retrieve the mounts," said Elbiona.

"Yes, we alternated them on the return trip to make it back as swiftly as possible, Warden," said Karragin.

"Odd that the grondle left the Aarindin," the warden replied with an arched eyebrow. "From what I recall, they like horseflesh. Whenever we discovered a grondle camp, the bones of humans and their mounts always littered the site."

"I can't say that I understand why the grondle left them, but we found the bodies still warm. It's possible we arrived only a short time after their deaths," said Karragin.

Elbiona considered each of them, then leaned forward and whispered, "There is more to your story than you are divulging. Tell your father I don't need to know all the details, but that I don't like being managed. Now, do you have a plan regarding how to give the news to their families?"

Nolan watched his sister, amazed at her calm demeanor. At times like these, he envied her composure. *I would likely ramble on like a child caught with his hands in the cookie jar.*

Karragin kept a placid, composed expression on her face as she nodded. "Yes, there were some small personal effects in their saddlebags. We couldn't recover the remains of their bodies. Reddevek directed us to leave the area of the attack without delay. I thought perhaps an escort could deliver their things with the news. If it would help, Nolan and I could make the journey."

Elbiona sighed. "Well, I'm certainly not sending you both back to the Borderlands. Not yet, anyway. And we might have to consider splitting you two up."

Nolan blanched at the implication that somehow keeping Karragin and him in the same quad would cause trouble. Karragin, however, reasoned out her concern. "You think it's dangerous keeping the only two children of the regent in the same quad at a time when grondle have returned?"

Elbiona nodded, and Nolan felt the color return to his face. The warden continued, "That's a matter for another time, though. I think you both should be present to deliver the news to the families. Perhaps Chancle could suggest someone to accompany you to make the group feel more like a formal delegation. Let me speak to him." She thumped the table with the tip of one finger. "That's your next mission. Deliver this . . . version of the events, then return. By the time you get back, I should have all the Outriders mustered at the Pillars. Find me there, but under no circumstances are you two to venture back out to the Borderlands. Understand?"

"Yes, Warden!" they replied in unison.

"I like your father well enough, but I can't imagine what losing either of you would do to the man. The Giver knows he never asked to be regent."

The turn in the conversation surprised Nolan enough that he blurted, "Were you friends with Father before he accepted the position?"

"I was," said the warden with a distant expression. "Those were stressful times. I hope your discovery doesn't mean a return to anything like the Abrogator's War. In the years that followed, your father managed the kingdom with more grace than the Giver normally affords a single person. He kept Aarindorn from falling back into a civil war as the great houses banded together to hunt down any who were affiliated with the Usurper.

"In the first year, most of the Lellendules fled the kingdom, while the Endules retreated to the western duchies. The next year, the Outriders policed the kingdom. Your father somehow steered us back to a place where we could have reasonable conversations. Eventually, reparation talks were completed, and we all started to move forward again. But any of us who knew him from before the war could see the strain the position placed upon him, and I won't add to it. I figure your trip to Beclure and Dulesque should only take a week. I'll provide you with papers ordering your prompt return within that time, just in case any of the nobles in those duchies seek to detain you."

"Yes, sir," said Karragin.

"One last thing," said the warden. "I don't know what really happened in the Borderlands. I do know that I passed on Berling because he was a rich, lazy snob. Velda was not much better. And both of them came from high families with certain sentiments. You stay together and watch yourselves. If possible, let someone else do the talking. Go there, present their families with anything of value, and return. But always be on your guard. I can't have two of my best Outriders tangled up in political games."

"Yes, sir," they said in unison.

True to her word, Elbiona managed to convince Chancle of the strategic importance of a formal delegation to honor Velda and Berling. The next morning, he met them as they exited the dining hall.

"I have business in the western duchies and have need of a few able-bodied Outriders," said Chancle as he reached forward and ran his hands over the crisp, silver embroidery of Nolan's new uniform. He continued to straighten up Nolan's tunic with friendly familiarity. "Would you two happen to know of any available just now? It seems Elbiona has most of the Outriders engaged in preparations for a trip to the Borderlands."

Nolan smiled and shared a sidelong glance with Karragin. "We just happen to be available and also have business in Dulesque and Beclure," he said, grinning. "But I admit, I didn't think the warden had that much pull."

Chancle laid an arm around Nolan's shoulder, gave him a warm squeeze, then stepped back. "Well, I wasn't kidding when I said I do have business there. Your father has tasked me with a diplomatic mission of my own. I didn't plan on leaving for another week or so, but once I learned what Elbiona intended for you both . . . Well, I can't let my only two runelings face grieving families without moral support. I mean, what kind of runefather would I be?"

Runeling. Nolan giggled a bit at the term and leaned into Chancle as they walked. Used to formalize the relationship between a mentor and any youth yet to undergo the Rite of Revealing, the term signified a special bond. Over the years, Chancle had become more than a mentor. He'd acted the part of uncle and even parent whenever the demands of the kingdom preoccupied their father. Even though both Karragin and he had completed their rites of passage, Chancle still liked to fall back on the term as one of endearment.

As they walked, he realized for the first time that he felt anxious about facing the families of Velda and Berling. Did the traitors act on their own, or under direction from someone else in the duchy? Having an official from Stone's Grasp, especially Chancle, made him feel at ease about the trip.

Karragin arched an eyebrow and allowed the slightest curl of the side of her mouth, a practical full-toothed grin as far as Nolan was concerned. "Will you accompany us, or will we accompany an official delegation?" she asked.

"Oh, you will most definitely accompany me, Karra," he answered. "I mean, sleeping on a bedroll under the stars sounds heroic, but you can't expect that from the rest of us. No, you will just have to ride alongside my small but significant entourage."

"Does that mean what I think it means?" Nolan asked. He felt his ears lift from the fullness of his smile.

"It means wagon cots instead of bedrolls, hot breakfast in the morning, and possibly a sip of fifteen-year-old resco at night," Chancle said with a wink.

Nolan whistled. Chancle rarely exaggerated. Any resco predating the Abrogator's War was a rare and expensive commodity. "When do we leave?" he asked.

"Well, Elbiona expects you to join with the Outriders within seven days. It will likely take you two days to ride from Beclure to the staging area between the Pillars of Eldrek. Given all that we need to accomplish, we need to leave this afternoon if you can manage," said Chancle.

"Do we provision ourselves?" Karragin asked.

Chancle gasped as if the suggestion wounded him, then leaned in close and whispered, "What do you take me for, a common Llentrell? That lot might find something noble about traveling on Outrider rations, but I think the vice regent can do better."

Karragin offered, "If we don't have to provision ourselves, we can be ready in a few hours."

"Good. It's settled then. Why don't we meet at the west gate one hour after high sun?" Chancle suggested.

Several hours later, Nolan and Karragin accompanied Chancle and his entourage, though the term "entourage" simplified the small delegation Chancle had organized. Chancle himself rode an Aarindin mare, and stout workhorses pulled not one but five covered wagons.

Nolan remembered the feeling of adventure from the few times he'd traveled with Chancle in such luxury. A coachman manned each wagon and also carried out the menial tasks of setting camp, preparing meals, and even grooming the mounts. Three other women, attendants from Stone's Grasp, rode along, though Nolan had no idea why. Inside the vehicles, ingenious craftsmanship allowed two separate cots to unfold. When the cots were stored away, food and provisions stacked easily into the carriages. By Nolan's reckoning, they carried enough provisions to feed five times their number.

The afternoon ride proved easy by Outrider standards, yet they covered a good portion of the journey. They stopped two hours before sundown for camp and shared a hearty meal of roast mutton, warm bread, and crownberry cobbler. After eating, they sat around a fire, and Chancle pulled out a horned zendolin from an ornate case. Nolan gasped in recognition; the priceless instrument was a relic from before the Great War.

Their runefather looked up with a sly grin, enjoying the rare chance to catch everyone off guard. "What?" he asked. Karragin stared back at him with her deadpan face. "I submit to you that this wonderful instrument is not meant to gather dust in storage. Rather, it's meant to be played. And since I have been practicing, and since it's mine, I choose to play it."

To emphasize his point, Chancle plucked and strummed the twelve double strings. Some secret in the instrument's crafting, lost after the Great War, allowed the strings to harness zenith and amplify the sound. As such, he could simply press the strings with his left hand, allowing his right to rattle and tap the body in primal beats as he performed a haunting melody, "The Sword Cuts Both Ways."

The familiar song had Nolan clapping his hands, and he thought he even heard Karragin humming along. As he played, the coachmen and attendants joined them around the fire. They all spent the next hour mesmerized by Chancle's rattle and strum. He played several favorites, including "The Snow from the Mountain," and then even a few bawdy tavern songs like "The Road to Aarindorn" and "Resco, Resco, Resco!"

The last one had the coachman joining in the chorus. After a time, Chancle stared at the fingertips of his left hand as if they had betrayed him. "Well," he said, "I do love to play for a captive audience, but I fear I've let my calluses run soft." He shook his hand and wrinkled up his nose. They retired for the night.

Nolan and Karragin shared a carriage in relative comfort, especially when compared to their sojourn into the Borderlands, and after a hot breakfast the next morning, Nolan turned to find his belongings packed. One of the coachmen had groomed his Aarindin the night before and saw to its feed and water. *A fella could get used to this.*

He gestured, and the Aarindin lowered its belly to the ground to allow him to mount. Chancle still used a saddle, but Karragin had insisted they not depart from protocol. Though saddles made for a comfortable ride, the Outriders never used them, favoring stealth over comfort.

One of their training drills involved riding an Aarindin to the crest of a hill and commanding the horse to lay on its side. In this fashion, they practiced how to hide among tall grasses or brush while carrying out surveillance. If discovered, they could use the Aarindin for cover or direct the horse to rise while remounting.

"For us, the saddles are pointless," Karragin had said. Nolan understood the simple truth of her words. He knew the saddles would only be discarded once they left Chancle's company, but his aching groin muscles made him envy Chancle's saddle more than a little. Thankfully they rode at a relatively mild pace, stopping only for quick breaks. They camped in a similar fashion that night and, by the middle of the next day, crested a hill to look upon Beclure.

One of the larger cities in Aarindorn, the duchy served as the home for many high families in the Endule line. Cousins to the Lellendules, the Endule families often raised gifted healers, scribes, and historians. Many Endules lived in Stone's Grasp in clerical jobs or filled the ranks among the healers and scholars at Callinora in northern Aarindorn.

Elevated in the Great Crown, Beclure's steep dirt roads wound through tracks of forest and crossed bridges spanning deep ravines. Because of the unique geography, the duchy required no walls. Instead, all labor and materials contributed to tall stone buildings of two and three stories with timber framing and conical roofs. The buildings seemed to erupt from the forest as they approached the main bridge over the last ravine.

Chancle took the lead and addressed a guard. The young man wore a dark green tabard over a tan shirt and trousers; a short sword strapped to his side appeared more for show than defense. The Beclurian crest adorned his left shoulder. He looked notably flustered by their unannounced arrival, but Chancle's gentle nature put him at ease.

After exchanging pleasantries, the guard sent a messenger ahead and offered to escort the vice regent. Chancle assured the young man he knew how to navigate the duchy, and they continued. The main road, wide enough for the carriages to pass, wound through the small city.

"When we arrive, allow me to make introductions and gauge the temperament of the Endules," said Chancle.

"Should we be worried?" asked Nolan.

"Worried? Not at all," said Chancle with a wink. "But we are wandering a bit into the wolves' den, and sometimes they bite, but not too hard. The Duchess Endera is an acquired taste. If she corners you, be careful of her questions. Like your father, she can sense when someone is telling half-truths, but she has to touch you—her gift requires physical contact."

"Would she be so bold as to attempt to read someone without letting them know?" asked Karragin.

"Not normally," said Chancle, "but we bring news that will strain her sensibilities, so be prepared for anything."

They rode on in companionable silence. "What's the population of Beclure?" asked Nolan.

Chancle replied as if anticipating the question, "The last census a few years ago placed the population just over nine thousand, though we think that underestimates their actual number. Both Beclure and its sister duchy, Dulesque, serve as the trading hubs for an unknown number of communities that live mainly in the Great Crown. In winter, when the trees are bare, you can see their cookfires and lanterns like stars in the sky."

Nolan did notice a good number of homes recessed in tiers higher in the mountains. They rounded a three-story stone building to find the road open onto a vast paved square, where locals busied themselves on routine errands. Some shopped at vendors while others entered and exited the different storefronts.

Chancle led them to the district house of Beclure, a grand four-story building with massive double doors. A small group of people dressed in formal Beclurian attire exited the district house in heated conversation. At their center, two women deflected questions. The taller woman wore a dark green dress with the crest of Beclure. Only a hand shorter, the other wore similar attire but with the crest of Dulesque.

Upon seeing Chancle, they both strode forward. The taller woman bore a striking resemblance to Velda: high forehead, dark brown eyes, and square shoulders. The shorter woman pursed thick lips together under a thin nose and had black hair in tight curls. She had to be Berling's relative.

Chancle smiled with soft eyes. "Duchess Endera and Duchess Phelond. We did not expect to find you both on this summer day."

Endera descended the wide steps with catlike grace. Even her walk resembled Velda's. "Cousin," she spoke the words with a hint of questioning suspicion, "what occasion brings the vice regent to my doorstep, and with such an entourage?" Her initial smile melted as she appraised Chancle's escort. Her eyes lingered unnaturally long on Nolan and Karragin.

Chancle leaned forward on his Aarindin. "We are here for several reasons, Endera. Perhaps we could speak inside."

"I would normally exchange pleasantries with you, Cousin, but you travel in strange company," said Endera. "I see before me the Outrider who stole the title of prime from my daughter. And unless I'm mistaken, that's another of the regent's . . . children at your side. Why don't you first tell me why these two Outriders are in your company and without my daughter."

Chapter Eighteen: The Moorlok

Bryndor knelt to inspect paw prints set deep into the soil, the only clue left from the slaughter of a milk cow. Between what he thought must be the pads of toes, mud creased up unnaturally. It reminded him of the sharp spines of the Korjinth Mountains from an elaborate three-dimensional map. Not the kind of map he and Lluthean crafted, but more like the elaborate works found only at the formal school in Riverton.

He withdrew from that distant memory and focused on the paw prints. The creases of mud separated not four but five distinct rounded pads set deep in a radius around a sizeable hind pad. He thought the prints must belong to something like a bear. The width of the imprint stretched well beyond the measure of his hand.

He stepped lightly around the bloody carcass of the cow, his nose wrinkling against the smell of decayed flesh as the stench assaulted his senses in the crisp morning air. Numerous smaller footprints also peppered the mud. They resembled dog tracks and clustered around a hind quarter dragged thirty paces off. *Those must be scavengers, but what made the big prints?*

He compared the unnatural depth of the tracks to the ones left by his horse and found the two set into the soil in a similar fashion, though any number of conditions could alter the impression. Perhaps after the rain, the soil had softened.

The rains had eroded most of the large tracks, but a few of the prints still ended with curved grooves that plunged deep into the mud. His index finger disappeared into the cold soil as he probed the depth of the curve, unable to plumb the bottom. He assumed the hooked furrow must be the natural imprint left by an unnaturally large claw. He wished he'd taken the time to learn more about the art of tracking. *Maybe then I could tell more about what happened here.*

"If we linger here, the flies will start becoming less attracted to what's left of that cow and more attracted to you," Lluthean chided.

Bryndor stood and surveyed the rest of the farm pasture with a sigh of unease. Morning sun shimmered off the pasture ground, silhouetting the dew-slicked grass. He felt too frustrated to appreciate the simple beauty. Their opportunities to earn the constable's bounty occurred only after they completed daily chores, which included managing the farm animals, drafting copies of their maps, and finishing any tasks for Aunt Rona. *Grind me, it's like they know all we want to do is join the hunt, and they're looking for ways to keep us busy.*

This made only the second time in as many weeks that they'd managed to leave the house. Other groups of men from Journey's Bend patrolled the areas around the town every night only to return empty-handed. Few, though, ventured very far into the Moorlok. The thick wood pressed against the south side of the Korjinth Mountains and served as the northern border for Journey's Bend. Something about the strange black, craggy peaks gave rise to all manner of superstitions among the locals. He recalled a night on the Tellend farm when three sows each birthed full litters of stillborn piglets. Markum had cursed the event, saying, "On nights when the moons dip below the Korjinth, foul things happen."

He gazed at the dark peaks in the afternoon sun. *They're just mountains. No different than the ones in any other part of the world.*

He drew his attention back to the tracks and the rotting carcass. Lluthean interrupted his thoughts. "You alright, Bryn?"

"The rains have already washed away a good portion of these tracks, or other farm animals have ridden over them." In affirmation of his point, his gelding shifted its stance, generating a sucking sound as it lifted one hoof from the mud. "I'm no tracker."

"You think we waited too long?" asked Lluthean.

"Perhaps," said Bryndor. "But you know as well as I do that folks in the Bend don't ever go very far into the Moorlok. It seems to me the woods are the most logical place to search. Most of the attacks are among farms like this one, north side of town, pressed against the woods. You and I both know it's silliness that keeps them from going in."

Lluthean nodded. "I go where you go, brother. But if we don't turn up something by week's end, Whirik is going to recruit more help from the margrave. This might be our last crack at it."

Bryndor nodded and glanced at the shadow cast by Lluthean in the sun. On his horse with his Logrend bow slung over a shoulder, he thought Lluthean's silhouette might pass for a heroic adventurer, except that he was juggling billow seed pods in the air. The contrast made him smile. *Some things never change.*

"You're right," said Bryndor. "Let's at least make a day of it."

The brothers left their geldings to graze in the closed pasture and walked north to a stand of oak trees. The oaks' stout trunks defined the end of farmland and the edge of the Moorlok. Beyond the trees, thick nettles, thorny underbrush, and immense stands of timber formed a tangled, unwelcoming wall.

Twenty head of sheep wandered close to the geldings, their pleasant mews echoing across the green. A flock of starlings chattered in the tree line. He noticed a few squirrels frolicking in the upper branches of an old oak, dangling from the edges of one tree and nimbly hopping to another. He hoped their easy play did not mean they had chosen the wrong farmstead.

"You want to sit or walk?" asked Bryndor.

"Well, you're the one with the plan, brother. I'm just here to impress the ladies," Lluthean quipped.

Bryndor guffawed. "It'll take more than the hide of some beast slung around your shoulders to turn the eye of Sadeen Tunkle."

Lluthean pocketed his billow seeds. "You saying I haven't already caught her favor?"

"I'm saying you can't shine a turd." Bryndor giggled, then dodged away from Lluthean's bow, which swung in a lazy arc meant for Bryndor's backside.

"Takes one to know one!" Lluthean shot back with a single eyebrow cocked. Instead of replying, Bryndor chewed his cheek. This familiar banter could go on for hours, and the two needed to move ahead with their plan.

"You're the one with the skills," Bryndor said, eyeing Lluthean's bow. "Up you go."

He cupped his hands to give his brother a boost up the thick trunk of a burr oak. Lluthean slung his bow over one shoulder, hopped once, and was deftly thrown up to a low-hanging branch. From there, he picked his way to a natural fork high in the trunk.

"Can you see well enough if I'm able to flush anything from the woods?" Bryndor asked.

"Yes. It's a better view than last week." Lluthean surveyed the area. "Which way are you going?"

Bryndor pointed north into the dense timber, then made a zigzag gesture with his hand to indicate how he would sweep the area to try and drive their prey out into the open. Lluthean nodded his agreement and settled his bow across his lap.

Bryndor made his way into the Moorlok, leaving behind the chatter of the farm and the flock of birds. The dark woods smelled faintly of wet leaves, and squirrels cackled high above in the autumn canopy.

He chose his steps with ease, nibbling at an annoying sliver of dry skin on his lower lip. As the grasslands gave way to briar and deadfall, progress would slow for most, but Bryndor found the terrain comfortable. He settled into familiar habits, advancing his way through game trails and moving on light feet through the ancient wood. He planned to climb to the top of a long rise in the woods, then switch back to drive out ... *What? A bear?*

His mind wandered, thinking about what he might discover. Local hunting parties occasionally gathered and often landed fox or deer. The men would return, slapping each other on the back for a job well done, but they'd never found a predator large enough to account for the killing seen so far.

Bryndor imagined that only a monster born from children's tales could devour a whole cow or sheep. He'd even begun to wonder about Sadeen Tunkle's belief in the untamed, the mischievous boys raised by wolves who tricked the unsuspecting to their death. But the tracks this morning had left him imagining a large bear. *Grind me with a sharp stick. If it is a bear, what am I doing out here alone with just a bow and a knife?*

The memory of those tracks tickled Bryndor's mind. Something about the prints had him feeling unsettled, but he was not an experienced tracker. Ever vigilant to his surroundings, he continued his stealthy ascent up the hillside.

He wondered what the locals would think if they succeeded. Though Journey's Bend frequently welcomed new settlers, he and Lluthean had always felt slightly removed from their neighbors. Part of that detachment certainly lay in their strict upbringing under Kaellor and Rona's care. Certain habits, like the appropriate use of a knife and fork or the ability to read, felt marginally alien whenever they mingled in town.

Part of their separation also stemmed from their unusual stock; he never found it difficult to pick out his family in a crowd. Now that their mantle seemed to be fading, he imagined that many of his peers and perhaps even a young woman or two might finally become more welcoming if they succeeded in this hunt. More perhaps than all of these factors, though, Bryndor simply believed that whatever they found, they could handle.

He stopped and glared back down at the farmstead. At the tree line, Lluthean had made himself comfortable in the burr oak with his bow across his lap. Bryn smiled as a flock of starlings nearly startled him out of his perch. A wave of the birds rushed past the aged oak and out into the open sky of the pasture below. The flock undulated in a mesmerizing dance. Like a swirl of black ink, they eddied in rhythm over the pasture. They swayed first one way then another before landing in a small stand of trees on the other side of the field.

Bryndor chuckled to himself and continued his ascent into the woods. After walking for the better part of a half hour, he began to descend the hillside, cutting a path slightly southeast. A soft chorus of frogs chirped, and he found a small mountain stream. The frogs became silent as he hopped over the shallow water but resumed their calls as he left the creek behind.

He rounded a clump of dense undergrowth and walked along a small ravine. It appeared to be a dry creek bed. He followed the gully and found himself staring into the open maw of a dark cave that cut into the terrain. The entrance was a large dark cavity about five feet high, and the dirt before the cave appeared worn smooth, compacted by use, like a game trail.

At the periphery of the trail, he spied what he'd been searching for. *Bear tracks.*

He walked over and knelt to examine them closer; they looked similar to his untrained eye to the tracks from the farm. He felt the same sense of unease. Bryndor studied the cave until the hairs rose on the back of his neck, and a wave of goosebumps shivered through him. Something was suddenly not the same and set the skin between his shoulderblades crawling. *Why is my heart pounding like a rabbit's?*

He drew long, slow breaths and strained to hear as he took in his surroundings. He'd walked so far into the woods that he couldn't see the farmstead below. *I should get Llu, and we can sort this out together.*

As the thought crossed his mind, he realized the change: silence. The distant chorus of frogs from the stream had ceased. The calls of squirrels and forest birds were now distant.

Strange . . . suddenly, it feels like I'm the one being hunted.

He considered retreating but instead climbed the small gully to a gnarled tree. He began to pull himself up to the trunk. In the moment of his next heartbeat, something massive knocked him to the ground. His bow skittered into the underbrush, and a crushing weight struck him in the back.

As he fell forward, a vice clamped down on his right shoulder. Stinging pain lanced through his woolen tunic and streaked down his arm, and a burning numbness settled into the fingers of his right hand. The sound of snapping arrows from his quiver jolted him to his senses.

His attacker was balanced on top of him as he lay prone. Reaching out, he grasped a tree root and used it to pull himself to the side. He grunted a primal sound, then yelled. As he shifted, so did the weight of his attacker.

The vicelike pain in his right shoulder tightened. More of the arrows from his quiver snapped, and something sharp seared along the flesh under his right shoulder blade. The strap of his quiver pulled so tight he found it difficult to draw a full breath.

Bryndor's fear response surged. He became aware of a deep, malevolent growl accompanied by the smell of fetid breath. He struggled to roll his right shoulder under himself, but the creature held him tight. Surrendering to instinct, he rocked back. The strap of his quiver and part of his tunic tore away. The beast released its grip and tumbled down into the gully.

He turned to discover an enormous wolf. The huge animal stood tall enough to challenge him face to face. Silver and black hackles stood erect from its neck, its long ears were pinned back, and its black lips were snarling, revealing a broad muzzle with overlapping, sharp fangs. The feathered shaft of an arrow stuck out from between its jagged upper teeth. It shook its enormous head, spitting out fragments of feather and wood, then pawed at the arrow shaft wedged in its mouth.

The distraction gave Bryndor time to retreat a few steps, but his legs felt tremulous, and his bowels had turned to water. His hands found a stout branch, and he wrestled it from the underbrush. He turned just in time to meet the charge of the wolf.

The momentum of the beast made him stumble back, but he jammed the limb forward and struggled with both arms to hold the branch between him and the wolf. The beast straddled him and pressed a massive paw onto his chest. One of its hind paws clawed into the front of his thigh. The weight of the thing pressed the wind from his lungs, but he managed to keep a fork of the branch wedged in its jaw.

Grind me! I'm an idiot!

The giant wolf drew back for another charge, allowing him to gasp a lungful of air. The predator paced a slow arc in front of the cave. It growled at something in the dark recesses of the den, then turned back to him with hackles raised. Bryndor frustrated its lunges by swinging the large branch. His throat became sore from screaming, and he tried to retreat.

The beast circled him, preventing escape. The wolf seemed to judge his fatigue and eventually bit down on the branch. With a savage shake of its head, it started to pull him toward the cave.

The struggle sapped his strength, and as his forearm muscles cramped, he lost ground. Though the pain in his right shoulder had eased, his right hand felt weak and numb. His grip on the branch was made all the worse by the slick spittle of the wolf. With a violent jerk, the beast pulled back, and Bryndor lost control of the branch.

The wolf tumbled back, and Bryndor struggled to regain his balance. He panted from the exertion, his right arm heavy and numb at his side. The wolf drew its lips back and seemed to smile as it let out a savage growl. The creature gathered its hind legs under it and prepared to pounce once again.

Bryndor reached to his belt and unsheathed a long hunting knife, then turned his right shoulder away from the wolf. The animal sprang, and Bryndor staggered back. His knife plunged into the beast's underside. Claws seared across his neck as the monster stopped short of ripping his throat out. It howled in pain, but the wolf did not retreat. Bryndor found himself pinned once again under the enormous weight of the creature.

This is it; I'm going to die!

Bryndor watched as the wolf slowly lunged forward again to rend the flesh from his neck. In that desperate moment, something from within his chest erupted. Prickly heat fountained from his core and out into his arms. A wave of power surged through him, and his heart thumped a heavy beat.

In the space between heartbeats, a small part of his awareness separated. He smelled the rich aroma of the autumn leaves, marveled at the immense size of the animal before him, and noted with an odd detachment how the cold forest soil leeched heat from his back. That small detached part of his mind also wondered what people would find after his death.

The intense burning flickered over the skin of his arms with a dazzling blue light and surged into his hands. His heart beat again, and a thunderous clap filled his chest and reverberated down his extremities. The concussive force vibrated, stinging as it coursed across his shoulders, down the length of his arms, and even along his torso to his legs.

In a mixture of pain, fear, and surprise, he roared a loud, primal shout of desperation, "Raaaaaaaaaaaa!"

A sphere of intense, brilliant blue flame erupted from his palms, striking the beast in its chest. The strange blast released a concussive force that hurtled him several feet back along the ground.

The wolf staggered back from the force of the violent detonation. Wisps of smoke rose from its singed muzzle. An angry red and black eschar appeared along its chest, and the air felt sticky with the reek of singed hair. The beast released a hoarse cry of pain as it tried to step on its front left leg. The deformed limb flexed up under its chest.

Bryndor's head swam with vertigo, and scintillating lights streaked at the periphery of his vision. Somehow, the sudden release of the blue fire had leeched the last of his strength. With no small amount of effort, he stumbled to his feet and staggered to find his balance, too confused to do anything but catch his breath. He stared at the wolf as he took slow steps back.

"That's it! Stay! Just stay, and I'll go." He offered the words more like a plea than a command.

The wolf turned away from him and peered into the cave for a few seconds. It looked like it might retreat and seemed to wobble on its feet as it coughed black and bloody soot. However, the beast snarled and bared its fangs again. Despite its broken leg, the wolf leaped forward faster than Bryndor thought it could manage. It landed on top of him.

He drove his knife into the eschar on the wolf's chest. The blade passed through the thickened hide and twisted as it met bone. Something popped, and he lost his grip on the handle. With the last of his strength, he latched his thumbs under the beast's jaw bone and tried to push its snapping teeth away.

The wolf shook its head, then pulled free. The beast dove to gorge upon Bryndor's neck, and he felt a thump vibrate through his chest. In the corner of his vision, the fletching of an arrow sprouted from the wolf's side. Sharp fangs plunged into his shoulder again, but the head of the wolf seemed limp. He felt another thump and another. Two more arrows appeared in the beast's side above and below the shoulder. The wolf sighed and collapsed.

"Bryn? Seven gods, Bryn!" Lluthean yelled, racing up the hillside.

Bryndor tried to answer but labored even to draw breath under the beast's dead weight. Lluthean dropped, panting, next to him. Bryndor turned his head and started to see streaks of light at the periphery of his vision. He felt his face flush like when he'd hung upside down from a tree as a boy. He gazed at Lluthean, bewildered.

"No, no, no, no!" In a panic, Lluthean shouldered the enormous beast off his brother. Bryndor gasped a full breath, and with it, the pressure subsided from his face.

"Thanks," Bryndor panted, "I thought I was dead, Llu." He lay on his back beside the corpse of the wolf, panting.

Lluthean sighed in relief and sat back, gasping in equally heavy breaths. After regaining his composure, he answered, "Paint me with sheep dip, I thought so too. How bad are you hurt?"

Bryndor remained prone for a moment, testing the movement of his right arm. His body felt unusually weak and heavy. He wondered if he could even turn over on his own. His hand opened and closed but felt odd, and his fingers tingled as if he'd slept on his arm awkwardly. Scratches and cuts too numerous to count burned along his back and legs.

The act of sitting up surprised him with pain. For a few minutes, he warred against his stomach and eventually lost, turning to his side to vomit.

As the adrenaline of the moment wore off, a searing burning spread from his jaw down to his shoulder. His tattered clothing clung to his skin from sweat and blood.

"I can't tell. My arm feels weird; how do I look?"

Lluthean flashed a toothy grin. "Like one of the mangled sheep from the farm, and you don't smell much better."

Lluthean set his bow and quiver down to assess his brother's wounds. He lifted away parts of Bryndor's tunic. "The cuts on your neck and shoulder will scar, but the bleeding isn't too bad."

He then peeled back the material of Bryndor's trousers. Congealed blood released to reveal parallel, serrated cuts in his thigh.

"I don't think it's down to the muscle, and it's not bleeding much," said Bryndor after a brief inspection. "Mogdure's teeth, it stings a lot."

"Aunt Ro is gonna have a fit when she sees you," said Lluthean. He tore the front of his shirt away and applied it to Bryndor's neck and shoulder wound as a compress. He wrapped the rest of the shirt around Bryndor's thigh, using the arm sleeves to tie it into place.

"Too tight?" Lluthean asked.

Bryndor wrinkled his nose and grunted. "No, it's alright. Help me stand."

Satisfied with the makeshift dressings, Lluthean pulled Bryndor forward to his feet. Bryndor stood a moment, testing the soundness of his balance. His head whirled for several seconds. Once the feeling passed, the burning sting of all his cuts flared. Whenever he moved, dried blood pulled at the fresh wounds. He limped in a lazy circle but did not sense anything more serious in his injuries. He stopped and looked at his hands as if they were not his own, half expecting more blue light to erupt.

"You alright?" Lluthean asked.

Finding no explanation for the strange eruption, Bryndor shrugged. "Something happened to me, Llu. Something . . . saved me," Bryndor tried to explain.

"Yes, it was no small amount of Lutney's luck, I think." Lluthean giggled.

"No. Well, yes. By the All-Mother, yes," said Bryndor, "but more than that. There was something else. Something sprang out of my hand and hit that thing like a thunderbolt."

Lluthean cocked his head to the side. "I did hear a thunderclap, but I figured a storm was coming over the ridge. That was you?"

Bryndor shrugged. "I think so. I don't know, but something definitely happened to me."

Bryndor searched the upper canopy of the timber, expecting someone to descend and explain it was all a trick. After long moments and no forthcoming answers, he released the notion. "Let's have a look at this wolf of ours."

Lluthean heaved the beast onto its back to better assess its size. The creature stretched out on the ground in a silhouette longer than Bryndor was tall. The wolf's monstrous head lifelessly rolled over, following the momentum of its corpse. A strange purple tongue protruded from the side of the creature's jaw.

Lluthean retrieved Bryndor's knife from the beast's underside, where it had wedged between two ribs. He wiped the blood on the wolf's pelt and re-sheathed the blade.

"Lucky blow there," said Lluthean.

They both stared at the strange, fresh burn along the wolf's chest and left side. "That's fresh; I can still smell the burned hair. Did you do that too?" Lluthean asked.

Bryndor nodded and chewed on his lower lip. "Yes. I can't explain it, Llu, but I think maybe something of the power Kae was talking about saved me."

"What did it feel like? How did you do it?" asked Lluthean.

"That's just it. I didn't do anything," said Bryndor. "I felt this surge of anger, or maybe I was so scared, I don't know. And then this blue fire erupted from my palms."

They both stood in silence for a time. Bryndor inspected the three arrow shafts protruding from the side of the wolf. "Nice shooting, by the way. How did you know to come up here?"

"I saw something dart from the next farm over into the Moorlok. It was big and fast. I ran up here as fast as I could," he answered. "Bryn, this is like no wolf I've ever seen. It's huge, and its coat is black, not like any of the grey ones I've seen before."

Lluthean grasped the paw and held it out against his hand. The pads stretched beyond the tips of Lluthean's fingers. When he pressed into the paw, long claws curled out. "That's weird. They retract like cat claws. Animal this size, no wonder it fed on livestock nearly every day," Lluthean surmised.

"Aye, there's that, and it's got a litter. Look here." Bryndor pointed to a row of engorged nipples on the wolf's underside. They both looked apprehensively at the cave entrance.

"I think I've had enough adventure for one day," said Bryndor.

"If there is a litter in there, we should end them now. One of those things nearly sent you to the Drift, can you imagine more?" asked Lluthean.

"I'll wager you're right. Why don't we at least rustle up the horses first? We can pack the wolf; I didn't go through all this not to get our reward, and maybe you will manage to win Sadeen's favor after all. Besides, I think I have flint in the saddlebag. If we have to go in, let's not go in blind," suggested Bryndor.

"Torches then, sounds good. Only you rest here. I'll be back with the horses," replied Lluthean. He dropped a few arrows, a small pouch of food, and a water satchel to the ground near his brother. "You lose your bow?"

Bryndor craned his neck and saw the bow adjacent to the tree he tried to climb. He pointed, and Lluthean retrieved it. The weapon appeared unblemished.

"Alright, wait here, and I'll be right back," said Lluthean.

Bryndor nodded and settled down against a tree trunk. Beams of sun spilled through the canopy of the Moorlok and warmed his face. He watched a shirtless Lluthean deftly pick his way down the hillside.

The summer winds gusted, lifting the smell of wet leaves up to him. Bryndor noted his cuts seemed to sting less, and the feeling was returning to his right hand. He fingered the edge of the shirt scrap Lluthean had applied as a dressing and counted himself among the lucky.

If he were honest with himself, he had to admit that he'd never really expected to find the beast that plagued the farmsteads. He and Lluthean had simply enjoyed the adventure of the hunt and one another's friendship more than anything else. *By the All-Mother, what were we thinking? Somehow we walked right past confidence to outright stupidity.*

That they found the beast and then dispatched it was a wonder only slightly smaller than realizing just how close to death he'd walked this morning. The gravity of the events turned over in his mind as he studied the wolf, admiring the animal's power and size. Its pale blue eyes stared into the distance. Without the growling and snarling, the creature appeared somehow noble. He inspected the singed hair and recalled the very peculiar release of power he'd experienced in the struggle.

He rubbed involuntarily at his palms, expecting still to find some remnant of the dazzling blue light, a mark, or soot perhaps. But his palms revealed only familiar weathered calluses.

Still, what was that?

He tried to remember the feeling at the moment that the fire surged through his body, but it all seemed lost in the chaos and excitement of the struggle.

Perhaps Uncle Kae will have an explanation.

Unable to discern any clear answers, Bryndor withdrew his attention from the puzzle and found himself unable to resist gazing at the forest canopy. Though the Moorlok Wood could be a treacherous place, the natural foliage made it seem less ominous. He followed the course of a thick vine winding up a tree trunk. Wherever the vine turned back on itself, a cluster of red flowers erupted.

The late morning breeze swayed the treetops and caused some of the red petals to flutter to the ground. The forest awoke again with chirping birds and cackling squirrels, and Bryndor found himself wanting to sleep—but sleep felt against his better nature. There could well be danger residing inside the cave. At that notion, Bryndor snapped his eyes open.

Grind me for a fool! Sometimes I'm as dumb as a sack of hammers.

He wondered if he had allowed himself to actually fall asleep or only momentarily drift to that place between wake and sleep. Just then, something stirred from within the shadows of the cave. Bryndor strained to identify any details, but all he could see was something moving close to the ground. With a grunt of pain, he shifted to a kneeling position, picked up his bow, and nocked an arrow.

The strain to draw the bow was more than he expected. The muscles in his right shoulder ached in protest. But slowly, steadily, he drew the bowstring, thumb flush to cheek. He waited. Ten seconds. He waited. Twenty seconds. Sweat beaded up on his forehead, and his right arm trembled with spasms of pain and fatigue. He began to cramp and couldn't hold the arrow nocked any longer.

A small mass of fur tumbled out of the cave mouth. Bryndor gasped and let the arrow fly errantly well above its intended mark. As the arrow skittered against the backside of the cave, two black wolf pups startled from their wrestling. The morning sun seemed a surprise to their eyes, and they blinked and squinted.

One of the pups discovered the corpse of its mother and began to tug playfully at her ear until it realized there was no response. Eventually, both pups made their way to a teat and tried to nurse, but both stopped, bewildered, within minutes. Bryndor observed them with empathy as they tried to elicit a response from their mother. The first pup returned to pulling at the ears of the corpse, and the second sat back and let out a small bark.

Bryndor considered the sight before him. The anchor of guilt pulled his throat into his chest, and he swallowed in an attempt to dismiss the feeling. Hunting a monster that decimated livestock was one thing, but watching the scene before him drained most of the glory from the morning's events. He started to understand some of the creature's strange behavior during their struggle.

He whistled to announce his presence, and both pups perked their ears. He whistled again, and they turned uneasily, sniffing at the air. Bryndor dropped to all fours to seem less intimidating, then reached into the small pouch Lluthean left behind and tore off a piece of salted pork. He tossed it to the pups, who sniffed it warily. After a moment of indecision, both found the meat desirable and entered a tug-of-war to fight for the scrap. The larger pup won and went to work chewing up the hardened meat. The smaller one sniffed the air again and crept forward, picking its steps with caution as it approached.

Bryndor tore another piece of pork and held it at arm's length. The small pup investigated. Eventually, the offer was enticing enough that it took the meat from his hand, then retreated a step. By this time, the larger one had approached, looking for another handout.

Bryndor smiled and eased back to a sitting position, his shoulder too stiff to remain on all fours. For several long minutes, the three observed each other. The wind rustled around Bryndor's back toward the pups, and they once again eagerly searched the air for information about him. Something in that information caused one of them to creep forward.

Amazed, Bryndor recalled the amount of saliva he was bathed in during his struggle with the mother. "I wonder?" he questioned out loud.

He removed a strip of his torn shirt from near his neck and playfully dragged the cloth on the forest floor. The tease was more than one pup could ignore, and it pounced upon the object in play. The other sat back for a bit, then joined the game. In minutes, he became enthralled, watching both pups tumble over each other in circles.

"Found yourself a few friends, I see." Lluthean's greeting startled the game to a halt, and both pups sniffed the air at him nervously. "Any more inside?"

"I've no idea. These two tumbled out on their own. I think they smell their mother on me," Bryndor answered.

"Hah!" Lluthean chortled. "That the first time you ever had the scent of a woman wrapped around your neck, brother?"

"I'm serious, Llu. How else would you explain it?" Bryndor answered.

"Just tell me you didn't name 'em already," Lluthean said flatly.

Bryndor chanced to pet the larger one behind the ear. "No."

The two brothers watched as the pups turned their attention to the strip of cloth and resumed another game of tug-of-war. Lluthean brandished a hatchet in his hand and watched the innocent play.

"Something feels wrong about butchering pups," Lluthean mumbled.

He looked to Bryndor, who replied, "I don't think I can do it either. It's likely folks will have questions about this beast. The pups might help answer them, I guess."

"I suppose," Lluthean replied, then placed his hatchet back into a saddlebag and removed a small coil of rope. They tried to lift the carcass onto the gelding, but Bryndor's injuries prevented him from being much help. The sheer mass of the carcass proved too much for Lluthean alone.

Lluthean watched the pups wander back into the cave, then withdrew his knife. He plunged the six-inch blade under the midline of the rib cage and made a neat incision down to the bladder. He reached in and maneuvered the knife to free up the chest organs, then sat back. "Now there's something you don't see every day."

"What's that?" Bryndor asked.

"Grind me sideways if the lungs aren't cooked solid," Lluthean said. "Parts of the guts too. I've lost track of how many deer we field dressed over the years, and I've never seen that before."

Bryndor recalled the strange bloody soot the beast had coughed right before it died. He watched his brother pull out the beast's organs onto the forest floor. "Where's all the blood?" Bryndor asked.

Lluthean tapped the flat of his blade on the massive heart. The red organ bounced like normal, but the lungs appeared grey and firm. "I think . . . I think it's all seared in or something. That's stranger than a frog with nuts! How did you do that, Bryn?"

"I told you, I'm not really sure. Are you done, or can we go home?" he asked.

"Give me one minute," Lluthean answered. He tossed a rope over a stout limb, secured it to the carcass, then looped the other end around the pommel of Bryndor's saddle. He walked the horse forward, and the carcass lifted from the ground with the makeshift pulley. In minutes, he had the wolf secured onto his own mount.

Bryndor watched it all with admiration. "What made you think of that?"

Lluthean shrugged. "I don't know. I remember seeing deckhands do something like that in Hammond to unload a ship's cargo. They used a pulley wheel and donkeys. I thought it was worth a try if we could lighten the load." He kicked at the cooked organs on the ground as he spoke.

Lluthean's dapple gelding nickered nervously and pawed the ground, but he grabbed the reins and calmed the animal. With no small amount of effort and pain, Bryndor mounted his own gelding. The brothers eyed the pups napping near the cave in the late morning sun.

"Might be best to leave them to the woods for now," Bryndor suggested.

"I don't imagine they can cause any harm, and if anyone in town needs more answers, I believe we can find this cave easy enough," Lluthean agreed.

Lluthean eased his mount down the gully and around the thickets of briar. Bryndor followed. The summer sun fell light on their backs as they painstakingly traveled back home.

Chapter Nineteen: Laryn on the Hunt

Laryn clambered along a steep hillside of shale. The thinning mists made her descent down the Korjinth a tedious struggle. By the time she stumbled through the darkness to the tree line, she felt defeated. Instead of looking for another bank of clouds to travel, she pitched a lean-to, stripped off most of her heavier clothing, then climbed inside a bedroll and collapsed.

She awoke the next morning to a chorus of birdsong. She lay awkwardly on her belly, and everything ached, from the small muscles in her feet to the muscles at the back of her neck. *That's what I get for being a side sleeper.*

She rolled to her side, slow and cautious, surprised to discover that her breathing felt unlabored. The tingling in her fingers had diminished from the day before.

She shifted her weight and grunted as more muscles revealed their deep aches. With a significant effort, she shrugged out of her bedroll, then stared through a canopy of dense trees. To her surprise, hanging directly over her meager camp, a kevash tree drooped with branches laden with unpicked fruit. *How far down did I come?*

She grounded herself in the moment, in her breathing, and in her surroundings. After allowing her senses to awaken further, she began gentle stretches and worked out the major areas of pain. The reward of the fresh kevash motivated her to stand. She plucked a ripe fruit, then wandered out to a clearing. The valley loomed well below her. The village, or where she thought it should be, seemed insignificant from her vantage point. *Good, not all the way back.*

By the sun's position in the sky, it neared late morning. She emptied her pack of all but a knife and some twine, then plucked a few more pieces of fruit. After dressing in her cumbersome outer layers, she scouted the area. Surveillance of the mountainside revealed that she could likely find this camp again. A rockslide scarred the adjacent area directly down from where she stood. The rest of the valley remained uniformly covered in a dense canopy of green.

The trees thinned as she climbed up the mountainside. Just as she walked out of the tree line, she stumbled upon a cluster of small plants clinging to a rocky outcropping. Closer inspection showed that the plants lacked the fuzzy plume or the thick roots of Broga's beard. So she continued.

A dense, clouded mist rolled in from the west, and she allowed herself to fold into it. Familiar cold vapors pressed against her, leaving a kiss of moisture on her cheek. The ethereal swells carried her, weightless, and deposited her near the ridge.

In the daylight, she had no awareness of the clashing currents of zenith and nadir. *At least I can't hear the death sighs.*

She decided to check her snares and managed the walk along the ridge with greater ease this time. While her breathing pulled in deep, rapid breaths, she didn't suffer the exhaustion like the day before. She found all three snares, each undisturbed. She stared at the last one in frustration until a faint hissing sigh tickled her senses. The warning motivated her to leave the high place. She caught a random cloud bank and moved back down the ridge.

Laryn wandered back and forth, searching outcroppings of rock and vegetation. Her hunt proved unsuccessful, though a rotting log at the top of the tree line provided a comfortable spot to rest in the afternoon light.

The sun loomed just above the western peaks as she finished a bit of dried meat and the last of her kevash. She removed the peel in one complete rind. *Hmm, that's supposed to be good luck.*

She tossed the green kevash ball and tracked its course as it bounded along the tree trunk. The pitted peel ramped up into the air, following the curve of the tree base, then disappeared under a cluster of deep purple leaves.

She startled to a standing position, then rushed over to the plants and squatted down for a closer inspection. The cavity left in the ground by the tree's root ball lay blanketed with the strange growth. Tan, tubular roots allowed each plant to sit perched on top of dead tree roots and rocks. The structure supported fleshy, thin leaves that appeared green near the stem. As the leaves curled back, they faded to blue, and purple hues stained the tips. A purple, feathery flower tufted the top of the plants.

Sometimes the Giver gives.

She used a small knife to pry up three of the plants. They released from their perches with ease. Feeling a sense of accomplishment, she considered a return to her snares, but long shadows began to climb across the valley. Instead, she walked along the tree line until she discovered the familiar scar in the mountainside. A short descent led to her bedroll and supplies. She made a small fire and relaxed for the night.

The next morning, she awoke feeling less of the effect of the high places. The tingling in her hands had vanished, and her breathing at rest felt almost normal. She enjoyed another breakfast of fruit and the last of her dried meat.

A quick inspection showed that her stash of Broga's beard remained fresh in her pack. She packed her bedroll and climbed up out of the tree line. The sun shone bright and clear without a cloud for miles. She stood long moments, hoping that the wind would usher in mists to allow her to fold and slide up to the ridge, where her snares sat. The air hung unusually still, and the skies darkened to the west. *Storm's coming.*

She kicked her foot against loose shale, considering her options. The absence of significant cloud cover made her descent and escape from any severe storms a risky endeavor. Patting at her heavy outerwear to reassure herself, she tried to gauge her odds. If inclement weather caught her in the high places, she didn't know if the layers would keep her warm enough.

"What have you come all this way for? Go, just go," she said to nobody in particular. With her pack hoisted over a shoulder, she began the arduous climb in the thin air. Four hours later, and after numerous stops to catch her breath, she reached the ridge where her snares lay.

She almost tripped over the spike of the first snare. Something had come along and removed the valley rat. The loose shale and rock revealed no clear tracks, so she spent the next two hours walking in ever-wider circles. If a clouded leopard had consumed the bait and succumbed to the bandle root, she meant to capitalize.

The entire time, she kept track of the darkening skies. Dark blue clouds gathered above the western peaks, and a cold, moist wind gusted across the Korjinth. She knew it was still midafternoon, but the storm made it appear much later.

With renewed urgency, she climbed back to the ridgeline and walked toward the next of the two snares. The second one remained undisturbed. She dismantled the trap, tossed the rat carcass far down the slope, and recovered the stake and twine. As she crouched, gathering her supplies, motion flickered in the corner of her vision. She turned to see a dark shadow shifting close to the ground near the last snare.

Laryn quickstepped just below the ridgeline and circled around toward where she thought the last snare was. She peeked around a boulder without making a sound. Hunkered over her trap, a large black panther chewed on the bait. Her heart raced so loud she feared the elusive animal might actually hear it, so she froze.

A solemn feeling occupied her mind as she watched the creature. Sleek black fur rippled over powerful shoulder muscles. Occasional hues of midnight blue undertones appeared along its flank. The tension of the encroaching storm combined with the thin air numbed her concentration, and before she realized what she was doing, she spoke out loud in frustration.

"Grind me. You don't have any spots."

She thought she only mumbled the words, but the large cat looked up with a feral growl. Its ears pinned back, and it hunched close to the ground, prepared to pounce. Before she could turn to run down the mountainside, the cat lunged. The beast arced with alarming speed, and she fell back, expecting the worst, but the snare caught around its hindfoot, and the panther tumbled to the ground.

In a rage, the beast twirled in violent circles wrestling with the snarc. It thrashed about the lash for several long moments and tried to chew the bitter material, howling the entire time. After several moments, the panther stopped and gathered itself by the stake.

A growl, more of an angry whine tainted with fear, carried across the ridgeline. It remained in a defensive crouch but occasionally pulled at its trapped hind leg. She sat next to the large boulder, wondering how long she should stay. The wind gusted, and her chin felt numb. The sky had turned from late afternoon to night in those tense moments as the last of the day's light vanished behind a massive dark wall of storm clouds.

"Fall asleep," she whispered. "Just fall asleep, and I'll set you free. Then we can both get off this ridge."

She felt defeated. Elder Miljin had said she had a limited window before this storm rolled in. Guilt prevented her from leaving even as she watched the storm clouds churn just overhead.

From the roiling thunderhead, familiar keening tones echoed as currents of zenith and nadir collided. In the relative darkness, a brilliant cascade of sparks illuminated the panther's silhouette. Something about the release of power caused the panther's coat to flare for two or three seconds . . . with white spots.

Not a panther after all. Now that was worth staying for!

Laryn leaned forward to inspect the leopard. It seemed more relaxed and lay with its belly flush to the ground, but it was still awake. She decided to retreat behind the boulder, hoping that if the creature remained relaxed, the bandle root might take effect.

Tucked out of the wind, she watched the mesmerizing dance of the ribbons of zenith. She thought she felt rather than heard the rasping friction as the counter-currents ran against one another and then collided in bursts of sparks. The explosions released long, melancholy wails across the canyon.

Time became elusive to her awareness. The ethereal songs released by the otherworldly collisions entranced her. She lost track of how many times the currents clashed or how many different echoes resonated through her body. Rain started to spit against her cheek, and still, she lingered until a crack of thunder and lightning stunned her to awareness.

She startled as if waking from a long nap, feeling bewildered. It took her a few moments to make sense of her surroundings. She stood on wobbly legs and rounded the boulder.

The leopard lay on its side, either dead or asleep. She made numb fingers retrieve her small knife and stumbled toward the creature. Relieved that it remained still, she made quick work of the snare.

The wind drove the rain against her face like razors of ice. Despite the onslaught, the leopard didn't move. The only sign of life occurred when another eruption of nadir and zenith made its pelt flare with white spots.

Now that she knelt next to the creature, she got an accurate sense for the size of the leopard. "You're just a cub, aren't you? I can't leave you out in this weather."

She grunted as she lifted the cub into her arms. She felt the leopard's shallow breaths and sighed in relief. The creature weighed at least forty pounds, and she struggled to carry it back the short distance to the ridgeline. By the time she crested the ridge to begin her descent, her arms were threatening to cramp.

A sibilant moan carried across the barrier. Something that sounded like two sheets of metal sliding against one another crescendoed over the wind, erupting in a brilliant deluge of sparks. The air smelled sterile and dry for a moment, and just down the mountainside, something else flared with white spots. Something much larger than the leopard she was struggling to hold in her arms.

"Oh grind it all, is that your mother?"

Laryn dropped to a knee and gently placed the cub on the ground. She backed up a few paces. Her numb fingers trembled, but she grasped the hilt of her knife. Irregular flashes of lightning allowed her to track the approach of the adult leopard.

She continued to retreat up the mountainside. Another collision of zenith and nadir caused the leopards' coats to illuminate. The adult stalked past the body of the cub. In the darkness between lightning strikes, she strained to hear any sign that the adult was approaching.

Another eruption of zenith colliding with nadir illuminated the great cat, and Laryn could now clearly make out the silhouette of the predator. Luminous eyes peered back at her as it gathered large paws under its coiled muscles.

"Go! Take your cub and go! Leave me alone!" she shouted.

At her shoulder, a massive shadow appeared. Before she had time to react, a familiar howl moaned across the mountaintop. Lightning skittered across the sky, revealing the muscled contours of a majestic wolvryn with a silver muzzle.

"Ghetti? Oh, thank the Giver, but you almost made me pee!"

Laryn glanced back down the mountainside. The adult leopard circled back to the cub, picked it up by the fur of its neck, and retreated into the darkness.

They stood there together for several minutes. The wolvryn's rumbling growl served as a threat to any other predators.

Laryn wiped the stinging rain from her face. "Time to head back, Ghetti."

She took no more than two steps when the wolvryn jerked her back. Ghetti released her hold of the material at Laryn's shoulder and lowered herself to the ground. Laryn considered the majestic creature. Biting winds ruffled the fur along her flank and neck, but the wolvryn appeared unconcerned. She yawned at the dark sky and turned her massive head to gaze back at Laryn.

"I don't understand, Ghetti. What?" She stumbled over her thoughts. "We can't stay here. I can't stay here."

Laryn started down the mountainside again, but Ghetti crept forward on her belly to block her path.

"You act like you want me to ride you. Ghetti, I can't ride you. You're as big as a horse, but I don't think . . ." Another hissing sound tore through the night, followed by a violent, dazzling cascade of lightning that seared across the sky.

Laryn adjusted her pack and threw a leg over the wolvryn. She leaned forward and grabbed fistfuls of fur. Before she could say anything, she felt herself lurch forward. The sensation reminded her of folding into the clouds. In the darkness, she became disoriented. It felt like they were falling. She turned her head to the side to get her bearings, but the motion only caused a strange whirling, tickling feeling in her core.

After a few seconds, the sensations dissipated. The wind felt warm, and she sensed her weight on top of Ghetti for the first time. The wolvryn cantered through dense forest with all the grace of a riding horse. They surged over a hilltop, and Ghetti leaped off the mountainside. They fell only for a second, then Laryn sensed the familiar weightlessness of folding into the mists.

Ghetti panted lightly but never slowed enough for her to dismount. Laryn marveled at the way the wolvryn negotiated the terrain. With little effort, she bounded over hillsides. Time and again, they leaped without hesitation out into the night, into the mists. In but a few minutes, Ghetti trotted to the front steps before her hut.

Laryn felt her boots scuff the ground when the wolvryn stopped and lowered her belly. She felt a little disappointed that the journey had ended but quickly dismounted. She dropped her pack and turned to offer the matriarch her thanks, but the wolvryn had already soundlessly bounded off.

Laryn stood alone. In less than an hour, she had endured the life-threatening storms of zenith colliding with nadir, stared down an elusive wild cat from the Korjinth, and rode a wolvryn. All that, and she'd forgotten to collect any samples from the leopard. She dropped her head in despair and discovered that strange, short strands of black fur covered the front of her outer coat. She rolled a few of the hairs between her fingers. They felt soft and smooth, not like coarse wolvryn hair.

"Yes, yes, yes, yes!" she shouted and stomped her feet in a private victory dance. Before anything else could interrupt her success, she retrieved a small brush. In minutes, she'd gathered up a handful of the leopard fur. She closed her fist and repeated her small dance.

"Is this a private celebration?" asked the familiar voice of Elder Miljin.

She turned to produce her trophy. "I'm back, and have I ever got a story for you."

The elder approached, climbed a few steps, then turned to regard her. "Stories are nice, but have you the two items we need?"

"I do, Elder," she answered. Her smile widened ear to ear.

He seemed to consider her words for a time. "Well then, come in and tell me your story."

They stepped into her small hut. Laryn described her adventure while she placed the handful of leopard fur into a small pouch. She then produced the Broga's beard, setting the plants carefully on a windowsill. As she unpacked the twine from the last snare, her fingers ran across something sharp. She stopped her story to investigate. A single sharp tooth, a fang, lay embedded in the twine. She held the object up for the elder's inspection.

"I think that might be from the leopard cub. It tried to chew off the snare," she said.

Elder Miljin leaned forward. "May I, Laryn?" He studied the fang, turning it over in his palm. "If this really is the fang of a clouded leopard, then you have surely put my adventure to shame. May I keep this to study it for a time? I will return it soon."

"Sure, I don't have a use for it," she said as she relaxed back onto her bed. "Oh, but I haven't got to the best part."

The elder pulled his eyes from the fang and cocked his head to the side, prepared to listen.

"I rode Ghetti through the mists!" she said. "There was this other leopard, not the one I caught, another one. I think it was the mother. Anyway, I don't think it took too kindly to what I did to the cub, even though I was just trying to get the poor thing off of the mountain ridge. Just when I thought this mama leopard was going to give me trouble, Ghetti showed up and scared off the leopard. But then the clash of zenith and nadir became more intense, and . . . I don't know how I would have made it back without Ghetti."

Elder Miljin smiled passively. At that moment, she felt a bit like a young child telling a fabricated story.

"It's true, all of it," she signed.

He gestured, *"I believe you, child. I just don't understand why it took you so long."*

She gestured back, exasperated, *"So long for what? I was only gone the two days!"*

Now his smile beamed. *"So long for you to figure out that you could ride the wolvryn."*

Chapter Twenty: A Second Crack of Thunder

The walk back through the Moorlok unfolded without further adventure. Lluthean led his gelding along well-established game trails to avoid as much of the thorny underbrush as possible. He already itched in several places where tall nettles had brushed against his exposed skin. Just when he started to regret giving up his shirt, they rounded the stand of oaks that marked the edge of the Moorlok and the entrance to the farm pasture. His gelding quickstepped and nickered in annoyance as two balls of black fur tumbled onto the field.

"Would you look at that," he said. Bryndor didn't answer, and Lluthean looked back at his older brother. He rode with his head down and swayed a little in the saddle. *Mogdure's teeth, you look rough, brother.*

"Bryn?" He spoke his name more as a question.

Bryndor lifted his head, and Lluthean sighed in relief, then pointed at the pups.

"They followed us all the way here?" Bryndor asked.

"I only just now realized it," Lluthean answered. He squatted down and wriggled his fingers playfully. The smaller pup approached and allowed him to scratch it behind the ears. The creatures sniffed with interest at the smells of the farm.

"If you can round them up, we should probably take them home. Kae will know what to do." Bryndor sat erect and stretched with a grimace in the saddle. "I don't imagine any of the farmers will be too interested in allowing them to run free."

Lluthean lashed his lead rope around a branch and collected the smaller pup. It licked at the sweat along his neck and chin, making him giggle. "I've got a burlap sack rolled up in my saddlebag. If I can get them into it, can you manage them on the saddle?" he asked.

"We can only try and see," Bryndor answered. Lluthean handed the smaller pup to Bryndor.

It took him a few minutes, but eventually, he corralled the larger pup. After the short chase, he walked back to find the small one asleep in Bryndor's arms. The larger pup unrolled a long purple tongue and yawned. With little resistance, he placed both into the oversized sack and looped the drawstring around Bryndor's saddle horn. Bryndor adjusted their weight in his lap. They watched for a moment.

When neither pup moved or yelped, Bryndor shrugged and nodded. "Let's go while we can," he said.

Lluthean led them along a dirt road past several farmsteads, then through the west side of Journey's Bend. They made for an unusual sight. His shirtless, welted appearance was one thing, but Bryndor looked mortally wounded. Dried blood had congealed on all of his clothing in a mixture of burgundy and brown stains. Lluthean glanced back to the carcass draped across his gelding. *I can't believe you killed that thing, Bryn. It's massive.*

On their way home, he glanced back at the wolf several times, as much to make sure it remained on the saddle as to remind himself how enormous the beast was. Surprise took him every time he realized the size of the thing. Draped over his gelding, the beast's head and tail still brushed the ground.

They passed by a tavern, the Bashing Ram. One of the barmaids, a round woman named Della, stepped out with a broom in hand to sweep the front boardwalk. She called out as they passed, "Lluthean! Lluthean Scrivson. What manner of trouble are you two dragging into the Bend this afternoon?"

Lluthean looked over his shoulder but continued walking. "We're not bringing trouble, Della; we're ending it. Tell the constable, my brother and I killed this thing. He can come to our place to see for himself."

Della took one look at the unusually large wolf carcass, then disappeared inside the tavern. Before he'd walked the length of the boardwalk, three men and a woman all rushed out to see the brothers. Lluthean continued along the block and to the outer edge of town. He answered their excited questions patiently, and before he left the outskirts of town, he turned to address the gawkers.

"I think we can all agree this is the biggest wolf any of us has ever seen," said Lluthean. "I can't imagine anything else killing the livestock of late. Right now, my brother needs the attention of my Aunt Rona and some rest. We can answer more questions from Constable Whirik later."

They left the crowd behind and continued on the familiar road home. The farther they walked, the more he realized Aunt Rona would likely give them the rough side of her tongue when she saw Bryndor's injuries. The realization and his brother's relative silence made him feel restless. He slapped the long end of the lead rope against his thigh in rhythm with the gelding's walk.

"So Bryn, what are you going to do with your share of the reward?" he asked.

After a long pause, Bryndor answered. "I hadn't really thought about it. You?"

"Now that I'm done saving your sorry ass, I plan to double it, maybe cards at the Ram." Lluthean winked.

Bryndor smiled back but remained quiet. Lluthean grew more concerned. Bryndor was usually up for a round or two of word games in good humor. He led the geldings past a bend of the Shelwyn River, then along the ivy-covered stone wall around their farmstead. He grabbed the reins of both mounts and studied his brother's face. Bryndor looked slightly pale, weary, and tired. "You feeling alright?" asked Lluthean.

Bryndor drew a deep breath in and grunted more than a little as he lifted his head to view their home. "Yes, just achy. I'll manage."

"I'll stable the horses. Why don't you get cleaned up, and we'll see to our reward later," Lluthean offered.

"Thanks, Llu," said Bryndor. He dismounted and staggered a few steps, then seemed to collect his balance. He stepped with a slight limp toward the porch.

Rona barged out of the front door to meet him. "By Malldra and her Seven, what have you boys gotten yourselves into this time?"

One look at Bryndor's wounds drained the heat from her voice. Lluthean paused, expecting a tongue lashing. Instead, Rona waved him on to the barn. She rushed forward and placed one of Bryndor's arms over her shoulder. Together, they disappeared inside.

Lluthean counted himself lucky twice over: once that Rona was capable of tending to Bryndor's wounds, and twice that he'd gotten away without a berating. *Might need to test my luck at the Ram tonight.*

Lluthean led the mounts into the barn. He heaved the wolf carcass over the gate of an empty stall. His gelding nickered in what he thought seemed like appreciation at having the weight removed. He ushered the horses to familiar posts for grooming.

He placed a small mound of hay, a ham bone, and a saucer of water in a pen at the back of the barn. The sleepy-eyed pups rolled out of the bag and sniffed at the air. Both stretched and yawned, then explored their new kennel.

"Scout might not look too kindly on roommates, so don't get too comfortable," he said.

In short order, they began gnawing on the gristly ends of the hambone. Satisfied they could not escape the pen to cause any problems, he tended the geldings. He spent more than the usual effort in their grooming. *The longer this takes, the more time Ro has to cool off.*

Once he finished, he approached the house with trepidation. Inside, Bryndor rested in a large chair by the hearth. As Lluthean entered, Bryndor cocked an eye open. Rona must have ordered him stripped down to his smallclothes, and in the time it took him to stable the horses, Rona had cleaned off nearly all the dried blood. His hair lay disheveled, and his clothes rested unceremoniously in a pile on the floor. Purple bruising stained the front of his right shoulder, merging with the darkened lacerations, which crossed to his neck. Clean bandages were stained pink along his thigh and shoulder, but he looked better.

A steaming cup of tea steeped on the table near him. Lluthean sniffed at the concoction and wrinkled his nose. *Why can't medicine be more like herbal tea?*

"Does that taste as bad as it smells?" he asked.

Bryndor turned the edge of his mouth in a subtle smile. "Yes, but believe it or not, it helps dull the pain."

"Where is Aunt Ro, and what did she have to say?" he asked.

"She's out back, gathering the herbs to make more of this." Bryndor pointed at the teacup emitting the foul aroma.

"That makes sense. You don't look so good." Lluthean scratched absentmindedly at a raised welt along his rib cage. "Have you talked with Kae yet?"

Bryndor shook his head. "No, Rona said he took Scout to Riverton again and was to visit the Tellends before returning home."

At the mention of her name, Rona entered the common room with a basketful of Maedra's pitchers. The purple-flowered plants bloomed wild around their homestead. She took one look at Lluthean, then sighed.

"I can't say that I'm too happy about the trouble you two got into this morning, but at least you don't look as bad as your brother. Turn around, let's have a look at you."

She directed Lluthean in a circle. She pulled at his ears, lifted an arm to inspect his rib cage, and leaned in to smell him. "By the All-Mother, is there any part of you not covered with nettle-bite?"

Lluthean lifted a pant leg to show normal skin without any signs of the welted rash that had spread across his torso. He scratched at a particularly itchy patch on his side. She slapped his hands away, then nodded with what he thought looked like a small bit of disgust. "It's a good thing you only used your shirt to make Bryn's dressing. Now stop that. You'll only rub in the resin."

She set down her basket and walked to a cupboard to retrieve a green bar of soap and a small towel. "Listen to me and do exactly as I say, or that rash will be ten times worse in the morning. Soak in the river, then get out and lather up from head to toe. Let the soap dry out without rinsing. Sit in the sun. Wait a good half hour, then rinse; that should remove most of the plant resin. Now off with you!"

Lluthean brooked no argument. He knew better than to try to argue with his aunt. *Besides, her herbal cures usually work out for the best.*

A short walk down a familiar trail led him to the banks of the Shelwyn. He disrobed, dipped in the river, then lathered up from head to toe. The bar of soap felt unusually gritty but had a pleasant floral smell.

He stood on the riverbank in the afternoon sun. To pass the time, he skipped river stones for a while but soon became bored. Skipping stones was always more fun when he and Bryn tried to outdo each other. So he settled for whittling a small piece of driftwood. In a short time, he'd carved the rough shape of a duck.

After a while, his skin drew up in strange cobblestones from the caked layers of soap. He set the carving to drift away and dove into the river. After rinsing, he emerged to see the welts reduced to a faint pink rash. *Thank Maedra, Aunt Ro knows her herbs.*

He pulled on a fresh set of trousers and was waiting for the sun to dry him when he heard a woman scream. He climbed up the bank to peer over the edge to see Sadeen Tunkle slowly backing away from three young men. The Hawklin brothers circled her, oblivious to his presence.

Bruug reached for Sadeen's shoulder, but she slapped his hand away. The bully spat on the ground with casual indifference, then said out of the side of his mouth, "Don't gotta be like that, Sadeen. Besides, looks like you even brought me a present." He snatched a small basket from her hands and unwrapped two loaves of bread.

"That's not for you, Bruug Hawklin. It's for them that paid fairly for it!" Sadeen protested. "Give it back!"

"Oh, I'll give you something." Bruug smiled and tossed the basket to the side. He began to pull at the drawstring in the front of his trousers. "We all know you want it."

"I don't know what you're talking about," Sadeen said with less certainty. "Leave me alone, or I'll—!"

"You'll what?" Bruug cut her off. "You try to tell anyone who might listen, and it's your word against the three of us. Now come on; let's see what you been hiding under that dress all summer."

He grabbed a fistful of the dress at her shoulder. She tried to pull away, but Rusn stood behind her and shoved her forward. She stumbled and fell to her side, the front of her dress tearing apart. She screamed and struggled to keep herself covered while the Hawklin brothers chuckled.

Lluthean acted on instinct. In one fluid motion, he hoisted himself up the riverbank. His hand found a dirt clod. As he stood, Rusn and Heff glanced his way, but Bruug stood with his back turned. Lluthean threw the clod of dirt, and it struck Rusn in the face. He crumpled to the ground, groaning.

Lluthean charged ahead and tackled into Bruug just as the larger man turned. He collided into Bruug's midsection, but the brute deflected him. They spun around, and Lluthean's momentum caused him to tumble back into the river in a tangled mess with Bruug and Heff.

All three struggled and thrashed in the dark waters. Lluthean stood to catch his breath and caught a meaty fist across the jaw. He threw a wild elbow as he reeled back and felt the crunch of bone as he caught Heff in the nose. Then Bruug fell on him. The larger man punched through the water, mostly landing glancing blows.

"Never should have!" Bruug threw more punches. "Crawled off of your farm, boy!"

Lluthean struggled to get his feet under him. The dizzying effect of Bruug's punches and the strong current made purchase on the slippery river rocks difficult. He gasped and choked as a gulp of river water burned into his nose and then his lungs. Bruug kept raining blows down on him and tried more than once to grapple him, but without a shirt on, Lluthean managed to wriggle free.

Lluthean kicked out, catching Bruug in the groin. The space created allowed Lluthean to find his footing and start to wade back to the shallows. Heff stood in ankle-deep water, issuing a challenge and waving him forward. Streams of blood ran from a swollen nose and down the Hawklin's chin, and his upper lip swelled. Up the bank, Rusn staggered away, crying something about his eye.

One down, two to go.

Just then, a stout branch cracked into the side of Heff Hawklin's head. Sadeen grunted as she threw all her weight into the swing. She knelt topless on the riverbank holding the stout limb. Heff's neck snapped to the side, and he dropped to the riverbank. She nodded at Lluthean, ignoring her nakedness.

Two down, better odds.

"Bitch! I'll kill you as soon as I'm done with this one!" growled Bruug.
"Watch out!" shouted Sadeen.

Bruug lunged forward and found a firm hold, his burly arms snaking around Lluthean's torso and neck. The muscled bully squeezed and submerged Lluthean's face into the water. Lluthean felt something sharp and painful pop along his rib cage. He gasped, and another lungful of water burned into him. He felt Bruug drag him into deeper water and pushed and kicked off the river bottom in desperate attempts to break free of the surface. Sharp rocks cut into his feet as a distant sensation. He bit down without restraint on Bruug's forearm and tasted blood.

Dimly, he became aware of Bruug screaming, but the larger man still refused to let go. Lluthean felt a throbbing sensation pound from his chest to his head. His lungs burned, and he ached to draw in fresh air, but Bruug held him underwater. Panic overwhelmed him, and then the burning urgency to draw a breath dissipated. A strange calm feeling settled in his mind. He became oddly detached and, at the same time, aware.

His feet slid over a large round rock, and he felt strands of moss sift between his toes. Bruug thrashed and rolled him back enough for his eyes to break the surface of the water. He could count the individual drops that splashed before him. Then the strange break in time ended.

In an instant, a wave of vigor erupted from his chest and coursed into his arms and legs. The sensation surged with stinging pain that amplified into an intense, hot burning. With a scream into the water, he released the feeling. An odd vacuum erupted between him and Bruug, accompanied by a deafening clap of thunder. Then he tumbled ass over eyebrows through the air and landed upside down on his back in the mud of the riverbank.

Through blurry eyes, he saw the muscled bully fly like a rag doll to the opposite side of the river. A shower of river water landed all around him, and several small fish floated to the surface on their sides. He turned his head in confusion, trying to make sense of what had just happened. He watched as the current carried the stunned trout downstream.

From the opposite bank, Bruug lay still for several moments, then struggled to his feet. He swayed like a man given to the bottle. The bully took one look at Lluthean before scurrying up the riverbank and disappearing.

Lluthean tried to draw a full breath, then began a violent coughing episode to clear the river water from his lungs. Each time he coughed, sharp pain lanced through his ribs on his right side. He eventually heaved and emptied the contents of his stomach. Panting with splinted breaths, the simple act of remaining on his side seemed to be all he could manage.

With more effort than should be required, he rolled to his back. He felt like the world shifted underneath him as waves of vertigo rolled across his awareness. *If this is how Bryn felt after that wolf attack, small wonder he looked so rough.*

Dirt scattered near him as Sadeen descended the riverbank. He tried to open his eyes and realized they both had swelled enough to prevent a clear view. He tilted his head back to see better. She finished tying the remnants of her shirt into a knot to cover herself, then gasped and knelt beside him.

"That bad?" he asked. Sadeen pulled a trembling hand from her lips and touched his forehead. Her fingers felt warm as she brushed the hair from his face.

She leaned back, inspecting his wounds. "You have more bruises than I've ever seen on one man, and we need to bandage the cuts on your feet, but you'll live, I expect."

At the mention of his injuries, he searched the riverbank for Heff. "Are they gone then?"

"Rusn took a dirt clod to the eye, and Bruug ran off. Heff came to in time to see you do . . . whatever that was to Bruug, and he ran off as well," she said. "Wait here, and I'll be right back."

She scurried up the riverbank, then returned with her basket. "Those cuts on your feet need to be cleaned. Slide them into the water."

He followed her command and slid his feet ankle-deep into the river, and grimaced as she began picking mud and sand from the wounds. The stinging pain on the soles of his feet felt small compared to how much his entire face throbbed. After a few minutes, she ripped the tea cloth from the breadbasket in half and wrapped both of his feet.

"No tellin' when the Hawklin brothers might return. We should get you home. Do you think you can stand?" she asked.

With her help, he rose to his feet, and they began the slow return home. His eyes had swelled so much that he could barely see out of a thin slit from his left. Numerous bruises ached and throbbed, though none felt as bad as the throbbing in his head or the catch in his ribs whenever he took a deep breath.

The return home took a long time, and he limped along in silence. He focused on walking on the sides of his feet and timing his steps with shallow, splinted breaths.

"Lluthean?" Sadeen asked, interrupting his concentration.

"Huh?" he grunted.

"Was that thunderclap the good fortune of Maedra, or did you . . . ?"

Lluthean shrugged. "Maedra? What would the goddess have to do with that?"

"She controls nature, silly," she answered. "You know, thunderstorms and such."

"Let's go with that. It makes the most sense," he said through gritted teeth.

The familiar fragrance from the vines crawling over the stone hedge outside their home oriented him. "Thanks for your help, Sadeen. I can manage from here. Maybe my Aunt Rona can see you safely home."

The clamor of a galloping horse prevented him from speaking further. Lluthean tilted his head to allow him to peer out of his one good eye. A man dismounted the horse and stepped close. He recognized his uncle's boots and voice.

"What have you gotten yourself into today, Llu?" he asked.

Lluthean tried to grin, but the attempt just made his cheeks ache. "You're the third person to ask me that, and all for different reasons."

"Never mind, let's get you inside." He felt Kaellor lift him off his feet and carry him across the yard. A part of his awareness found it slightly embarrassing to have his uncle carry him in like a small child, but he released the notion as the stinging pains in his feet subsided.

As they crossed through the front door, he heard Rona gasp. "I don't know," Kaellor said to her unspoken question.

Lluthean felt himself lowered onto what he thought must be his bed. His entire body ached with bone-deep pain and overwhelming fatigue. In moments, he surrendered to sleep.

He awoke several hours later and felt like one of Rona's used tea bags: bogged down and utterly spent. A wave of dizziness caused him to lurch whenever he turned his head. The muscles in the base of his neck and shoulders threatened to cramp as he moved, and something wet and heavy covered his face. He pulled back at a dressing and found he could see better out of his left eye.

A wrap of some kind splinted his chest. It forced him to take in shallow breaths but controlled the worst part of the sharp pain of his ribs when he moved to sit. He tested, placing his feet on the floor. Thick dressings padded his feet and made standing bearable.

He limped into the common room and found Bryndor reclining back in a chair and grimacing as Rona applied the finishing touches of a tincture to the wounds on his neck and shoulder. The pungent aroma of devil's tail wafted across the room. Rona replaced a clean dressing on the wounds, then stepped back to inspect her work. Bryndor wore more bandages than clothes, but none of them showed any bloody drainage.

Lluthean limped over to the table and took a seat as Kaellor walked in through the front door.

"By the Seven Llu, you look worse than me," said Bryndor.

Lluthean turned to respond, but the muscles in his neck ached too much, so he just stared ahead. "I think I gave as good as I got." He recalled some of the particulars of the scuffle with the Hawklin brothers. "Maybe."

Lluthean could feel Bryndor's stare and finally turned just enough to catch his gaze. His brother wore a look of either frustrated judgment or puzzled annoyance. "What?" Lluthean asked.

Bryndor finally smiled and nodded in resignation.

"It's not like I went looking for trouble, Bryn. You sort of had to be there," he tried to explain.

"Alright, boys, tell me what happened, all of it," Kaellor directed.

Lluthean looked at Bryndor, who had rested his head back. Sweat gathered on his brother's forehead, and he looked a little pale. "Which part do you want to know, Kae?" Lluthean asked.

Kaellor took a seat and rested his hands on the table in an oddly formal posture. "The Tunkle girl filled us in on the Hawklins," he said. "I saw her safely home. Between her father, brothers, and the constable, the Hawklins will not bother anyone again any time soon. But I'm not talking about any of that." Kaellor leaned in with an intense expression. "Tell me about the thunder."

Chapter Twenty-One: Licking the Wounds

Bryndor labored to pull himself forward to answer Kaellor's question. His body sagged as if his limbs were filled with wet sand. Fatigue worse than a winter flux had settled into every muscle, and he grunted with the effort. "How did you know about the thunder? Weren't you in Riverton?" he asked.

"I was in Riverton this morning," Kaellor replied, drawing out the words as if puzzled, "but I was well into the Bend when I heard a thunderclap. And there is not a cloud in the sky."

"It's been a day full of Lutney's mischief," said Rona from the kitchen, where she was muddling purple flowers in a pestle.

Bryndor looked at the foul-smelling medicinal tea Rona was making him drink. He wondered if the concoction had addled his wits. "Now that you mention it, there was another thunderclap this afternoon."

"Another one?" Kaellor pulled at the chin hairs of his beard. A deep furrow formed on his brow. "Tell me everything that you two have been up to today."

Bryndor surrendered to achy fatigue and allowed his head to rest on the back of the chair. He was inhaling to relay the events of the morning when Lluthean spoke up.

"We slew Whirik's beast, Kae," said Lluthean. He tried to gesture grandly but grimaced in the simple act of turning his head. "We figured, who better to win the constable's reward than two dashing young princes with a heart for adventure?"

Kaellor seemed unmoved by Lluthean's attempt at levity and simply reached across the table and grabbed Lluthean's wrists, inspecting his injuries.

255

"Skip the dramatics Llu, this is important," said Kaellor. He walked over to Bryndor and started inspecting all of his dressings, even lifting up the bandage on his leg. The wound stung a little when exposed to the air, and Bryndor sucked in a breath but found himself more disturbed by his uncle's strange behavior. Kaellor seemed to make eye contact with Rona, who only shook her head in a negative response.

Lluthean continued, "Well, since we sort of had the morning off, we thought to take a last crack at Whirik's reward before he recruits soldiers from Riverton. You know, for all the livestock killings. Anyway, Bryn tracked this huge wolf to its den, a cave up in the Moorlok. The beast surprised him. There was a struggle. He got bit and scratched up a bit. Bryn did most of the work, and I helped a little at the end. But between the two of us, we took the beast down. Its carcass is just inside the barn." Lluthean gestured casually with his thumb.

As Lluthean relayed the story, Kaellor finished his assessment of Bryndor's injuries. "Nasty business there, Bryn. The devil's tail should prevent any corruption. You can thank your aunt for keeping an ample supply."

"I used a one-third dilution instead of the one-fifth," Rona echoed from the kitchen. "It surely burns a little, but I didn't want to chance a weaker tincture allowing rot to set in."

A little? Mogdure's balls, Ro! It felt like liquid fire!

Kaellor nodded and turned to Lluthean. "That's not all of it, Llu. Tell me about the thunder," he said.

The brothers both answered at the same time. "It happened to me when I . . ."

Bryndor looked to Lluthean, confused. "It happened to you too?"

Lluthean shrugged with a weak, guilty smile. It reminded Bryndor of the time Rona found him eating the last crumbs of an entire pie she had baked for the market.

"It happened to me when we fought the wolf. Only, this wolf," said Bryndor, "it's not just big, Kae. It's huge. We had no business tangling with it. But by the time I realized that, the thing had already cornered me. It was a mother protecting its litter. I should have died, but right when I thought it was going to kill me, this—"

"Release of power erupted and saved you," Kaellor said with a sigh.

"Yes, how did you know?" Bryndor asked.

Kaellor turned, ignoring his question. "And I gather from what Sadeen told me that the same thing happened to you, Llu?"

"Yes, Bruug had me underwater, and I thought he was going to drown me. Then, boom!" Lluthean said the last word and lifted his bruised eyebrows only to wince with a grunt of pain.

Kaellor palmed his beard in thought. "Where is this wolf now?"

"We carried the carcass back here," said Lluthean. "It's hanging over one of the stalls in the barn."

Kaellor stood and walked out. Bryndor watched him through the window. His uncle walked with an unusual brisk gait. After a few minutes, he exited the barn and stared oddly at the mountains to the north. He paced in a slow circle in the yard before returning.

Upon his return, he walked into the kitchen and pulled out a glass he rarely used. With shaky hands, he poured two fingers of whiskey, tossed it back, then poured two more. Kaellor was not a man who ever catered to drama, a fact they all knew well. The crack in his normally stoic demeanor made Bryndor feel apprehensive. *Always the calm center of the storm; where is that man now?*

Rona laid a hand on Kaellor's shoulder. "What is it, Kae?"

Kaellor sniffed long at the whiskey, then took a smaller draw and sat down at the table. "Each of you struggled for your lives today. How that occurred on the same exact day might very well have something to do with Lutney's mischief."

He glanced back over his shoulder to Rona, who arched an eyebrow, pleased to see him refer to one of the Southland gods. He continued, "I think it's very likely that in the moment of extreme danger, some part of your mantle frayed. You each channeled rune fire or something very near to it. Bryn, tell me what you felt at that moment when the thunder triggered."

Bryndor thought back to the odd moment just before the wolf lunged to finish him off. "I got pretty lucky. The wolf attacked me from behind and got a mouthful of arrow shafts. I was able to use a branch to fend it off for a little while, but the thing wrestled it away from me. All I had was my hunting knife. The wolf lunged at me, and it was like . . . I can't explain it."

"Like time stopped," said Lluthean.

Bryndor nodded. "Yes. I became aware of strange things around me, like the cold feel of the ground and the smell of old leaves. Then this intense burning feeling spread from my chest into my arms and legs. I didn't really do anything, and it just came out!"

"Boom!" Lluthean added.

"What exactly came out, Bryn?" asked Kaellor.

"It was a ball of blue light, and it sort of burst into the wolf like a ball of fire," he answered. "It burned into the wolf, Kae. Lluthean field dressed it, and the innards were cooked!"

"Mine was the same; only I was underwater when it happened," said Lluthean. "Instead of burning Bruug and me, it tossed us to opposite sides of the river."

Kaellor rubbed his eyes and sighed, then swirled the remaining whiskey in the bottom of his glass. "I don't think there can be much room for doubt, especially since it happened to each of you. That was rune fire. Nobody that I know of has called forth rune fire since the passing of your grandfather. Your father didn't even command that much destructive power. And so far from home . . . that's strange." He tipped the glass up and stared at the amber liquor.

"How did it feel right after?" asked Kaellor.

"I felt like I did when I took sick with fever a few years ago," said Lluthean. "I landed on the riverbank, and it was all I could do to lift my head and throw up. I couldn't even climb the riverbank to get home without Sadeen's help."

"That makes sense, I suppose," said Kaellor. He finished the last of his whiskey and pursed his lips to blow off the vapors. "It's no small miracle that you were in the water, Llu, or we might have to answer for the accidental death of that Hawklin bully. And I don't think the folks of the Bend would know what to make of a burned corpse. As it is, we can say Bruug had his wits addled when you got the better of him. It sounds like the other Hawklins didn't see it all, and Sadeen promised she wouldn't say a word. Besides, she thinks it was an act of the gods that saved you."

"Yes, she mentioned something about Maedra on the way home," said Lluthean.

"What do we tell Whirik about the wolf?" asked Bryndor. "Won't he think there's something odd about all the fur being burned away?"

Kaellor sighed and seemed to consider his words. "Well, first, that's not a wolf. You two might be the first ever to survive the attack of a feral wolvryn."

"That was a wolvryn? A real wolvryn? I thought those were just something you told us about to keep us out of the Moorlok when we were little!" Lluthean said with a dumbfounded expression. The bruising under his eyes made his bewilderment appear all the more haunting. Rona sat down at the table and stirred her cup of tea. She seemed to be staring into the brown liquid with unusual concentration.

"Yes," said Kaellor. "I thought they were hunted to extinction, at least in the north. And I've never heard of anything like them in the Southlands. Did anyone in the Bend see you bring it home?"

"Yes," said Bryndor. "Lots of folks."

"And I sort of invited the constable to come pay us a visit to see the thing for himself. You know, to get the reward," said Lluthean. "So, I suppose it's a little late to try to hide the thing."

"It's not the worst of our troubles today," said Kaellor. "You already dressed the carcass, and I can trim away the burned skin and fur enough that nobody should be able to tell once it starts to dry out. Whirik will be too busy the next day or two bringing the Hawklins to justice anyway. I heard they ran for Riverton to hide from the retribution of Sadeen's brothers."

Kaellor stood from the table and retrieved a skinning knife from the kitchen. "Mind your aunt, and I'll trim out the burned parts of the hide. You're not in trouble, but you both took injuries that will need some time to mend. Understand?"

"Yes, sir," they both replied.

Kaellor turned to leave for the barn, then pivoted back to face them. He tapped the hilt of the knife into his palm. "Oh, and boys, just what do you intend to do with those pups in the barn?"

Rona, who had lifted her teacup to take a sip, froze at Kaellor's question. "Did you say, pups in the barn?"

Lluthean put a hand on his ribs and stared at the table. Bryndor itched at the rough edge of the dressing on his shoulder before answering, "Well, they're just pups. We already killed the mother, and neither of us had the heart to kill them. It just seemed . . ."

"I understand, boys," said Kaellor. "No sense fretting about the small things. We'll figure it out in the morning."

Chapter Twenty-Two: Reddevek on the Trail

Reddevek stretched in the morning sun and felt his trousers slip on his hips. He tightened his belt a notch. He always lost a little weight on long rangings, but his current task had proved more time-consuming than any other.

Along the way, he had found no short supply of meat from snakes, birds, and rabbits. Every two or three days, he managed to stop and fish with relative success. He steeped rosehips, spruce needles, and licorice roots into tea and always stopped for patches of wild berries. Mushrooms and roasted crickets rounded out his fare most evenings, and he always retired for bed, feeling rather full. But engaging zenith so frequently and so far from home exacted a price, and he would need to consume at least twice as much food if he continued this way.

He allowed Zippy to graze for the better part of an hour, then broke camp. They continued down a mountain valley to the west. The game trails had made for easy travel farther up the south slope of the mountains, but as he descended, the different clusters of evergreens mingled with other trees and thick undergrowth, making the journey tedious. Every night, he preferred to climb back up the slopes to better gauge his progress.

They crested a short hill in the afternoon. Pine martens and squirrels barked at each other, and a chorus of birds volleyed songs back and forth, oblivious to his silent passage. He allowed Zippy to meander along a game trail and channeled zenith. He cast tendrils of his awareness out across the slope, searching for the pattern of the purple wildflower.

His net dragged over a few boulders, and a soft vibration like a high-pitched bell sang back along a delicate filament of zenith. Reddevek released his command of zenith and hopped off Zippy. Trail dust cracked at the edges of his mouth as he smiled for the first time in days. He clambered on top of the cluster of boulders and peered down across a small clearing. Something had felled a few of the mature evergreen trees years ago. *My guess would be a lightning strike based on those blackened trunks.*

In the open space left behind, clusters of plants with purple, pitcher-shaped flowers sprang up. He knelt and plucked a few of them and inhaled the sweet aroma. *Finally. But where do we go from here?*

He considered climbing back up the mountain slope to better survey the area but knew already from his vantage this morning that the dense forest obscured everything below the tree line. Zippy approached and picked large clumps of the flowering plant, content to graze in the open patch.

After a few peaceful moments, Zippy's ears perked forward, and he lifted his head to the west. A few seconds later, the unmistakable crack of a lone thunderclap echoed across the mountainside. Reddevek stared for several minutes at the southwest horizon.

He watched as treetops undulated, signaling the approach of a massive gust of wind. He grabbed Zippy's reins and signaled the Aarindin to kneel before leaning into the horse's flank. Dust and loose debris blew past him and up the slope of the hillside. A stronger blast of wind followed. Several seconds later, the wind stilled. A crisp, galvanic vapor permeated the air for another minute. Eventually, the sweet fragrance of the purple flowers carried back across the slope.

Zippy nickered with unease. "I know. It's gone now, but something, or more likely someone, released a blast of rune fire, or I'm a tender," said Reddevek.

The horse glanced at him with one dark eye. Reddevek chuckled, then threw a leg over Zippy's back. "Come on, Zip. The sooner we find the source of that, the sooner we can return home."

In moments, they were on their way southwest. Reddevek had no way to know how far away the source of the blast was, but he thought it might be several miles off.

They meandered up and down rolling forested hills, over streams, and through more patches of briar than he could count. In the late afternoon, another crack of thunder peeled across the cloudless sky. Reddevek dismounted and whispered in calm tones to the Aarindin. The gentle forest breeze remained undisturbed by this second eruption. *That one either came from farther away or perhaps from down in a valley.*

He pushed Zippy hard over the next two days and gave up on significant efforts to forage. Instead, he focused on finding the least encumbered path to the southwest. Two or three times an hour, he engaged zenith to survey the area.

They stopped each night, and he found an endless supply of nourishment from the wild berries, roots, and tubers. But when Zippy nuzzled him awake on the third day, he felt seriously ill. The way the Aarindin puffed breath through pursed lips made him think the horse was expressing worry.

"I'm awake; I'm awake, Zip. Just give me a moment," he said.

The horse nickered again, then wandered a few feet away to nibble at the undergrowth. He stretched his feet, and muscles in his calf immediately cramped. He drew his feet up to stretch, and the muscles along the front of his legs cramped.

"Ahh, Taker's nobby tits!" he yelled and sat up to both stretch and rub cramped muscles.

Several minutes later, and with a bead of sweat on his brow, he lay back down. His head felt light, and the ground felt like it was tilting. He remembered the lectures he'd given to tenders on the draft. In Aarindorn, the term described the sickness that came from channeling too much zenith. He knew well the risks of employing the full measure of his gift too often and so far from home.

Zenith existed in every living thing, but drawing it into one's self and shaping it exacted a price. Somehow, the connection to Aarindorn, or maybe its people, mitigated the toll. But isolated and separated from home meant he paid the cost himself. With sheepish understanding, he sensed that far too much of his essence had drained away from the exertion of the past few days. The pace he set, combined with a decrease in his ability to forage, had aggravated the condition.

And now, I'm in the first stages of the draft. If we don't find the source of that rune fire today, I'm going to have to stop to recover, and that could take a week.

With trepidation, he rifled through one of his saddlebags and found a small pouch holding a tan and white powder. He looked at the ground herb and sighed. Not once in his entire Outrider career had he ever considered utilizing vivith, but he felt pressed into a corner. He knew he could make a weak tea of the drug and should be able to continue, but that decision held risks. He knew strong Outriders in the past who had become addicted after just one dose. In the Abrogator's War, others had used the tincture and pressed themselves so hard they literally fell dead on their Aarindin.

He looked over to Zippy, who seemed to cast a judgmental eye in his direction. "I'm not there yet, Zip; I'm just thinking about my options."

He replaced the pouch and instead brewed a stiff black tea. After a potful of tea and a breakfast of tubers and berries, he broke camp. He felt a little better once mounted, but muscles along the small of his back and thighs threatened to cramp at different intervals.

He knuckled a particularly bothersome spasm in his back and almost missed the subtle change in the terrain. Though they walked along a game trail, no animal tracks littered the ground. No hoofprints, anyway. Instead, he noticed the occasional paw print of a large predator. Something tugged at his memory.

His heart quickened, and his fatigue dissipated. He dismounted and palmed his weapons; the handaxe and long saber still hung from his belt. Reassured, he retrieved his bow and slapped Zippy to send him back up the trail before continuing down the path.

Within a few hundred yards, the tracks appeared more numerous. He engaged his gift, and memories of his youth flooded his awareness. He recalled the last time he'd assessed the tracks of a wolvryn. He never thought he would see one again. His gift revealed that the tracks belonged to a lone wolvryn and that all of the paw prints were at least half a week old. He released his command of the flow and shrugged off a small wave of nausea. He felt too excited to allow the moment to be tainted by the draft.

He knelt to place his hand inside the paw print. "You're a big one, too." He surveyed the surrounding woods. Birds and martens chattered without care. *You were here. But where did you go?*

He walked back up the trail and recovered Zippy, then led him by the reins. The horse nickered softly but followed him without protest. The trail and the deep-set prints made for easy travel, and he followed the path without the need for his gift.

Eventually, he crested a hill and looked down at the mouth of a large cave. The ground before the cave entrance appeared compacted from use, but something else seemed unnatural.

He pulled at Zippy's reins, but the Aarindin whinnied and pulled back. Something about the area had spooked the animal. "Suit yourself. I'll be right back."

He walked the horse back several paces and lashed the reins to a small tree. Walking around the hillside, he approached the clearing before the cave mouth. He drew a deep breath and summoned his command of zenith once again, then cast the net of his awareness across the area. His gift revealed the tracks of a single adult wolvryn and two pups. Bits of wolvryn fur scintillated, sending vibrations back to him through filaments of his gift. A faint musty fragrance permeated his awareness, and he shivered at the memory of the last time he'd experienced the smell of the creatures.

Outside the cave, old bloodstains and trampled plants revealed a struggle. He thought the discovery could reflect the wolvryn dragging its prey back to its den until he noticed human tracks.

Two different sets of soft-soled leather boots interspersed the wolvryn prints. Tendrils of his gift sang when they ran across the old bloodstains, and the familiar resonance of a gifted traveled back to his awareness. And not just any gifted; only someone of immense power left behind blood that still thrummed with zenith after a couple of hours.

Reddevek sucked in his breath and released his grip on zenith. His head swam, and he fell to his knees. The draft caught up with him, and the world tilted. He slumped, overcome with retching and dry heaves. When the worst of it passed, he crawled forward and parted the trampled undergrowth. Mixed among the old blood, wolvryn prints, and human tracks lay a single horseshoe print.

The Outrider struggled to clear his head. He doubted the reality of the single print before him and stared at it for more than a minute. Cast in a clear outline in the soft ground, a whimsical capital *D* sat in the center of the print. "What's anyone from Dulesque doing all the way out here?"

Reddevek crawled forward and discovered more of the unique tracks. They mixed with the hoofprints of at least two other unshod horses, and all three led back to the south. He sat back on his heels, considering the new discovery.

Eventually, he grabbed a small sapling and pulled himself to his feet. The light-headedness that washed over him took nearly a full minute to dissipate. He staggered back up to Zippy and retrieved the pouch of vivith but once again thought better of it. After a quick gesture, the Aarindin knelt, allowing him to mount. They followed the hoofprints along a well-marked trail that led down a steep hill winding through the woods to the south. Within an hour, Zippy stumbled over bramble and onto an expansive field of grass cropped short by a herd of sheep.

Reddevek sat a moment at the edge of the pasture. *The regent's folly indeed. The horse is shod from a Dulescan blacksmith. Dulesque holds no love for anyone tied to the capital. Berling was from Dulesque. Grind me twice over. How did they know to send anyone here?*

Chapter Twenty-Three: Business in the Bend

Kaellor thought he'd woken early, but the whistle of a tea kettle announced Rona's activity in the kitchen. He dressed, then found her crushing more wildflowers in a mortar and pestle. The sweet fragrance of Maedra's pitchers carried across the room, and beams of early morning light reflected off the hammered metal wall above the mapmaking workspace. The bright yellow shafts combined with the aromatic poultice and made the room feel cheery. *Funny how light and smell can do that.*

He nodded as if to say hello. Rona smiled back, then nodded at the whistling tea kettle. He quickstepped into the kitchen, grabbed a hot pad, and removed the pot from the heat. A different scent, sharper and slightly sweet, permeated the steam. He looked into the kettle to see a full metal tea strainer bobbing up and down.

"How did you know I would be up so early?" he asked.

"It didn't take much imagination," she answered. "I knew you would want to meet with the constable this morning to control as much of the story as possible. Folks in the Bend will be anxious to see for themselves what caused all the trouble lately."

"Eggs?" he asked.

"Please, and maybe toast some bread," said Rona.

He walked out onto the front porch. Rings crouched at the end of the porch, prepared to pounce on a hovering butterfly. Two goats nibbled at grass at the far end of the yard near the barn. He walked around to the back of the house and opened the small chicken coop. Several hens clucked their approval and wandered out onto the lawn to begin a day of grazing. He retrieved four eggs and returned inside. A few minutes later, he served up spiced scrambled eggs and toasted bread with tea. Rona set her poultice to the side and joined him at the table.

They ate in companionable silence. "I'll get the carcass of the wolvryn into town. Do you need anything while I'm there?" he asked.

"Yes, please stop into the creamery and bring back some cheese and extra cheesecloth. I could use more for the poultices for the boys," she said, "and I am curious to know what Whirik did with the Hawklin boys."

"I'll find out," he said. He stood and cleared the table. "I shouldn't be long."

"I dosed the boys with just a touch of stilben root last night, so they should sleep a few hours yet. Maedra knows they need it to recover from everything," she said.

Kaellor peered into the rooms of his nephews. Bryndor lay in a deep sleep on his back. The dressings over his shoulder and thigh appeared dry. He sniffed at the wounds, relieved to discover the spicy, antiseptic smell of devil's tail and not rot. Kaellor resisted an urge to lift his bandages. *No good can come of it, and Ro has things well in hand.*

Lluthean lay on his side with his splinted rib cage protected by the mattress. A soft buzzing snore escaped the younger boy's lips; his nose was still swollen and congested from his injuries. He shifted his legs but remained asleep. The swelling around his eyes had dissipated, leaving dark purple bruising like a mask. *At least the shape of his face seems back to normal.*

His sense of apprehension caused the muscles between his shoulders to grab and tighten. *The day is just begun, and there's plenty more to it.*

He walked out to their yard and grounded his senses in the moment. The faint smell of horse wafted from the barn. In the distance, birds chirped. He practiced the simple act of breathing taught to him so many years ago when he'd trained in Aarindorn. After a few minutes of introspection, he mastered his lingering worry over the events of the prior day.

He walked out to the barn and peered into the pen holding the wolvryn pups. They curled around each other in the corner, still asleep. *I would love to know the truth behind your arrival in the Southlands. Let's hope the constable buys my version of events.*

He backed their small wagon alongside the wolvryn carcass and heaved it off the gate. The wagon listed to the side as the massive body careened onto it. He then lifted the hind legs onto the cart, and the beast's broad head rolled to the side. For a moment, he thought he saw sunlight reflecting from the eyes of the wolvryn carcass. Closer inspection showed that they were glowing with a pale blue light.

He cupped a hand over one of the eyes and sucked in a breath. *They weren't doing that when I trimmed away the singed fur last night. I can't very well let the constable see this. Convincing the man about a freak of nature is one thing, but something like this will draw far too much attention.*

He retrieved his skinning knife and tapped at one of the glowing orbs, expecting it to puncture and leak viscous fluid. Instead, the point of the blade vibrated and rebounded back with a high-pitched plinking sound. He applied the flat of the blade along the lower eyelid. The eyeball protruded slightly, and he pressed harder.

"Ho!" he exclaimed as the intact oval globe popped out of the socket and into the air. He caught the orb before it flew over his shoulder. Just smaller than the size of his palm, the eyeball still emitted a faint pale blue light.

He turned it over and ran his fingers along its outer edge. Like a small, perfect, crystalline egg, there were no seams or imperfections. *Creatures of zenith, no doubt. I wonder why I never knew about this.*

He removed the other eyeball with the same technique. The globe popped out of the socket to produce an identical glowing crystalline egg. He set the orbs on a small shelf and spent more time inspecting the remnants of the pelt, the nose, and teeth. Other than the massive size of the creature, the carcass held no further surprises.

He examined the oval orbs on the shelf once again. As the light of day brightened, the orbs dimmed and appeared like nothing more than curious glass trinkets. *Sorting that out will take some time.*

He hitched a gelding to the wagon and made his way into town, passing by several townsfolk out on morning errands. More than one person looked with interest at the carcass in the back of his wagon. He smiled at most, nodded at some, but made instinctual mental assessments of each as they passed.

Family of four, hands occupied with parcels, no visible weapons, familiar from the market . . . Matriarch of that farm near the Tellends, no threats there. Della and her brother from the Ram out to gather their supplies for the day.

Encountering no new faces or strangers, he made a straight path to the stockade in the center of town. As he tied the gelding to a hitch and climbed down from the wagon, Lawn Whirik walked out onto the boardwalk in front of the jailhouse.

The constable tucked his thumbs into the belt over his navy surcoat. "In all the commotion to deal with the Hawklins, I haven't had time to check in to see if the stories I heard about your nephews ring true."

The two men shook hands. "They are true enough," said Kaellor. "I brought you the carcass as proof."

Lawn walked around to the back of the wagon and inspected the body. He stood there long moments gazing at the size of the wolvryn. Without a word, he stepped forward and placed his hand against the paw. Finding that the pads extended beyond the length of his bony fingers, he raised his eyebrows, either in amazement or fear. Kaellor couldn't be sure. Next, he pushed back at the purple-lined lips to inspect the fangs, the most gruesome of which overlapped like three-inch-long curved ivory daggers.

The constable wiped his hands across his trousers and stepped back. "Have you ever seen anything like this before?" he asked.

"Not in my travels of the Southlands," said Kaellor. "But in the north, we had sightings of alpha wolves like this on rare occasions. They lived high in the Korjinth but came down to hunt during tough winters."

Lawn considered Kaellor's explanation. "That makes some sense, I suppose. I can certainly understand how a wolf this size would find easy pickings among farm animals. How did your boys manage it?"

"They'll both be scarred for the experience, at least Bryndor will be," said Kaellor. "Lluthean managed to walk out of the Moorlok without any injuries until he met up with the Hawklins."

At the mention of the rough family from the south side of town, Lawn screwed up his face like he'd just swallowed sour milk. "Yes, about that," said Lawn.

Kaellor looked over his shoulder to the jailhouse. "Don't tell me you let them go?" he asked.

Lawn sighed. "I never had them in the first place. Sadeen's father and brothers got to the Hawklin farm before I did. There was a brawl of sorts. One of the Tunkle boys got worse than he gave. Gruus stabbed him with a pitchfork in the back. In the back, of all things." The constable scratched along a skinny forearm. "What kind of man stabs a boy with a pitchfork in the back?"

You know very well who, and it's no surprise for how you've allowed them to run rough through town with no consequences. "Will the Tunkle boy recover?" asked Kaellor.

"It's too early to say," said Lawn. "He can move all his parts, and his mother says he makes water without blood, so that's a good thing. Gruus lit out of town with two of his boys on horseback toward Riverton. The youngest one, Rusn, is recovering at the Hawklin farm. He pretty much confirmed everything Sadeen said. He earned himself a broken leg in the fight with the Tunkle boys and will likely lose his eye. That's a fair price to pay for his part in everything."

"What do you plan to do about the others?" asked Kaellor.

"Sadeen's older brother and two cousins are already on the hunt to track down the Hawklins. If Gruus disappears into Riverton, they have my written report for the authorities there. I don't imagine he will ever be back, and Gruus's wife seemed actually a little relieved to be rid of the man." The constable leaned forward over the edge of the wagon. His shoulders sagged, and he hung his head for a moment.

Kaellor rubbed the back of his hand along the edge of his beard at his chin. "I expect you'll keep me informed if the Tunkles find them?"

"It's the least I can do, Kevold." He straightened up, appearing to recover something of his official title and bearing. "Don't you lose any sleep over it. I should have brought that family to heel years ago. I'll make sure they see justice one way or another."

Kaellor thought about some of the precautions he might need to take. Until the Tunkles apprehended Bruug and his sons, they posed a threat. *It's a shame we never took on a dog. Perhaps some snares around the perimeter of the house, and I'll check on the soundness of the wood beam barricade over the front door tonight.*

"I imagine you came to collect the reward?" asked Lawn.

Kaellor finished the mental list of the things he needed to secure around their home and tucked it away into a corner of his mind. "It's not mine to collect. I just wanted to give everyone in the Bend a sense of relief and find out about the Hawklins."

Lawn nodded in agreement. "If it's all the same to you, I'll need to show that carcass to the margrave as proof. It's a generous pelt. While I'm in Riverton, I could drop it by the tanners."

Kaellor pinched the chin hairs of his beard between thumb and forefinger. *How many people will believe my tale about an alpha wolf before someone wise enough comes asking more questions? More questions mean more people. Years of anonymity dashed away in the space of an afternoon.* The insulation between his family and the abrogators suddenly felt rather thin.

"How about this, Lawn," he countered. "Take the carcass to the margrave, but then dispose of it. We have no need for the fur, and I'm not even sure it would be suitable for outerwear. Besides, the expense alone isn't worth the trouble."

"Consider it done," said the constable. "I know the boys are nursing wounds, but the townsfolk are throwing a party. You know, to recognize the end of the threat. We are gathering at the Ram. Do you think they could make an appearance? Say, near the dinner bell? You don't have to prepare anything, just get them to the inn, and we'll take care of the rest."

Kaellor considered the best answer. Part of him wanted nothing more than for the entire affair to wash downstream like so much driftwood on the Shelwyn.

That wolvryn had everyone on edge, and more than a few folks are happy to see the most gnarled branch of the Hawklin family tree fall away. The boys do deserve some recognition, and Bryndor especially craves a sense of belonging.

"I think Rona and I can patch them up well enough for an appearance," he said.

With the issue settled, Lawn organized a few burly young men to transfer the wolvryn carcass from Kaellor's wagon to the constable's. Four men were just able to complete the task, and once Lawn welcomed onlookers, a sizeable crowd gathered.

Kaellor answered a few questions as politely as possible, reaffirming his belief that the creature was a rare alpha wolf and that things should return to normal in the Bend. He redirected queries about the encounter with the beast to his more significant concern for the Hawklins and the recovery of Sadeen's brother. His deflection found eager ears. Bruug, in particular, it seemed, had developed quite a reputation, and many were happy to learn of his departure.

After more than an hour of the tedious interaction, Kaellor excused himself. He stopped at the creamery, where he purchased cheese and cheesecloth for Rona's poultices and managed to remove himself from another litany of probing inquiries about the alpha wolf by explaining that Rona would be waiting impatiently for her cheesecloth. The shop owner seemed mollified both by his explanation and his promise to attend the party.

He navigated the backside of the crowd, which had continued to grow outside the jailhouse. He caught bits and pieces of conversation from the constable. "Yes, I'm sure, it's an alpha wolf, from the mountains . . . you can see for yourself they're as real as you and me . . ."

Though he took comfort in Lawn's acceptance of his explanation, the stiffness that gathered in his shoulders and back relaxed only when he drove the wagon along the ivy-covered stone wall outside their home.

He set the horses to graze and walked inside to find Bryndor and Lluthean reclining in chairs. Discarded bloodstained bandages lay on the floor, replaced by clean ones. Rona hummed in the kitchen, busy with her medicinal tea.

Bryndor turned his head, grimacing with the effort. "Good morning, Kae." A half-smile played across his face.

"It's good to see you both up. How do you feel?" he asked.

"Thanks to Ro, I'm better," said Bryndor. He sat up straighter in his chair and sipped at a cup of tea. He screwed up his face and wrinkled his nose, but it seemed more from the taste than any genuine discomfort.

"And you?" Kaellor asked with a nod to Lluthean.

"Yes, better," Lluthean grunted. "I can see out of both eyes today. But I think I'll stay clear of Bruug Hawklin for a while."

Red bruising stained the whites of Lluthean's eyes, making him look even more ghastly. Kaellor knelt to inspect his nephew. He pressed thumbs around Lluthean's eyes, nose, and face. Satisfied that none of the delicate bones had shifted, he stood.

What are you looking for? You're no healer, and you wouldn't know what to do if you thought his injuries were more severe.

"The Hawklins won't be a problem," said Kaellor. He reviewed his conversation with the constable. "And everyone seemed agreeable to the idea that the wolvryn was a rare alpha wolf from the mountains. They want to see you both tonight for a recognition dinner of sorts."

At the mention of a party, Lluthean stood up. He knew better than to complain, but the flushing of his cheeks betrayed his discomfort. He limped more than walked into the kitchen with his empty cup. "More tea, Ro?" he asked.

Ro arched an eyebrow and considered her nephew. "You said you wouldn't drink any more of this foul poison."

"That was before I knew that the people had demanded an audience!" said Lluthean. He grabbed at his sore ribs as he spoke. "Please, Ro? The stuff tastes worse than it smells."

"And it smells like the backside of a dead—" said Bryndor, but he stopped when Rona cocked her head, challenging him to continue. "Like something unsavory."

"However," said Lluthean, "it helps a lot. So, can I please have a bit more?"

"May you please?" Rona corrected.

"Yes, please. May I please have a bit more of that amazing medicine, Aunt Ro?" Lluthean asked.

Kaellor felt reassured to see some of the boys' playfulness and vigor return. He spent the next few hours checking on the security of their home while the boys rested.

The stout wood barricade they lowered over the only door at night needed no adjustments. He walked the perimeter of their farm. Just beyond the chicken coop, thick briar and bramble pressed against the fencing. *A Hawklin would have to be pretty motivated to come in this way.*

Unfortunately, the rest of their property provided little defense against an intruder. Anyone with a desire could easily walk through the pasture in which the horses grazed or come through the wide entryway between the ivy-covered stone wall. He considered that their best defense might be to set up a watch at night.

A familiar voice interrupted his thoughts. "Everyone in town is talking about the Scrivson boys, so we thought to come see for ourselves."

Kaellor chided himself and turned to see Markum, Emile, and Harland Tellend on their horse-drawn wagon. *You're so lost in your head, you didn't even hear them coming.*

He stepped forward to offer Emile a hand down. She shooed him away and hopped down from the wagon with an agility that defied her age. Standing barely five feet tall, she peered up at him with bright eyes surrounded by sun-wrinkled skin.

She held a basket filled with Maedra's pitchers and a few other herbs. "How are the boys, Kae?" she asked.

"Thanks to Ro's poultices and medicinal tea, they are on the mend. Why don't you come inside and see for yourself?"

The Tellends wandered inside. After their initial shock at seeing the severity of the boys' injuries, they settled into the kind of conversation bred by history and familiarity. Emile produced a sausage bake, a pie tin brimming with scrambled eggs, herbs, and sausage. Rona added jam and bread, and they crowded around the table.

"Now then," said Markum. "Suppose you tell us exactly what happened yesterday."

Chapter Twenty-Four: Politics in Beclure

Karragin stood beside her mount outside the district house in Beclure. She felt thankful for the small entourage accompanying them from Stone's Grasp. Hours before, Chancle had convinced the Duchesses Endera and Phelond to accompany him inside. Within a short time, hysterical wailing and cries of grief began piercing the thick walls of the district house.

She glanced to Nolan, who appeared to be attempting to hide in the shadow of his Aarindin. *I wasn't sure how we were going to tell them. That's one favor I owe you, Chancle.*

She and Nolan waited outside, enduring the awkward scrutiny of the locals walking through the central business district. Nolan became frustrated by the leering and retreated inside one of the covered wagons.

Just when she thought about joining him, a thin man dressed in tailored grey clothing trimmed with dark green accents greeted them.

"Good afternoon, and please forgive my delay. I only just learned of your arrival," said the man with a polite bow. "I am Commissioner Leveck, and it's my pleasure to welcome you to the district house of Beclure."

"Your welcome is most appreciated, Commissioner," said Karragin. "My name is Karragin Lefledge."

"Yes, I know. The vice regent informed us of your arrival," said the man. His mouth twitched with an odd tic, and he pinched the seams of his vest with nervous repetition. "He was only just able to extract himself from what I can guess was a heated conversation. My sincere apologies for your delay here. Had I known, I would have seen to your comfort immediately."

"I understand," said Karragin. "It's not your fault."

The commissioner seemed noticeably put at ease by her acceptance of the delay. "Thank you," said Leveck, "still, I feel that we must make amends. If you would allow me small liberty, I could see to the comfort of your entourage?"

Karragin placed her thumb and index fingers in her mouth and released a curt, loud whistle. Nolan exited one of the covered wagons with a bewildered expression.

"The covered wagons belong to the vice regent," said Karragin. "If you can direct them to an inn, I suspect they are more than capable of managing their affairs. My brother and I are escorting them as representatives of the Outriders, and we need no special accommodations."

Leveck paled at her apparent rejection. "Please, the vice regent awaits you in the dining hall. He gave me explicit instructions. If you would both accompany me inside?"

So, it's acceptable to risk offense to the regent, but the Taker's ire if you cross the vice regent? Thank the Giver Chancle holds some influence west of Lake Ullend, or we would still be waiting, I think.

Karragin nodded in acceptance of the invitation. The commissioner snapped his fingers, and several servants rushed down the steps of the district house. One man led the Aarindin away while another approached one of the wagon drivers. Karragin retrieved the sack holding the grondle horn, then she and Nolan followed Leveck inside.

The double doors led to a wide hallway with portraits of high families on the walls. Stern faces glowered down at all who passed. She recognized the family crests of Lellendule and Endule. They walked down the length of the hall to a set of glass double doors and passed under a portrait of the Duchess Endera Endule. The painting captured her sitting while surrounded by several children. Velda stood at her right with a thin smile. *You smiled like that just before you tried to kill Nolan, like a cat anticipating the pounce.*

Leveck pushed open the double doors and ushered them into a formal dining hall. Chancle stood in discussion with several people dressed in formal attire. Men wore grey or black vests and surcoats trimmed with dark green, and women wore high-quality dresses embroidered with delicate stitching across the shoulders and wrists in patterns common to the western duchies.

Chancle excused himself and approached them. Despite having endured what must have been a stressful conversation, he appeared his usual cheery self. His compassionate eyes held no sadness. Instead, he beamed a reassuring smile framed by a smartly manicured beard.

"I fear I owe you both an apology," he said, then waved a server over. The man held a tray with fluted glasses full of a faint green liquid. "Care to sample this? I found it refreshing; they call it cold spruce tea." He lifted a glass and sipped.

Karragin tilted her head, removed two glasses, and handed one to Nolan. She sniffed at the tea. It held a strange tangy aroma mixed with a subtle hint of pine. She sipped once, surprised by the delicate flavors: tangy, then oddly minty, then just a whiff of pine at the back of the mouth.

"If there is more of this tea, then you're forgiven," said Nolan. He'd already drained one glass and swapped the empty flute for a full one from the server.

"Is everything alright, Chancle?" Karragin asked. "Think nothing of the wait. That's part of the job. But I didn't expect you to bear the responsibility of extending formal condolences to the Endules. Warden Elbiona—"

"Elbiona sent you on a diplomatic mission without all the necessary tools to fend off the wolves," said Chancle. "I, on the other hand, fight off wolves for the greater good of Aarindorn on a regular basis."

"What exactly did you tell their mothers?" she asked.

"I told them the truth," said Chancle. "Velda and Berling died defending a village in the Borderlands from a crush of grondle."

"We heard their grieving," said Nolan with puffed-out cheeks.

"Did they accept your explanation? You were in here alone with them a long time," said Karragin.

Chancle gazed around the room, then drew his soft oval eyes to hers. "It went about as it does any time a parent learns of the untimely death of their child. I imagine that they will have specific questions for you, but the grondle horn should go a long way to satisfying any doubts they might have."

The ringing of a high-pitched dinner bell interrupted further conversation. A manservant stepped forward. "Ladies and gentlemen of the realm, if you would find a seat, Her Grace the Duchess Endera of Beclure and Her Grace the Duchess Phelond of Dulesque shall join us shortly."

Chancle led them over to a long table with seating for twenty. The servants placed name tags for all the people in attendance—except Nolan and Karragin. The open chairs left the Lefledge siblings at the end of the table, far removed from any position of importance. Chancle and other guests of high status sat close to the duchesses. *And frankly, that suits me just fine.*

By both their attire and physical similarities, Karragin surmised that Endules occupied most of the other seats at the table. She recognized Phelond's husband, Duke Bexter. The rotund man had married into the family and rarely attended court affairs. She remembered something her father once said about his keen eye for trade. She had trouble identifying the names of most of the others. By their casual banter and relative lack of anything approaching despondence, she guessed that the duchesses had yet to share the news regarding the deaths of Berling and Velda.

As the servants placed appetizers on small plates before the guests, Endera and Phelond entered the dining hall. All in attendance stood while the two women assumed seats at the far end of the grand table.

Phelond nodded once toward Karragin and Nolan. Her eyes still appeared swollen, and her nose unusually boggy and red. *And who can blame her? It's a small wonder either of them attended us this evening. I wonder why they didn't share the news with the others here?*

Endera flashed a stony glance to their end of the table but carried on a quiet conversation with Chancle and the others sitting close. Karragin nibbled at the appetizer, some type of light cheese with a crownberry compote. She vaguely recognized the flavors as she considered the room. *How many courses are served for a diplomatic occasion? If they serve soup next, this could be a painful eight- to twelve-course ordeal.*

Nolan must have developed the same distaste for formal dinners, as his shoulders slumped when the servants arrived with bowls and a large tureen. They ladled out the savory broth for each guest.

Karragin blew across a hot spoon in preparation to sample the soup but fumbled her spoon in surprise at the duchess's voice, which cut through all of the small conversations in the dining hall. "How do you find the food, Outrider?"

So, it's Outrider—not daughter of the regent or escort of the vice regent.

Karragin looked to Nolan, who seemed to be searching for something in the bottom of his soup bowl. She turned to address the duchess. "Your Grace, it's quite generous, far more than we are accustomed to in our responsibilities. Thank you for including us." She looked down the table to Endera with her usual, calm expression, feeling more than a little thankful for her mother's resting asshole gaze.

That's about all you'll get from me, so go back to your soup.

Color flared across Endera's cheeks as if the woman could sense Karragin's thoughts.

Chancle attempted to deflect the conversation to a lighter topic. "The soup is complex. I might have your cook share the recipe to take back to Stone's Grasp."

Endera stared back at Karragin without blinking and replied, "Yes, I'm sure that can be arranged, Cousin."

The duchess sipped her soup, then raised her voice again. "Outrider, the vice regent made the purpose of your visit clear to Her Grace, the Duchess Phelond, and me. But I would like to hear from you directly."

So much for fighting off the wolves, Chancle. Father always said the best way to engage trouble is head-on.

"That Nolan and I are in attendance is not a coincidence, Your Grace. As the only surviving members of the quad, it seemed appropriate to express our condolences to Velda and Berling's families personally. What would you like to know?"

More than one spoon dropped into a bowl as different family members registered the significance of Karragin's words. Duke Bexter, in particular, appeared overwhelmed and gaped first to Karragin, then to his wife, then back to Karragin. Soup ran down his chin and dribbled onto the front of his grey vest.

"Did she just," the duke stammered. "Did I just hear? Why am I only now learning of this?"

The Duchess Phelond stared, wordless, into her lap. Fresh tears streamed down her cheeks, and her shoulders quivered with soundless sobs, confirming the duke's fear.

Endera regarded her cousins from Dulesque with a look of disgust, then gripped a handful of tablecloth, causing crystalware to shift across the table. Chancle reached forward with a grunt to catch Endera's full crystal goblet before it tipped over. Beyond his effort, the dining hall had fallen into somber silence.

"Appropriate," snapped Endera. She clipped the word with theatrical venom, filling the dining hall. She held an expression one might make after swallowing a piece of bitter cheese. "That's such a useful word, is it not? It makes one wonder how *appropriate* it was to place a novice in the position of prime. Maybe if someone more *appropriate* led that particular ranging, then two Endule children would not have perished. Maybe my questions themselves are not *appropriate*. What do you think, Prime?"

Karragin locked any frustration away behind the wall. She remained detached from her emotion and approached the conversation like a game of king's gambit. *The game only continues when all players participate. So, don't play, don't even look at the cards. Just walk away.*

"I think that you have a right to ask those questions and more, Your Grace. No one can measure the depth of your loss, so I won't offer you condolences and expect that to make one shred of difference. I personally know that it doesn't. But you have our sincere sympathies all the same."

Good Karra, neutral tone, calm. May that be the end of this. She dipped her spoon into her bowl but stopped halfway to her mouth.

"I do have questions," said Endera with a sharp tone. "Like, how appropriate was it to task any of the Outriders to the Borderlands? Or how appropriate was it to allow two Lefledge children, raised without the compassion and common sense of a good mother, into the Outriders in the first place? The entire situation smells like nothing more than the regent's folly."

And just like that, the barrier cracked. Before Karragin realized what she was doing, her gift flared with intensity, and a hot current surged out from her arca prime and into her arms. She barely resisted the urge to smash a fist through the furniture. Instead, she stood with slow purpose, grabbed the sides of the table, and lifted the entire mass. She balanced it parallel to the floor and lifted the far edge just below Endera's chin.

Several people gasped and pushed back their chairs. Aside from the creaking timbers supporting the span of the table, the hall remained silent. Endera stared slack-jawed at Karragin, and much of the color had drained from the duchess's face. Karragin held the table long moments and waited. She glanced to Chancle, who just shook his head and threw his napkin into his soup bowl, then pinched the bridge of his nose.

Not sorry, Chancle. Sometimes you have to punch a wolf in the nose to get it to stop biting.

"Your Grace," Karragin said with a placid, effortless expression. "Your behavior implies that you are under the delusion that you are the only person in this room who ever lost someone in the service to the kingdom. Since that is not the case, let me educate you. You insult my family when you should have asked me about the friendship Velda and I developed on the ranging, how she offered me support and guidance. You should have asked me the specific way she sacrificed herself for the good of others so that you could remember her heroism. You should have asked me about what a wonderful friend and mentor Berling was to my brother.

"We came here out of respect for the friends we lost and because of the bond between Outriders. You're grieving now, but if you think you can speak ill of my mother or father to my face and not expect a significant response from me . . . well, I think you can see you are wrong. In the future, I suggest you choose your words more carefully. One never knows how the daughter of the regent might respond without the constant nurturing of a good mother."

Karragin dropped the table, and the massive piece of furniture thundered to the floor. Glasses tipped over, and soup splashed across the tablecloth from every bowl. The room remained silent for several seconds, and Karragin stifled her gift, relieved to discover none of the fatigue she'd encountered in the Borderlands.

She walked to the far end of the table and unwrapped the grondle horn, then placed it in front of Endera. "Velda told me that you have some affinity with the gift, an ability to discern if someone is telling the truth. Go on, channel. Tell me when you are ready."

Endera swallowed hard, then seemed to regain some of her composure. The duchess reached a hesitant hand forward and placed it on Karragin's forearm. Light scattered across the runes visible above the neckline of her dress, and Endera nodded that she was ready.

Karragin looked directly into Endera's gaze and maintained her tranquil expression. "You can choose to believe what you want to about me. But know this, Nolan and I, we didn't kill your daughter. We didn't kill Berling. I admired Velda's skill, and Berling was an exceptional medic. Grondle have returned to the Borderlands, and that's a problem bigger than anyone in this room. If you intended to wound me with words about my father and mother, then congratulations. You did."

Karragin lingered there, unblinking, studying the older woman. The duchess released her hold and sank back in her chair, appearing deflated as an empty wineskin.

Better an empty one than one threatening to burst at the seams.

Endera cast her eyes to the floor as they welled with tears.

"It's clear that our presence is only adding to your family's stress. Enjoy the rest of your dinner. We can see ourselves out, and I will pass along your respects to the regent." She turned to find Nolan standing at attention at the far end of the table. The two walked back down the wide corridor of the district house. Somehow, the portraits of the line of Endules felt less stern and more somber to her.

Just as they reached the door, Chancle's voice interrupted their exit. "Karra, wait."

She turned to watch the man who was nearly her uncle rush down the hallway. She expected a rebuke, but he smiled as he approached, and that left her confused. He settled gentle hands on her shoulders, looked into her eyes, then gave her a warm embrace.

"I sometimes forget how much of your mother you have in you," he said. "You handled that very well."

She felt the slightest wrinkle of a frown crease her brow and ran her tongue along the scar of her upper lip. "So, you're not angry with me? I fear I've left you with a bit of a diplomatic mess."

"Believe it or not, I think you framed the conversation much better than you realize," said Chancle. "In thirty seconds, you demonstrated more guile than that woman has in all her years. You managed to intimidate her physically, of course. Then you laid bare her shameful behavior before her family. That should keep the old wolf from biting for a long time. You managed to remind her that you are the regent's daughter, a matter of no small consequence. And then, that last masterful bit allowing her to read you . . . perfection."

He waggled a playful finger at her. "And here I was, thinking you were poorly equipped to handle it all. You've learned a thing or two at court with your father, I think."

She relaxed and bent her mouth in a half-smile. "Thanks for that. Will you be alright without us? I think Nolan and I would prefer to gather our things and rejoin the Outriders."

"I will manage just fine," he said. "I knew you would both depart once the official condolences were given. If you need any provisions, assign the cost to my entourage before you leave."

They exchanged embraces, and Chancle opened the door for them. "When will I see you again?" he asked.

Karragin shrugged. "I'm not sure. Warden Elbiona seemed uncertain how to deploy us in the field, but the appearance of grondle in the Borderlands could change everything."

"Well, until we cross paths again, eyes to the horizon," he said.

"Eyes to the horizon," they replied in unison, then stepped out into the night.

Chapter Twenty-Five: A Warden Meets a Guster

Reddevek followed the tracks with the Dulescan insignia to the end of the farmstead. They continued through a wood gate and onto a dirt road that wound into a small town, and he soon lost them amid numerous other horse and wagon ruts. Just the thought of engaging his gift made a swell of bile rise in his throat, but he swallowed back nausea and gathered his concentration to draw on zenith once again.

Channeling the force came easy, but shaping it to his will used all his concentration. After a struggle, the familiar tingling sensation cascaded across his arca prime. He filtered his gift to the pattern of the horseshoe print. To his awareness, a faint trail like a light blue haze glowed on the road. Visible only while channeling zenith, the path now appeared clearly.

He directed Zippy forward and followed the trail into town. They trotted past a large inn and several storefronts, then turned onto a road leading to the northwest side of town.

In the distance, the illuminated trail wound around a hill and disappeared but seemed to follow the road. Reddevek lost command of his gift and slumped forward. A throbbing headache erupted between his temples. He thought Zippy was moving to the side of the road, then realized the Aarindin, in fact, stood motionless.

Man of no knowledge . . . Sometimes you really are a stupid monk. All this way only to be overcome by the draft like a tender.

He dry-heaved again as the sickness overwhelmed his senses, then directed Zippy into the shade at the east side of the large inn. Somehow, the Aarindin sensed the seriousness of his condition and knelt with its belly to the ground. Reddevek threw his weight to the side, landing on the ground with all the grace of a newborn bull calf.

He lay there the better part of an hour, and the dizziness subsided. His head pounded with the thunder of a herd of Aarindin galloping, and such tremendous fatigue saturated his muscles that he could only manage to crack an eyelid open when a woman approached.

"A strange boy inside said a man out here needs help. You sick, mister? We don't need outsiders bringing anything contagious into the Ram." A middle-aged woman with unusually burly shoulders dried her hands on a stained apron and leaned casually against the wall.

"Not sick. I just overextended myself to get here," Reddevek grumbled.

The woman glared at him with a suspicious eye. "My name's Della. My brother and I run the Bashing Ram here. Now don't get excited, I'm gonna check you for fever. If you ain't sick and you got coin, we can get you a room and maybe something to eat. Does that sound fair?"

Della waited for him to nod his agreement, then stepped off the boardwalk and knelt beside him. She placed her cheek to his forehead a moment, then stood back up. "No fever and you don't smell of the bottle, so you're welcome inside."

Reddevek struggled to get to a sitting position and leaned his back against the side of the inn. "I could use a room and something to eat. I just need a moment to recover."

Della cocked her head to the side and walked away without further words. A moment later, two men and a youth approached. They wore similar work attire to Della, and at least one of them smelled like smoked meat.

"Hello, Stranger. My sister Del says you might need a hand inside. Name's Ingram. I'm the pitmaster. This is Steckle and his son Feth." The chubby pitmaster smiled with ruddy cheeks and held out a hand. Reddevek clasped it, and the man hoisted him to his feet.

"Feth will stable your horse for a few copper nugs," said Ingram. "He sure is a fine-looking animal."

Reddevek nodded and handed Zippy's reins to the lad, then clicked his tongue twice. Zippy stood up, startling the boy. Feth regained his courage and took the reins. "Name's Red. You have my thanks."

"Cracked corn, oats, or just hay, Mister?" asked the boy.

Reddevek removed his travel pack, then flipped a silver mark to Feth. The youth snatched the coin, wide-eyed both at its weight and make. "Curry and brush him down. Feed him all three; he deserves more for getting me here."

Feth bowed low. "Yes, sir! What's his name?"

Reddevek sighed. He really hated for anyone to think he was the one who had named the horse. "Zippy. He goes by Zippy."

"Zippy. That's, well, that's a great name! Come on, Zippy, let's get you sorted out," said Feth. Without pause, he turned and led the Aarindin around the back of the inn.

Ingram and Steckle each supported a hand under Reddevek, and between the three of them managed to escort him inside to a table. As his eyes adjusted to the dim light inside the Bashing Ram, he noted that Della and her brother kept a clean inn. Though he sensed the faint aroma of old beer through the savoriness of smoked meat, his feet stumbled across clean floorboards. He flopped back into a chair and offered his thanks, along with another silver piece.

"Food and water, please," said Reddevek.

Steckle produced a mug and pitcher of water. After Reddevek drained two mugs and poured a third, Della served a heaping plate of smoked meat accompanied by sliced potatoes and warm bread. The warden raced to consume the food, occasionally stopping for another gulp of water. The proprietors observed him for a short time, then returned to the business of managing the inn. Della disappeared with Ingram into the kitchen, and Steckle made a show of wiping the clean bar.

With his appetite satiated, Reddevek relaxed back and assessed the taproom. Eight other round tables sat empty. A flight of steps ran up to a hallway that, he assumed, led to rooms for rent. He pushed back, noting a small portion of his strength had returned. He wandered over to the bar and took a seat.

"Your partner, Della," he said her name cautiously, uncertain if he remembered it correctly from her introduction. When Steckle nodded with a smile, he continued, "She and her brother serve the best food south of the mountains. So why is the taproom empty?"

"We don't get customers before midday meal very often," said Steckle. "Within an hour, I expect things to change. Get you something more substantial to drink? We import our ale from Riverton; it's the best around."

Reddevek nodded, then watched the barman disappear down a set of steep steps into a cellar. He returned a moment later with a foamy mug and proudly set the tankard on the bar. Reddevek lifted the ale and pulled a long gulp in. The cool, amber liquid splashed the back of his tongue with a refreshing wave. He wondered if the food and ale tasted so good because of his recent relative starvation or if the Bashing Ram actually did serve the best food south of the Korjinth. He realized that the latter might be true.

"What brings you to the Bend, friend?" asked Steckle.

"Is that the name of this town?" he asked.

"Journey's Bend, but folks around here just call it the Bend," said Steckle.

Reddevek peered back across the taproom. He shrugged off a feeling that someone had followed him, then remembered the Dulescan horseshoe print he'd followed through town.

"I suppose you could say I'm looking for someone," said the warden. He walked back to his table and rummaged through his travel pack to retrieve the small journal and the drawing of the compass rose provided by Therek Lefledge. He displayed the image for Steckle's inspection. "Anyone around these parts make anything like this?"

Steckle leaned forward with a frown. "You're the second stranger this week asking about the Scrivsons," he said.

Reddevek resisted the urge to press the man for details and pulled a generous gulp of mead instead. He set the tankard down and turned his intimidating gaze on the barman.

After a moment of silence, Steckle swallowed hard and continued, "Not long ago, another traveler from up north came asking about them. At least I assumed as much by his tall stature and blue eyes. Anyway, the both of you are in luck. The Scrivsons live just at the outskirts of town to the northwest. Kevold and his nephews, Lluthean and . . . Bryndor, I think, was the older one's name." The barman tapped a nobby finger on the journal. "That's the symbol they place on their maps. I'm sure of it."

Reddevek rarely encountered anything that surprised him anymore. He'd witnessed atrocities carried out by hordes of grotvonen during the Abrogator's War, bore witness to the mistreatment of the poor in the slums of cities across the Northlands, and lost too many friends to count to the randomness of life. But he did not expect to hear the names of the Aarindorian princes spoken so plainly. He glared at the barman with alarming intensity, shifting from his dominant eye to the other. Steckle took a step back and withered under the scrutiny of the warden's gaze.

"When did you last talk to this other traveler?" he asked.

"Oh, not long, perhaps an hour or so before you collapsed on our doorstep," said Steckle.

Reddevek pushed back from the barstool, then retrieved his throwing axe and a curved sword from his belongings at the table. He wolfed down one last mouthful of bread soaked with the juices from the meat platter. "Any chance you have a kettle with hot water in the back?"

"Sure, Mr. Red, right away," said Steckle. He swirled a cloth around the inside of a clean mug with a nervous eye to Reddevek's weapons. The barman disappeared into the kitchen and returned with a pot, then poured hot water into the mug.

Reddevek removed the small pouch with ground vivith and sighed in resignation. He knew he couldn't reasonably continue without significant rest.

Just a few more hours, that's likely all I need.

He dropped a single tea bag of the drug into the hot water and stirred it with one thick finger. The water felt hot enough to steep the tea. He waited a few minutes, crushed the teabag against the inside of the mug, then downed the drink in one large gulp. The bitter liquid immediately caused his mouth to draw up, leaving him feeling parched, but he also felt somewhat renewed. He tucked the pouch of vivith into a saddlebag.

"I trust you can see my things get to a room?" Reddevek asked.

"Yes, Mr. Red, with what you gave us already, you're paid up for at least three days," said Steckle.

"I need to get to the . . . Scrivsons? Is that what you said their names were?" Reddevek asked.

"Yes, Mr. Red," said Steckle with a nervous tenor to his voice.

"They might be in danger. Can you tell me the best way to their place?"

Steckle stared into the bottom of the empty mug he was feverishly overpolishing. The barman opened his mouth to speak but seemed conflicted. He licked at beads of sweat gathered on his upper lip.

Reddevek sighed. He knew he wasn't good at the softer side of interrogation. Awkwardly, he placed a beefy hand over the barman's. "I'm not here to hurt that man or his boys. They are kin to my kin, and I need to make sure they are safe from that other traveler."

Steckle looked down at his hand, then back to Reddevek, considering the words. "Sure, I understand," he said. "They live on a small farmstead just northwest. It's not a long row to hoe to get there. There is a walking trail that runs right up to their place. Or you could follow the winding dirt road until you come across a stone hedge about shoulder high that's overgrown with flowering ivy. It will be on your right. You can't miss it. If you hit the river, you've gone too far."

Reddevek rapped his knuckles twice on the bar. "Good. You folks have any kind of militia or law around here?"

"Yes, Constable Whirik," said Steckle.

"You better get the constable and anyone else who can help, and fast." He turned and strode back out to the boardwalk without waiting for Steckle to respond.

As Reddevek strode out of the Bashing Ram, his legs felt invigorated, and the headache diminished to a dull throb. For now, at least, the vivith had dissipated most of the symptoms of the draft. He chose not to risk channeling zenith again, trusting Steckle's directions. He walked across the boardwalk, then along the only road leading to the northwest. The road meandered more west than north, and Reddevek easily found the footpath Steckle had referred to.

After five minutes, he discovered another horseshoe print with the Dulescan insignia. The finding incited him to jog a short distance down the path, axe bouncing against the side of one hip and sword on the other.

As he ran, he wondered what trick of the vivith made him feel so edgy. His heart thumped with an unusually fast pace, and his hand felt oddly tremulous on the hilt of his axe. His thoughts seemed to bounce from one plan of action to the next, and every moment was flavored by a sense of hypervigilance. A skittish, hollow feeling settled in his stomach. He swallowed what felt like dust.

Is that the drug? Why would anyone ever want to feel this way? I'm like a fart in a skillet.

Reddevek pounded a fist to his chest, more to distract himself from the thumping of his heart than anything else. He continued on the footpath northwest over a few hills that wound through clusters of timber. Eventually, the path merged back to the dirt road, right along an ivy-covered stone wall. He turned through a break in the wall to discover a modest home.

A horse barn stood off to the right side. A saddled bay horse stood by the barn nibbling at the grass. A woman sat alone on the front porch in a chair but seemed not to notice him. He moved behind the bay, and the horse nickered softly but seemed content to crop the grass. Reddevek ran a hand along one of the horse's front legs, then enticed the animal to bend and lift its leg. The weathered horseshoe revealed the familiar, whimsical *D* at the apex of the shoe.

Reddevek circled behind the barn and approached the home from the side with no windows. He crept along the side of the house to the porch and just listened. In the distance, a few chickens clucked, frogs croaked, and birds chirped in the nearby timber. A goat walked around from the backside of the home and bleated softly at him, then contended itself to nibble at the weeds just beyond a fence.

He heard a creaking floorboard and audible footsteps, so he peered over the edge of the porch. The woman seemed still, unmoving.

Something isn't right, and it's not the vivith. Or is it? I've been as nervous as a rabbit in a wolf den ever since I drank that poison.

He lifted the axe from his belt loop with one hand and held the saber in his other. A man exited the home and strolled onto the porch. Reddevek backed behind the corner of the house, stealing a quick look as he did. The man wore plain grey traveling clothes and looked like someone from the north: tall and lean of stature compared to most he met below the Korjinth. Reddevek watched as he pulled a wood rocking chair over and sat down next to the woman. He couldn't see the stranger's face, but he did see the clear outlines of gold and silver runes on his exposed wrists.

He resisted the strange urge to walk forward and introduce himself. The man sat, just staring at the woman. Neither of them said anything. Reddevek looked past the stranger's shoulder at the woman. Her round face was pale, her head had slumped forward, and a line of drool hung from her slack-jawed open mouth onto needlepoint that she held in her lap. Her breaths came shallow and infrequent. Reddevek remembered seeing other people breathe like that.

Right before they fade away to the Drift.

The stranger leaned forward and plucked a small dart from the side of her neck. No bigger than a thimble, Reddevek hadn't even noticed the object until the man plucked it out. He pocketed the dart in a leather wallet and put the wallet inside a pocket in his tunic. The man used two fingers to shove her forehead back. The woman's face came into view as her head rocked back to rest on her chair's back.

A rich, calm voice filled the silence. "It's a shame you couldn't be more accommodating, really. I've come all this way for a reunion. The least you could do is tell me when Kaellor and the heirs will return."

The woman stared at the stranger as she breathed in that strange manner that reminded Reddevek of the dying.

"No?" asked the man. "I shouldn't be too surprised. I have a friend in Callinora who makes this stuff. He calls it a paralytic, though I suppose I will have to tell him to adjust the potency."

The strange man leaned forward with a cloth to wipe the drool from her chin and blot a stream of tears from her cheeks. "I mean, you can't even seem to blink. How am I supposed to learn anything from you in this state?" The man sighed with theatrical drama to nobody. "By the looks of you, I think you are about to slip away. Don't worry, though. I will wait right here for Kaellor and the boys."

Reddevek had heard enough. He took a deep breath, set a foot up to the porch, and lunged forward to cleave his axe into the man's backside. The maneuver seemed simple enough, but the warden felt his body leap completely over the stranger, past the woman, and out onto the hard ground.

His head slammed into the dirt, and he tasted the salty, metal tang of blood. He spit and stood just in time to see the remnants of zenith flare across the arca prime above the man's shirt.

The stranger stood with casual indifference and leaned forward on the porch rail. "You are . . . Reddevek? You've changed over the years. I knew I smelled an Outrider. Allow me to introduce myself. My name is—"

"Vardell," growled the warden. "You washed out of the Outriders years ago."

And it's just my luck; you're a guster. That's why I flew clear off the porch.

Vardell's lip twitched with brief irritation. Then his expression returned to one of amusement. "Oh, the Outriders were too small for me. And Elbiona was always so formal, so stiff. Where you play games pretending to protect the kingdom, my employer allows me to do things to shape it."

"And just who is your employer?" the warden asked.

"Right to the heart of the matter. You really are a blunt weapon, aren't you?" said Vardell. "Tell you what, you turn and walk out of here now, leave me to my business with the heirs, and I won't have to kill you."

Reddevek tilted his head to the side. The man held no weapons, but he stood next to the woman on the porch. "The woman, is the poison reversible? Let me take her into town for a medic." *Maybe I can protect the heirs as well.*

Vardell giggled. "You are so provincial. First, the poison is not reversible. It's a shame, really, but couldn't be helped. These Southlanders can be stubborn, and this woman is not the least among them in that regard. Even if there were a way to save her, there are no medics in this backwater town. By the Giver, Warden, have you been so focused on the trail that you failed to notice we aren't in the Northlands anymore?"

Reddevek slumped his shoulders. The act of appearing defeated and not crouched like a cat prepared to pounce required all of his concentration. He made a show of securing his saber back on his hip, then turned as if to walk away.

"Give my regards to the regent," said Vardell, but his sarcasm ended with a surprised, high-pitched grunt.

Reddevek took two steps, pivoted, and threw his axe sidearm at Vardell's head. The weapon rotated along a deadly trajectory. Sunlight glinted off the blade. Silver, haft, silver, haft . . . but at the last moment, Vardell managed to channel zenith. The man dropped to the floor of the porch and used a sharp current of air to deflect the blade. The weapon wedged into a header above the front door.

Reddevek charged forward in a serpentine pattern, weaving his way across the yard. He'd dueled a guster once years ago, and his training returned unbidden. He ran to close the distance. If he could reach the man, he could put a quick end to the fight.

Vardell stood and appeared to hurl invisible balls at the warden. Puffs of dust erupted where the warden might have been if he'd run a straight path. Reddevek evaded five of the blasts of air. His foot reached the first step, and instead of leaping forward, he twirled. He made to clear the last step, avoid Vardell's oncoming attack, and cleave his sword into the man's neck.

Reddevek craned his head around. His eyes found his target, the joint where the collar bone met the breast bone. He rolled his wrist, turning the edge of the saber for the killing blow and tightening his grip for the deed. But Vardell staggered back and threw both his hands wide.

Dust and debris along the porch billowed forth with a blast of air. The woman flew against the porch rail like a lifeless doll, and a dense wall of compressed air struck Reddevek's chest. The force felt more like getting thrown from an Aarindin or running headlong into a boulder. The burst of air barreled him off his feet and threw him to the end of the yard. He landed on his ass right in the middle of the opening of the ivy-covered wall. Something in the small of his back cracked, and an intense, sharp pain erupted down his butt cheek.

Reddevek tried to roll, convinced that fire or hot coals were searing his backside. The motion caused the pain to intensify.

"Ahh, grind you sideways! What did you do to me? I'll send you to the Drift, Guster!" Reddevek peered back at the porch through eyes obscured by tears. Vardell sagged against one of the wood support beams along the front porch, clearly exhausted but still very much alive.

Chapter Twenty-Six: Some Paths Lead to Dark Places

Kaellor bounced in the front seat of the Tellends' horse-drawn wagon. The wheels spun fast enough that the individual spokes appeared blended as one round disc and seemed to roll backward. He bookended Emile, who rode between him and Markum in the front seat of the wagon. Something Lluthean said made Harland and Bryndor laugh in the back. After the stress of the last few weeks, it felt good to hear the boys laugh in good company.

If their mood was any indication, Rona was going to miss out on a fun night. But after a long afternoon spent sharing stories around their table, she'd begged off attending the party and planned to craft another compass rose in needlepoint.

Despite their injuries, the boys managed to dress and beat him to the wagon. Kaellor understood their enthusiasm and felt more than a little pride when he considered how the town might respond to their accomplishments.

They followed the road into town, winding around forested hills and eventually pulling up to the front boardwalk in front of the Bashing Ram. Kaellor offered a polite hand to Emile, and this time, she received his offer with grace. He watched the boys extricate themselves from the wagon. Both of them required assistance from Harland and moved with all the agility of infirm seniors. *It seems the ride here leeched a bit of their vinegar.*

"Boys, see to a table with Emile," said Kaellor. "Markum and I will be in straightaway."

Bryndor nodded stiffly and accompanied Emile inside. Kaellor climbed back into the front seat, and they rode around the back of the inn to the stables. The young stablehand, Feth, walked out from one of the stalls, a bucket with oats in one hand and a curry comb in the other. Kaellor smiled at the lad then sucked in a breath.

From the darkness of the stall, a majestic black head emerged, followed by a long sleek neck. An Aarindin nuzzled the boy. Feth dropped the bucket to the ground and giggled. "Zippy, wait," said Feth. "I have plenty more where that came from, but you're makin' a mess."

With furtive glances, Kaellor searched the dark corners of the stable, alert for any unusual movements. Two common horses nibbled at hay in other stalls. He swallowed hard, finding his mouth dry.

"Boy, that's a fine horse; how long has it been stabled here?" he asked.

"A man named Red arrived this afternoon. He gave me a whole silver piece just to groom and stable his horse. Isn't he just about the most amazing horse you ever saw?" asked Feth.

Kaellor stepped into the stall and walked around the Aarindin. Zippy contented himself to chew mouthfuls of oats. The outline of a handprint with a *B* branded the horse's chest. *That's a zenith brand, or I'm a monk. What is a Balladuren Aarindin doing here?*

"What is it, Kae—Kevold?" asked Markum.

Kaellor looked over to his friend but couldn't convince himself of the truth of the horse before him. So many questions raced through his mind. *Is it simply chance? Why here and now, when their mantle is fraying? I suppose, most importantly, who is Red?*

"Boy, did the rider use a saddle?" Kaellor asked.

Feth scratched his head. "Not really. He had some saddlebags but no saddle."

Kaellor felt a strange cramp in his gut like he might have to race to the privy to drop mud. An Outrider could manage the journey without a saddle, but what would one of them be doing all the way out here?

"Is there any chance you still have that silver piece? I would love to see it," said Kaellor.

Feth pulled out the coin but held it in a clenched fist.

"It's alright; you hold on to it. Please, I just want to see if it has any marks I might recognize," said Kaellor.

Feth nodded once, held his hand forward, and opened his fist. An Aarindorian silver mark lay on the boy's palm with an outline of Stone's Grasp on one side and two moons over mountains on the other.

"Are you alright, mister?" the boy asked.

Markum's thick hand rested on his shoulder. "What is it, Kevold?"

Kaellor rubbed a hand across his face, surprised to discover it peppered with tiny dots of sweat. "Boy, where is this Red just now? Is he inside the Ram?"

"Mr. Red?" asked Feth. "Yes, he looked like a fella in bad need of food and drink. My dad helped him inside."

Kaellor nodded his thanks, then turned and walked through the back door of the inn. Muggy air spilled out, carrying with it the rich aroma of baked bread and stew. Della looked up from her counter, brandished a rolling pin like a cudgel, and glared at him.

"You know better than to surprise me in my kitchen, Mr. Scrivson," she said.

Kaellor held up both hands in a pleading gesture then placed a finger before his lips to garner silence. His eyes searched the kitchen. She worked by her brother, Ingram, as he tended a spit over hot coals. They both looked at him with curiosity.

"Please, I need your help. A man arrived here today on a large, black horse. He goes by the name Red. It's possible he is looking for the boys or me," said Kaellor. "Did he take a room? Is he here now?"

"What would this fella want with you, Mr. Scrivson?" asked Ingram.

"I'm not sure," said Kaellor. "Maybe he is just passing through. It is a very long story."

Della and her brother considered him for a few long moments. Eventually, Ingram shrugged. "Folks in the Bend stick together. The All-Mother knows we owe both of those boys for everything they've done in the last few days. Let me ask Steckle. You stay here."

Ingram wiped his hands on a grease-stained apron and walked into the taproom. After only a moment, Steckle returned with him. At the same time, Markum came in through the back door to the inn.

"Mr. Scrivson," said Steckle. "It's good to see your family here. That Red fellow left for your place and seemed to be in a dark mood. He gathered weapons and told me to get Constable Whirik. I don't think he had good intentions."

"How long?" Kaellor growled. Something in the grim determination of his voice made the barkeep pale. "How long ago did the man leave?"

"I imagine he should be there by now," said Steckle. "But we sent for the constable, and your family is safe here."

"Everyone except Rona," said Markum.

Kaellor grabbed two knives from a butcher block—a cleaver and a boning knife. "I'm borrowing these, but I'll get them back," he said to Della. "Markum, keep your family and the boys here. Send the constable and a few men once they arrive. I'm going to get Ro."

Without waiting for a response, Kaellor barged past the burly-shouldered farmer and back to the stable. Feth had just finished unhitching Markum's horse from the wagon. "Boy, do you know Rona Scrivson?"

"Sure, Mr. Scrivson, everybody loves Ms. Rona."

Kaellor nodded. "She might be in danger, and I need to reach her as soon as possible. Which one of these horses can get me there the fastest?"

Feth frowned in concentration. "Smart money would be on Zippy, the big black one; only I don't know if he would take to the saddle too kindly."

The boy led a dapple mare from one of the stalls. "Take this one. She belongs to Ingram. She'll get you there fast." In less than a minute, they had the horse saddled, and Kaellor raced her up the footpath toward his home.

He slapped the mare and encouraged her to gallop the entire way. They sped along the footpath and through the forested hills. He considered how he should approach their home. Maybe he should ride through the pasture and come in from the barn side. There were no windows from that way. Or perhaps he should wait for the constable and others to arrive. *But if anything happened to Ro, I could never forgive myself.*

Kaellor drew the mare to a stop alongside the ivy-covered stone wall. He hopped down and tucked the cleaver behind his back belt, then secreted the boning knife along his forearm and up his sleeve. He was considering doubling back to come in through the pasture when a gust of wind blew dust through the entryway of the ivy-covered wall and onto the road. A second later, a man flew by as well, landing on his backside in the middle of the road.

The stranger grunted when he landed and cursed, "Ahh, grind you sideways! What did you do to me? I'll send you to the Drift, Guster!"

Gold and silver runes adorned the man's arms and neck, merging with a furrowed scar on the right side of his face. He wore the soiled outercoat of an Outrider. Kaellor crouched behind the stone wall, and the man turned to look straight at him. *I know those eyes, that scar. Red is . . . Reddevek? Thank the Giver.*

The man recognized Kaellor as well and held a hand out, then made a chopping gesture to stay.

"I'm not an Aarindin, but I think you want me to stay?" Kaellor whispered.

Reddevek gave a short nod, then lay back down, panting. "Something in my back or my hips is broken; I can't get up."

"Who did this to you?" asked Kaellor.

"Vardell. He's alone," said Reddevek. The Outrider grimaced and looked pale.

"What about Rona? The woman who lives here?" asked Kaellor.

Reddevek shook his head. "I can't be certain, but Vardell poisoned her with a dart."

Kaellor grabbed the cleaver and charged through the opening, leaping over Reddevek. He turned onto the front yard to see a man dressed in everyday traveling attire. A small part of Kaellor's awareness screamed for caution. A body, possibly Rona, lay draped over the rail of the front porch in an unnatural position. The man looked tired, and the glowing outline of his arca prime appeared at his neckline.

Behind him, Reddevek yelled, "Wait, dammit, he's a guster!"

Hot anger washed over Kaellor and prevented him from registering Reddevek's warning. He charged forward and threw the cleaver. It flashed end over end and flew above Vardell's head, clanging against the front of the house. The assassin stepped to the side and channeled just as Kaellor reached the front step.

Kaellor's feet flew out from under him, and his head struck the ground hard. Dazzling lights swam across the periphery of his vision, accompanied by a wave of nausea. He lost all sense of direction as his body flew back and slammed against the ivy-covered wall.

Vardell funneled a continuous column of air directly at him. The pressure made it difficult to draw in a breath. Kaellor gritted his teeth and struggled to see the assassin through squinted eyes. He forced shallow breaths but found all he could manage was a gasp. Dirt and debris gusted against him, bearing down with terrible persistent force. The tall man walked casually forward.

The runes at Vardell's neckline flared and pulsed, clearly visible through the dust devil surrounding them both. His eyes blazed with a crystal blue luster. The Aarindorian yelled over the conjured whirlwind, "You look like him. Maybe you are, and maybe you are not, but I don't have time for questions. Sorry, friend."

Vardell stepped forward, holding a dagger, and raised his hand to strike. He grunted, and his eyes widened in surprise. Both men, Kaellor and Vardell, fell forward. Dust and debris settled to the ground as Vardell's conjured windstorm dissipated. Kaellor rose to his hands and knees, coughed the dirt from his lungs, and strained to make sense of his surroundings. Through tear-streaked eyes, he squinted.

Vardell lay facedown with a dagger embedded between his shoulder blades. A ruby gemstone adorned the hilt of the weapon. An emaciated girl with hair like fine straw and wearing as much dirt on her cheeks as her clothing stepped forward and removed the dagger, then walked over to Reddevek.

She stood over the Outrider, wiped a small amount of blood from the blade, and waved it in front of him. "I suppose you'll be wanting this back now, Red?"

Reddevek considered the girl but remained on his back. "Ranika? What are you—did you follow me all the way here? You've got more stone in you than most. Keep it; you've earned it." The feral man chuckled. "I knew someone followed me here, grind me a new one."

Kaellor observed their interaction for a moment, then struggled to his feet. He lurched to the porch; the world seemed to roll and sway. Rona lay awkwardly on her back, draped over the porch rail. Her neck was twisted at a strange angle, and a ridge of bone tented her skin unnaturally at the ribs beside her spine. Kaellor supported her like he would a newborn as he labored to set her gently on the porch, then swallowed back a wave of nausea when he heard the bones of her rib cage grind like sandpaper.

He tucked a few errant grey strands of hair under the scarf she wore as a bonnet, then made himself look upon her face. All the life and cheery color were gone, leaving her ashen and grey. He imagined her opening her eyes to smile. He stared at her fragile, still form, waiting for her to draw breath, willing some part of her to come back to life. *Ro, open your eyes. Breathe. Smile for me, Ro.*

A hot surge of grief threatened to well up in his throat, but he muscled it down and embraced a cold numbness. He walked over to Vardell and kicked the man in the ribs. He expected the man to be dead, but the assassin grunted.

Kaellor knelt and rolled Vardell over. The Aarindorian looked at him, eyes white with fear, and panted.

"My legs, I can't move my legs," he stammered.

"When you use the Giver's gifts for the Taker's purpose, that's a risk, I suppose," said Kaellor. "What's your name?"

"Vardell." The assassin swallowed hard. Sweat glistened his pale face. "Vardell Becks of Dulesque, Your Highness."

"I think we can both agree that you don't really think of me as Your Highness, so let's drop all that silliness. Tell me, can you feel this?" Kaellor stabbed the boning knife deep into Vardell's foot. The blade punched through with a stabbing, shearing noise.

"I feel . . . there's a sharp pain in my back, between my shoulder blades," Vardell said, then started to whimper.

"Can you not move your arms then?" Kaellor asked. "Can you even feel this?" He removed the boning knife and held Vardell's hand up where the man could see it. With a slow, curious probing motion, he drilled the knife into the hand, boring a hole clean through. Hot blood pumped from the wound and onto the man's face.

"By all the dead in the Drift, is that my hand?" Vardell cried.

Kaellor wiped his bloody hands on Vardell's shirt then tore the garment apart to inspect his arca prime. Gold and silver runes intertwined in a whirlwind pattern that centered on his chest, then ran to his arms.

"How about here; can you feel this?" Kaellor twisted the point of the blade into the man's nipple, but Vardell didn't seem to register the injury. Next, he flicked a finger in the man's eye, and Vardell cried with alarm and pain. "Alright then, something to work with, I suppose. Vardell, is it? You took a knife to the spine. It's going to be the end of you, but how you go is up to you, and I can still cause you terrible pain."

To emphasize his point, Kaellor twisted the blade into the man's right outer ear. "Who sent you, and why did you come here?"

Vardell panted and whimpered in pain. "I can't say. Just kill me and be done with it! Please, I have poison darts in my front jacket. Push one into my neck. Leave me to the Drift."

Kaellor cocked his head to the side, considering the man's words. He held the tip of the knife in front of Vardell's right eye. "I popped the eye out of a dead wolvryn once, and do you know what happened? The whole globe popped out like a crystal egg. I wonder if you're full of that much zenith?"

Vardell looked at the blade in horror. "Wait, I want to tell you! I have an answer! Wait! I'm a member of the Lacuna. I took the contract from an anonymous party. The money was too good to pass up, half now and half when I returned with evidence of your death. All I had to do was follow the Outrider at a distance. I wasn't even sure he was going to be able to find you, but then someone used rune fire, and the pieces sort of fell together."

Vardell closed his eyes and whimpered. "I've told you all I know. Please just give me the poison."

"The woman on the porch, why did you kill her?" asked Kaellor. "She had nothing to do with any of this."

"It was a mistake. I only meant to put her to sleep," said Vardell. "The distillation was too strong. I would have let her go."

"But you didn't," said Kaellor. "Do you know what happens to the gifted if they enter the Drift stripped of their gift before they die? They wander forever, disconnected, alone, too ruined for the Giver and too weak for the Taker to bother with."

Kaellor stood and grabbed two fistfuls of the man's hair and dragged him back against the ivy-covered wall. He propped the man up to make the assassin watch. Vardell yelled, then began crying hysterically as Kaellor began to cut.

"What are you doing? What? Madness! Stop—no, you don't have to do this; just let me go!" Vardell screamed and sobbed.

Kaellor used the boning knife to remove the man's arca prime, then pared away any parts of flesh marked with silver or gold runes. The task took a long time, and all the while, Kaellor continued, neatly trimming away any vestiges of the man's gift. Vardell's whimpers and sobs barely echoed in the periphery of his awareness. He finished the task with no more concern than if he were skinning a deer. Finally, he tossed the skinned symbols into the dirt at the man's side.

He stood and walked back to the porch to retrieve Reddevek's axe, which was still embedded above the door. His hands, sticky with blood, gripped the weapon. Something about the friction of his fingers on the haft felt . . . right. As he walked back to Vardell, he caught a glimpse of the Outrider and the girl kneeling beside him. Both of them seemed to consider him with wide-eyed acceptance.

"Vardell Becks of Aarindorn, I am sending you to the Drift without access to your gift, where you will wander forever alone, disconnected from zenith, disconnected from the Giver, and likely to be shunned even by the Taker."

Kaellor knelt down, ignoring the man's pleas and whimpers. He grabbed a fistful of the man's hair, craned his neck to the side, and swung the handaxe. One chop, and blood spurted and foamed from the man's airway. Two chops, and a satisfying crunch traveled up the haft as the axe blade cracked into bone. A third chop, and the head came loose. Kaellor tossed Vardell's head into the dirt as the decapitated corpse listed sideways, pumping dark blood onto the ground.

Chapter Twenty-Seven: Sorrow and Vengeance

U pon learning that Kaellor and Rona might be in danger, Bryndor began running home from the Bashing Ram. The scabs of his recent wounds throbbed and burned, but after a few minutes, the pain subsided. His attention turned to sprinting the footpath. He arrived along the front gate moments before the Tellends and Lluthean.

He couldn't make sense of the grisly scene before him. An outlander with gold and silver tattoos lay on the ground panting in pain. A girl squatted beside the stranger. She fingered a knife and looked like a cat ready to pounce. Her demeanor softened when Bryndor stepped past. Just inside the ivy-covered walls lay a beheaded corpse. Dark stains congealed on the body, and next to that gore rested a mound of bloody flesh and the head from the carcass.

By all the dead in the Drift, what happened here?

"Bryn! Wait! You should wait for Harland and me!" shouted Markum Tellend. The stout farmer stepped beside him, holding a pitchfork. Markum inhaled in either revulsion or surprise. "Mother Maedra, protect and keep us."

They stood there long moments, their trance unceasing until Emile and Harland arrived, supporting a limping Lluthean. Bryndor hurried into the barn and retrieved an old blanket. Ignoring the yelps of the pups, he returned, used his foot to roll the head closer to the corpse, and covered both.

With at least a part of the macabre scene obscured, he turned to Kaellor. He realized that his uncle had not moved since they arrived. Kaellor sat with shoulders slumped on the front steps of the porch, cradling

Rona's body in his lap. Together, they approached him with caution, and all the while, Bryndor struggled to make his feet move, afraid they might both be dead.

"Kae? Kae, are you alright?" asked Bryndor.

Kaellor turned their direction but held a vacant stare. He was covered in blood, and a purple welt swelled on his forehead. Emile took one look at them, then took charge of the situation. "Harland, get Lluthean to a chair. Markum, get me a pitcher of water, and Bryn, I need some rags." She ordered them about with a soft tone, but they all followed her direction, thankful to have something to do.

When Bryndor returned, they stood in a somber semicircle around Kaellor, watching as Emile attempted to remove the dried blood. Bryndor watched closely every time Emile removed the rag, thankful to find his uncle free from life-threatening injury.

"I couldn't save her, Em. I wasn't fast enough," said Kaellor with a soft voice. He looked up to Bryndor and Lluthean, a hollow expression in his eyes. "I'm sorry."

Bryndor had no words, and his shock prevented him from forming any questions. He felt numb and struggled to understand that the woman who appeared to be sleeping on Kaellor's lap would never wake up. He kept imagining her opening her eyes and waited with disbelief, expecting to see her move.

Emile tossed the blood-stained basin of water off the side of the porch. "There's no help for it, Kae. Get inside and get out of those clothes," she ordered.

Kaellor seemed to recover something of himself and laid Rona's head gently on the porch. He disappeared inside and returned a moment later with a clean shirt. Somehow, the action had brought a return of the man Bryndor expected to see.

"Wait here a moment. I'll be right back," said Kaellor.

Bryndor watched his uncle walk over to the foreigners with comfortable purpose. Kaellor squatted down and seemed to introduce himself. They shared a few words, and the girl sheathed her knife. After a few minutes, Kaellor stood and addressed them. "Everyone, this is a friend of mine, Reddevek of Aarindorn and Ranika. Reddevek was injured and needs a place to rest up. Markum, can I impose on the Tellends to see him to a room at the Ram? Tell Della I'll cover the cost and be in to settle up later."

Kaellor offered a brief account, reviewing what he knew of the assassin and Rona's death. The Tellends accepted his explanation, then transported Reddevek and the girl back to town. After seeing them off, Kaellor returned to the porch where Byndor sat by Lluthean.

The three of them shared a long silence.

Eventually, Kaellor cleared his throat. "Markum and Harland are going to meet us up on the hill north of here, the one that overlooks the river valley. I'll hitch Scout to the wagon, and we'll take Rona up there. It's where she would want to be buried. I know you both have injuries to mend, but there's no help for it."

With a grunt of pain, Bryndor helped Lluthean to his feet. Together, they wrapped Rona in a blanket, placed her in their wagon, and the three of them rode off to the burial site. The Tellends arrived in time to help dig the grave. After placing Rona's shrouded corpse, they layered stones until the cairn stood shoulder height.

Bryndor placed a heavy river stone on the barrow. After the first hour, his muscles had loosened up, and he quickly learned how to avoid movements that caused his scabbed wounds to pull or sting. Lluthean seemed not to fare as well. Any time he twisted or bent forward, he grabbed at his ribs or grimaced in pain. To his brother's credit, he never complained. None of them did. They just kept retrieving heavy river stones and hauling them up the hillside.

They carried out the dreary labor without words, each person contributing what their stamina allowed. The sun began to set as they finished building the stone barrow, and even though Bryndor placed a good number of the stones himself, the whole thing felt surreal, like it was happening to someone else.

Maybe later, Aunt Ro could make a—. Bryndor stopped mid-stride and let his heavy stone plummet to the ground. He cursed the sting that threatened to wet his eyes, then chewed his lower lip until the salty mineral taste of blood ran across his tongue. He sucked at his teeth and clenched his fists repeatedly. Long moments passed in which he remained paralyzed by grief. Eventually, he retrieved the stone and placed it at the apex of the cairn. The five of them gathered around and stood in companionable silence.

Markum wiped sweat from his brow with a beefy forearm. "It's an awful thing to have to do this, but I'm glad we could be a part of it, Kae. Ro was like a sister to us," said the burly farmer.

Kaellor nodded. "Did Emile reach the rector? I can't say that I could pick the man out of a crowd, but Rona would be happy if he could speak the blessings of the Seven."

"Mother said the rector was returning from Riverton tonight and should be able to perform a service in the morning," said Harland.

"I thank you both for your help then," said Kaellor with a nod to Markum.

They stood in awkward silence for a few moments, then Lluthean said, "Can we say something now, Kae? While it's just us who knew her the best?"

Kaellor placed one arm around Lluthean and the other around Bryndor. His words carried across the hillside in a tone more like a lecture than anything rendered from heartache. "Rona Scrivson was the best among us. She came into our family at a time when we needed her the most and made our lives here possible. My words can't explain how she modeled kindness, patience, and love. We would never have made it in the Bend without her, and I'm not sure yet how we will go on. It wasn't right what happened to her, and so I ask whatever Southland gods might be listening to find her in the Drift and give her the same comfort she afforded us in this life."

After a brief pause, Markum cleared his throat. "Rona Scrivson, may you rest in fields covered with your favorite flowers, may the wind be ever at your back and the sun light your way. Wherever you land in the Drift, you surely deserve nothing less."

They stood long moments in silence, and Bryndor worked to swallow the thick feeling in his throat. Eventually, his voice became steady enough to speak. "I don't think I know all the things I'm going to miss about you,

Aunt Ro," said Bryndor. His eyes and nose stung again with the threat of tears. "And it feels like there isn't anything that can fill the empty space inside where you should be."

Lluthean removed three billow seeds. He splinted his ribs with one hand, and with the other, juggled the three seeds a few times, then let them clatter among the stones of the cairn. "I'll miss . . . everything, Aunt Ro. But I think it's like Bryn said."

After several more minutes of silence, they rode back to their home. Constable Whirik sat on their front porch and stood as they approached. The man hooked a thumb into his doublet and held his hat in hand.

The yard looked familiar, unchanged, even. Rings lounged at the constable's feet; goats nibbled at clumps of grass. Bryndor stared at the window and imagined Rona's smiling face appearing there any moment. His gaze then lingered on the front door, where he half-expected her to barge out and berate the three of them for allowing their clothes to become soiled. Everything looked commonplace, but without Rona, nothing felt right.

Someone had removed the corpse of the assassin. A dark stain of blood in the grass next to the stone wall was the only sign of the struggle. Markum and Harland offered to unhitch the wagon, leaving the three of them to address the constable.

"I've got no words to express my condolences to your family, Kevold," said the constable. "I spoke to the other stranger, or I tried to. He wouldn't say much except that you acted in self-defense."

They all stood in silence. Whirik waited for Kaellor to acknowledge his statement. Sensing no new information, the constable continued, "Well, I don't think it's too hard to see that's the case when a stranger turns up on your property to cause you harm. While I can't say I can begin to understand the wounds the man received, it seems he met a just end nonetheless."

Whirik reached into his pocket and retrieved five gold crowns. He grabbed Bryndor's wrist, turned his palm up, and slapped the coins into his hand. "I'll trust you two to divide that up. It's the reward for bringing in that wolf."

The constable took a step back and placed his hat back on his head, then tucked his thumbs back into his vest. "Well," said Whirik, "the party at the Ram was canceled, and I have some loose ends to tie up. I'm sorry for your loss. If you need anything, let me know."

"Reddevek, how is he?" asked Kaellor. The constable turned a questioning eye to him. "The Northlander with the girl, you said you spoke to him."

"As I said, he wouldn't tell me much, and he can't get out of bed without some assistance," said the constable. "He'll survive, I imagine, but who can say how long it will be before he walks on his own."

"Let him know I'll be by soon enough," said Kaellor.

After Whirik left, Emile walked out of their home with puffy eyes and a swollen red nose. She hugged them each and muttered something about stopping over tomorrow evening for supper, then climbed into her family wagon with Markum and Harland. And just like that, the three of them stood alone.

Bryndor felt like his feet were rooted in place. He had no desire to walk into their home without the sound of Rona's humming or the smell of one of her teas. Lluthean must have felt the same, and they both stood in place, studying their own feet.

"Listen, boys," said Kaellor. "While Rona would be none too surprised at our collective sorrow, she would suffer none of it." He waited for them both to look up. "Llu, we need to splint your ribs, and then let's change all your dressings. After that, I'm going to brew some of her stilben root tea. I think we could all use some help getting to sleep this night."

Bryndor was thankful that his uncle had outlined a plan. Otherwise, he might have stood in their yard all night. Even so, something in Kaellor's strange detached manner itched at the periphery of his awareness. He shrugged off the feeling too spent from the day's events to consider it further.

The next morning still felt incomplete. They ate a simple breakfast, but the bread chewed hard, the cheese crumbled, and none of them thought to make a morning tea to wash it all down.

After breakfast, they joined the rector for a formal service. The man kept his words brief and cast blessings over the barrow, after which they endured the well-wishes of the townsfolk who attended the ceremony. The Tunkles attended, and Sadeen stole a private conversation with Lluthean. Even the Hawklin matron came to pay her respects.

They spent the next few days trying to find ways to distract themselves from the empty silence. Lluthean crafted small maps on high-quality vellum in earnest. Kaellor busied himself with long-neglected repairs around the farm. Bryndor scribed larger reproductions of the Southland map and tried his hand in the kitchen. His version of tea seemed either too weak or too strong, but they all appreciated his effort.

The week carried on as they adjusted to this new strange half-of-a-life. Twice a day, they played with the wolvryn pups, taking them out for walks and even lounging with them in the hay. Their time spent with the creatures seemed to distract each of them from darker thoughts. Bryndor thought he would need to return them to the Moorlok soon.

I don't know how long we should wait. Too long, and they'll become dependent on us. Too soon, and they won't be ready to fend for themselves.

They sat on the front porch and watched the smaller cub drag the larger one around by the ear; then both tumbled in a fuzzy ball. Lluthean giggled, and even Kaellor revealed a half-smile for the first time in a week, and the obligation to return the pups to the wild melted.

On the morning of the seventh day after Rona's death, Bryndor awoke to the smell of flatcakes and bacon. He and Lluthean stumbled into the common room together. His heart skipped at the thought that Rona might be the one making the meal, and by the way Lluthean barged through his door, he must have had a similar notion. They discovered Kaellor sitting at the kitchen table.

"Good morning," said Kaellor. He poured dark tea into three cups, and chunks of raw honeycomb were already warming on stacks of flatcakes divided onto three plates.

"What's the occasion, Kae?" asked Bryndor.

Kaellor gestured to their chairs, "Food first, then we talk."

They accepted his direction and made quick work of the meal. Bryndor sipped at the tea, a perfect brew of Rona's stout. He drained a cup and poured himself another. Something in the dark liquid warmed his belly and awakened his senses. The familiar taste put him in a mood to smile for the first time all week.

Lluthean rolled a coin back and forth across his knuckles. Bryndor watched Kaellor, waiting. *If I know you, Uncle, there's a plan to all of this. An announcement or a proposal, something, will follow.*

He looked at his brother from the corner of his eye just in time to see the coin flying toward him. Bryndor caught the coin before it struck him in the temple and arched an eyebrow at Lluthean, who tilted his head in respect. All the while, Kaellor sipped at his tea.

"Alright, Kae, let's have it," said Bryndor. "Before I catch a random flying object to the head." He flicked the coin back at Lluthean, who snatched it with ease.

"Fair enough," said Kaellor. "The assassin that killed Rona was one of two men from Aarindorn; the other is an old acquaintance of mine, Reddevek."

"Is that the stranger with the gold and silver tattoos?" asked Lluthean.

"He is," said Kaellor.

"How is he managing?" asked Bryndor.

"He's made of tough stuff, but he will not be able to travel for a long time," said Kaellor. "If I'm right, Reddevek was tasked by the regent to find us and then convince us to come back to Aarindorn. I will need to prepare for a long journey."

"You plan to go back then?" asked Bryndor. He became aware of something in Kaellor's stance, a rare glimmer of uncertainty.

"Yes," said Kaellor, "but you are both of an age to make your own decisions. If you decide to stay, you could make a good life down here. I'm sure the Tellends would be happy to check in on—"

"We're coming. At least, I am. Nothing here feels right without Aunt Ro. Besides, you always said we're at our best when we stand together," Bryndor said.

Lluthean offered a theatrical sigh. "What will Sadeen do without me?"

Kaellor exhaled, and something in his countenance changed. His shoulders drew back, and he raised his chin, possibly to argue, then nodded with acceptance. He looked like he did when coordinating plans for a cartography endeavor, one set high in the mountains and deep in the middle of winter.

"When do we leave?" asked Bryndor.

"Tomorrow. If none of us are staying, I am signing the property over to Harland," said Kaellor. "I'll grab provisions. You have the day to prepare."

Lluthean stuck out his lower lip. "Why so fast?"

"We are not just returning because of the regent," said Kaellor. "The man that killed Rona came here for us, the three of us. Someone from Aarindorn sent him here. I mean to find out who and exact some justice."

Bryndor sat back in the chair, considering his uncle's words and the strange dark expression that had settled across his face.

Chapter Twenty-Eight: The Prince and the Warden

Seven days after his encounter with Vardell, Reddevek still required significant assistance from Della and her brother just to rise from bed. With the aid of a crutch, he managed to navigate to the chamber pot, but changing position caused flares of sharp pain in his lower back and right butt cheek. If he tried to pivot or bear weight with the right leg, pain seared all the way down to his toes.

Della thought he must have broken a bone in the small of his back or maybe his pelvis and had offered to send for a healer from Riverton, but he declined. He didn't trust the Southland healers to do anything but relieve him of coin, a commodity of which he found himself in short supply.

A soft knock at the door interrupted his thoughts. "Who is it?" he answered.

Thin fingers pushed open the door, followed by Ranika's smiling face. She walked into the room with a bounce in her step. She wore an oversized shirt tucked into trousers, and from the side still resembled a boy more than a little. Della had taken the girl under her wing and saw that she bathed and ate, but Ranika refused to consider wearing anything resembling a dress.

"Good morning, Nika," said Reddevek. "Ms. Della know you're up here?"

"No, but I already finished helping her in the kitchen." The girl fingered the hilt of the ruby-encrusted dagger she wore on a belt sheath.

"Don't tell me you used my dagger to peel potatoes again?" Reddevek arched an eyebrow. He thought back to their first meeting in Callish. Something about the girl's impish nature always made him want to smile. He'd never met anyone quite like her.

She walked over and sat next to him on his bed. Her light frame barely moved the blanket. "It's no good for peeling, but it is for chopping!" She slashed a hand onto his bed.

To resist the edge of a smile that started to pull at his cheek, he puffed out a breath of air. "What brings you up here this morning?"

"There's a Northman come to see you. The man from that home where we fought Vardell," said Ranika.

He thought back to the events of that afternoon and how this malnourished gutter rat had basically saved his life. Since then, Ranika never strayed far. He had plenty of time to think about how she must have trailed him through the wilderness. He imagined that she was accustomed to meager rations. What he couldn't figure out was how she'd managed to follow him without his awareness.

"When will you be able to ride Zippy, Red?" she asked.

"When I can manage to walk down the stairs on my own two feet," he said. "Nika, how is it you followed me all the way here, and I never knew it? You say you snuck into my camp at night more than once."

Ranika nodded. "I ate your leftovers and gave Zippy treats sometimes."

"How did you come and go without me knowing?" he asked.

She puckered her lips to the side, thinking about his question. "Well, I got real good at hiding myself in Callish. If you make yourself small, nobody pays attention to you. If they don't pay you any mind, they don't beat you or take what's yours."

"And why didn't you just tell me you were there?" Reddevek asked.

"Because you would have sent me back, and I could see you was a man going somewhere," she said as she kicked her legs back and forth on the edge of the bed. "And somewhere was bound to be better than Callish."

Reddevek mentally retraced his journey through the Southland forest. His gift should have revealed some sign of her passing. *Maybe I was so focused on finding that plant that I just missed it?*

A knock at his door interrupted his thoughts. "It's open!" he said.

Kaellor Baellentrell entered the room. The two men regarded one another, and the prince seemed almost uncertain. "Nika, why don't you let Master Kevold and I have a private word? I'll make it up to you with cards later this afternoon."

"No problem. Feth is gonna show me how to shoe a horse, and then we're gonna walk Zippy!" The girl bounced down off the bed. She made a point to check and secure the knife in its belt sheath, then scampered down the stairs.

Kaellor's stiff posture relaxed. He closed the door, set a leather satchel on the floor, then reached for a chair with a raised eyebrow. "Be my guest, Your Highness," said Reddevek in answer to the unspoken question. "Forgive me; I'm not able to get around too easy."

"Thanks for that, Reddevek," said Kaellor, thumbing back to the door. "Besides the boys, there's only three others down here who know my real name. And in that light, let's drop the formal titles. I haven't answered to those for over a decade, and I don't intend to start now."

"I figured that the only way you managed to remain hidden all these years meant you adopted a new identity," he said. "Only thing I don't understand is why you let the heirs use their birth names."

Kaellor sighed as if expecting the question. "Their parents crafted a rather unique mantle. I can't say I understand how, but the binding suppressed not just their gift but also their very identities. Until just this past month, their mantle kept anyone from remembering them. Anyone who met them forgot about them by morning."

"That had to be a strange blessing," said the warden. "Nobody remembered them?"

"Just their aunt and a family the boys grew up with here in the Bend," said Kaellor.

"When did that change?" asked Reddevek.

"It started to fade over a month ago while we were in Hammond, a kingdom far to the south," said Kaellor. "We took a job finishing a map of the southwestern coast and collected census information for the king there. When we returned, it became obvious that even relative strangers remembered them."

Reddevek grunted and raised his eyebrows. "A month ago? That's about the time the regent had his vision, the one that set me on the path down here to you."

"How is Therek these days?" asked Kaellor.

"He manages to hold the noble houses together, but I don't think he cares much for the job. He sent me here to find you and convince you to return with your nephews."

"I can't say that I am surprised," said Kaellor. "A month ago, I would have turned you down. Life down here is comfortable. The heirs have a small fortune waiting for them in Riverton, and both have mastered cartography."

"Your Highness, ahh, Kaellor, Therek believes Aarindorn will thrive only with a Baellentrell on the throne," said Reddevek.

"Did he see that in one of his visions, too?" asked Kaellor. "You don't have to convince me. The boys and I decided to return if for no other reason than to investigate who sent that assassin."

"That task might be more difficult than you expect if he really belongs to the Lacuna," said Reddevek.

"Who are the Lacuna?" asked Kaellor.

"They are a sect that sprang up after the Abrogator's War. We think they have guilds in every duchy across the kingdom, and their members cut across all the major families. They deal in black market goods, vivith, stolen merchandise, and occasionally kidnappings. If there is a brothel turning a profit, you can bet the man collecting the fee is a member of the Lacuna," said Reddevek.

"Why does Therek allow them to exist? Surely he has the means to eliminate such a dark element?" asked Kaellor.

"We tried several times to place an Outrider on the inside, but they have ways of sniffing out imposters," said the warden. "Since they stick to low-level crime, the regent decided not to pursue them any further."

"Are the Lacuna loyal to any particular house?" asked Kaellor.

"They are loyal to anyone with the coin," answered Reddevek. He shifted with a grimace, moving his weight off of one butt cheek to the other. A flare of hot pain shot down from his back into his groin and throbbed in his right ballsack. He gripped the sheets and clenched his teeth. "I hope something dark finds Vardell in the Drift and grinds him sideways, at least three times and with a very pointy stick."

"That bad?" Kaellor asked. "Is there anything I can do to help?"

The pain subsided, and Reddevek wiped beads of sweat from his lip. "It only hurts when I move." He realized he was panting and allowed his breath to slow as the pain receded. "I heard what you said to him, to Vardell, about the Drift. Was any of that true?"

Kaellor shrugged. "I don't actually know. Probably not, but I wasn't sure I could cause him enough physical pain, so stealing any peace he might have before he died felt like a small amount of justice."

Kaellor reached into the satchel and removed two tins, one with hand-painted yellow flowers, the other with purple pitcher-shaped flowers embossed on the outside. "Rona, the woman Vardell killed, had a talent for herbs and teas. The yellow one is a faint stilben root tea. You'll know it as bandle root up north. It's not enough to cause you to fall asleep, but it can likely make your nights better. The other one is Maedra's pitchers. It smells bad and tastes worse. Brew it once a day as strong as you can stand, and it should speed your recovery."

Reddevek looked at the prince. *Who is this man? The Kaellor I knew always lurked in his brother's shadow and seemed content to avoid responsibility. Only his dead fiancé could coerce him to greater things back in the day.*

"The years down here seem to have been good for you. If I might ask, how are the heirs?" asked Reddevek.

"Bryndor, the older one, is thoughtful, resourceful, and responsible. He never stops until a job is done, and he always seems to find his way to doing the right thing without being told," said Kaellor. He reached down and produced a flask of liquor. He walked to a small table and retrieved two small cups.

"Lluthean is still young and has yet to inherit his brother's ability to see the world from another's point of view. But where his brother labors under a burden of responsibility, Lluthean thrives in the moment. He's got a crafty mind and an uncanny memory. You should see that lad draft a map. It's like his arca prime is cartography."

Kaellor splashed a finger of amber liquid into each cup and handed one to Reddevek. They clanged the glasses together, and Reddevek tossed the liquor back. The liquid burned his throat then evaporated, leaving a caramel honey taste on his tongue. The drink kindled a subtle and pleasant burn in his stomach.

"A man could get used to that, but it reminds me of resco," said Reddevek. "One splash cures the rot; two makes you brave."

"Three grants a dreamless sleep, and four grants the grave," Kaellor finished the rhyme but kept a neutral expression.

Either he's more broken than he lets on, or he's more stoic than the regent's daughter.

"I haven't thought about resco in years," said Kaellor. "This is Malvressian honey-cut; only it burns more like a good bourbon. One more?"

"As long as you don't tell Della," said Reddevek as he held up his glass. Kaellor splashed more of the liquid into the cup and sat back. "If you don't mind me asking, how have the heirs come into their gift without sitting for their Rite of Revealing?"

"They haven't. Their arms are as bare as mine," said Kaellor.

"I thought . . . I'm certain I felt rune fire, just before I arrived, out in the forest," said Reddevek.

"You likely did," said Kaellor. "I think that part of their mantle frayed, allowing some of their power to leak out. If I'm right, they have each channeled something like rune fire once, but only at the point of death."

"Two in a generation; two that can command rune fire? That's unheard of." Reddevek sipped at the honey rum considering the possible repercussions of the prince's words. "The Usurper, Tarkannen, what happens to his banishment if their binding fails altogether?"

"I'm not sure," said the prince. "Therek Lefledge might be able to shed some light on the situation, and that's another reason to return to Aarindorn."

"I ran into a crush of grondle in the Borderlands on the way here," said Reddevek. Kaellor looked at him without surprise. Reddevek explained, "We hunted them to the Drift in the year after the war. It's the first sighting in more than ten years. With everything else you're telling me . . . coincidence is the virtue of a monk."

"Man of no knowledge," recited Kaellor. "Benyon Garr used to call my brother and me that when we trained together with the gift." The prince stared off into the distance for a moment. "I have been away too long. What can you tell me of the journey back?"

"When will you leave?" asked Reddevek.

Kaellor ran a knuckle back and forth across the silver strip of beard in the center of his chin. "I was hoping to leave in the morning to take advantage of the favorable weather. The boys and I are no strangers to the road, but I would prefer to avoid making camp in the winter."

Reddevek tossed back the last of his rum, nodded his thanks, then sighed. "Part of me wants to talk you into waiting until I can join you, but another part of me knows that Therek needs you back as soon as possible."

"How bad is your injury, Warden?" asked Kaellor.

"It's better than last week, but even a tender would know I'm not going to be able to ride for at least a month, maybe longer," said Reddevek. "You should take Zippy, my Aarindin."

Kaellor considered the offer, then waved his hand. "It's a kind offer, but I've become accustomed to the saddle, and I don't imagine a spirited Aarindin would take too kindly to that."

They spoke for several more hours. Reddevek recounted his journey, including his encounter with Karragin's quad. They then discussed current politics and reviewed the last few years of Aarindorian history.

A knock on the door interrupted their conversation. Della walked in with a tray of food, cocking an eyebrow at the bottle of rum.

Kaellor replaced the liquor in his satchel and bowed deferentially to the woman. He turned to Reddevek. "Well, Master Reddevek, I have made arrangements with Della and Ingram to see to your room and board and that of your horse. It's the least we can do for all your trouble. Do be sure to take that tea at least once a day. Rona would be pleased to know it was put to good use. Until next time, eyes to the horizon."

Chapter Twenty-Nine: Goodbye to the Tellends

Kaellor entered Constable Whirik's offices with the deed to his home in hand. He had already amended the title naming Markum and Emile Tellend as the new owners. While Whirik notarized the simple document, Kaellor deflected several of his questions with vague responses. Eventually, he indicated that he and the boys had an offer to work for the Kingdom of Hammond, far to the south. As Whirik handed the document back, Kaellor realized he felt no remorse. He puzzled at the realization that a certain part of him had always known he would stand here one day completing this transaction.

Have I always known I would leave? What did I think was going to happen to Rona? He thought about the large deposit waiting for them all in Riverton and realized a significant part of him had planned to stay. *But something in me seems eager to return. Giver's blessings, when did that happen?*

He rode to the Tellends' farm next. Harland Tellend waved to him as he approached. He dismounted Scout and greeted the young man.

"Good morning, Harland. Where are your folks? I was hoping for a moment of their time."

"Sure thing, Kae." The young man tossed a pale of leftover greens to a few pigs, hopped back over a wood fence, and joined Kaellor.

"Maybe we could sit at the table inside?" Kaellor asked. "I have a few things I wanted to go over with you all."

Harland walked to the side of their home and yelled to the backside of the house, "Mother, grab Father, Kae is here!"

The young man led Kaellor into the modest home just in time to see Markum and Emile walk in from the back door. Emile wore an apron, gloves and held pruning shears. They both kicked dirt from their boots, and Markum set a weathered hoe in the corner. Kaellor tapped the rolled document in his hand.

"And here I thought I was being productive today. Your family's work ethic shames the rest of us," said Kaellor.

Emile set a kettle over flame and filled it with cider. The rich cinnamon aroma filled the room. "The weeds in the garden don't take a day of rest, though, by the All-Mother, I surely wish they would."

"It's not really a good day for weed pullin'," said Markum. He wiped sweat from his sun-leathered brow. "Need a good rain for weed pullin'; wet soil makes for easy work."

"Hoe when it's dry and pull when it's wet?" Kaellor asked.

"I'm glad to see that all that traveling you do hasn't made you forget some of the things we taught you," said Markum with a grin. "Can you stay for lunch, Kae? I have a cheese wheel in the cellar just begging to be sliced open. We've plenty to fill your belly."

Kaellor weighed his options for the conversation he had planned. He'd hoped for a quick goodbye, but a light lunch was less time than these dear friends deserved, and at least as much as he could accommodate. He placed a hand on the farmer's broad shoulders. "Far be it from me to pass on the famous Tellend hospitality." He sat down at their kitchen table.

"I see you're already prepared for winter." Kaellor nodded out the window toward a generous pile of split wood stacked neatly against the side of the cottage.

"We have to do something to keep out of Em's way," said Markum. "Harland split most of that, but between the two of us, we managed to get ahead this year. I think winter's comin' earlier than most expect."

Kaellor knew not to doubt the man's intuition about the weather. "What makes you say that?"

Markum sat down and scratched his belly, then shrugged. "It's just a feeling, but you didn't ride out here to ask me about our winter preparations. Is everything alright? How are the boys?"

Just like a Tellend to speak plainly and with a care for me and mine. Kaellor tried to force a smile, but it felt hollow. "They're mending; we are all adjusting. But I do have a purpose in coming here this morning. I came to ask one last favor, share some good company, and say goodbye."

Both Markum and Harland cocked their heads to the side, considering his words. Kaellor almost laughed at the two of them sitting side by side and so eerily mimicking one another's gestures. Emile broke the silence by placing mugs before them all and pouring hot cider.

She joined them at the table. "Since it's a serious conversation then, a toast," she said. "We give thanks to the All-Mother for those that truly love us."

"May the All-Mother warm the hearts of those who don't," added Markum.

Emile continued, "And if cold stone still dwells in their hearts."

Then they all joined the toast in a chorus, "May she turn their ankles that we may know them by their limping." They clanged mugs and giggled.

Markum retrieved a wheel of cheese and, in a few minutes, had set a large platter of the aromatic yellow curd with thick slices of bread and spiced dry sausage. They each nibbled from the plate.

"Now, what's this about goodbye, Kae?" asked Emile.

Kaellor sipped at the cider, thinking about how best to approach the conversation. *Just getting here was the hard part. Now that you're here, best to get on with it.*

"Since Rona's death, the boys and I have decided to return to the north. I intend to discover who sent that assassin. But even then, there are lots of other questions that need to be answered, and I'll never find the answers down here. I don't want to get into all the specifics, but I wondered if, well, I don't think we will return for a long time if—" He struggled to find the right words. The Tellends, like all those in the Bend, carried themselves with an independent pride.

"You need someone to mind your place," Markum finished for him. "Say no more, Kae. I'm sure Harland would be happy to keep an eye out for squatters."

"Shouldn't be a problem at all," said Harland with a mouthful of bread.

"That's just the thing." Kaellor lifted his eyes from the table with a soft smile. "I don't want you to simply mind the home; I want you to have it. Here, I already amended the deed with the constable. All you have to do is sign it and return it to Whirik to make the transition smooth." He handed over the rolled parchment.

Markum swallowed hard and blinked once. "You . . . you really are leavin' then?"

"Yes," replied Kaellor softly. "The homestead, it will be empty. You could sell it, or it would make a good home for anyone you saw fit. I don't mean to presume you might want to live there, of course." He picked his next words with care. "But it would be a shame to let the place fall apart."

Markum and Harland each cocked a proud eyebrow in question, and Emile broke the awkward silence. "Kae, if you are sure you are leaving." She put a gentle hand on Markum's shoulder to still his tongue. "We would be honored to care for the place until you return. It is a wonderful home and so close to the water."

"No, Emile. I need you to know if you move there, it's yours—unconditionally," Kaellor said, dusting off a memory as he continued, "Do you remember when we arrived at your doorstep all those years back?"

"Remember?" Markum chuckled. "We were havin' a giggle yesterday at how haggard tired and run-down you looked with two whelps on your back. You blew in with a rainstorm and lit up the smile on my Em's face like no other."

"I remember too," said Kaellor, "and I also remember how you welcomed me like I was your son. You introduced me to the fine people in Journey's Bend, to Rona. I'll never be able to repay you the kindness. But it would be a start if you would accept the home. Honestly, you three are the only thing close to family we have in these parts. It feels right leaving the home in your hands."

"I don't know," said Harland. Kaellor could sense the proud man's reluctance to receive such a gift.

Markum sat back with beefy arms folded across his belly for a moment. Then he leaned forward onto the table and smiled. "Em is right," said Markum. "It's a wonderful gift, Kae. Say no more. Let's just enjoy the afternoon."

They retired to the front porch, where rockers and a swing afforded easy conversation. Markum puffed the last bit of his sweet Riverfield tobacco, Harland sharpened the blade of a shear, and Emile knitted. Kaellor took stock of the day, making sure to mark this memory of the place he had called home for a time.

Their conversation lingered several hours, as things always do with good and true friends. When Kaellor clasped Markum in a goodbye shake, the old farmer pulled him in warmly, and the two embraced in a firm hug.

Emile wiggled her way in between the two and pushed a covered basket into Kaellor's arms. "Can't a lady get some lovin' here?" She giggled. They embraced one last time, and Kaellor waved goodbye as he saddled up Scout for the short ride home.

Chapter Thirty: Symbolic Gifts

Lluthean wandered out to the barn and ushered the two geldings to the side pasture while the wolvryn pups yipped with excitement. As soon as he opened the door to their pen, they tumbled out of the barn. He giggled at their exuberance. The larger one, a male, chased a chicken to the side of the house. The smaller one, female, stayed beside Lluthean. She whined softly and stretched up from her hind legs, begging for attention.

Lluthean grimaced, splinting his ribs, then bent to pick her up. His pains had eased in the last week, but if he turned too fast or coughed, a sharp stab reminded him of the injury. All the swelling in his face had resolved, leaving him with bruises and sore muscles, but he didn't think Bruug had caused him any other lasting injuries.

The pup licked at his neck, and he rewarded her affection by scratching behind her ears. She rolled in his arms onto her back and stretched. Sunlight filtered through her coat; the fluffy, darker outercoat of a puppy had begun to shed, and thick, wavy, silver-white fur was emerging. He tilted her up for a kiss, and she licked his nose. Her eyes drew him in. In the last week, faint blue outer rings had appeared, and dark purple shards of color radiated out from her black pupils.

"A girl could get jealous watching the two of you."

Lluthean turned to see Sadeen walk around the edge of the stone wall onto their property. She tucked a lock of sandy brown hair behind her ear, and her freckled cheeks peaked with her smile as the wind caught at the hem of a summer dress at her ankles. He masked his surprise at her appearance by setting the pup down. She trotted over to Sadeen, then ran after the other wolvryn on the far side of the yard. Sadeen turned a sly gaze his way.

"I saw your uncle in town gathering supplies. Does that mean the famous Scrivsons are leaving again?" she asked.

"Yes, we have another contract in the south," he said.

"It's a bit late in the season to be roaming the countryside, isn't it?" she asked.

"Perhaps," he said. "But I think we could use something to distract us from Rona's death."

"How long will you be gone this time?" she asked.

"I'm not sure. We might not come back, Sadeen," he answered.

"I figured as much. What's Bryndor doing?" she asked.

He puzzled at the strange question. "He's packing for tomorrow."

Sadeen sighed as if his answer had settled some obvious question. She started walking, and he followed her back to the barn. "Sadeen, what?" he asked.

She turned him and pushed him back onto a pile of hay. He fell back with a pained grimace, the stab of pain in his side flashing once. She giggled and gently straddled him. Her thighs felt warm on his hips. She leaned in to kiss him before he could organize his thoughts further. He didn't know he could become excited so fast. In an instant, he became more than a little aroused and embarrassed. His fruits shifted, and it felt achy and hot and wonderful.

By the All-Mother, she's sitting right on it!

She smelled like apple blossom, and her lips felt wet. She leaned back and regarded him. "That will have to hold you until you come back. If you ever come back."

For the first time, possibly ever, his mind felt numb and tingly—so much that all he could do was nod agreement. She leaned forward, and they kissed once more. Everywhere their bodies touched monopolized all of his attention. She weighed very little, but he became intimately aware of the pressure of her breasts on his chest.

She rubbed her temple against his, and he turned to kiss her neck, but she pulled back again. "That's about as far as we should go. I'm not the type for a fast grind in the hay."

For the first time since she threw him down, he felt straw poking his back in a few places. He ignored the itchy discomfort, drawn into her brown eyes.

"I wish we weren't leaving," he said, feeling more than a little sheepish.

She arched her brow and smiled, then brushed a lock of hair off his forehead. "I know. Me too."

Further words escaped him as a weight fell upon his lower legs. Sadeen giggled again as the two wolvryn pups rolled across the floor of the barn. One of them plunged its nose into his pant leg by the ankle. Without warning, Sadeen stood up, leaving Lluthean sprawled in the hay with the wolvryn pups tangled in his legs. She adjusted her dress and brushed the straw off, then threw a glance down at his fruits with a look of appreciation.

It took him more time to disentangle the pups and stand. The pain in his ribs flared anew with any movement. He looked over to see her one last time, and she leaned back through the barn door opening and blew him a kiss. "Don't you forget me, Lluthean Scrivson. I won't forget you."

He stepped to follow her but stumbled over his own feet, landing oddly in the hay. He lifted his head to see both pups regarding him with heads turned to the side. Once again, he struggled to his feet with guarded motions to avoid aggravating his fractured rib.

By the time he wandered out of the barn and out onto the road, he could only barely see the top of her sandy brown hair bobbing a light step over the top of a hillside. And then she was gone.

He called the pups back, fed them, and kenneled them back in the pen, then walked back into their home to find Bryndor kneeling on the floor, examining the contents of a saddlebag. Lluthean sat down in one of the common room chairs, his mind still oddly numb. Bryndor reached up with a frown and removed a shaft of straw from the top of his hair.

"What have you been doing?" asked Bryndor.

Lluthean ran his fingers through his hair, releasing a few more errant bits of straw. "Saying goodbye to Sadeen."

Bryndor turned his head to the side in disbelief. "Did you at least let the horses out while you were romping with the pups in the barn?"

Lluthean stared long at his brother then grinned.

"You feel alright, Llu?" Bryndor asked.

"I'm fine," he said. He sat there a while longer, then retrieved his saddlebags and started to organize the contents on the kitchen table. They had most of their things packed when Kaellor returned home late in the afternoon.

He entered with a basket under his arm. Lluthean considered the bundle. "Going away gifts for anyone in particular?" he asked.

"No, these are from the Tellends; early Harvestmoon gifts. They ought to serve you well on the journey ahead." From the basket, Kaellor withdrew two wool tunics. They were dyed a forest green with toggles near the v-neck. The stitching and embroidery around the collar revealed tedious attention to detail.

Lluthean whistled long and low in appreciation as he pulled the tunic overhead, admiring the fitting. "I almost feel like royalty in this. So, what did we get them?" He grinned.

"Well, for starters, our love and gratitude," said Kaellor. "But when we leave, I have arranged that the Tellends should own the homestead. I withdrew coin for our journey but left enough to provide the Tellends with a small dividend from our holdings in Riverton. I could think of no others who deserve it more. I hope you approve?"

It was an odd question. Usually, Kaellor would not find it necessary to consult the brothers regarding important business decisions.

"Right-fine choice, Kae. Like you said, no one more deserving," replied Lluthean.

Kaellor nodded. "I was thinking on the way over here that—well, I want you two to know I am aware that I am asking everything of you. To leave this place and return with me to Aarindorn, it's a lot. I remember the day I left. It was difficult."

Kaellor's eyes lost their focus, and he seemed preoccupied for a moment. "But we landed in a good place, and whatever becomes of the weeks ahead, I want you both to know how proud I am of you. I'm still a little shocked at how easily you agreed to come with me. I guess I expected if this day ever arrived that I would have quite the argument on my hands."

Lluthean stood and eyed his brother, who nodded in agreement. "Seems like the right time to me," muttered Bryndor, who then retired to his room.

"Kae, I don't think we have ever once really been able to say thank you and have it mean what it needs to mean." Lluthean picked his words slowly. "I don't think we ever imagined what those times must have been like for you. And like Bryndor said earlier, you gave up no less for us, how could we possibly do anything except jump at the chance to go?"

Bryndor returned with a large object in his arms covered by a blanket from his bed. "Llu's right, Kae. So here is your early Harvestmoon present from us."

Bryndor set the heavy object on Kaellor's lap, then removed the blanket to reveal a new saddle. The leather was freshly oiled, and the metal bindings reflected the firelight. Kaellor ran his hand over the pommel and seat in disbelief.

"Oh, and one more thing," said Lluthean. He walked into his room and returned with the Logrend sword and scabbard.

Bryndor removed the saddle, and Lluthean laid the sword and scabbard into Kaellor's hands. Kaellor ran his hands along the leather sheath. Etched deep into the neck of the scabbard and stained a dark brown, scrolling, artistic symbols now decorated the casing. Kaellor turned it over and saw his name scrolled down the backside.

He removed the Logrend sword to discover similar intricate symbols running the length of the blade on one side and again his name on the other. He ran fingers across the engraving in question.

"We thought we needed to change it, to mark it as yours. So we had one of the local gilders show us the basics," said Lluthean. "We engraved the scabbard then copied that template onto the blade."

Kaellor's expression remained aloof and contemplative. "If you don't like it, we can have it buffed out, Kae," said Bryndor.

"I've never seen such a thing. It's perfect," muttered Kaellor. "But, where did you come across such knowledge?"

"Not all of our lessons come from you." Lluthean smiled. "And together, we found the time to design the scabbard."

"As for the saddle, Kae, you have needed a new one for a long time," explained Bryndor. "We bought it with some of the reward money."

Kaellor sat, silent and misty-eyed. After a few moments, he abruptly stood and hugged them both.

"I fear you have caught me empty-handed," Kaellor said wryly, "but thankfully, Harvestmoon is still weeks away. Come then, let's get our things packed."

Without waiting for a response, he retired to his room. Lluthean looked to Bryndor, who shrugged.

"Is he going to be alright?" asked Lluthean in hushed tones. "When was the last time he smiled?"

"It was before the day he killed the assassin from the north," said Bryndor. He chewed on the inside of his lower lip. "We all need time to adjust. Maybe Kae needs more time."

Lluthean took comfort in the calm way his brother assessed their uncle. Bryndor stifled a yawn. "Good night, Llu."

Bryndor retired to his room, leaving Lluthean alone in the common room. He ran his finger along their desk, then traced the marks carved on the beam near the door. Kaellor had recorded most of the marks, documenting the boys' various growth spurts over the years. One of the entries was in Rona's handwriting. He turned toward the kitchen with a desire to share the memory of that day with her, but the kitchen, like his uncle, remained shrouded in somber shadows.

Chapter Thirty-One: A Hint of the Gift

Bryndor startled awake as his uncle shook his shoulder with a firm hand. "Bryn, Bryn, wake up!"

Bryndor sat up and squinted from the first light of the morning. Once Kaellor seemed convinced that he would rise, he rushed into Lluthean's room. Bryndor stumbled out into the common room to watch his uncle.

Kaellor stood by their humble dining table and waited for Lluthean to join them. His younger brother, shuffling his feet, finally arrived. Kaellor stood with a stiff posture and frowned at them both.

"What is it, Kae?" asked Lluthean.

Kaellor set the Logrend longsword on the table. The morning sun gleamed off the blade. As Kaellor grasped the sword to turn it for inspection, the sunlight reflected into Lluthean's eyes.

"Whoa! Down there, snapper!" Lluthean quipped at the sudden blinding flash.

"Yes, sorry, Llu," said Kaellor as he laid the sword down.

"Kae, what's on your mind?" asked Bryndor. Dark circles ringed Kaellor's eyes. *I would guess you didn't sleep at all last night, and you seem edgy today.*

"This here, on the crossguard and down the blade." Kaellor tapped the engravings on the sword. The design undulated in an intricate pattern and circled under the bindings to the pommel. "Look, this is important. I need to know. Who really engraved the sword? I have not seen these markings in, well, decades."

Puzzled, Bryndor picked up the end of the sword as if seeing it for the first time, then handed the pommel over to Lluthean. "We did, Kae, both of us. The gilder showed us the basics but thought our design was too elaborate. He also thought we would have to soak the blade in caustic alchemics to cast the pattern into such hard metal. But we managed pretty well without any of that. Most of the time, it was a one-man job, but we took turns," explained Bryndor.

"First, we burned the design into the scabbard. Then, just like copying the maps, used that as a template," said Lluthean.

Kaellor squinted his eyes, weighing their words. "You did it? You both did it together?" He stared at them for a long moment, then sat down. "Alright then, tell me about the symbols here at the pommel, the crossguard, and running up the side of the blade. These runes, in particular, are what I'm talking about." Kaellor prodded.

"The frilly engraving?" asked Lluthean through a stifled yawn. "Well, we sort of thought it needed something to mark the sword as yours. So I started it, and Bryndor finished it. We used a fine engraver and took turns with the etching. If you don't like it, we can just burr it back down smooth. But you're sort of stuck with the scabbard as it is."

Kaellor sighed. "So, just to be clear. You two drew these symbols? First in leather and then in metal; you two crafted the runes?" Kaellor tugged at his beard and eyed them with disbelief.

Bryndor raised the longsword with both hands and held it pommel up, blade down, appraising the weapon with a fresh skeptical eye. The engraving revealed the familiar design on one side and Kaellor's name on the other. "Yes, we did it. But I don't see what you're bothered by there, Kae. It's just a decorative pattern. We simply thought the sword needed something there."

Kaellor looked from Bryndor to Lluthean and back, then steadied both hands on the table. He appeared to wrestle with a heavy decision. *As if we haven't done enough of that this week already.*

Eventually, he sat down and looked at them both. "When you decided the sword hilt needed something, tell me about that moment. Tell me about the very time you placed the first rune."

"What are you getting at, Kae? What rune?" asked Lluthean.

"Here, on the crossguard! These . . . engravings, these are power runes representing the Aarindorian symbol for the guardian," Kaellor said the words slowly and with an emphasis that left Bryndor wondering if he was impressed or angry.

"Llu, only artisans exceptionally strong in their gift can craft these symbols in leather, and to create them in metal is another thing altogether. The act alone requires a master of the gift and a significant investment . . ." Kaellor's words trailed from his lips, and he looked at his nephews as if seeing them for the first time.

After a long, silent moment of searching Bryndor and Lluthean's eyes, Kaellor leaned back. He appeared oddly defeated. "My goodness, I believe you. You really have no idea what you've accomplished here, none at all." A wistful expression played across his face. For the first time since Rona's death, he seemed lighter.

Bryndor relaxed at the change in Kaellor's demeanor, and Lluthean scratched his belly while catching his first true morning yawn. "Sometimes the Giver gives," murmured Kaellor. "So, when exactly did you two lay these engravings down?"

"Well, about one to two weeks back, I'll wager," Bryndor answered.

"That seems about right," added Lluthean. "It was one of the days you left for Riverton."

"We started drafting maps, but one of us got distracted," said Bryndor with a sidelong glance to his brother. "Llu pulled the sword out to sharpen the blade, so I began to doodle."

Lluthean continued, "Then we sort of took turns pretending to swing the sword, and it felt like it needed something more. Together we made the design, then transferred it to the scabbard. The rest was just hours of etching."

Kaellor shook his head again. "Llu, what I have been trying to tell you is that these are not just etchings or engravings. You two changed the weapon; you made it a thing of power. Now it's a weapon I could only dream of. Somehow, you altered it with your gift. And that means it must have been leaking through the mantle longer than I realized. The Giver take me. Two weeks ago?" Kaellor asked.

Bryndor nodded. "If zenith played some part in all this, how come we didn't feel anything like that thunderclap with the wolvryn? I didn't even see a spark."

"Channeling zenith isn't all about lightning bolts and thunder. Sometimes the strongest action is evoked from the smallest gesture." Kaellor sighed. "I thought about postponing our trip until Reddevek could join us, but we have to leave this morning as we planned. If your mantle is failing, then it's possible—" His intense frown left no question that he considered the issues grave.

"What's possible, Kae?" asked Lluthean.

"Time . . . need more time," Kaellor responded in a contemplative tone. "Look here, are you both packed?"

They both nodded. "Alright then, I'll explain everything on the road. First, you need to ride over to the Tellends and say your goodbyes. They know some part of our plan but don't tell anyone we ride north. We leave as soon as you're both ready."

He sheathed the Logrend sword, grabbed his new saddle, and marched out to the barn. Lluthean watched for a moment, then wandered back into his room to get dressed.

After the intense conversation, Bryndor stood in the empty, quiet room. He imagined Rona standing in the kitchen, brewing tea, and Kaellor next to her, chopping vegetables for a stew. He inhaled once. Faint traces of herbal tea and stew wafted from the timbers. He smiled, then dismissed the memory and prepared for the day.

Chapter Thirty-Two: The Sandbar Camp

Three men sat astride mounts watching the late summer sun climb over the distant tree line of the Moorlok. Bryndor and Lluthean rode their familiar dapple grey geldings, and Kaellor sat astride Scout. The constant whisper of the Shelwyn River accompanied by a few songbirds echoed over the river valley they had called home for the last twelve years.

Bryndor turned in his saddle. The wounds upon his neck, shoulder, and thigh had healed, but the unforgiving scabs pulled and stung when he rotated his head too far. He eyed his uncle, who sat in quiet contemplation. Mounted with his new saddle and gear, Kaellor Baellentrell wore the title of Prince of Aarindorn for the first time in twelve years and looked every bit the part. Something about his bearing gave Bryndor a sense of security, and he smiled appreciatively.

Kaellor turned, rubbed the chin hairs of his beard with the back of his hand, and addressed them both. "We ride south out of town, then break east until we reach the Shelwyn. We'll follow the river back north through the Moorlok, then pick our way east along the south spine of the Korjinth. I'm figuring at least three weeks for that much of the journey. From there, we'll book passage aboard a ship from the coastal city Callish. That's when the fun begins."

"Callish? The Callish? The rum-filled, pirate-laden, loose-women Callish?" asked Lluthean. "Count me in. If only a part of that is true, I need to see it!"

"Well," replied Kaellor, "at least a third of it is true. It's hard to imagine that city as dry. More than a decade is a long time for a harbor city, and a lot can change. Let's keep our eyes to the horizon and see what we see, shall we?"

The three set out at a trot, letting the horses warm in the morning sun. After they cleared the edge of town, they rode three abreast. By late morning, the fields of Journey's Bend yielded to the foliage of the Moorlok. Lluthean took the lead, with Kaellor and Bryndor following. The horses managed the trail with ease, though they could not travel faster than a trot along the unpredictable river edge.

Kaellor eventually broke the silence. "Llu, I had assumed the stiff leather pouch off your saddlehorn was a new way to pack an oddity until I saw the black nose peeking out."

Kaellor looked back to Bryndor. "By the Giver, do you have one too? A wolvryn pup?" he asked over his shoulder.

Bryndor nodded with a shrug and checked his own package to see that it remained secure. He'd had the idea to divide one of the broad, cylindrical map cases. They had never found a use for the case before, and its rigid structure allowed the pups a portable den in which to travel. He lifted up the flap of cloth over the pup's head, who lay nestled into a ball while in a deep sleep.

"How do you propose to keep them confined to those pouches?" asked Kaellor.

"Stilben root," said Bryndor proudly, "we gave them each a piece wrapped in table scraps this morning, and they've slept ever since. I figure once we travel far enough away from home, we can turn them loose with no harm done."

Home. The notion made Bryndor drift back to the moment he'd stood alone in their empty common room. Home was the place you returned to, a familiar place, a safe place. Now, he traveled to this new home with uncertainty. He had so many questions, but they would have to wait until a break in the journey.

After traveling most of the day, evening found the men at a quiet sandbar along the banks of the Shelwyn. They tethered and groomed their mounts, falling into familiar patterns from so many other trips through the Southlands. They made a small camp around a fire and used their saddles as recliners, then shared a bit of jerky and dried fruits, courtesy of Emile Tellend.

"You suppose the pups will do alright out here?" asked Lluthean. They had released their charges into the woods when they began to stir a few hours back. The pups immediately began sniffing out their new environment, and the trio had quickly left them behind.

Bryndor sat facing the forest and smirked. "I don't think you'll have to wait long to find out." He pointed at the tree line. Two balls of sable fur lingered at the forest edge, then crept forward onto the sandbar. After lapping at the river water, the two seemed to have no trouble making themselves at home wrestling near the campfire.

"I was afraid of something like that," said Kaellor. He fed the smaller pup a piece of jerky, then lifted the creature unceremoniously to examine between its legs. "This one's a girl. How about that one, Bryn?"

Bryndor slapped at his thighs, welcoming the playful tumble of the one he'd carried for most of the day. "He's all boy. But what do you mean, Kae?"

"Remember what I told you about the wolvryn when I was a boy? Spend enough time with them, and they sort of pick one person and bond to them." Kaellor set the female down, and she scurried over to Lluthean.

"Strange though, nobody could ever figure out how to breed or domesticate them. Once every few years, a pup would wander down out of the mountains. Their numbers among us were never very large, and by the time I was of an age to even consider taking one as my own, they were hunted to near extinction."

Lluthean frowned as he played with the female pup, who was tugging at his boot string. "What changed to bring all that about?"

Kaellor responded, "To understand that is to begin to scratch the surface of the home to which we travel. Many in Aarindorn find truth in the writings of prophecy. In the time before your births, some came to believe in a complex prophecy called the Abrogator Derivation."

"That sounds like a terrible math equation," said Lluthean. "After all the calculations we made to complete the maps near Hammond, I hope you have a better explanation."

Bryndor smiled with understanding. They had managed to cover a lot of ground today, unfettered by measurements and distances or the need to draft a map. This felt like the most relaxed camp he could ever recall. He ruffled the fur of the male pup, who pawed playfully back at him.

"The derivation is a branch of prophecy, Llu," said Kaellor. "Old prophecy is never passed down as a single string of events. In *The Book of Seven Prophets*, there are forks of prophecy, of different possible outcomes. Seemingly random events confirm one branch and destroy another. If a falling star crosses the path of the red moon and not the blue, then one fork of prophecy is proved. If a child survives a random case of the flux, then one branch blossoms while the other withers."

"How did we get from talking about extinct wolvryn to whatever it is we are talking about now?" asked Bryndor.

"I'm getting to that point," said Kaellor. Irritation flavored his tone. "The Abrogator Derivation is a major branch of prophecy that allows for the possible resurgence of Tarkannen and all the abrogators. Your parents, among others, believed that this particular fork could only manifest after a wolvryn scarred a highborn son of Baellentrell or Lellendule."

They each sat contemplating Kaellor's rather complex explanation. Bryndor listened to the popping embers of the campfire and watched a tongue of flame lick in and out of a small knothole in the driftwood as he scratched at the scabs at his shoulder. His thumbnail caught an edge that peeled back and gave a gentle tug. A surprisingly large piece of scab released, leaving pink skin underneath. He flicked the brown crust into the fire. *We just had to go stomping about the Moorlok.*

Bryndor sighed and considered his uncle's explanation while chewing on the side of his lip. He looked at Lluthean, surprised he hadn't made a sarcastic remark. His brother lounged back against his saddle with only half of his attention occupied by the wolvryn pup. With squinted eyes, Lluthean seemed to be waiting for Kaellor to explain more.

"What do you believe, Kae? About prophecy and all that?" Bryndor asked.

Kaellor looked into the fire for a long while. "We've spent all our time among people in the Bend; people who appreciate the significance of something you can see and hold: a sturdy hammer, a cord of firewood. So much of the Baellentrell past involves things you can't see."

Kaellor stirred the campfire and added another piece of driftwood, then continued, "Prophecy is a funny thing. I have seen some prophecies resonate with truth, and others go so far astray as to scatter the entire notion like ash in the wind. The point is, Tarkannen believed it was true and acted on his belief. For my part, I think people act of their own free will. I like to think each person is responsible for his or her own life. Life is what you make it, regardless of what someone hundreds of years ago said it should be."

Lluthean surmised, "But not everyone in Aarindorn saw it that way, so the wolvryn—"

"So the wolvryn were hunted to extinction in a silly notion to prevent the Abrogator Derivation," answered Kaellor.

"But you still carry that book, Kae," said Bryndor, pointing at Kaellor's pack. "Do you think the wolvryn scarring me is responsible for making this derivation thing possible?"

"By the Giver, no, Bryn," said Kaellor. He appeared frustrated and exhausted by the conversation. He paused a few moments and seemed to master his aggravation.

"That's just the opposite of what I'm saying," said Kaellor. "I've seen prophecy be wrong too many times to be even remotely reliable. But others in Aarindorn don't feel that way. If I want to understand the people we are going to mix with, I need to remember some of the things they value, like this book."

"Alright, what exactly does that book say?" asked Lluthean.

Kaellor sighed again, then reached into his pack and withdrew the small black leatherbound book. He tilted the book to read by firelight, then turned a few pages, searching for the one he desired. Light from the campfire flickered across the gold embossed lettering, *The Book of Seven Prophets.*

Kaellor recited from the text, "When the wild wolvryn scars the highborn one, the channelers of nadir will rise. The tethers that bind can leech or sustain. The chance for confluence emerges, but only from balance. The sundered bindings will unleash one who rules from the void. Seek the bearer who carries the burden, then look to reveal the Eidolon." Kaellor snapped the book closed. "It goes on and on from there with countless possibilities."

"I didn't get all those words, but that first part sort of felt like it could be a reference to Bryn," said Lluthean.

"Some believed it to be so," said Kaellor. "Your parents thought it was possible it referred to one of you. The problem was, some found the possibility of the prophecy so troubling that they closed their minds to all reason and the experience of the past. They hunted the wolvryn with religious fanaticism. Their intentions were, I think, to prevent the very possibility of the Abrogator Derivation."

Kaellor stretched weary arms overhead with a contagious yawn that spread to his nephews. "I'm bushed, men. We have a long row to hoe and plenty of time to talk more. Mind a little shut-eye? We need to set a rotating watch until we're certain no one followed us from the Bend. If one of you can pull the first shift, I'm happy to be up later?"

"I can go first. There's too much buzzing around in my head to fall asleep fast," said Bryndor. He tossed more driftwood on the fire and stirred the coals.

"Wake me up halfway through if you need," said Lluthean before settling down for the night.

As Bryndor hunkered down against his saddle, the male pup nuzzled up against him for warmth. He looked over to Lluthean; the female had wedged itself into his armpit. Bryndor found some comfort in the affection of the pups. He wiggled around to make a comfortable impression in the sand, buried his nose against the pup's neck, and mulled over Kaellor's words. *If wolvryn were hunted to extinction, how will people act when we return with you?*

Chapter Thirty-Three: To Chase Through the Shadows

Volencia Lellendule stood on her private balcony. Situated on the north wing of a large coastal estate with windows looking toward her homeland in Aarindorn, she commanded an unobstructed view of Callish. She placed her hands on the cold stone railing and cast her gaze down across the port city. More than eight ships sat at anchor in the bay, rocking back and forth, their crews waiting to load or unload cargo.

She considered how much the city had changed in the last decade. In that time, whole districts had sprouted up, and no fewer than eight businesses owed their financial welfare to Volencia and Mallic's unique talents. They employed their skill with nadir among their connections with the seedier side of Callish, and made the ship of a competitor sink while concealing the contraband of a partner.

A breeze carried the sour tang of the ocean to her alcove, and she wrinkled her nose. She never understood why so many people claimed to like that smell. She reached for the cold stone anchor in her center to find her reserve of nadir, then cast a web, like an umbrella, across the balcony. Delicate, black filaments no more substantial than spider silk settled around her, then dispersed. In an instant, the brine smell dissipated, replaced by air devoid of aroma and humidity.

She sauntered to a flowering potted plant and plucked one of the fragrant red buds. She held the flower overhead and tapped it with a finger, releasing pollen and a sweet fragrance, then tucked the bud behind her ear.

Far below, commoners milled about in mundane daily activities. From her vantage point, the warren of tents and vendors in the central bazaar appeared less like the center of Callishite trade and more like a mosaic design.

She turned to a servant who stood in the shadows at the back of the balcony. *What was her name again? Shass? No, that was her sister, the one Mallic ruined. Why do I ever bother to remember their names; he never allows one to remain in service long enough to matter.*

"Fetch me a cocktail, something with lime in it," she ordered. The servant bowed and disappeared down a spiral staircase at the back.

She turned back to the bazaar. As evening approached, columns of vendors and customers filed out of the expansive market and into the convoluted tenement blocks. *Mallic was right; they actually do look like termites from up here.*

As if her very thought summoned him, her partner appeared at the top of the spiral steps. He carried a serving platter with two drinks and handed one to her, then kissed her on the cheek. She received the greeting, looking past him to discover that the servant had returned. *And that's why he's acting the prince. It's not for my benefit, of course, but for hers.*

"I thought I might find you up here," said Mallic. "Looking down on all the little people?"

"It's a way to pass the time," she replied. She sipped at her cocktail. Finding the blend appealing, she raised her glass to the servant then turned to gaze out across the city once more.

"That will be all for now, Vesta," said Mallic.

She rolled her eyes. *Vesta, that's right.*

Mallic stepped forward and leaned out over the balcony rail, interrupting Volencia's appraisal of the city. He waited for her to lift her eyes away from the harbor view. "We'll take dinner in, what, an hour or so?" he asked Volencia but spoke loud enough for Vesta to hear.

Volencia considered the long shadows cast to the east. By her estimate, the sun should fall in an hour, allowing them to release the shadow chasers once again. She tilted her head to acknowledge his plans for dinner.

He turned back to Vesta. "Yes, one hour will suffice." The servant disappeared down the spiral steps.

Once she felt certain that none of the help could eavesdrop, Volencia turned to regard him. *He hasn't taken the opportunity to bore me with his exploits, so I must have been right.*

He swallowed a large gulp of his cocktail, then twitched his head to the side involuntarily. He puckered his lips, then set the glass down on the stone rail. "I should have known better than to share one of your drinks. Always just a little too much lime for me."

He turned to lean with his hips against the rail. She held out her hand, palm up, waiting.

"Yes, yes, here you go," said Mallic as he slapped a thick gold coin into her palm. "It went about as you expected. I managed to follow one of them for no more than a half a mile before my horse fell behind. Later in the night, I did catch a glimpse of one of them, but they move so fast I couldn't tell if they were coming or going."

Each night since their encounter with the shade of Tarkannen, they had released the shadow chasers. The shade of their master had indicated that they should wait until the sounding to deploy the creatures, but Mallic was impatient and took it upon himself to send the hounds out on patrol.

Each morning the silent creatures returned with no evidence of finding their prey. Tonight, she held out hope for a different result, as this was the first time they were releasing the chasers since the sounding last resonated, indicating a fraying of another layer of Tarkannen's banishment. *And if his binding weakens, then so too might the mantle that obscures the heirs.*

She thought back to the first night she dropped the three globes onto the ground. They'd fallen with unnatural weight and sunk into the mud. All three globes had glistened with the same mercurial surface that slicked the blood pool immediately before the shade of Tarkannen appeared.

She remembered her wonder at watching the globes swell and morph into hounds. Each stood nearly four feet tall at the shoulder with a broad neck and oversized paws. Corded muscles and sinew protruded through thin, black, hairless hides. Their eyes looked like solid black marble; they reminded Volencia of the dead expression of a snake.

"You know that they leap from one shadow to the next and that distances are irrelevant," she said. "What made you think you could possibly follow one of them?"

"I don't know, but I did learn something useful," he said.

She waited for him to share his revelation. *He just wants me to ask, but I won't, and he knows it.*

She sipped at her cocktail and made a pretense of investing her attention in the drink as she looked down past her drink to his feet. Inside his soft leather boot, he tapped one toe with annoyance. *You can tell a lot from a man's feet.*

Finally, he sighed. "They don't hunt as a pack. They split up and travel the shadows in different directions."

That makes sense, I suppose. They're constructs, ripped from the Drift, and given a purpose. Just because they look like hounds doesn't mean they act like them.

When the shadow chasers returned at dawn after that first night, she had probed one with a tendril of nadir and discovered that the beasts were composed of constructed nadir. She didn't understand it, but she felt certain that her master had coalesced strands of nadir into solid constructs, then trapped something sentient inside each one.

They released the hounds every night and collected them at dawn. In the full light of day, they seized up then curled in on themselves, shrinking into the unusually dense globes.

"I suppose that allows them to cover more ground while they search for the Baellentrells," said Mallic. "I wish they had a way to communicate with us, to tell us what they found or where they searched."

"All in due time, Mallic," she said. "Remember, Master would not offer such a gift lightly."

He paced back and forth across the alcove, then brooded at the railing while they waited for the sun to vanish behind the western horizon. She smiled to herself, realizing that his impatience and discomfort were lightening her mood. *Somehow when you suffer, I simply feel . . . better.*

Sensing that enough light had faded, she walked over to a small round table and removed the three mercurial globes from a leather satchel. They dropped to the stone floor, emitting strange tones, like low-pitched chimes. In seconds, they began to tremble and vibrate, then uncurled and assumed the forms of the large hounds.

Mallic walked forward with a torch in hand and watched as the hounds each flickered from one shadow to the next. One vanished only to reappear at the back of the alcove, while another materialized where the first had stood. They continued to jump from shadow to shadow with such speed that each appeared more a blur than a distinct creature.

"I swear, I'll never get used to that," said Mallic.

"Stop toying with them and put that away," snapped Volencia. She crouched down and flared a burst of nadir into the air, allowing the strands to spray in a cloud that lasted a few seconds, then dissipated. The gesture caused the hounds to gather before her.

"You have the scent. You know our prey. Return at dawn. Now, go!" she ordered.

With unnatural speed, the hounds shuddered, as if flickering in place, then disappeared into the shadows, chasing through the night. She stood straight, tossed back the last of her cocktail, and purred, "Ready yourselves wherever you are, sons of Baellentrell. Very soon, I think, your death arrives on silent shadows. Very soon, indeed."

Chapter Thirty-Four: The Warnings of the Wolvryn

Lluthean awoke on the sandbar and thought he might still be dreaming. A dark, thick fog rose along the river bottom. The morning chatter of birds pierced the grey blanket, but the murk obscured the tree line. The curtain of fog made it impossible to determine the position of the moons or even the sun. The camp felt isolated in the eerie haze.

Any apprehension he felt melted as the female wolvryn pup wandered over. She pounced on his boots as he tried to dress and busied herself chewing on any loose end of string or leather. He rolled her onto her back, and they made a game of wrestling. She gnawed at his wrist while he tickled her belly. Her sharp teeth poked through the cuff of his sleeve, but he freed himself before she drew blood. He looked across the ash of the campfire to see Bryndor enjoying the same kind of play with the male pup.

Kaellor's voice cut through the fog. "If they are coming with us, give them names. From what I recall, they thrive on a strong bond with one person. You'll need to be telling them apart at an early age."

Lluthean picked up the female and peered into her thoughtful blue eyes. Once again, the strange shards of purple that surrounded her pupil intrigued him. *What name can I give to such a beautiful creature?*

"Neska. Definitely, Neska." Lluthean grinned.

"The courtesan from the child's tale, 'Old King Walsh'? That Neska?" asked Bryndor with disbelief flavoring his expression.

Lluthean answered with a grin, "There were none more beautiful in all the land, and she did save his life at the end of that story! Besides, I think she likes it. Look at her wag her tail."

"Pshaw, she just wants your breakfast," Bryndor chided. "Alright, Kae, tell me the name of a great Aarindorian king or hero."

"There are several to choose from: your parents, the first King Eldrek Baellentrell, or maybe his brother Borullian, the warrior. There was also Kelledar Lellendule," Kaellor answered.

Bryndor lifted the male pup's chin and eyed him. The pup cocked his head to the side. "Boru. You look like a Boru to me."

They stood on the sandbar after packing up the small camp. Lluthean removed the stilben root they stored in a small pouch and prepared two doses of the sleeping herb before kneeling to give Neska her treat. Instead of taking the bait, she snarled with hackles raised. She bared her teeth, and before he could react, she snapped at the air beside him, missing his hand by inches. The stab of his cracked rib grabbed him as he rocked back, confused by the sudden change.

Despite his surprise, he couldn't help but giggle. Her growl sounded more like an angry squirrel chattering than the savage, rumbling snarl of her mother. *What's got you all riled up? Don't like the name Neska after all? I suppose we can change it.* He reached a cautious hand forward, but she pinned her ears back and bared her teeth.

"Wait a moment," said Kaellor. "Look, something has both of them worked up."

Lluthean turned to see Boru retreating toward the brothers, ears pinned back and releasing a growl of warning only slightly less humorous than Neska's. The wolvryn persisted in their strange vigilant state, appearing irritated by something unseen in the fog.

"I don't hear anything," said Kaellor. He withdrew the Logrend sword.

"It's something about this fog," answered Lluthean.

"No, it's more," said Kaellor. "I don't hear *anything*: no birds, no squirrels, nothing. Something is wrong. Quickly, Lluthean, grab your bow. Bryndor, mind the horses!" Kaellor directed firmly.

They acted without question. Bryndor grabbed the reins and held the horses together, Lluthean knocked an arrow, and Kaellor brandished the longsword in both hands. Several silent moments passed, and again, the pups snapped at something unseen in the fog. One of the dapple grey geldings nickered nervously and pawed at the ground.

"Kae," Bryndor whispered, "have a look at this."

Kaellor pivoted in a slow defensive circle. "Llu, go see what he's talking about."

Lluthean strained to see from where he stood, but the roiling haze obscured anything beyond their immediate vicinity. He walked to Bryndor, whose attention was focused on the ground, and knelt to examine the sand. Just behind one of the geldings, set deep into the sand, lay a set of large paw prints.

"Kae, something big left fresh tracks behind the horse," said Lluthean.

"Another wolvryn?" Kaellor asked.

"I don't think so," said Lluthean. "The paw prints are big, but not that big. There's a lot of them, but maybe we didn't see them last night."

"No," said Bryndor. "There are too many to miss; those are fresh."

All three men strained their ears at the silence, trying to make sense of the situation. The wolvryn continued their puppy growls, and both seemed to follow something in the fog. Lluthean stood behind them, watching. A massive dark head, like a hound's, materialized at the edge of the mists just behind Kaellor.

Without thinking, Lluthean drew and fired. He gritted his teeth, trying to ignore the sharp rib pain in his side. The arrow shaft flew past Kaellor and disappeared into the fog. A noise reminiscent of stabbing a shovel into dirt indicated that he'd hit something. A strange growl, like the rasping sound of metal against metal, echoed through the fog.

"Dammit to the Drift, Llu! Warn me!" Kaellor said. After a pause, he seemed to rein in his anger. "What did you see?"

"I'm not sure," Lluthean answered. He already had another arrow nocked and was straining to see anything through the haze. "I swear, in the fog, I saw the head of some beast, like a dog, but not like any dog I've ever seen."

Another hound appeared at the visible edge of the fog, flickering into view and then moving. "There, just ten feet out. No, now there!" said Lluthean. He released the tension in the bowstring but kept training his sight to different places in the fog.

"I can hear them running around us, but that doesn't sound like any dog to me," said Bryndor.

"I just saw one too," said Kaellor. He continued to pivot slowly and held the longsword in a defensive stance. "By the Giver, they're fast! I saw one; then, in a blur, it was gone."

A long minute passed with the only sound that of the wolvryn and the loping footsteps of something heavy running around the perimeter of their camp. By the sound of the beast, he could only discern one attacker. *But it can't be that fast, right? Here one moment and there the next? There must be more than one?*

Lluthean watched the pups. Instead of straining to see through the fog, he focused on their movements. The wolvryn held their ground, snarling. First, they glared in one direction, then another. Boru continued to growl in one direction, and in a moment, Neska joined him.

Trusting instinct, Lluthean drew and released another arrow just as the head of a dark hound appeared. The beast screeched more than growled, either in pain or anger; he couldn't tell. Then it disappeared into the fog again.

"The pups can sense whatever is out there, Kae," he said, nocking another arrow. "I just shot another one by following their lead."

Kaellor stepped closer and watched the wolvryn. As the pups tracked the circular path of something, he struck. He pivoted and lunged forward, swinging the longsword in an overhead arc. The sword split the air and parted a furrow in the sandbar.

"Mercy and goodness, I saw it at least," Kaellor uttered in surprise. "It's some kind of black hound." He recovered and resumed his defensive stance.

Long moments of silence unfolded, interrupted only by the wolvryn pups growling. Kaellor continued to use the pups to target and made several long slashes through the air. He never made contact with anything solid.

Lluthean rattled the fingertips of his right hand against the bowstring. The rhythmic feel seemed to still his nerves. He searched the edges of the dark fog, sweeping in deliberate, slow semicircles. As he peered to his uncle's right, he sucked in a breath against the pain and loosed an arrow at a dark object leaping toward Kaellor. The arrow found its mark, but the hound seemed unaffected and continued its approach unabated.

Without turning, Kaellor dropped to a knee and reversed his grip upon the sword. Using what appeared to be an awkward thrusting motion, he stabbed backward at his hip. The sword impaled the beast, but the momentum of its charge knocked him to the ground. All three men trained their eyes on the hound from the Drift.

Muscles rippled under its sleek, hairless hide as the longsword pierced through the beast's broad chest and protruded through its front shoulder. The creature writhed and vibrated on the ground. As it did so, two bloodless arrows dropped from its body to the sand.

Kaellor rolled to his feet. They watched as the hound continued its strange tremulous motions, but the longsword did not dislodge. The hound then tried in vain to bite at the hilt of the weapon. Kae stepped forward to grasp the sword, and the hound snarled in defiance. It turned to regard them with strange, murky black eyes.

Lluthean used the beast's distraction to shoot again. At such a close distance, he landed a perfect kill shot into its chest. Once more, the hound undulated and seemed to vibrate, and the arrow fell from its torso to the ground. The beast continued to screech, but the sword remained embedded in its chest. The creature staggered forward, teeth bared.

"Alright, one more Llu. Be ready; I'm going to try for it," Kaellor directed.

Lluthean pulled the bowstring flush to his jaw and sighted the beast down the arrow shaft. He allowed his gaze to linger only a moment on the beast's empty black eyes, then loosed. The hound recoiled as the arrow sunk into its eye.

Kaellor pounced. With a primal growl, he grasped the hilt in both hands and pulled it in a slashing motion. He shifted his hips and used his weight to push forward into the beast. The sword sliced deep into the hound and cleaved a third of the creature away. The pieces fell to the ground, and the dismembered limb melted into an oily pool that seeped into the sand.

Kaellor whirled the sword back around to the wounded hound with a two-handed swing. His slash chopped cleanly through its spine and deep into the muscled neck of the beast. The rest of the hound's corpse withered into an ink-black slick around Lluthean's unmarred arrows.

Kaellor resumed his defensive stance, and all three of them strained their senses into the fog. Long minutes passed with no further attacks. The sun began to burn through the haze, and both Neska and Boru returned to casual stances.

The adrenaline of the event left them in a vigilant state, and they stood their ground for another half hour. Eventually, the birdsong and morning squirrel chatter returned. The fog thinned enough to reveal countless tracks at the periphery of their camp. Lluthean retrieved his arrows, and Kaellor finally sheathed the Logrend sword.

"Any notion of what that was, Kae?" Lluthean asked.

"No," Kaellor replied, "but the way it seeped back into the ground smacks of something from the Drift."

"I thought there were several of them—that one moved so fast. I count it a blessing there was only one," Bryndor said.

"The blessing is this Logrend sword and the guardian rune you placed on it," Kaellor said, then sheathed the weapon. "Llu's arrows had little effect, but something about this blade held that creature fast. The sooner we put distance between us and this sandbar, the better. Let's move along. Keep a wary eye to the horizon."

Lluthean considered dosing the pups with the stilben root, then thought better of it. "Bryn, the pups were the only warning we had of that hound. Do you think you can manage that one without the stilben root?"

Bryndor hoisted the male pup up and settled him into the makeshift travel pouch. "We can only try and see. If he becomes unmanageable, we can always try the stilben later. For now, I like the idea of another set of eyes and ears."

With the pups settled into their travel pouches, Lluthean felt relieved to leave the sandbar behind. They continued their journey in vigilant silence, ever watchful of the tree line.

Chapter Thirty-Five: The Abrogators' Strategy

Volencia stirred with anticipation in the early morning hours. She sauntered barefoot out to the balcony where they had released the shadow chasers the night before. The chasers always returned just before dawn to the spot where they were released. Mallic already stood at the railing, overlooking the harbor city. As the sun threatened to peek over the eastern horizon, two of the hounds appeared from the shadows at the back of the alcove.

Volencia bent down to inspect the constructs. Neither seemed injured, but only the two had returned.

"Where is the third chaser?" she asked. But the hound only cocked its head and stared with its dead eyes toward the railing.

Mallic took a step closer. "Maybe they just need a little incentive," he said.

She felt thin filaments of nadir gather as he prepared to channel. But before he took action, the two remaining chasers began to shift and vibrate. In seconds, they had returned to their spherical shapes, immobile on the ground.

Where is the third one? Did it find a Baellentrell, I wonder?

She retrieved the mercurial globes; they leeched the heat from her palm. It was like holding a tin cup full of glacier water.

"It's a shame they remain active only at night," she said, then placed the spheres into a leather pouch.

"It's a far greater shame that they can't speak," Mallic responded. "I would love to know if the remaining hound was successful. Even if we knew where to search for the Baellentrell spawn . . ." The abrogator paced back to the balcony rail, brooding.

Volencia considered his words. Her achievements came not by birth but through cunning and forethought. After relinquishing her birthright to support her cousin, she had acquired the ability to channel nadir and discovered power well beyond anything she would have attained in her former life.

She reviewed several possible scenarios that might provide them more information. *If we had held onto a portion of our old gifts, Mallic might have been able to sense them empathically.*

But from what she sensed of the chasers, they carried no actual emotion. They were sentient, but she never sensed any sign of joy or fear in the creatures. When she had probed one with a tendril of nadir, the hound vibrated and shivered. The probing seemed to cause it pain and root it in place. However, when she finished, the hound had remained still, as if her invasion had not even occurred.

She continued to ponder a way to track the hounds. With a sly smile, she glanced to Mallic. She had always considered the man beneath her. He relied on his ability to inflict pain to coerce and manipulate people. On occasion, he could contrive more insidious designs to blackmail victims, but most of the time, he acted more like a blunt weapon.

"Do you recall the trinket we used to collar and track the captain, Captain Mundle, a few years back?" she asked.

"Yes. We used it to ensure that he traveled to the northland port and back with those useless tomes. As I recall, you thought they would contain information that would help us release our master," Mallic replied sarcastically.

Volencia dismissed the condescending tone in his voice. Mallic's jibes had lost their ability to sting her years ago. "Think, Mallic. Or do you only use that head of yours to molest the girls? Where is the trinket, the necklace? Perhaps it can be placed on one of the hounds when we next activate them to track it."

Mallic seemed to consider her words. "Alright. It should be in the study."

In the underground level of their estate was the study, within which the abrogators plotted and schemed. Though, the term study undersold the size and scope of the library, with its vaulted ceilings and numerous shelves. Several side rooms branched off the main chamber. Some held laboratories used for arcane rituals. Others had borne witness to her torturous experiments with new poisons.

Volencia had once crafted a poison that spread through the tears of one person to another. She'd tested the concoction on young lovers several times until she felt satisfied with its potency. She had administered the poison to one of the pair, then locked them into a dungeon-like room. A shard of nadir had provoked enough pain to evoke tears from the poisoned individual and render death to them both.

They searched the alcoves of the underground study in earnest. "It is here," said Mallic. He withdrew a plain brass chain from a simple wooden box. The library held many such boxes, intermixed with texts and scrolls, stacked along the shelves.

"Good, let me see it. I believe we can augment this to allow us to spy where the shadow chasers travel," she said.

Mallic handed the object to her. The simple brass chain had no clasps, and to the unlearned, appeared to hold little value. Volencia reached into a pocket of her dress and withdrew a small oval pendant with a pink crystal in its center. She looped the chain through the pendant and back upon itself. She tugged at the chain, testing its strength. Reassured, she turned and dangled the chain and its pendant before Mallic.

"A glimmer crystal. Not a bad idea. Sneaky, I like it," said Mallic.

He did not offer remarks of admiration often, but Volencia's crafty idea would allow the two to discern the general direction of the shadow chasers. In addition, through a scrying bowl, they could observe what the hound saw.

"I thought we might at least see the Baellentrells when the hounds take them," said Volencia with satisfaction. "Did you use the last of the scrying crystals?" She knew that he had dipped into their supply in his voyeuristic pursuits of a lover in the previous month.

"I can refine more, but it will take me a few days," said Mallic.

"You should get started then." She turned and left him to the task.

Over the next two days, Mallic sequestered himself in the library and used a filter of nadir to remove impurities among the scrying crystals. Volencia attended to a few messages from their army of street rats and informants.

She used the network of informants and spies to keep track of ships entering and leaving the harbor. She also tracked new business developments in Callish. She paid more, however, for leverage. Knowledge of the unfaithful tryst of a high council member or the bastard son of a prelate could often be used to encourage an affluent member of Callishite society to grant Mallic or Volencia certain favors.

Volencia retreated to the study two nights later to find Mallic preparing the scrying bowl. To view anything with clarity, he'd had to polish the bowl and fill it with refined ground crystals.

As the sun set, Mallic opened the pouch and removed the two shadow chaser globes. He dropped them to the floor, where they began to vibrate and morph into the familiar hounds. The two beasts sat before their masters, awaiting instruction. Volencia placed the necklace around one of the hounds.

"Tonight, hunt your prey together. Kill them and return," she said.

The beasts looked at her with emotionless eyes. Just when she began to doubt their understanding of her command, they obediently vanished into the shadows. After a moment, Volencia approached the scrying bowl. The ground crystal powder filling the bowl remained still.

From her pocket, she removed a second glimmer crystal identical to the one the chaser now wore. With care to avoid contaminating the refined crystal, she placed the oval pendant in the center of the bowl. As it sank, the crystals began to swirl and rise into the air.

Dark and murky images formed in the swirling cloud above the scrying bowl. The chasers traveled with such blinding speed that the images were blurry and provoked a wave of nausea. Volencia swallowed back the sour feeling and continued to observe as the chasers roamed through the city shadows of Callish and emerged into one of the local farming villages. She stared, amazed at how fast they spirited themselves from one shadow to another.

"The heirs are not likely to be found so close to the city. Perhaps we could retire for a bit and return later to observe their progress," said Mallic. Volencia agreed, and the pair left the scrying bowl while the images continued to dance inside the crystal cloud.

Chapter Thirty-Six: A Cave in the Korjinth

Kaellor watched Lluthean crest a small rise along a game trail, then disappear around a small copse of trees as his gelding trotted down the incline. *He has the most uncanny ability to find the trails.*

The last two days of travel had unfolded without further immediate dangers. Gradually, they'd left the tangled undergrowth of the Moorlok and entered vast tracks of pine and spruce. They had pushed far enough north that they'd ridden in the shadow of the Korjinth Mountains for most of the morning. Kaellor craned his neck to consider the black peaks erupting from the forest valley. The terrain reminded him a little of Stone's Grasp: dry air, the smell of pine, and majestic canyons.

Thinking of Aarindorn left him unsettled. For a brief time, after they'd finished the job in Hammond, he felt . . . happy. He had struggled for years to find a sense of contentment in the Southlands. At least, he thought that's what he had been doing.

Since Rona's death, his unsettled mind had left him restless. He felt the loss of her friendship, of the way she grounded him and gave them all a sense of home. Some mornings, he awoke feeling eager to return to Aarindorn. Those notions always withered by midday under a sense of guilt. Other mornings, he awoke fearing the danger his nephews might encounter if they really did sit at the center of the Abrogator Derivation. More than once, he considered turning them around, knowing they could still have comfortable lives in the Southlands.

At the end of most days, a simmering anger fueled his desire to push on. *Rona deserves a measure of justice, and I'll have it if I have to personally slaughter every member of the Lacuna myself.*

He rode in silence and thought about the trust his brother had placed in him. *Japheth. If you knew how much time we wasted in the Southlands only to return, would you have ever sent us away?*

He sighed and tried to lift his mind to lighter things as he urged his mount to follow Lluthean.

It wasn't a waste. The boys have had a productive life full of experiences. But where would we all be today if we never left? What are we even returning to?

His mind wandered back to his conversation with Reddevek and the man's descriptions of Aarindorn. He pondered the Lacuna and considered different ways to infiltrate the organization. Those thoughts led him back to dark places as he imagined how he would deal with the people responsible for Rona's death. His hands cramped from clenching the reins, and Scout nickered in discomfort. He loosened his grip.

One problem at a time. Save your retribution for the day we actually arrive in Aarindorn.

He made himself recall some of the first lessons taught by his training master, Benyon Garr. It was challenging while riding, but he became aware of how tight all his muscles felt. He relaxed his neck, shoulders, and then as much of his back as he could manage. *Be present, center on what's here. Place your focus into the things you can affect.*

"Smells like rain," said Lluthean. Kaellor leaned back in his saddle in mild surprise.

Meditation is good Kae, just don't lose your awareness of your surroundings.

Kaellor looked across a small valley where a stream cut through the forest. The past two nights, they had picked defensive locations to camp, seeking out rocky outcroppings and dense tree stands and picketing the horses close. The terrain before them provided several reasonable options. He searched the skyline. Dark blue storm clouds gathered, and a breeze laden with the smell of rain chilled the air.

"Let's push on a bit. This close to the mountains, we might find a shelf to protect us from the rain. See what you can find," said Kaellor.

Lluthean nodded, then encouraged his gelding to trot up the north side of the valley closer to the black cliffs.

Within the hour, they stumbled across a deep-set cave with a large open mouth. Both of his nephews seemed reluctant to approach, and Bryndor scratched at the scabbed wound of his shoulder.

"Are you both alright?" he asked.

They sat in silence for a moment before Bryndor said, "It sort of looks like the cave where we found the wolvryn."

They each dismounted, and the boys set the wolvryn pups on the ground. The pups had spent the last few hours dozing in their makeshift pouches, and both investigated the terrain with tails wagging.

Neska sniffed at the ground along a game trail while Boru scampered up the small incline. Before any of them realized, he had disappeared into the dark shadows of the cave. He reappeared a moment later, yawned, and sat at the cave mouth.

"After the way they alerted us to that hound from the Drift, I trust his nose," said Kaellor. He withdrew his Logrend sword. "Wait here, and I'll have a look."

Inspection revealed an empty, deep cave. No tracks marred the entrance, though a few scattered bones and what he guessed was dried scat indicated some animal had used the cave in the past. His eyes adjusted, and the dim light revealed a chamber twenty feet high; plenty of room to tether the horses, make a fire, and establish a comfortable camp out of the elements.

Kaellor knelt and scratched Boru on the backside of his neck. "Come on up. It's safe, and there's plenty of room to get the horses out of the rain."

They shared in the responsibilities of making camp. Tonight, Lluthean tended to the horses, picketing them close by to graze and then getting them settled for the night inside the dry cave. Kaellor gathered firewood before the anticipated rain. A natural depression inside the cave entrance served as a firepit.

Bryndor foraged for food. Typically they hunted small game: coneys or squirrel. He returned to the cave with a small deer slung over his back, and his pockets bulged with some kind of tuber. Kaellor eyed his nephew curiously as he wandered into camp.

"I see you're finally getting the hang of the bow," said Lluthean. His tone was teasing, but his raised eyebrows betrayed his admiration.

"I can't really take much credit," said Bryndor. "I was gathering knotweed and even found a bunch of red berry. I stood up, and the silly thing startled away from me. It tried to jump the creek bottom only to break a leg. I ended its misery. Besides, the pups need more than jerky and scraps."

"Sometimes the Giver gives," said Kaellor.

"And just in time. My belly's been growling louder than Neska," said Lluthean as he rubbed his stomach in anticipation.

Bryndor made short work of the animal, and they were soon roasting the venison over a low fire. The three sat in a semicircle around the campfire facing the mouth of the cave while the wolvryn pups gnawed on meaty bones Lluthean gave them.

Bryndor sat up straight and stretched with a groan, indicating his muscles felt as sore as Kaellor's. "Kae, how did you manage to make this journey with two toddlers?" he asked. Using his saddle as a backrest, he arched back, stretching.

"It was a journey far easier to speak of than to accomplish. Sometimes though, the Giver smiles on the deaf and the dumb," Kaellor answered. "There was a time when a fairly regular flow of wagons traveled from Callish to the west coast. The trail is far to the south along the plains; the travel is easier by far but adds another few weeks. I hitched myself to a family traveling by wagon, then headed north. I wagered that Journey's Bend was remote enough to stay in and fell upon the good graces of the Tellends. That first couple of years, I don't think we could have managed without them."

"I can't imagine," said Lluthean while he rubbed Neska's belly.

I wondered how long it would take for them to choose. Kaellor watched the pups. Neska followed Lluthean, close as a shadow. Whenever they stopped for a break, Boru sought attention and reassurance from Bryndor.

"Just keeping an eye on Neska challenges my attention." Lluthean chuckled. "So, Kae, tell us more about Aarindorn."

"What do you want to hear about?" Kaellor asked.

"More about runes and the gift would be nice. Tell us about magic!" Lluthean said with an extravagant wave of his arm.

Kaellor fingered his beard. "Alright, only we don't call it magic. Magic is for the mummers and jolly men. We channel zenith."

He picked up a stick from the fire's edge and used the charred end to draw thin bands encircling his forearm. Inside the bands, he traced delicate symbols. He continued adding small charcoal marks like branches off a vine. He wove the symbols around a larger rune he drew in the center of his forearm. When he finished sketching the intricate pattern, the embellishment adorned most of his forearm.

"This is the symbol for balance. Most Aarindorian children, but not all, inherit the ability to channel zenith. Sometime after age five, bits and pieces of the runes first appear and slowly weave into the full symbol. The combination of the runes makes a unique tapestry for every person."

"On my other arm rested the rune for judgment, on my shoulders lay the runes of perception and service." Kaellor withdrew the guardian sword and tapped the hilt and pommel. "And these runes were entwined on my chest."

"And those runes have what to do with magic exactly?" Bryndor asked.

"Nothing," said Kaellor with an edge of irritation. "It's not magic."

"It's channeling zenith," said Lluthean with a haughty tone that made them all smile.

He does manage to keep things light. "If I may continue?" Kaellor asked.

"Sorry, Kae," said Lluthean.

Kaellor waved off the apology and continued, "The symbols determine how a gifted can channel zenith. Some people can foretell and even shape weather. Others move water, heal people, or grow plants. The exact nature of your ability to channel zenith is shaped by the combinations of the runes you inherit. But it's this symbol, called the arca prime, that identifies your strongest ability." He pounded a fist to his chest.

"So, one of your runes was a guardian symbol?" asked Bryndor.

"Yes," Kaellor replied.

"How come we never see people in the Southlands with these runes, Kae?" Bryndor asked.

"Several reasons," said Kaellor. "To begin with, not everyone in Aarindorn is gifted to channel. There are many Aarindorians who never manifest runes but raise children who do. One never knows whether a child will inherit the gift at birth.

"Next, I suspect that after the Abrogator's War, Aarindorn closed its borders. I have heard of other people using different means to channel zenith. But in Aarindorn, it's through the pattern of our runes. Remember Reddevek, the man from the north?"

He waited for them to nod. "His runes ran across his arms and chest, then up to his cheeks and temples."

"Those gold and silver tattoos? He had a nasty scar, but I don't remember him doing anything special," said Bryndor. "Was he bound as well then?"

"No," said Kaellor, remembering the man's blue eyes. "It would be hard to cage that animal. You just arrived late, but I suspect he channeled more than his share of zenith just to find us."

They sat watching the embers hiss and pop. A log collapsed into coals. Kaellor stirred the embers then placed more wood, stoking the flames. "Where were we?" he asked.

"The arca prime," said Lluthean.

"Ah, yes. That last rune manifests after a gifted enters a trial called the Rite of Revealing," said Kaellor.

Lluthean chuckled. "If revealing means we have to prance around naked, I'm not too sure how much I want to inherit this gift."

Kaellor felt his cheek draw up into a small smile, the stress of the day wilting under Lluthean's persistent merry disposition. "The Rite of Revealing is the Aarindorian way of ensuring that no person inherits their full abilities before they are of an age and maturity to handle it. Typically in their late teenage years, a gifted will petition for the rite. Once granted, they spend the night in the inner sanctum before the statue of Aarlenian Baellentrell. The rest is for you to experience for yourselves. Every person's rite is as unique and varied as their runes."

"What could you do when you channeled, Kae?" Lluthean asked.

"Channeling through the guardian symbol was frustrating. It manifested mostly in times of duress." Kaellor withdrew to distant memories for a few moments. "My abilities allowed me to perceive unique weaknesses in my attacker's defenses in combat once. Another time I was able to . . . radiate a sort of blast wave that repelled an advance against your father and me."

"Who attacked you, Kae?" Lluthean asked in surprise.

"No one," he said. "I was training in a sparring exercise. I left for the Southlands with you both before I was ever really challenged to use my gifts."

"How did you channel—I mean, I guess I don't understand how it works," said Lluthean

"I recall that a feeling of power welled up inside me once like a warm sense of strength, and when I had need, it just seemed natural to release it," replied Kaellor.

"What do the runes feel like?" asked Bryndor.

"Sometimes, as you grow, they itch a little. They reflect light, but you can't really feel them," Kaellor responded.

"Did we have any of these symbols?" asked Lluthean.

"No. Your parents fashioned the mantle for you both, hiding your gifts and identities before any of your symbols appeared. But there do tend to be patterns that run in families. Both your father and I carried runes of enlightenment, service, and perception. Your mother carried runes of strength, truth, and mirth."

"Mirth, that sounds like my arca prime," said Lluthean.

"That assumes we even have runes," said Bryndor. "What was our father's arca prime, Kae?"

Kaellor recalled the last time he saw his brother's rune deep in the lower recesses of Stone's Grasp so many years ago. "Your father was rare. He bore the gift of sacrifice. All his life, we were left to question the nature of his power until the night he banished Tarkannen. Only your father and his unique gifts accompanied by your mother's strength could defeat the Usurper."

Kaellor lost himself remembering days gone by, his brother, and the life he left behind. The embers hissed as Lluthean stirred the coals and added a piece of wood.

"And our mother?" Lluthean asked. "What was her main gift?"

"Mind you, I never actually saw hers," Kaellor explained. "But your mother's arca prime was courage. And I think there was no better match for your father in life."

Their conversation ebbed for a time, and they sat in companionable silence, watching the wolvryn play. Boru dragged a leg bone from the deer over, waited for Bryndor to reach for it, then began a game of tugging it back and forth. Neska began to chew on top of Lluthean's boot. He pulled his leg back and offered her a scrap of deer hide as an alternative.

"Are there any runes of belching?" Lluthean eventually asked. "Because if there are, I want that one. I shall smite me enemies with a blast from me belly!" He leaned back, tapping his abdomen. Bryndor chuckled, and Kaellor felt his cheeks warm with a genuine smile.

Bryndor fanned his hands at his brother. "As long as thine air dost come from the top end and not the bottom, dear brother!"

Kaellor couldn't help himself and sounded a deep laugh. *What is it about boys and fart jokes?*

As if in answer, Lluthean lifted a leg and released a high-pitched squeaky fart into the night. More laughter echoed through the cave. Their laughter continued so long that his sides ached, and his beard gathered tears. As the conversation settled, Boru gave up on his game of tug-of-war with Bryndor, and Neska curled up against Lluthean for the night. Kaellor eased back, daydreaming of runes, training exercises with Japheth, and happy days.

Chapter Thirty-Seven: Crown Beetle Hiccups

Nolan and Karragin pushed the Aarindin hard to place as much distance between themselves and Beclure as possible. They had covered more than half the distance to the other Outriders by the time they camped for the night. By midday of their second day of travel, they crossed a path wide enough to allow the horses to walk two abreast.

Karragin stopped her mount to gaze north, toward Aarindorn. She sat calmly in the saddle, but Nolan couldn't read her expression.

He hopped down and cursed that his leg had stiffened up on the ride. He channeled zenith, activating his arca prime. A myriad of light blue, wispy images flooded his awareness, and he scanned the tracks of numerous horse-drawn wagons and humans passing in each direction. He studied the images for several minutes.

"It's a road, a new one," he said.

One of Karragin's eyebrows twitched. "Tell me the Giver's gift allows you to see more than just that."

Nolan squinted at her through unruly ginger curls. He stepped forward, intending to fetch one of the sliced, smoked mutton portions they had left over from their visit to Beclure. Karragin's mount nipped at him, and he withdrew his hand.

"Did he do that, or did you encourage him to?" asked Nolan.

Karragin folded her arms, and he thought he could see the last flicker of zenith as it channeled across the runes on her forearm.

"Tell me what you saw, and we'll see about this road first. Then we can think about food," she said.

Nolan nodded. "The wagons traveling south are heavy, and the tracks heading back home are light, like they left their cargo. There were at least twenty, maybe more, and they used common horses, not Aarindin. Whoever came this way took great care to remove the stumps, and they collected all the lumber."

"This must be part of the road to the Borderlands," said Karragin. "Father planned to open the road and investigate trade. Let's use it for now, but stay alert."

Nolan gestured, and his Aarindin knelt down, allowing him to mount. They made swift progress south. Within a few hours, the sounds of hammers and axes announced the presence of an expansive camp between the Pillars of Eldrek.

The smell of fresh-cut pine mixed with cookfires. Massive stacks of logs rested on one side of the clearing; supply wagons and tents clustered at the other. Men and women labored at different tasks. Some prepared food while others hefted axes and trimmed the logs. A group of laborers set a log on what appeared to be the first floor of a timber-framed structure.

A gruff voice called over the din, "Elbiona said to keep a lookout for you two!"

Nolan recognized the voice and turned to see Benyon Garr approach from a large tent. Their old mentor smiled a gap-toothed grin and stood with hands on his hips. They directed their Aarindin to his tent.

"Hello, Lord Garr, it's good to see you," said Nolan.

"And good to see you both as well," said Benyon. "How did you find my new road?"

"It's coming along nicely, but what's all this?" asked Nolan.

"This group here will finish the framing of the command hall. Those boys there," he said, pointing at a group of men with shovels, axes, and other hand tools. "They start work on the palisade this afternoon."

"This isn't just a road; it's a forward staging area," said Karragin. "What happened?"

Benyon scratched his frizzled beard. "You're right, Karra. How long have you two been separated from the Outriders now?"

"A little over a week," she replied.

"That makes sense, I suppose," he said. "Cutters, the axemen from Stellance, began construction of the road but suddenly went missing. The warden investigated and found signs that a crush of grondle has pushed into the forest between the Pillars here. Grondle, of all things." He spit between the wide gap of his front teeth.

Benyon seemed to withdraw into himself a moment. "It only took your father, the regent that is, part of a day to send us down here."

Nolan looked across the clearing and scanned the horizon. The Pillars stood over a mile apart, and dense stands of timber pushed up to the white cliffs.

"Do the plans call for the palisade to span the entire distance between the Pillars?" he asked.

"They do now, my boy," said Benyon. "But don't you worry about that. While there's a lot of work to do, just the mention of the grondle has most in the kingdom eager to see the barrier completed."

"Where is the warden, then?" Karragin asked.

Benyon shielded his eyes to the sun and gazed to the south. "Ride through the timber to the south a few hours, and you should find the rest of the Outriders."

"Thanks. We should take our leave," said Karragin.

"Eyes to the horizon then," said Benyon.

Karragin nodded, and Nolan repeated the salutation, "Eyes to the horizon, Lord Garr."

They followed well-worn trails through the timber and reached the Outrider camp. A central conical tent dominated the camp, ringed by small individual Outrider tents, each with an Aarindin picketed nearby. They dismounted and entered to find Warden Elbiona taking a report from a lone Outrider.

She stood behind a central table in the large commander's tent. The warden dismissed the Outrider, a young man. Nolan couldn't place his name but thought for sure he was a medic. *What's a medic doing giving the report of a prime?*

The medic drew up short as he made eye contact with Karragin and Nolan. He nodded once, then prepared to exit the tent.

"Wait, Tovnik," said Elbiona. "This is Karragin and Nolan Lefledge. She will be your new prime. Find Amniah and let her know. You four can get to know each other later."

Tovnik sighed, then shifted the empty medic satchel to his other shoulder to shake hands with Karragin and Nolan. Brown hair matted to his forehead, and he held an empty medic pack over his lean frame.

He acted like the exchange cost him more than he cared to release. "A pleasure to meet you both," said the young man. "I can bring Amniah by in a few hours. She's in the stitch tent."

Nolan noticed for the first time that Tovnik's midnight blue uniform held dark stains spattered on the lower tunic and pants. A smear of blood at his neckline indicated the likely nature of the stains. "It looks like you had an eventful day?" asked Nolan.

Tovnik looked to the warden, who nodded consent. "Our quad tried to assist another, Berwek's group. They took heavy casualties. We lost Berwek's entire group and two from our quad but saved one before the last grondle fell."

Karragin turned her head slightly at the news. "We lost six to bring down how many?" she asked.

The medic pursed his lips, then said, "We lost nine. A third quad was involved. Nine Outriders to bring down four grondle and maybe twice that number in grotvonen."

Nolan shifted his weight back as if the words had altered the feel of the ground beneath him. He wasn't sure what impacted him more, the loss of nine Outriders or the casual mention of grondle and grotvonen. He tried to remember what he knew about the grotvonen, but all he could do was participate in the group silence.

Karragin broke through the somber veil that had settled in the tent. "Leave Amniah to rest, for now. We can meet in the morning after you have had time to recover."

Tovnik tilted his head with an exaggerated gesture as if to say, "Finally." He stepped to the side to depart.

"Tovnik," said Karragin as she placed a hand on his arm, "blood stains your dagger. What is it from?"

"It's grot blood," he said with a rueful look. "One tried to surprise me while I tended to another Outrider."

Karragin pointed to her Aarindin. "In my saddlebag is a portion of sliced, smoked mutton. Take it and give half to Amniah; you look like you need to replenish yourself. But leave me your dagger for now."

Nolan's stomach grumbled at the thought of losing the chance to sink his teeth into the tender, smoked meat, but he had to agree with Karragin's gesture. He watched the medic leave the tent without further words.

"I can see the value to trading field rations for real food, but why the dagger?" asked Elbiona.

"Nolan might be able to use it to learn something of the grot scent," said Karragin. She handed him the knife, hilt first.

"In camp less than ten minutes and already straight to business," said Elbiona. "I knew there was something special about you. You made exceptionally fast travel to get to Dulesque and Beclure. I didn't expect to see you for another week."

"We had the good fortune to be able to address both families in Beclure," said Karragin.

Elbiona rocked back and folded her arms. "That can't have been easy."

"As you know, the vice regent accompanied us," said Karragin. "He gave the visit a certain diplomatic tone, so we were able to offer our condolences and explanations, then depart."

The warden leaned back as if waiting for more. She looked to Nolan, who decided to defer to his sister's explanation. *Don't look at me. I think I prefer chasing grotvonen to getting into that mess again.*

"You two," said Elbiona. "Two nuts that didn't roll far enough away from the tree. Alright then, step up here, and we can review operations to date."

They approached the table to view a map of the southern portion of the kingdom, the region between the Pillars and the immediate Borderlands. Four figurines in the shape of Aarindin rested on the table, scattered in a random fashion.

"These are the places on the plain where we encountered grondle," the warden explained. "Without Reddevek, we've been unable to determine if this is a single crush roving the Borderlands or different groups. I'm counting on you to help us out there tomorrow, Nolan."

Nolan felt his face flush at being compared to Reddevek. Elbiona continued to talk, but none of the words penetrated the fog of his anxiety about having so much responsibility thrust upon him. Karragin must have sensed his unease because she tapped a boot against his foot, drawing him back to the conversation.

"We know from our reconnaissance that the grondle left the area shortly after killing the cutters from Stellance," she said. "Even without a tracker, most of us can find a trail left by a crush of grondle. But somehow, the grot manage to skirmish us several times a day. We have yet to find where they get in and where they muster. Starting tomorrow, that is your mission."

Nolan tapped the blunt handle of Tovnik's dagger into his palm. *It beats night watch.* He looked down at Karragin as she studied the map. She looked up and nodded.

"When you range, assume the enemy is looking for you as well. Travel in quad formation, ghost protocol. Any questions?" asked Elbiona.

Nolan groaned inwardly. *Ghost protocol is the worst. No fire to cook by, no tents, just bedrolls.* He already missed the lavish wagons of Chancle's entourage.

"Two, sir," said Karragin. "Nolan's ability—it's accurate. With that dagger, we'll discover something of the enemy tomorrow. How often should we return to base?"

"I will leave that to your discretion, but for now, I expect to see you once every three days."

Karragin nodded, then tongued the scar on her upper lip. "If we encounter grotvonen or grondle, what are the engagement parameters?"

"Your mission is to observe, gather intelligence, and return here," said Elbiona. She leaned in for good measure. "Under no circumstances are you two to be found in heavy engagement with the enemy. If an opportunity presents itself, get word to us here so we can send in an organized strike force. The last thing I need is to manage a couple of adventure-hungry

Outriders. I know you've been in the field, but I've half a mind to separate you and send one of you back to Aarindorn, except I'm already down two primes and have no tracker. I shouldn't have to tell the children of the regent just how much risk I'm taking."

They took their leave and settled in for the night. Nolan found small comfort in his bedroll. He sat knee to chest, thinking about what the morning might bring. On a whim, he channeled zenith through his arca prime. The rune vibrated and tingled with warmth as he activated his tracking sense. He directed his focus to Tovnik's bloodied dagger.

After a few minutes of concentration, he felt his gift identify a pattern in the blood. A faint sensation, something like the mineral taste of blood coupled with rancid meat, played across the back of his tongue and assaulted his nose. A thin blue haze trailed off to the south and another to the west.

Satisfied that the source of the grotvonen lay in the distance, he released his gift, then searched for something to remove the foul taste that lingered on the back of his tongue. All he found in his pack was a bit of dried fruit. He paced around his tent, chewing the tangy bits and trying to settle his mind. *Everyone is counting on me. Not Reddevek, but me! Taker's salty balls, I'm not ready for all this!*

Another Outrider walked toward his tent. Her dark Outrider uniform would have allowed her to hide in the shadows, but she ducked under a tree branch with lithe steps and walked into the light of Baellen. At first, he thought she might be Warden Elbiona; her black hair was cropped short in a similar fashion, but the moonlight silhouetted her subtle curves and played across a more youthful face. She set a small rucksack on the ground, appearing to grunt in pain. A fresh bandage was wrapped around her leg. "Mind if I introduce myself?"

Nolan forgot about the scent of the grotvonen and swallowed an unchewed lump of dried fruit. He coughed, and his eyes teared as he tried to speak. "Please, excuse me," he sputtered, coughed some more, and finally recovered.

"My name is Anniah. I understand that Tovnik and I will be joining your quad tomorrow."

"I'm not the prime. That's Karra's job," said Nolan. They shook hands.

"I know, it's just an expression," said Amniah. "I hear you're a tracker. I'm a guster. So you'll find the trails, and I'll hide them. Ours, I mean, our trails."

She stood without expression and seemed to wait for him to acknowledge—*Something? What am I supposed to say? Did I miss something there?*

"I've never trained with a guster," he said. "You push the wind? How does that work exactly?"

She shrugged. "When I channel zenith, I can feel strands of air like spider webs. I gather them up and push or pull them. I can't move big things yet. But someday."

They stood in awkward silence until a rumbling growl erupted from Nolan's stomach. Amniah cocked her head to the side, then reached into her rucksack and produced a pastry rolled into a pocket larger than his hand.

"The sliced mutton was yours, wasn't it?" she asked.

Nolan took the proffered pastry and sniffed at it curiously, surprised by its weight. The savory spices caused his stomach to gurgle even louder. Amniah lifted the left side of her mouth in a half-smile. "Well, go on silly, it sounds like you need it."

"Thanks," he said. He bit through the flaky dough crust into some kind of ground sausage mixed with onion, potato, and spices. Nolan moaned with pleasure.

"By the Giver," he mumbled with a full mouth. "That's about the best thing I've ever tasted. What is it?"

"Stellancian meat pockets. You like them?" she asked.

"The smoked mutton was good, but these are amazing," said Nolan. "I think I could move to Stellance for these alone. Where did you come by them?"

"My mother makes them," she said. "They only last a day or two unless you can bake them again. But I understand we'll be traveling under ghost protocol, so I'm passing them out tonight."

At the mention of the protocol, Nolan glanced to the dressing on Amniah's thigh. "We heard a little about the attack. It sounds like it was pretty bad."

Amniah looked down at her leg, then back up. "It was."

More silence followed. *Talking to this one is just weird. Does she ever smile? It's like her face never moves. She and Karra will get along grand.*

"Can you tell me anything about the grondle or the grot?" asked Nolan.

"Take the body of a man, a big man. Cut it in half at the waist and mash the top part onto the body of a bull where the neck should be. Then replace the man's head with something that looks like a bull, and you've got yourself a grondle," said Amniah. "They have these black slits on the chest and shoulders of the bull part. I think they use them to breathe and to smell. If they smell blood, they rage."

"What about the others?" asked Nolan.

"Grotvonen are more cunning," said Amniah. "Most of them stand only four or five feet tall, hairy things with beady black eyes. They walk funny."

"What do you mean?" asked Nolan as he licked his fingers.

"Have you ever seen a traveling glee-man with trained dogs?" she asked.

"I've seen jesters and traveling minstrels who used dogs as a side act," said Nolan.

Amniah nodded once. "You know how those dogs can walk on their hind feet? A grot is a little like that. It's like they can walk on two feet, and I think that allows them to hold weapons like spears and knives. But they are faster on all fours."

She tipped her rucksack upside down, and the last meat pocket fell into her hand. She handed it to Nolan. "Are you sure? It's your last one," he said.

She just nodded.

He broke the meat pocket into two and offered her the larger portion. She took the smaller one and sat down with her back to a tree trunk. He watched as she picked out and discarded bits and pieces from the filling on the inside.

He looked at what appeared to be large pepper flakes and assumed those gave the meat its spice. "You don't like the pepper flakes?" He took an oversized bite, anticipating her slow response.

Amniah kept picking through her meat pocket. "They're not pepper flakes; they're crown beetle wings. If I eat too many, they give me hiccups."

Nolan felt something slightly crunchy in the filling and chewed twice more, then swallowed hard. Without thinking, he channeled zenith and coerced the power through the rune on his right forearm. He used the enhanced awareness to filter through the meat pocket and sensed several familiar herbs, stone-ground flour, meat, onion, potato, but nothing poisonous. He released his gift and sniffed at the pocket. The aromas begged to be consumed, so he shrugged and devoured the last bit.

He sat down next to her with his back to the tree trunk, one knee bent to his chest and the other extended. "If that's the last real food we eat for a long time, at least it tasted good." He sighed in contentment. "You mentioned that the grot are cunning. What do you mean?"

Amniah finally took delicate, small bites of her portion. "They use weapons, small spears and knives mostly. And they wear crude armor. Their hair bristles out from gaps in the armor. I don't think their armor was meant for them; I've never seen a grot with well-tailored armor. They attack in ambushes and groups, usually after the grondle ride in. Standard hornet nest attack."

Hornet nest, what ever is she talking about? Nolan stared at Amniah, waiting for more. The silence drew out, and he inhaled to move the conversation to something else when she spoke up.

"Sorry, some of the military talk is new to me," she said. "When I was a kid, you could throw a hornet nest at a group of bullies if you were fast. It kind of reminded me of how the GG attack. Shock troops up front, marauders in the rear. Anyway, the grot talk to each other and follow a command structure."

The GG? Oh right, grotvonen and grondle. "Amniah, how many times have you fought them?" asked Nolan.

"Just the one time," she said.

"One battle, and you learned all of that?" Nolan asked. He turned to look at her. She, in turn, swiveled her head to look directly into his eyes but said nothing.

"How did you manage to notice all of that in combat?" he asked.

"I used my eyes. I gusted as much as I could and used my eyes," she said as if that explained everything.

His next question was interrupted by a loud hiccup. He tried to speak again only to hiccup again, and then again.

"Hmm," said Amniah. "You've got crown beetle hiccups." She stood with a grunt and rubbed at the bandage on her thigh, then dusted off her trousers.

"Are you familiar with pine needle tea?" she asked.

"Yes—*hic*!" he squelched.

She picked a sprig of green pine needles and handed them to him. "That's about the only thing that ever cured my hiccups. Be sure to use the green needles; the dried brown ones aren't as potent."

"Thanks!" he gasped out. She turned to leave, stepped around the bough of a tree, and disappeared into the shadows.

What a strange girl.

Nolan busied himself with brewing a strong cup of pine needle tea. He sipped at the spicy hot liquid and thought about everything he'd learned. In short order, his hiccups resolved, and he found his bedroll more than comfortable. He forgot about his uncertainty and felt oddly content. He tried to remember what had caused him so much stress before Amniah arrived and couldn't before sleep found him.

Chapter Thirty-Eight: Conflict in the Cave

Thunder rumbled over the mountain valley and vibrated through the cave, making for a fitful night of sleep. Kaellor stirred the hot coals during his watch and added wood, making the cave glow with warm, amber light. He walked to the mouth of the cave and admired the fury of nature.

Crackling flashes of lightning stabbed across the night sky, illuminating the forest valley for brief moments. The rain fell in a heavy curtain, but the cave kept them dry. He stood for a few long moments, watching the lightning dance across the night sky. A long streak of blue-white energy branched overhead and left the mountain valley illuminated for two long seconds. That's when he saw it: the outline of a hound. He strained to see it again at the next lightning flash, but it had vanished.

Taking no chances, he rushed back into the cave and grabbed the Logrend sword. He then roused the boys, the urgency in his hushed voice quickly drawing them out of their slumber. Lluthean grabbed his bow and Bryndor, a hunting knife.

"Wake the pups; they might be of help," Kaellor directed.

"What is it, Kae?" Lluthean asked as he and Bryndor eyed the cave mouth.

"My eyes might be playing tricks on me, but I thought I saw another one of those hounds when the lightning flashed," said Kaellor.

Bryndor added more wood to the fire, illuminating the cave in a brighter glow. He set a thick burning stick closer to the cave mouth. "Maybe they won't come in if there is a fire," he suggested.

Light skittered across the sky, followed by a chorus of thunderclaps that echoed over the mountain valley. After several long minutes, Kaellor relaxed his guard, but they all three continued to watch the front of the cave.

"Maybe it passed us by," suggested Lluthean.

Kaellor nodded. "Perhaps. Just to be safe, I'll continue to watch."

Their temporary ease ended with a throaty growl from Boru. Neska joined him, baring her teeth. Flickering back and forth across the cave entrance, a black hound moved about with blinding speed. It seemed to pause in one place for a moment, then blink to the other side of the cave mouth.

Lluthean drew his bow and shifted his aim, trying to fix on a target. Bryndor stirred the fire, and the blaze illuminated the dark hounds. At the back of the cave, the horses whinnied in nervous protest. Kaellor turned to see that a hound had appeared in the shadows cast by the mounts. He stared into deep black eyes that seemed hollow. The hound blinked again and was gone.

"One just appeared in the shadows behind the horses," said Kaellor. "It was there a few moments; then it was gone. It just blinked away."

The hound returned to the shadows at the cave entrance, darting back and forth. Only now, two of them stalked across the opening. "Dammit to the Drift, there are two of them. Alright, Llu, keep an eye to the back. They must use the shadows somehow," said Kaellor.

"We could loose the horses and recover them in the morning; then there would be no shadows in here," suggested Bryndor.

"I would rather not, but we might have to," said Kaellor.

Thunder continued to echo with increasing intensity, and lightning flashed with frenzy across the night sky. The twang of Lluthean's bow interrupted the silence between thunderclaps. One of the shadow creatures appeared in the dark silhouette cast by a gelding and charged. At the same time, the other beast charged from the mouth of the cave.

Once in the light, the beasts moved like normal hounds. Their ability to blink from place to place seemed only to apply to the shadows.

Kaellor chanced a glance to the back of the cave. The hound there had paused and was vibrating in place. The arrow Lluthean had shot dropped from its shoulder to the stony cave floor. This pause gave Lluthean the chance to nock another arrow. The beast charged, and Lluthean's second arrow missed its head by a breath.

Kaellor turned to the hound charging in from the mouth and calmly ordered Bryndor, "Mind your brother!"

He held his ground as the beast charged forward.

One chance.

The shadow hound leaped for Kaellor's throat. He dropped a knee and impaled the creature through the chest. The momentum of the charge caused him to stagger back, but he held his grip upon the weapon. With a fluid turn, he followed the beast overhead and kept the sword embedded in the hound.

The hound howled an unnatural, grating screech of pain and struggled against the blade. Kaellor wrestled with it, trying to stay away from the violent thrashing of its hind claws. The hound tried to free itself, and intense vibrations ran down the blade, thrumming into his hands. Despite a numb feeling in his forearms, Kaellor maintained his grip, and the Logrend sword held the beast in place.

In the desperate struggle, he fought to gain enough leverage to slice through the beast but only managed to skewer it to the ground. He hesitated to withdraw the weapon. The stalemate continued while the hound thrashed savagely, attempting to get to its feet.

Kaellor sensed his forearms tiring. *This can't continue; I have to end it.*

He eyed the campfire and, without a second thought, put his weight into pushing the hound onto the fire. The beast continued to howl and thrash, sending coals and sparks skittering across the cave floor. The hot embers seared his hands, and he had to hide his face behind his arms. Thick acrid smoke erupted from under the hound, but he held fast, blinking back stinging tears.

The beast clawed hind legs at the coals and tried to roll away, but Kaellor kept his grip, and slowly, flames began licking around the hound's body. The creature's vibrations slowed, and its howl became one of panic. All the while, he held the beast over the hot coals and flames, giving it a slow, agonizing death.

BRYNDOR FOLLOWED KAELLOR'S direction and turned to see the shadow hound closing on Lluthean. Lluthean's first arrow shuddered to the cave floor, released by the creature's strange vibrations. His second arrow flew errantly to the back of the cave, and then the hound leaped at Lluthean, its muscled jaws clamping down on his left shoulder.

Bryndor watched the beast rip into his brother while he raced forward. Lluthean fell back and drove an arrow into the belly of the hound with his fist. The creature screeched and thrashed its head savagely. Sharp hind claws raked across Lluthean's chest and abdomen, and crimson streaks erupted through his shirt.

Just steps away, Bryndor was preparing to lunge at the hound when a flash of blue light erupted from Lluthean's palm. A deafening thunderclap erupted in the cave, and the surge of rune fire threw them all back several feet. Lluthean slid back on the floor, Bryndor staggered a few steps, and the hound hurtled back against the cave wall.

Scout whinnied and raced out of the cave with the dapple grey geldings in tow. Bryndor struggled to maintain his balance and avoid being trampled. He turned to find the hound recovering to its feet. Wisps of smoke curled away from its snout, but the creature shook its head, dug its claws into the ground, and leaped again at Lluthean.

Bryndor charged headlong and dove at the beast, tackling it in midair. They tumbled into the shadows and blinked away. He felt his weight lurch back and forth. As the beast careened through the shadows, his body felt weightless for a brief moment. When they reappeared at the cave mouth, he nearly lost his hold on the creature as his weight returned.

He grappled the hound around its thick neck, trying to break its windpipe, but the solid mass of the beast seemed unaffected. He wrapped his legs about the creature and held fast. It felt like hugging a cold boulder on a winter day. The hound exuded no body heat and leeched the warmth from his core. His senses recoiled from the fetid smell of the creature.

The hound continued to blink about the shadows of the cave in a frantic attempt to shake him off. His vision blurred, and he became so disoriented he had to close his eyes. He gripped a large hunting knife and deftly slid the weapon up toward the hound's neck, conscious not to release his grip.

Slowly, purposefully, he began to saw back and forth. The beast blinked to one more shadow, then lurched to a halt. Bryndor felt his weight slip forward, but his other hand caught the chain of a collar. He grasped the chain and repositioned his weight, keeping his legs wrapped around the creature.

As he sawed through the hairless hide, the beast tried to blink and vibrate to dislodge the solid object. But Bryndor kept the knife blade in place and continued the deliberate sawing motion. The hound shook and trembled more violently, but he held fast and continued to pull through the beast's neck. The blade rasped against something that felt like bone, and he pulled with all of his strength. The hound collapsed into an oily pool, leaving Bryndor shivering, exhausted, and holding a chain looped through an odd pink crystal pendant.

He struggled against nausea and dizziness to his hands and knees. In the middle of the cave, Kaellor was holding the other hound skewered and pinned over the campfire.

"I can't hold on much longer, Bryn, Llu!" Kaellor gasped. Lluthean sat back on his knees, pale.

Bryndor made a fast assessment of his brother. "I'll help Kae. Tend to those wounds, or you'll bleed to death," he said.

Because of the dizziness, a clumsy, staggering crawl was all Bryndor could manage. He struggled to his feet and grasped the Logrend sword. Thick smoke stung his eyes, and the heat of the embers scorched the hair on his knuckles.

How did you manage to hold on so long, Kae?

In answer to his question, Kaellor fell to his side, overwhelmed with wracking coughs. Bryndor continued to hold the beast to the fire. Through squinted eyes, he watched as the hound stopped writhing. A strange flare of green flame erupted, consuming the rest of the creature's body. The beast melted into another oily slick, leaving the taint of rotten, burned meat in the cave. Bryndor let the sword fall to the cave floor, then slumped to his knees in exhaustion.

Chapter Thirty-Nine: Follow the Blood Pigment

H*"ok shareth*!" Mallic cursed in the Callishite tongue. The abrogator threw his hands up and funneled thick cords of nadir against the vaulted ceiling. The foundations trembled, and Volencia stilled his agitation with a hand on his shoulder. He dismissed the currents without harming the vast library.

I'm glad there are limits to his control. She knew that it was unlikely he could damage the stone walls and columns enough to bring down the structure, as his chaotic release of nadir had remained unfocused. If he had desired to cause real damage, a surgical strike through the base of one or two columns would accomplish the task.

She focused her attention on the crystal scrying cloud and the image of a burly youth, possibly a Baellentrell, recovering after decapitating one hound and then burning another.

Mallic reached a hand forward in a mock attempt to snuff the life from the young man. The crystals shimmered and swirled around his hand, losing their defined shape. Once he removed his hand, the images reformed. He collapsed into a leather armchair with a defeated sigh. Volencia just grinned and continued to observe the three men in the cave.

"Those hounds failed, we failed! Master will not be pleased," he blubbered with his face in his hands.

"Mallic, all is not lost. We finally have a sense of what they look like and where they are located. I think this might be the first opponent worthy of our time," said Volencia.

She sauntered over to the sounding, where a silver disc floated above a basin of water. She ran her fingers across the engravings that circled the sounding in a spiral. The engravings resembled those in the blood pool and featured garish creatures with tusks and horns frolicking in scenes of sodomy, death, and gore.

"Did you feel it?" she asked.

Mallic looked up with a question on his face. "I was too lost in the scrying. Did the sounding emit?"

"Yes," she replied. "The device pulsed once when that runeling touched his gift. It looked like attenuated rune fire. If he was able to channel zenith, even for a moment . . ."

"Then another layer of the banishment has peeled away," said Mallic with excitement.

She laid the palm of her hand on the silver disc, willing it to gong again. Every time the sounding emitted the haunting tone, a layer of the binding holding Tarkannen in the Drift fractured. They had no idea how many times the sounding would need to echo through the library before his release. *But one more echo is one step closer.*

She turned back to the scrying cloud. The crystals coalesced with clarity around the larger young man. He knelt near the remnants of a campfire. An older man lay on his side, coughing and possibly vomiting. *That must be Kaellor.*

The larger youth wrapped the pendant around the pommel of a saddle and tended to the wounds of the thinner young man. Sitting side by side, the scrying crystals defined their faces with more clarity. *Brothers, definitely brothers—same jawline and eyes. Perfectly convenient that all three travel together.*

She turned back to Mallic. "If they keep the chain, we have the means to track them. We could dispense of them ourselves."

Mallic's look of defeat melted, giving way to a wry smile. "Master will know we failed when the hounds return to the Drift. But if we can find them ourselves—"

"Our redemption lies in the demise of those three," Volencia finished.

"Do you have the locator globe? The one we used to track Captain Mundle?" asked Mallic.

"Of course," she answered. She pulled a small globe from her pocket. Currents of silver liquid swirled through the sphere, and a fine red powder twirled in a funnel in the center. She held the object still, and the powder gathered along one side of the device.

She tilted her head, indicating Mallic should follow. They walked through the library, down dark corridors, and up to her private balcony. Once at the top, she held the globe up in front of her. The red pigments gathered along one hemisphere of the device.

"West," she said. *Have they lived in the Southlands all this time? I thought for sure this would direct us across the sea to the north.*

"They are in the Southlands?" Mallic asked. A skeptical look of confusion creased his brow. "All this time, and they were down here, in the Southlands."

"Until their binding began to splinter, we had no means to know where they lived," Volencia snapped, her sharp tone betraying her own frustration at the realization.

She pocketed the globe. "We should ride out in the morning. One of them is injured; they will not be able to travel very fast."

"Alright," said Mallic. "I wish we knew what direction they are traveling in. In the morning, then." He rose and retired to his chambers.

Perhaps there is a way to tell what direction they travel. Volencia returned to the library to inspect the basin once again. She searched the images, hoping to get a sense of the moons in the sky. After a few moments, she realized her folly. *It's a cave.*

She reached into the basin to retrieve the glimmer stone, then changed her mind. *There is always a chance the images will reveal something new. There is enough refined crystal to power the device for several days.*

She palmed the locator globe and withdrew the device once more. The mercurial fluid sloshed back and forth inside the delicate sphere, and the red pigment swirled within. She held the globe still, and the pigment faintly gathered to one side, indicating that the brass necklace, and her prey, were in the west. She smiled in satisfaction, then retired to her chambers.

Chapter Forty: Three Would Mean the End

L luthean propped himself back against a slope on the inside of the cave and clutched a shirt against the deep gash on his shoulder, trying to control the worst parts of the bleeding. From his brief inspection, the wound was grisly, but strangely enough, it caused him little pain as long as he didn't move. *Funny how the deep cuts do that. Slip and cut deep with a knife, not much pain at all. But nick a finger on a thorn and suffer.*

He shifted his weight, and the shallow cuts along his torso and abdomen flared with burning pain so intense that he didn't notice the stitch from the healing cracked rib.

His head felt oddly light, like he'd drunk a tankard of ale on an empty stomach. *Maybe I just need to close my eyes and sleep a bit.*

Something warm lapped at his hand, and he looked down to see Neska licking dried blood from his skin. He rewarded her with a reassuring scratch behind the ears, then looked around the cavern. The thunder and lightning had faded, but steady gentle rain continued to fall across the mountain valley.

The sulfurous, smoky taint of burned flesh lingered so heavily that Lluthean thought he could almost taste something of the hound they'd put to flame. He licked sweat from his upper lip, but the salty taste only masked the acrid smoke a little.

Looking across the cavern, Kaellor lay on his side, incapacitated with long spells of coughing. Eventually, he got to a sitting position. His hands and forehead looked reddened, and much of his beard was singed away. Soot stained his clothing and gave him the appearance of a man who worked the mincs.

Bryndor tried to get to his feet but stumbled like a drunkard for several minutes.

"Are you sick?" Lluthean asked.

"Something about riding on that hound; the way it blinked about made me dizzy," said Bryndor. "But the worst of it has passed. How's that wound?"

The makeshift dressing hung heavy with congealed blood. While Lluthean thought the dressing adequate, he realized it must be saturated as occasional drops of blood spilled from the fingers of his left hand. *That can't be good. After this long, it shouldn't still bleed, should it?*

Kaellor's voice cut through the stillness of the rain patter. "Bryn, get the bottle of devil's tail from my pack and use it to tend your brother's wounds. That's likely to cause infection if—" His words trailed off as he succumbed to another spasm of coughing. He staggered to the cave entrance, where he violently emptied his stomach.

Bryndor quietly retrieved the bottle from Kaellor's pack and approached Lluthean. He seemed hesitant. Eventually, he squatted down and lifted the dressing covering the wounds. He sucked in a breath and just stared at the gashes.

"I know, it's bad, isn't it?" asked Lluthean.

For long moments, Bryndor chewed on the inside of his lower lip. Eventually, he sighed. "Mogdure's teeth, you weren't supposed to kiss the damn thing."

Lluthean smiled back but could not think of a witty retort through the haze of pain. He watched Bryndor remove a clean shirt from his pack and tear it into strips to clean the wounds.

Bryndor swallowed hard. "This is going to hurt something fierce, but there's no help for it. That's one nasty bite. I don't think we should chance the same dilution Aunt Ro used for me back home."

"I would sooner drink that stuff than bathe in it," Lluthean said. Bryndor sat back on his heels, waiting. Lluthean looked up from the wound to Bryndor's eyes. "Well then, are we men or are we mice?" he asked.

Bryndor gave him a half-smile. "Umm, squeak up?"

Lluthean answered back in a high-pitched voice. "Squeaky squeak!"

Bryndor turned the devil's tail upside down and doused one of the dressings with the tincture. "I'm sorry, Llu. Are you ready?" he asked.

Lluthean nodded and watched his brother apply the devil's tail with steady resolve. As the oily substance splashed into his shoulder wound, Lluthean imagined hot molten metal dripping into his shoulder and burning a hole into his back. He gasped, too surprised by the sense of burning agony to scream.

The searing pain radiated into his torso and down his left arm. He looked down to check that his thumb and forefinger were not sizzling on hot embers. Bryndor rubbed at the wound, and a more intense wave of pain flooded his awareness. His head swam as he gasped and fell into darkness.

BRYNDOR PANICKED WHEN Lluthean slumped back but then realized he'd only fainted. He still drew deep breaths, and his chest vibrated with his heartbeat. *Dammit to the Drift, Llu!*

Bryndor took advantage of Lluthean's unconscious state. He brought back memories of watching Aunt Rona care for their small cuts over the years but had little experience managing anything so grisly. Edges of the skin flopped back as he scrubbed, revealing fatty, glistening globules. Deep in the wound, he thought he could see the fibers of muscles.

The sight made his hands tremble, and he swallowed back watery saliva. He decided to douse the wounds with devil's tail liberally, then continued to scrub. He removed a few bits of necrotic, dark flesh that would no doubt contaminate the injuries further. His mouth watered as if he might heave, but he swallowed back the rising bile.

His ministrations aggravated the bleeding, and dark blood pooled in the wounds and ran down Lluthean's arm. Bryndor remembered Rona using ash once to stop the bleeding of a goat mauled by a dog.

He rushed to the firepit and grabbed two handfuls of white wood ash. He rubbed the ash into the large shoulder gash, the shallow cuts on his torso, and then held pressure with strips of the clean shirt. The bleeding slowed, then stopped, allowing him to fasten the dressing in place. When he finished, Lluthean seemed to rest at ease.

Neska crept forward to lay beside Lluthean, placing her head on the top of his hand. Bryndor reached over and gave her a reassuring pat.

"He'll be fine, Neska. He's tougher than you think, but keep an eye on him."

She crawled closer on her belly and rested her head on Lluthean's abdomen. Bryndor turned to find Boru wagging his tail. He dusted off his hands and carried the bloodied dressings over to the fire pit, then sat down next to the warmth of the fire.

"Come here, boy." He gestured, and Boru jumped into his lap, smothering him with licks. The two sat on the cave floor, playing a game of tug-of-war with a piece of leather. After finding his spirit rejuvenated by Boru's playfulness, Bryndor rose to check on Kaellor.

His uncle sat just outside the cave mouth, shivering in the rain and letting the steady downfall wash away the ash and soot. Bryndor stood just inside, watching him. A small stream of rainwater splashed down from overhead, and Kaellor sat directly under the deluge.

"Why don't you come inside, Kae? If the chill seeps into your bones, you'll wake up sorry in the morning."

Kaellor had stopped coughing, and the soot was mostly washed away. He turned a ruddy face to Bryndor. Small white blisters had appeared on his lips and forehead, and his hair and beard withered in strange curled clumps. He nodded and came back into the warmth of the cave.

Kaellor walked over to inspect Lluthean, who still lay sleeping. A pink hue blushed through the bandages on his shoulder, but they appeared to be holding. "No easy task there Bryn, you did well."

Lluthean's face was still pale. "Should he still be asleep, Kae? I think he lost a lot of blood before I got to him," said Bryndor.

"It's more than that, I think," said Kaellor. "He released rune fire, and that can exact a price."

Kaellor reached forward, assessing Lluthean's color and warmth. "He's breathing easy; let's let him rest for now," he said.

After changing into dry clothes, Kaellor applied a salve to his burns, then joined Bryndor around the firepit.

"I found this on one of those hounds," said Bryndor.

He handed over the brass chain with the pink crystal pendant. Kaellor inspected the item. He turned it over and over in his hands, then tugged as if to snap it, but the chain held.

Kaellor handed the chain back with a grunt. "That's no ordinary necklace," he said.

Bryndor stared into the strange pendant. From within the pink gemstone, smoky wisps of vapor drifted in and out of focus. "I can see that," he said.

"The crystal is only part of it; look closely at the chain links. They're each engraved with symbols," said Kaellor.

Bryndor fingered the chain, turning it in the firelight. Tiny symbols engraved on the inside of the links reflected the amber light.

Kaellor rubbed at the burned parts of his beard. "That points to trouble for us."

"How so?" Bryndor asked.

"I had hoped that our first encounter a few days ago was just random, a fluke. But after tonight, I think it's clear that those hounds are from the Drift. They were likely sent to find us. Just knowing that one of them wore a collar means someone or something sent them," he explained.

"Have you ever seen anything like those hounds or this chain before?" asked Bryndor.

"No and yes," said Kaellor. "I've never met the likes of those hounds before, but their empty black eyes and the way they could travel the shadows—no natural animal can do that. They carry the taint of abrogators. As for that chain, I have seen its like. It's imbued with power. Perhaps someone uses it to control the beasts. I don't know what to make of the crystal. For now, let's keep it in a pouch."

Bryndor nodded, turned, and placed the necklace in his saddlebag. Kaellor stood up and walked back over to Lluthean. He inspected Lluthean's chest and arms, then covered him up with a blanket.

He returned to sit near the fire. "Just checking to see if the mantle still holds. How about you?" he asked.

Bryndor frowned in confusion. "I'm fine, Kae."

"I'm not talking about injuries. Runes, glyphs, did any of yours show up?" he asked.

Bryndor rolled back his sleeves and checked his chest; the skin remained bare. Kaellor grunted.

"Did you see it?" asked Bryndor. "He released the same blue light I did. I think it saved him, just like with me and the wolvryn, blue light and then a thunderclap."

"I felt it. But I'd wager you had more to do with saving his life than anything else," Kaellor replied.

"If the mantle fails, how will we know?" Bryndor pressed.

"Oh, I don't imagine you'll miss it," said Kaellor. "Symbols and runes should appear across your arms and chest."

Bryndor wasn't sure if he should be happy that his arms were still bare. *Maybe if we had access to our gifts, we wouldn't be here now.*

Boru crawled into his lap, turned a circle, and curled into a ball.

"Kae, the first time there was only one. Tonight there were two. What if . . ." Bryndor let the question hang.

"If three come tomorrow, then there is nothing to be gained by losing sleep over worrying about it now. All the same, though, let me take first watch, and you get some rest," said Kaellor.

Bryndor nodded and tried to relax with Boru nestled between his legs. He leaned back against his saddle and watched the rain continue to fall. Kaellor sat facing the cave entrance, holding the Logrend sword across his lap.

Bryndor closed his eyes, and as his mind drifted, he heard his uncle mutter to himself, "Guardian, indeed. Three would have been our end."

Chapter Forty-One: Riding With Desperation

Kaellor thanked their good fortune in finding the cave in the south face of the Korjinth. Over the next two days, the rains continued, and the dry shelter allowed them to recover. Lluthean's wounds dried, but he still appeared pale and weak, and Kaellor continued to endure spells of uncontrollable coughing.

The first day after the attack, soot-stained his phlegm. By the morning of the third day, he found himself able to draw air without deteriorating into spasms of hacking cough. The blisters on his burned face and hands dried and caused him only small discomfort.

Bryndor returned from foraging with Scout and the other two geldings, explaining that he'd found them nibbling at grass in the valley not far off. The horses seemed reluctant to enter the cave but remained picketed nearby while the three of them recovered.

The rains cleared by the morning of the third day, and a bright sunrise invited them back to the trail. After a light breakfast of wild berries and roasted game, Kaellor found Lluthean rolling Neska onto her back and rubbing her belly. "Do you feel up to traveling today?" he asked his nephew.

"I think I can manage. The sooner we are away from here, the better." Lluthean smiled, but the deep circles under his eyes betrayed his fatigue, and his complexion still appeared sallow.

"I understand. I think I've had my fill of cave living for a long time," Kaellor replied.

Bryndor and Kaellor packed the horses. After Lluthean mounted his gelding, Bryndor placed Neska into the round open saddlebag. In the last week, she'd grown too large to curl up into a ball in the carrier they'd made and now sat with her front paws on Lluthean's lap.

"What did you feed her in the last three days?" asked Lluthean. Bryndor smiled and grunted with the effort of lifting Boru into his own saddlebag.

"It's in their nature," said Kaellor. "They grow faster than weeds the first year. Have a look at their paws. Big feet for big animals."

A familiar twinkle flashed in Lluthean's eyes. "And you know what they say about a man with big feet."

Kaellor smiled. *I sort of walked into that one. Still, if he's found his wit again—that's a good sign.*

Bryndor answered his brother. "Indeed, big feet, bigger boots, right?"

"Well, some of us would know what I mean, right, Neska?" Lluthean added. Neska cocked her head at Lluthean. He gave her a reassuring touch behind the ears.

They left the shelter at an easy walk under the morning sun, continuing their trek along the base of the Korjinth range, heading ever eastward. The days welcomed their journey with fair skies and warm weather, and though guard duty made the nights tiresome, they unfolded without further danger. They filled their time recounting stories from Journey's Bend and talking more about the home to which they were returning.

"So, the ruling families in Aarindorn have always been Lellendule or Baellentrell, never another?" Bryndor asked.

"Not since the shaking of all Karsk in the Cataclysm," Kaellor answered. "When the mountains rose, separating the north and south, chaos, famine, and disease spread across both continents. Eldrek Baellentrell emerged as our first ruler. He possessed our family's first magical gift. Some legends say he journeyed to the Drift and wrestled the gift from an ancient power. Others say the Giver rewarded him because he was virtuous and stood as the only person at the time capable of uniting our people.

"Nobody really knows how he inherited the ability to channel. But with it, the histories say he founded Aarindorn. He must have believed that no one family should automatically govern the kingdom, so he created restrictions and tied the strength of the gift to the service of the people. Then he ensured that every one hundred years, the strongest of the gifted and the seat of authority, would pass from one family to another. His most trusted friend back in that time was Kelledar Lellendule," Kaellor recited the old history lesson, somewhat surprised that he could recall most of the details.

"What happens if a Lellendule and a Baellentrell marry or have children? Wouldn't that disrupt the neat division?" asked Bryndor.

"There have been a few such unions, but the nature of the gift prevents any such union from bearing children. While those relationships were discouraged, some occurred nonetheless," Kaellor replied.

"Kae, if our parents held the throne, and you left, who assumed the throne in your absence?" Bryndor asked.

"Arrangements were made for our second cousin, Therek Lefledge, to assume the seat as regent. He was a good and trusted friend to your parents and me. He possessed a knack for ferreting out a lie or a bluff." Kaellor chuckled. "More than once, he frustrated your father in games of chance. At any rate, I expect he still holds the seat. His authority would return to the oldest son of Japheth upon his death or our return."

Bryndor stopped his horse up short. Kaellor looked back over his shoulder; Bryndor looked like he'd swallowed too much of one of Rona's bitter medicinal teas.

"Surely this regent, Therek, will not turn that kind of responsibility over to the likes of me?" Bryndor asked.

Lluthean slapped him on the back as he rode past. "You're just now getting that? We covered this back in the Bend."

Bryndor nudged his gelding forward to walk beside Kaellor. Some of his color had returned. "Therek will have no trouble returning the throne to you," said Kaellor. "As I recall, he assumed the position only under protest."

Kaellor stopped his mount to make eye contact with his nephew. "Besides, Bryn—the strongest and best rulers among us are those who possess not only the gift but a sense of obligation and service to the people. That you look upon the station as a responsibility and not a windfall, well, that fact alone tells me you would make a good king."

Bryndor chewed on his lower lip. "But if Therek can channel—"

"He has lesser gifts, but as he is not a Baellentrell, he will never be able to marshal the strongest aspects of channeling on behalf of the kingdom. Those abilities and their obligations fall to us. That's just the way Aarindorn works," said Kaellor.

He doesn't think of himself as a king yet, but give him time to adjust, and he will.

Kaellor observed Bryndor as they walked. His nephew was silent and distracted, and an errant branch nearly unhorsed him as they turned around a bend of the game trail Lluthean was leading them on.

Kaellor laughed and gave him a gentle clap on the back. "Bryn, relax. You're putting the cart way ahead of the horse. Until we get there and you have the chance to learn more about Aarindorn firsthand, it does you no good to get all worried."

"That's easy for you to say," said Bryndor. "We're from Journey's Bend. What do I know about being a king?"

Lluthean chimed in, "You know, being the youngest definitely has its advantages."

"No arguments from me there," Bryndor replied.

Kaellor said nothing but caught Lluthean's attention with a wink as they rode on. Later that night, Kaellor sat on guard around the campfire and thought about the friends and relatives he'd left behind. His mind returned to the present at the sound of Lluthean mumbling in his sleep.

At first, the mumbling seemed innocent, but after several minutes, Kaellor frowned and rolled his nephew over to check on him. Lluthean tossed restlessly, and his shirt was stained dark with sweat. Kaellor felt his forehead, surprised to discover him in the grip of a high fever.

"By the Giver," he blurted in surprise. He peeled back the dressing across his nephew's left shoulder. He had not checked the wound for two days, believing it was mending well and stared aghast at the margins of the deep bite that curled in with gruesome black edges. A thick black scab of corrupted tissue cracked, emitting foul-smelling pus. Kaellor withdrew with a wrinkled nose.

Lluthean's entire left arm looked red and swollen, with unnatural dimples and puckering. Kaellor lifted the limb, surprised by how heavy it felt. The elbow resisted bending, and Lluthean groaned from the manipulation.

Kaellor rummaged through a saddlebag and found the last of the devil's tail along with a teabag of Maedra's pitchers. As he prepared the tea, Bryndor woke from the noise.

"Is it my turn, Kae?" Bryndor yawned awake.

"No, but we have a serious problem," Kaellor nodded toward Lluthean, who lay semiconscious and mumbling. "He's taken a fever—and look," Kaellor directed, lifting the bandages.

Bryndor covered his nose with his sleeve. "Goodness, that's awful."

"When was the last time he changed the dressings?" Kaellor asked.

"I don't know. I asked him if he needed any help two days ago, and he said he could manage. I've never seen anything like that. Is it serious?" Bryndor frowned with concern.

"It very well could be. Help me get this tea into him; then we'll redress the wound with the last of the devil's tail. We need to cut a litter. We might be able to get to a village with a healer of some kind," said Kaellor.

Bryndor moved without question, understanding the urgency in Kaellor's tone. Together, they coerced Lluthean to choke down most of the tea. Kaellor felt his heart quicken at seeing how weak Lluthean appeared and had to grab a handful of Lluthean's hair to keep his head propped up to administer the tea. The process was tedious and threatened to choke his nephew.

They redressed the wound with haste. This time, all Lluthean managed was a soft moan when the devil's tail splashed into the wound. The tincture removed most of the odor, but the curled, blackened eschar and the way Lluthean's arm swelled left no doubt about the seriousness of the infection.

"I can't understand why this took so long to fester. I thought it would have done this on the first day or two if it was going to be a problem," said Kaellor.

"Maybe it's because of those hounds. They weren't natural. Maybe it has something to do with that," Bryndor suggested.

"Perhaps. At any rate, we need to hurry. Grab the hatchet, and let's cut a litter," Kaellor directed.

They worked in silence and with an urgent fervor. By sunrise, they had Lluthean rolled onto a litter and the litter set to tow behind a horse. They broke camp without eating. Kaellor towed Lluthean while Bryndor tethered Lluthean's gelding behind his own horse. Neska jumped on Lluthean's litter, and they made slow progress. The tea seemed to have a calming effect on Lluthean, but his fever persisted, and he slipped further into unconsciousness. The three clumsily picked their way eastward, careful to avoid steep and rocky terrain.

Kaellor led the way as they traveled but periodically looked back. He kept hoping that the continuous jostling of the litter would startle Lluthean awake. He imagined his nephew waking with a wickedly evil grin to announce the whole charade was a ruse. They would share strong words, but in the end, he would trade a thousand humiliations for his nephew to sit up and smile.

By evening, Lluthean's condition had deteriorated. They paused to consider their options. His breathing was shallow, and their efforts to coerce him to drink only caused him to choke. The fever still ran strong, but his body was now too weak to force a sweat.

Kaellor's mind rebelled against the bitter irony. Here they were, attempting to return to Aarindorn, where the healers would have little difficulty restoring Lluthean to full health, and he was powerless to stop the infection. He tugged at the burned edges of his beard as he considered their situation. The rage of emotion made the burns on his forehead flush with heat.

His thoughts cascaded from overwhelming worry to guilt, then anger. He felt his own pulse quicken and noticed a tremulous feeling in his hands. After several long moments, he realized fear was threatening to paralyze his mind. With deliberate effort, he forced his attention away from the troubling thoughts and regained command of his emotions.

Focus. Center yourself. He observed Bryndor, who had knelt trying to find comfort from the wolvryn pups but was equally distracted. With a heavy sigh, he considered their situation objectively.

"We have two choices, Bryn. We ride on, hoping to stumble across some settlement or small village. Or one of us can stay here while the other rides ahead. Both options pose a risk, and neither is the solution I would hope for," said Kaellor.

Bryndor looked back at his brother for a few long moments. "If—" His voice broke, trembling. He cleared his throat. "If he slips away, Kae, I can't be—I can't do that alone."

He looked up without shame; tears streaked the trail dust from his cheeks. "But I don't think I can stand the notion of not being near him if that happens."

Kaellor stepped forward, and they shared a warm embrace. *What have I brought us to? Giver help us. Don't let my anger be the death of this boy.*

He made up his mind to resist becoming overwhelmed again by the emotion of the moment. "Together then. Besides, I don't want to see what happens if only one of us is here if those hounds return. We should stick together."

His gaze drifted into the dark wilderness, and he recalled his own brother's parting words. *Eyes to the horizon.* The traditional salutation was offered in friendship and meant as a term of encouragement. He wondered if Lluthean would survive to hear his countrymen offer the greeting.

"Let's ride until we find help, no stopping," said Kaellor.

Bryndor just nodded. With grim faces, they mounted and continued their ride of desperation into the night.

Chapter Forty-Two: Karragin Becomes a Prime

Karragin walked through the Outrider camp in the early morning. She had already completed her morning routine of calisthenics and was searching for Nolan's tent. Only a handful of other Outriders stirred at the early hour, but she wanted to make an early start on their mission and knew rousing Nolan would be the bottleneck in getting started.

She discovered a young woman sitting alone on the stump of a recently felled tree at the edge of her quad's camp. *You must be Amniah.*

The guster stared at something in the distance. Karragin stepped closer and surveyed the camp and surrounding forest but struggled to discern anything unusual. Amniah swiveled her head, not unlike an owl, which Karragin found interesting, if not odd. The guster continued to look into the distance with vacant eyes.

"There is plenty of room if you would like to join me, sir," said Amniah. *So, you did know I was here.*

"Thanks for the offer," said Karragin. "Have you eaten already?"

Amniah blinked as if considering the question. It almost looked like she wasn't sure if she had eaten or not. After a moment, she shook her head, indicating that she had not.

"Would you like to join me then?" asked Karragin.

Amniah nodded, hopped down, and walked beside Karragin to the mess tent. They each grabbed a plateful of food from the assortment of eggs, bacon, bread, and dried fruit.

They sat at a mess table outside in companionable silence. *At least I think it's companionable. This one has a resting gaze that's harder to read than mine, only without the asshole part.*

After several minutes, Tovnik approached their table. He sat down without waiting for an invitation and attacked a pile of scrambled eggs and sausage. After a few mouthfuls, he looked up, swallowed half of his tea, then raised the cup in a half-hearted toast.

"Good morning. Where's the tracker?" he asked, then returned his attention to the plate.

Karragin studied the medic. The lean man continued to gorge himself on eggs and sausage. She guessed his age to be about twenty-five.

He eats more than Nolan. Where does all that food go?

Instead of answering his question directly, Karragin looked over her shoulder to Nolan's tent. The flaps remained closed.

"Amniah," said Karragin. "Can you thread the needle?"

The guster understood the question. Outriders able to gust practiced using their skills in several ways. One was a drill called "Thread the Needle," in which they propelled a small object, usually a pebble, along a very focused path to a target.

"That's actually one of my better skills," said the girl. "What do you have in mind, sir?"

Karragin tore off a small bit of bacon. "We are downwind of Nolan's tent, or else he would have beat us to the table. I wonder if you can entice him to rouse by letting him know what he's missing?"

Amniah nodded once. Her eyes flickered with light as she channeled zenith. The smoke of the cookfire funneled in a peculiar line against the wind and into Nolan's tent.

"That should do it," said Karragin. "More tea?" she offered to them both. By the time she returned, Nolan was walking on sleepy legs toward the mess tent. He'd managed to throw on his Outrider uniform, but an unruly cowlick above his left ear betrayed the fact that until only a moment ago, he was sleeping soundly.

Nolan made his way through the mess tent and walked to their table. "Mind if I join you?" he asked.

Amniah lifted both eyebrows. "Giver's blessing, that was fast."

Karragin smiled into her teacup and moved over, creating space for him to sit down. "Now that we are all gathered, let's review our mission parameters," said Karragin. "Nolan, have you had the chance to apply your skill to Tovnik's knife?"

"Yes, last night. I found two faint signals. One to the west and another to the south," said Nolan.

"To the south makes sense. That's where Berwek's group encountered them," said Karragin. She lifted her gaze to the west. Dense forest covered the expanse between the camp and the Pillar of Eldrek, marking the beginning of the Great Crown on that side.

Why would the trail of grot lead that way?

"We'll follow the trail west and learn what we can," said Karragin. "At all times, we are to avoid direct conflict. Our job is reconnaissance. We'll travel in quad formation, ghost protocol, with Nolan in the lead, Amniah and I on the flanks, Tovnik on rear guard. Any questions?"

"When do we leave?" asked Tovnik.

"We ride out in thirty minutes," said Karragin.

Nolan shoveled the last bit of scrambled eggs into his mouth, then stood and grabbed his plate. He rushed back to the mess tent and back to the table before any of them had a chance to leave.

He looked up between bites to answer their questioning stares. "We're under ghost protocol. This might be the only decent meal for three days," said Nolan. He returned his attention to his plate.

Tovnik tipped his head back, then stood and followed Nolan's lead, making another pass through the mess tent.

A half-hour later, they rode west out of the camp. Nolan led them through dense forest and undergrowth for several hours. They skirted north of the Pillar of Eldrek and climbed into the rocky foothills of the Great Crown.

After another hour, he stopped at the top of a hill and signaled them to gather. From the vantage point, the mountain range encompassed the entire horizon. Karragin looked northeast to where she thought Stone's Grasp should lay but couldn't make out the capital city.

"Lose the trail?" Tovnik asked as he brought up the rear.

"No, the opposite actually," said Nolan. "The trail winds farther up over this ridge. Beyond that, we will encounter valleys and canyons. This time of year, there isn't usually much snow, but we aren't exactly kitted for mountain travel, so I thought we should talk before I lead us too far down the rabbit hole."

Karragin sucked on her upper lip and withdrew into herself. She felt the currents of zenith ready to ignite her arca prime and magnify her strength, but she directed her attention to the minor rune on her left forearm. She sensed the rune's tingle and thought over Nolan's words.

"Well, up or down?" asked Tovnik.

"A moment, I'm trying to discern something," said Karragin. She focused her attention, drawing more zenith into her rune of foresight. After a few minutes, she sighed in frustration.

"Anything?" Nolan asked.

"Not this time," she said. "Stay in quad formation. Let's follow the trail as long as we can. If the grotvonen are in the Crown, inside our borders, that's not something we can overlook."

Nolan led them along passable game trails farther west. The path he followed slowly ascended one ridge, then went down a valley and up another ridge. By midafternoon, the air felt colder. Karragin licked her lips and realized how parched her mouth felt. She took a long pull of water, and they continued the slow climb.

They camped that first night by a stream and resumed their investigation the next day. Nolan periodically channeled to confirm that they were following an active trail.

Late in the day, they crested another ridgeline. Karragin realized that she'd lost count of how many canyons and ridges they climbed and had second thoughts about returning to base camp for better gear and a field report. To make Elbiona's three-day deadline, they needed to start the return trip soon.

Another valley, this one carpeted with short, green plants and wildflowers, stretched out before them. The fragrant blossoms were a strange departure from the crisp pine aroma carried on the arid gusts.

The rune on Karragin's left forearm tingled. *Now you want my attention?*

She dismissed her irritation and checked their surroundings. Sensing no immediate danger, she drew her attention inward once again and attempted to engage her rune of foresight. Receiving no clear direction from her gift, she allowed zenith to recede from the rune.

She looked forward to Nolan. He rode about a hundred yards in front of her. Too far to speak to, but close enough for her to see. Without warning, he dismounted and signaled for his Aarindin to lay down.

She tugged on zenith and linked to her Aarindin. The mount seemed relieved for rest and promptly lay down in a similar fashion. She signaled Amniah and Tovnik to perform the maneuver then crawled ahead, mindful to keep her head below the ridgeline.

Nolan lay prone behind his mount as he searched the valley below. "What did you find?" she asked.

"Nothing, but I had a hunch," said Nolan.

"I'm lying here in wildflowers for a hunch?" she asked.

Nolan continued to survey the canyon. "There shouldn't be wildflowers here. They can't grow in the shade of the pine and spruce."

"So? There aren't any pine or spruce here," she answered. "Are you catching the draft from channeling too long?"

He turned to look at her as if the answer was obvious. "I haven't had to channel zenith for the last hour or so; grot signs are everywhere. Doesn't it seem a little odd to you that there is an entire canyon without trees? When was the last time you saw something like this?"

Karragin looked back down at the valley. The moon of Lellen waned as a sliver to the south, but Baellen hung bright and full directly overhead. Closer inspection revealed occasional stumps among the clusters of shrubs and flowers. "When we discovered Benyon's road. You think someone cut down all the trees, all the way up here?"

Her mind followed Nolan's logic. *If the grotvonen are responsible for clearing an area this large, they have either been busy for a long time, or there are a lot of them up here.*

She realized that their walking along the top of the ridge had made them alarmingly visible if the grot did inhabit the canyon. She reached over and ruffled Nolan's hair.

"Good job, Tracker. Mother would be proud."

She analyzed the arc of the sun. "How much time before the sun drops below the horizon?"

"Less than an hour, maybe half," said Nolan.

I would rather be a lucky monk than a dead one. The Aarindin would struggle to remain down for more than an hour, and even then, when the animals stood, they would stumble about for a time.

We've already pushed them hard to get this far.

"Stay here until the shadows obscure your retreat, then come back. I'll tell the others," she said.

Karragin crawled back down the ridge to her mount and shared Nolan's findings with Amniah and Tovnik.

"That seems like a pretty thin reason to miss the warden's three-day deadline," said Tovnik. He pulled at a handful of wildflowers and thrashed them against his other hand, appearing unimpressed with any of the developments.

"I thought about sending one of you two back to report our findings to the warden, but you wouldn't make the deadline, and I'm not splitting up the quad," said Karragin. "So instead, we'll picket the Aarindin here and investigate this canyon on foot tonight."

Tovnik looked at the sky and held his tongue but shook his head in disbelief. Amniah just lay on her side, considering them both.

Karragin considered the medic. She didn't want to dismiss his concerns. He was her senior by several years, an experienced Outrider. But part of her wondered if his impatience reflected the fact that this was his last season with the Outriders. She knew he came from wealth; his family owned an estate in Stone's Grasp next to the curtain wall. *Is he lazy, nervous, tired, or bored?*

She considered all these factors, then turned her best resting asshole gaze on him. The medic looked back, but only for a second, then averted his eyes.

"Sorry, Prime, that was inappropriate," he said. "This feels a little like the trouble Berwek got into, that's all."

"Tovnik, you aren't going to hurt my feelings. Just tell me what you are thinking," said Karragin. "You're seasoned, but that only helps if you share it with me."

"I thought I was," said the medic. He rubbed his forehead with a hand.

"I've known monks who speak more clearly than you and with less attitude," said Karragin with a frank tone that sounded more contemplative than confrontational. "It's beneath a medic in his last season. Speak plainly or don't speak at all, understood?"

Tovnik blinked and flushed at being called on his poor behavior so openly. He recovered and nodded once without further words.

As the sun dropped below the horizon of the Great Crown, the temperature dropped enough for Karragin to see her breath. Nolan returned with a grin. His Aarindin staggered down from the ridgeline on wobbly legs.

"What are you grinning at?" asked Tovnik.

Nolan's smile wilted. He shrugged at the older man. "I was thinking about our good fortune because Baellen is full tonight. It beats exploring the canyon when the moons wane. You know, more light."

They all stared at him, even Karragin. He was right, of course; the full moon would make their reconnaissance easier, but it also meant that the grot could see them.

They walked the mounts back into the tree line and picketed them. They each carried bows, she and Nolan wore sabers, and Tovnik had a pack of medic supplies.

"Nolan has the lead, tight quad formation, so we can still speak, but assume ghost protocol. The grotvonen hear and see better than we do in the dark, and their sense of smell is unparalleled. Any questions?" she asked.

"Just one. How do you know all that about the grot?" asked Tovnik.

"I paid attention as a tender," said Karragin. She had trouble sensing any emotion from Amniah, and Nolan reverted to excessive optimism when he felt nervous. Tovnik kept his voice steady, but she sensed an undercurrent of unease in him. "Look, our objective is not to confront the grot, but to find out if they are here and, if so, what they are doing. That's all."

They crossed over the ridgeline and picked their way into the canyon. Nolan led them behind outcroppings of rock and, for the most part, kept them in the shadows. The hidden stumps of trees threatened to trip them at random intervals, and one of them stumbled more than once. When the sound of a clumsy step rattled into the night, they paused, waiting to hear if the grot or anyone else had noticed. A slight breeze from the west put them downwind of anything in the valley.

They snuck down through lush, knee-deep patches of wildflowers, winding their way farther into the canyon. Nolan crouched down then waved them forward. They crept up to him, crouching in the moonlight.

"What is it?" whispered Karragin.

"Wait. Watch," he said, pointing down into the valley.

She strained to make anything out in the distance. Small waves of wildflowers undulated as a strong breeze carried over the rolling dark hills. Something fetid and unpleasant carried on the gust as if a carcass lay rotting ahead of them. Strange clacking and guttural noises carried on the wind before fading.

Karragin felt a hand grab her forearm and turned to see Amniah. The moon of Baellen reflected off the whites of her eyes. *That's the most emotion I've ever seen from her.*

"That's them, isn't it, the grot?" said Karragin in a low voice.

Amniah just nodded.

"Wait here. I'm going to have a look," said Karragin. "Wait thirty minutes, then head back to the Aarindin. I'll find you if anything happens."

She crawled forward without waiting for any of them to give her counsel. After fifty yards, the strange clacking and guttural sounds became more distinct. She strained to make sense of the noises over the thrum of her pulse beating in her ears.

She made herself remember her training and thought about her breathing. It took a few minutes of acclimation, but eventually, she lost awareness of her nerves and focused on the sounds.

She cursed herself for wasting time and crawled forward with purpose, then rammed her forehead into the base of a broad trunk jutting just above the flowers. She struck the solid object hard enough to see stars and grunted in pain and surprise.

She froze in place. *You're a grinding monk, Karra! Did the noises stop before or after that?*

After a few minutes, the clacking returned. A small cloud bank obscured the moon, giving her more cover. She reached a hand forward and followed the side of the trunk. The massive edge tapered to a root. She crawled over the obstacle and slithered forward, then careened into the open air. She labored to pull herself back and, for a moment, teetered on the edge. The tree root acted like a fulcrum against her thighs, but nothing anchored her feet. She arched her back and slowly windmilled her arms but felt her weight inexorably slide forward.

On instinct, she channeled zenith and flared her arca prime. Her reflexes and strength ignited with power. She withdrew her saber and plunged it into the backside of the tree just as her feet toppled overhead. She hung there, dangling from her sword, cantilevered over a vast crater in the floor of the canyon.

With her gift active, the task posed no challenge, but she worried that her acrobatics had alerted whatever was making the clacking noise to her presence. She strained to see into the darkness, hanging there.

The deepest shadows lifted as the clouds moved past the moon of Baellen. Shafts of pale blue light revealed a cave at least twenty feet wide. It traveled into the ground at a sharp angle. Two tree trunks protruded from the cavern, and she watched as a lone grot climbed out of the darkness using the tree as a crude ladder.

The creature mumbled something guttural; then, two others clambered out of the darkness and down the makeshift tree-ladder. She hung there in the shadow of the cantilevered stump, watching. The grot lumbered forward a few steps then dropped to all fours, running on its knuckles and feet. It loped with dexterous speed, then hopped up alarmingly high to a large boulder on the opposite side of the cavern.

The beast sat in the moonlight, and she lost herself in studying the alien features of the thing. She guessed its height as not more than four feet. Pale skin stretched tight over strange saucer-shaped ridges of bone that housed oversized eyes. The lenses of the grot reflected the moonlight and made the creature's expression appear stuck in a state of wide-eyed surprise. The eye ridges merged with a broad, furrowed nose, and the grot sniffed eagerly at the air. Teeth jutted out at strange angles from a lipless mouth.

The beast wore scraps of chain and leather armor. Coarse hairs protruded at its shoulders and elbows where the padding gapped. In one hand, it gripped a small spear.

The smell of the grotvonen this close turned her stomach, but she found the opportunity to watch them too valuable. She perched there several more minutes, enthralled in her gift. More of the creatures climbed up and down the tree trunks, but none paid her any attention.

And then she felt the wind eddy about her, changing direction. The grot perched on the boulder sniffed hungrily at the air and looked in her direction, but she remained obscured in the shadows. Its large, triangular ears twitched, and it barked a guttural command followed by a clacking noise made when it rapidly clattered its teeth.

Several grotvonen scurried into the cave from the shadowed vicinity, but they were replaced by at least ten others who climbed out. These others assumed a defensive perimeter and barked back to the scout on the boulder in the same strange language.

One of the new grotvonen stared in her direction a few moments then howled. *I think I've overstayed my welcome.*

In answer to her thought, the creature hurled a spear directly at her. She pulled her body to the side, and the weapon wedged into something solid behind her. She flipped her feet back overhead and tugged at her saber. The maneuver made her visible, and the grotvonen howled as one. She chanced a look down; from the depths of the cavern, hundreds of eyes twinkled in the moonlight.

So many. We'll never outrun them all.

Karragin pulled her saber loose, then pulsed zenith through her arca prime. She leaped across the opening of the cave. Spears aimed at where she was just perched flew past her. She landed with a knee crunching into the rib cage of the grot scout on the boulder. She felt its bones snap and splinter. The beast squealed in surprise, gasped, then slid to the ground.

A chorus of growls and clacking echoed across the canyon. Karragin paid them no attention and dropped to the backside of the boulder. It stood perhaps ten feet high. *But all I have to do is roll it.*

She stabbed her saber into the ground then dropped to a knee. She heard a rustle of the ground cover as two grot ran to her side of the boulder. In a fluid motion, she grabbed her weapon and pivoted on a knee, feeling the blade cleave deep enough into the beast's midsection that it hit bone. She pulled the saber back in a slicing motion, then rolled to the next one. Her hand found purchase on its ankle. A faint part of her awareness recoiled at the feel of its coarse, oily hair.

In disgust, she pulsed zenith, flared her strength, and tossed the creature like a rag doll. It sailed across the mouth of the cave, howling until it landed against the other side with a crunch of bone, then fell, lifeless, into the cavern.

She dropped back beside the boulder and, kneeling, found the leverage to begin rocking it back and forth. She'd never forced herself to channel so much zenith for so long. Her pulse pounded in her ears from the strain, and she endured a mild sense of light-headedness. She continued rocking the boulder, each push and recoil gaining momentum. The sounds of the grot echoed louder around her. Finally, the massive rock crashed down into the hole.

She crouched with her blade in hand and released her command of zenith. The boulder careened into the cavern, carrying with it the crude tree ladders. The sound of snapping timber and rockslides split the night.

Something staggered her forward, and she nearly followed the boulder. A grotvonen landed on her back, its sharp claws raking across her shoulder. She channeled more zenith and sprang to the side. The beast tumbled off her to the ground but landed like a cat. Without delay, it bounded twice and leaped at her. She ducked and swiped overhead, removing one of its legs.

She charged at the next one and, at the last minute, lunged to the side. Her blade slashed against the backside of its neck as she passed, and it crumpled. She crouched defensively and counted at least six more, but they retreated to the opposite side of the opening to their cavern.

Karragin edged her way back up to the ridgeline, trying to keep one eye on the grotvonen and another on the rest of the valley, regretting ever committing to action in the dark of night. She moved slowly back, and the grot continued to gather on the far side of the entrance to their warren. Their howls changed from cries of alarm and pain to more guttural growls and the clacking of teeth.

What are you waiting for? You have the numbers. In the distance, running down the far side of the canyon, a horde of grotvonen raced in her direction. The creatures periodically changed from loping on two feet to bounding on four and covered the ground with alarming speed.

By the Giver, you really have the numbers.

Karra turned and looked back up the canyon. "Get to the horses!" she shouted.

She dashed back up the hill using zenith to maintain her strength and prevent the fatigue that would otherwise overwhelm her. She sensed arrows fly past her toward the grotvonen and heard them cry out in pain.

"Enough, go! Run!" she shouted. "There are too many!"

She caught up to Nolan, who stood and continued to shoot arrows. "What are you doing? Run!" She poured as much venom into her words as her breath allowed, took the bow from his hands, and swatted him on the ass as he turned. Closer to the ridgeline, Tovnik and Amniah shot more arrows until the siblings reached them. Then they all ran.

Karragin released her grip on zenith and fell back to bring up the rear. More than once, one of her Outriders stumbled on a rock or stump unseen in the darkness. Whenever that happened, she pulsed zenith and darted in to pick them up and keep them running.

They crested the ridgeline and sprinted downhill. In moments, they made the trees and then the Aarindin. As they worked to untie the horses, the grotvonen horde crested the ridgeline.

We'll never make it. Not in the darkness.

She channeled zenith into the rune on her forearm and linked to two of the Aarindin. The horses turned as she sent her simple message: *"Run home."*

Before they could mount, Amniah and Tovnik's horses bounded off to the east. She repeated the same command to the other two.

"Get to me quickly. We can't outrun them, but they might follow the Aarindin," she said in harsh tones.

Karragin cupped her hands and chanced channeling zenith one more time. Silver light scattered across the rune on her chest. Nolan understood and stepped into her hands. She tossed him eight to ten feet into the air. He caught a branch of the stout pine and climbed into the dense boughs.

"Now you Amniah, the same way," said Karragin. In under thirty seconds, she had each of them thrown up into a tree. She crouched and sprang up into another pine, narrowly avoiding catching a branch in the face. Less than one minute later, the first grotvonen loped under the boughs. A few paused to sniff the air, then chased off after the Aarindin to the east. From the safety of her lofty perch, she couldn't count how many of the beasts pursued the horses, but the initial wave of the creatures scampered by continuously for several minutes.

As Karragin struggled to control her breathing, a shimmer of light in the darkness caught her eye. She looked over to Amniah, who sat perched in the upper boughs of a spruce tree.

Clever girl. She's using her gift to send our scent with the Aarindin.

Karragin flicked a pine cone at Amniah. The guster caught the object with a column of air, then swiveled her head; her eyebrows creased in the faintest hint of a frown. Karragin made an exaggerated motion of grabbing at the neckline of her uniform then pointed at Amniah.

After a moment, she nodded once, then closed the top panels securely over her arca prime, preventing the escape of any light. A lone grotvonen loped past Karragin's perch and stopped directly under Amniah's tree. The creature appeared to search for something in the air, sniffing eagerly. Its wide eyes stared up into the boughs. After a few moments, the beast dropped to all four limbs and loped off. Karragin released the breath she didn't even realize she was holding.

They stayed in their perches, near frozen in the mountain air. More than once, Karragin considered descending to the ground, but groups of grotvonen kept wandering back and forth under their hiding places.

She lashed the buckle of her belt to the tree in case exhaustion overcame her. The balls of her feet ached and then fell asleep from standing, and she had to place her tongue between her teeth to avoid chattering.

Several painful hours later, morning arrived. Still, they kept to the safety of the trees. Two hours into daylight, she struggled to keep her eyes open. Just as she nodded to sleep, Amniah's voice startled her.

"None of the grot have passed our way since dawn. I think it's the light. Would it be alright for us to get down, Prime?" asked the guster.

Karragin cleared her throat. "Alright, let's drop. Drop and *ruchi*."

They each grunted and groaned as they made their way to the forest floor.

"What's ruchi?" asked Nolan.

Karragin circled a finger in the air and cleared her throat. "Rally-up and check-in!"

Each of them stepped forward. Amniah looked more pale than usual and had deep circles under her eyes.

"How long did you channel, Niah?" asked Karragin.

Amniah stared back without expression for an oddly long time. At last, she said, "Nobody has called me Niah since I left home. I like it. I stopped when the sun rose."

She looked at Tovnik. He did not appear as tired, but a large scrape decorated one cheek and forehead. A glob of sap stained the other cheek. Karragin recalled him falling more than once on their run up to the ridgeline. "How about you, Tovnik, any injuries?"

"Nothing a salve and time won't heal," said the medic. He adjusted the medic pack on his shoulders and rummaged through his satchel before producing strips of dried meat that he passed out.

"Nolan, anything to report?"

"Amniah's right; they don't like the daylight, but they were all over this ridge last night, Karra. I mean everywhere. Some might have tried to follow the Aarindin to the east, but most returned to that canyon just before dawn."

Karragin squatted down, then stood up again. She clasped her hands then grunted in irritation at the realization that the sap was threatening to keep her fists balled. She sniffed at the pine resin then recoiled. "I don't know what's worse, the feel of the sap or the smell of those things."

"The smell," Amniah and Nolan answered together. Their timing caused them all to smile.

"That was a colossal grot-grind. You all did well. Thanks for listening to me. Next time," Karragin said as she turned to Tovnik, "I'll listen to you."

The medic shrugged. "We all survived, which is more than I can say for the Aarindin."

"They'll be fine. I sent them home. I don't think even those creatures could catch a motivated Aarindin. If the grot follow them, it will be all the way to the Balladuren ranch."

They divided up their leftover arrows and made plans to walk north out of the Great Crown. As they ranged over forested canyons, identical to the ones that had brought them into the Crown, Karragin couldn't shake the feeling that she'd placed her quad in unnecessary danger. She tempered any thoughts of self-doubt with the knowledge that their discovery of the grotvonen threat was important.

How did so many gather inside our territory for so long, and to what purpose?

She turned the questions over in her mind and even flared zenith into her rune of foresight in an attempt to learn something more useful. No clear answers were forthcoming, and she tried to dismiss her concerns, but they kept at her, gnawing like a ravenous rat.

Chapter Forty-Three: Folding Beyond the Korjinth

Laryn sat on the edge of her cot, staring at her feet as she traced a symbol with her big toe into the dust of the floor on her hut. When she finished the last scrolling loop of the design, she stopped and stared at the rune with genuine surprise. Without thinking, she'd drawn the Aarindorian rune of the healer.

What was I dreaming that made me remember that? She waited for something, anything, to manifest in her awareness. After a few minutes, and with no clear understanding of why she had remembered the symbol, she swiped her foot across the tracing.

Perhaps that's just a ghost from the Drift telling me it's time to dust.

She stood and stubbed her toe on a small basket beside her front door. Ever since Elder Miljin revealed that her finding day was drawing near, younger children like Ellisina had shown disappointment. Conversely, the adults congratulated Laryn with genuine affection, and most mornings, she rose to fresh flowers and new gifts: finely woven blankets, new leather breeches, and small baskets of fruit.

She reached into the basket and retrieved a handful of tangy, dried fruit. She pulled her hair behind her ears and felt the skin of her cheeks draw back. The feeling reminded her that she was wearing face paint for the first time in years. The day before, Ellisina's mother and two others had stolen Laryn away for an afternoon of ritual adornment. Using richly colored pigments of red and deep purple, they took hours to embellish her skin with whirling dots. The staining would last for weeks.

She inspected her arms. The pattern began as faint tendrils at the wrists, coalescing into swirling patterns that wove up her neck to her cheeks. She grabbed a small hand mirror, one of her few belongings from home, and inspected the artwork.

Drab grey eyes stared back. *How do I always forget that? All these years and still, my own gaze surprises me.*

She stepped out of her hut in time to see one of the village matriarchs, Elgruh, deliver a new blanket to her front step.

She waited with her hands on her hips for the woman to glance back, then signed, *"You honor me too much, Elgruh. My basket overflows, and my arms can't carry all the gifts. Thank you."*

The woman nodded, smiled, then signed back, *"You might need more on your journey."* The woman walked back down the path that led to the gathering house.

And so the days unfolded with random visits by different Cloud Walkers. Some mornings, children greeted her with songs. Other days, a new gift found its way to her hut.

Everyone knew of Laryn's desire to see her future unfold. While only the spirits revealed any sense of that future, all the villagers felt sure that because she had learned the patience of the Cloud Walkers, only good things would follow.

At the end of the week, the entire village gathered for a feast in Laryn's honor. They converted the gathering house into an enormous buffet with roasted game and fowl, trays of wild fruits and melons, yams and roast tubers, and large platters of a dense cake drizzled with honey.

Laryn entered to find Ellisina with a small wolvryn hidden under the table. The pup licked her fingers clean of the honey drippings.

"Ellisina, you better be careful, or that pup will never leave your side, and your mother will have a fit," said Laryn with feigned reproach.

The girl leaned in close to whisper, "I know, that's why I let her lick my fingers."

Both of them giggled, and Laryn whisked Ellisina off her feet to join in the tribal dance ceremony. Men and women played drums or piped through reed stalk instruments. The elders led chants, and everyone mingled in dances under the roof of the gathering house.

After a communal chant meant to signal the start of the feast, Elder Miljin stepped forward. The olive-skinned elder stood on a small raised platform adjacent to the drummers and pipers. A new crop of butterflies wreathed his bald head; at least four sat fanning their deep red and purple wings in a slow cadence. He waited for the crowd to quiet.

With a mixture of speech and signing, he addressed the crowd. "My friends, many blessings and honor to our village. With happiness, we dance to honor our sister, Laryn, on the eve before her finding day. We dance and sing tonight to ask the spirits to guide her on a safe and happy path."

Several people whistled the happy chirps of bird calls, signaling their approval as the elder spoke. "And we join together to acknowledge that no matter where her path leads, she will know she can always return as an honored sister of the Cloud Walkers."

Elder Miljin stepped forward to the edge of the platform and held out a hand, welcoming her to step forward. She knelt on the platform, feeling humbled by his words. He blessed her with a gentle kiss on the forehead.

The drums and chanting started with renewed vigor. "I'm ready," she said.

"I think you have been ready for some time, but time was not ready for you." He smiled, then looked across the gathering house. "Try not to dance all night, though. I need to see you by sunrise at the spirit house. We will begin then, my child."

Laryn nodded, then rejoined the dancing. She retired to her hut hours later, weary from the food and merriment. Yet, as she lay on her simple bed looking at the blue moon of Baellen riding high and bright in the night sky, she found sleep elusive.

She awoke with a start from the soft tapping upon her doorframe. Her heart quickened with excitement, and she made fast work of dressing. She stepped outside with a travel pack on her back to find Elder Miljin standing alone in the predawn light, holding a small candle lantern. He offered her a piece of kevash fruit and smiled; the butterflies hovered about his shoulders, his silent companions in the dim light.

"Many blessings, Laryn, and honor to your house," he signed.

"Many blessings, Elder Miljin; honor to your house," she returned. *"Where did you find fresh kevash? I thought we ate the last of the harvested fruit earlier this week."*

She sank her teeth into the meaty pulp and felt the sides of her cheek tingle from the fresh, tangy-sweet juices.

The cherubic elder tapped his temple, setting a few more butterflies aloft. *"I still have a few tricks. It falls all year round if you know where to look."*

A sly smile played across his face as he said aloud, "Come child; the hour is fast upon us. The spirits are restless. But you will not need that pack where you are going."

Laryn set her travel pack down and followed as the old man walked through the village. Fragrant blossoms and vines clung to simple architectural huts that blended into the environment. An unusually thick cloud bank billowed around them, and she strained to find familiar landmarks through the silent, dense mists. The landscape appeared foreign and otherworldly; it reminded her of the first morning she'd arrived at the village. The quiet, proud, and beautiful olive-skinned people lived in a world of strange beauty.

I wonder if I'll ever be able to return. For a moment, sadness threatened to distract her, and her eyes stung with the threat of tears.

Miljin's resonant, soft voice encouraged her onward. "My child, do you recall the day of your arrival?" he asked as they walked toward the spirit house.

"I was just thinking about that day," she replied. "I camped at the foot of the mountains and awoke at the outskirts of the village on a day similar to this one."

"The spirits told me to welcome you and teach you our ways. When I found you sleeping outside of our valley, I decided it was best to bring you to our village unaware," he explained. "I was reluctant to trust the spirits. You are the first person from the outside to visit the Cloud Walkers, and I was afraid. After a very short time, I realized I was a fool not to trust the ancestors completely."

He climbed two of the steps before the spirit house and faced Laryn with a warm smile. "You are a daughter of the red moon, but you are also now a daughter to our people. Are you prepared to run with the spirits, Laryn?"

Run with the spirits? What does that mean, exactly? Despite her uncertainty, she nodded.

"Come then and let us see where the spirits take you." The elder held out a hand. She placed her palm in his, and they continued up the steps. She began to ask a question, but Miljin turned at the door, held up one finger, and signed, *"Inside here is only for listening. Trust the spirits, and your path will be made clear."*

Laryn nodded her understanding and followed him into the spirit house. Her heart quickened as she peered about the interior in wonder. The dim light revealed a simple room with a matted floor and no furnishings. Incense drifted across the room from small braziers in each corner. In the center, a small hearth filled with hot embers kept the spirit house warm.

Miljin walked on silent feet across the room and gestured for Laryn to sit near the coals. From a small shelf, he retrieved a wooden bowl adorned with decorative pigments like the ones used as face paint. The bowl brimmed with dried butterfly wings. He poured some into his palm, then blew the delicate, lacy structures over the hearth. The wings eddied about unnaturally on the warm air currents above the coals. When they finally descended, they spiraled and twirled.

Upon landing, each small wing puffed in a brilliant flash of light and smoke. Iridescent red wings produced pink or red trails of smoke. Others gave rise to tendrils of vapor with different hues of green. He continued to add different colored wings until a rainbow of colors mingled unnaturally in a vortex above the embers. The wispy currents then swirled about the room with a light flowery aroma.

When the bowl was empty, Miljin retrieved a few leaves from the sample of Broga's beard. The fleshy thin blue and green leaves landed on the embers and released what appeared to be normal smoke. Laryn wrinkled her nose at the strange pungent odor.

Next, Miljin removed several of the hairs from what she assumed was the black clouded leopard. He released the strands into the brazier, where they curled then smoked, smelling worse than the Broga's beard.

Finally, Miljin stood and signed, *"Now we welcome the spirits and see where they lead you, child."*

The elder grasped a long wooden pole with a hook at the end. He latched the hook onto a removable cover over the center of the room and slid back the thin reed panel. A round sky window opened, and the dense clouds pressed into the room, mixing with the wispy smoke inside.

Laryn swallowed, then realized she must have been standing slack-jawed for several minutes. From the mingling of cloud and smoke emerged poorly defined shapes. The apparitions of butterflies, birds, and numerous small rodent spirits mingled with the colored currents of smoke in the spirit house. Next, larger animals, deer and wolvryn, emerged from the clouds. Then human forms coalesced, and Laryn witnessed the embodiment of the ancestral spirits of the Cloud Walkers.

The ghostly apparitions of men and women joined hands and encircled Laryn. Each spirit looked back at her without expression. From the circle of spirits, an old woman drifted forward—the same woman from Mahkeel's calling with the wolvryn song.

The woman seemed to inspect the tendrils of smoke lifting from the brazier. She placed a hand into the vapor trails. Laryn watched as the black and grey columns slithered in a ring around the apparition's wrist, forming a dense bracelet. A dark blue ribbon entwined with the silver, mercurial band.

The ancestor looked up to Miljin with an expression of approval. Then she turned and offered the hand with the wristband to Laryn.

Laryn stood immobile. She wanted to mark the occasion in her mind, creating a memory. For years, she had longed for this moment, and she sensed as soon as she committed to action, she would be forever changed. The notion made her both excited and apprehensive.

After taking in the full measure of her surroundings, she looked to Elder Miljin, who nodded in reassurance. She then looked to the kind face of the apparition and grasped the spirit's outstretched hand.

A harsh, shearing sound that reminded Laryn of standing at the summit of the Korjinth filled the room. The bracelet slid from the ancestor's wrist to Laryn's. She stared at the strange band. It felt heavier than she had imagined it would be and tickled her with an odd vibration. The blue and silver bands wove around her wrist in a current of fluid motion.

The ancestor reached forward to draw Laryn's attention and pointed to the open circular sky window. Immediately, all perception of weight lifted as they folded into the clouds. The apparition blew a kiss to the south, as she had done on their previous encounter. The spirit then released Laryn's hand.

She felt an odd sense of being urged through the mists and surrendered to the sensation. Something unseen pulled her through thick cloudbanks to the south. A warm current caught at her clothing, and she allowed herself to drift farther.

As she floated through dense banks of clouds, she lost all awareness of space. Occasionally, she caught a glimpse of the top of a large stand of trees, but the dense ocean of clouds obscured her ability to sense any distance. Her stomach thrilled and fluttered at the speed.

Abruptly, the temperature dropped, and the mists thinned. Laryn felt like her breaths were capturing no air and began panting. She arced over the summit of the mountains and sped directly into thick currents of zenith and nadir.

Something pulled at her arm, and she looked down to see the apparition of the ancestral spirit lift her hand and hold her arm with the bracelet forward. The woman traveled beside Laryn and seemed focused on the warring currents before them.

As they plunged into the blue and silver streams, the zenith and nadir recoiled back, seeming to withdraw from the bracelet. Understanding the ancestor's intent, Laryn willed herself forward and propelled through the opening left by the separation of the flows. They surged ahead, and behind them, the currents collided. A wave of stinging pain washed over her, followed by a dazzling array of scintillating light.

Like looking at the sun too long, she felt momentarily blinded. Then she began descending, and a warm breeze removed the chill from the summit. Her breath returned, and the aroma of pine filtered into her nostrils.

Dense, grey clouds continued to obscure her vision as she descended. The mists cleared, but her ears still rang from the effect of traveling so close to the warring currents of zenith and nadir. Finally, the weightless feeling left, and her stomach settled. She stomped her feet then knelt, seeking reassurance.

At last, solid ground.

The strange bracelet continued to vibrate on her wrist. The clouds dissipated, and she stood to overlook a vast forested canyon. Tracts of pine and evergreen extended to both horizons.

Where did you bring me, and where did you go?

She searched for any sign of the spirit, but the clouds had dissipated, leaving her lost and alone.

Chapter Forty-Four: In the Coils of Nadir

Volencia checked the scrying stone once more before meeting Mallic. The crystals swirled above the scrying basin in a murky, formless cloud.

It must be inside a saddlebag or the grimy pocket of one of the Baellentrell scum.

She withdrew the locator globe and swirled the contents. Faint red pigment gathered to one side of the orb.

West it is.

She met Mallic at the stables. He had procured fresh mounts, two pinto geldings. She arched an eyebrow, appraising the animals. Nothing ever compared to the Aarindin of her youth, and Mallic's inability to purchase sound mounts had complicated more than one journey in their past.

She assessed the first horse. *Good confirmation, fair balance, coat sleek and shiny—not bad.*

She examined the mount's teeth and guessed him near five years of age. She looked back at the tracks the horses left, then began a brief inspection of the second mount despite Mallic's protests.

"They're the same Vol," he said. He cocked his head back slightly in that strange posture that always made him appear to be looking down the length of his nose. He folded his arms in a challenge. "Same breed, same age, same breeder, same everything, and I paid good coin. Can we just go before the streets jam with merchants?"

"Fine, I'll take this one then," she said and mounted the first horse.

"What's the difference?" Mallic asked.

Volencia looked down at the other horse's hind feet. "That one is splayfooted with a narrow base, four or five years older, and has a dull coat."

435

"What's that got to do with getting us from here to there?" asked Mallic as he mounted the other horse.

"The locator globe only designates their location as to the west; we have no idea how far we have to travel. We could be in the saddle for several days, maybe a week. If you plan to ride that horse, you are going to use a lot of nadir removing the animal's fatigue, and that assumes his aberrant gait doesn't throw your back into spasms along the way."

Mallic leaned forward in the saddle and pretended to speak to his horse. "Did you hear that? She doesn't think you can manage the journey as well as your twin there."

Volencia shook her head and kicked her horse into a trot. *Any idiot can see these are not twins. They're not even the same breed. This one's a Callishite strider. That one is just a pinto mixed breed. Honestly, all these years relying on horses, and he still hasn't learned the basics.*

Volencia pushed a hard pace. They employed nadir to remove their fatigue and that of the animals, and by midafternoon, Mallic began to show the strain of channeling nadir. If one channeled too much zenith, they risked the draft. Pull on too much nadir for too long, and one risked the frenze. Continued siphoning of nadir caused a sense of mild euphoria. However, prolonged excessive channeling led from that to a state of agitation to restless hypervigilance to eventual disorganized frenzy.

She watched the silhouette of his shadow on the ground. He rode with a fidgety nature. His shoulders and arms writhed with random movements, and he often rolled his neck in odd contortions. *How he remains in the saddle is no small miracle.*

She turned to look directly at him. His complexion was pale, and beads of sweat had gathered on his pale brow.

"You've been siphoning nadir for the last two hours. We should stop so you can both recover," said Volencia.

To his credit, Mallic nodded agreement with none of the sarcasm that usually flavored his responses. They rested only a few hours then pushed on. The Festian Plains extended west of Callish and supported numerous small farming communities.

By the third day out, the plains merged with pine forest, and rolling hills interrupted the flat horizon. They reached the foothills of the Korjinth a few days later.

Volencia periodically removed the locator globe. Pigments inside the orb gathered with increasing density, always indicating that their quarry lay to the west.

By the week's end, the red pigment settled like a small clot of blood in the mercurial fluid of the orb. The sight seemed to renew some of Mallic's vigor.

"It's like the orb knows we are out for blood, so it uses a signal to match our desire," he said.

The gentle pace she allowed for in the last two days had given him time to recover. She didn't think she would need him to subdue the prince, but their performance against the shadow chasers had surprised her. Better to overwhelm them than take any chances.

"I'm feeling better, and we must be close. Let's ride on into the night," said Mallic.

Dumb as a monk and twice as stubborn; you must be in the euphoria phase of the frenze.

She shrugged indifference. "As long as you mind the frenze. I don't anticipate having trouble with the Baellentrells, but I'm not playing nursemaid if you slip again."

Mallic didn't wait for her. He kicked his gelding forward, and they pushed their mounts to exhaustion, riding long into the night. The late summer air hung heavy and sticky. As the night progressed, the cooler temperatures gave rise to thick fog. A bank of dense clouds rolled off the Korjinth Mountains and saturated the foothills and valleys. Travel became hazardous, and the mounts began to stumble on the uneven terrain. Volencia lit a torch, but the curtain of vapor allowed her to see only a few feet ahead.

Mallic turned, and his head bobbed with the characteristic motion of the frenze. He sneered. "Extinguish that, you fool. Better to walk on foot and approach them with surprise than reveal our presence with a torch."

She considered a biting retort but only grunted, then released the light. *If it gets you to walk and stop channeling nadir, then I'll count it a victory.*

The abrogators dismounted and led their mounts on foot, making slow progress in the predawn hours. They climbed a rolling hill and emerged from a stand of trees. Mallic stopped and glanced at Volencia with a wicked smile. The muted sounds of approaching horses emerged from the fog.

Volencia held forth the locator globe. Bright, arterial-red color swirled inside the orb and streamed against the sphere as if trying to escape in the direction of the sounds. They sat in ambush for the approaching riders.

She felt a tingly vibration as coils of power rippled through her forearms. She rubbed at the sensation and inspected the snakelike sigils. They undulated, reflecting her anticipation.

They're coming, Master, and soon we'll have the key to unlock your binding.

They did not have to wait long. In minutes, two men emerged from the fog. They both led horses by the reins, and one of the horses pulled what appeared to be a litter. The older of the two panted. He muttered something to the younger man, then seemed to check on someone in the litter.

Though the fog muffled their words, she felt certain these were the same faces they had seen in the scrying cloud last week. She followed Mallic, and they crept around a copse of trees for closer inspection.

"Any change, Kae?" asked the younger man. Concern flavored his tone.

"No. He draws labored breaths, and they're shallow. Let's rest a moment here. Perhaps travel will prove safer once the sun burns away this fog." The older man reached around his saddle and withdrew a waterskin. After quenching his thirst, he turned to hand it to the other man.

Good, we have all three of them, Kaellor and the heirs.

Mallic shared a hungry look with Volencia, and she nodded. They stepped out from different sides of the cluster of trees.

"Maladictor!" yelled Volencia. She spoke the word, imbuing passion and strength to her intent as she channeled nadir, then unleashed her power. The power of abrogation coalesced and snaked forward.

"Look out!" the man she assumed was Kaellor yelled. His reaction was too late. She felt the extension of her will throttle him to the ground. She infused the tentacle into his chest and abdomen, and he writhed on the ground in spasms of pain.

She looked up to see the younger man, one of the heirs, throw a knife at her. Mallic stepped forward and tossed condensed nadir into the path of the blade.

The heir ducked under his horse only to reappear with a bow. He knocked the arrow. Mallic threw a dart of nadir at the horse, and it bucked then ran off. Smoke and the sickly sweet smell of charred hair and rotting flesh remained. The commotion of the bucking horse caused the heir to release the arrow overhead.

"Maladictor!" hissed Mallic. He threw his hand forward, and a tendril of nadir shot forth. Like a black cord of rope, the dark current lashed around the young man, constricting him, and he too fell to the ground in agony.

Mallic turned with a wicked smile of triumph. He cocked his head back. "More than twenty years of waiting for this? I've had more trouble from the street rats in Callish."

They continued to immobilize the men. Mallic walked around to inspect an older horse tethered to a litter.

"This one's unconscious. By the smell, I would say he's got one foot in the Drift already," said Mallic. He then rummaged through a saddlebag and found the glimmer stone and brass locator chain.

The horse attached to the litter pawed the ground but remained in place. The abrogators held the two men immobile on the ground, both contorting and grunting in expressions of pain.

Mallic watched the young man struggle against the jet-black bindings, then leaned down over Kaellor. The older man managed to resist the spasms of pain and get to his knees.

"Impressive," said Mallic. He looked back at Volencia. "Have you got him?"

How is he not writhing on the ground? Nobody has ever been able to withstand that much pain.

Volencia gave a curt nod to Mallic, then directed more malevolence into her channeling. She twisted the coils of nadir deeper into Kaellor's center. He cried out in pain but remained on his knees. Mallic dangled the brass chain before the man.

"Thanks for keeping this; it came in handy as we searched for you," said Mallic. "Nice work, Volencia. Master will be impressed."

A pup of some sort jumped off the litter and ran to stand beside Bryndor and snarl at them. Mallic kicked at the creature, but it scurried back and continued to growl.

"What are you waiting for then, abrogator?" said Kaellor with a gasp. He glared up through a tangled curtain of unkempt hair.

"We've searched for you three for years. Maybe I just want to enjoy the moment." Mallic stood then shuddered, and his arms and neck rolled and twisted involuntarily. He sighed and looked back to Volencia with an apologetic expression. "But you're right; it's time."

"Make the strike clean, Mallic. Tarkannen will want to see their heads," said Volencia.

Chapter Forty-Five: Laryn's Deliverance

Laryn picked her way down a rocky ledge and under thick pine boughs laden with dew in the predawn hours. Within minutes, her clothing clung to her skin and hung heavy on her shoulders. She shivered and tried to make sense of her surroundings. The crisp bite of conifer lingered in the air, and she heard something rustle just beyond the limits of her sight in the cloud-obscured forest.

Something about the muted sounds gave her pause. She deliberated a moment, then dropped to all fours. She crawled forward and strained her senses into the fog. Small pine needles poked into her palms, and she settled back onto her knees to remove the painful debris. While she worked, swirls of fog and mist eddied about, preventing vision beyond a few feet. A gentle breeze gusted, allowing the dense cloud bank to thin. A clearing emerged, and she spied two men leading horses. They pulled a litter with an obviously injured person.

The men appeared unkempt. Both wore simple clothing stained with dirt. The older man panted and lifted a gaunt face to survey the clearing. His shoulders slumped either in exhaustion or defeat, and she watched as he drank from a waterskin before handing it to his companion.

For an instant, she glimpsed the man's face through the mists: sharp grey eyes and a rugged jawline with an unkempt beard. The sight of him made something inside of her drop from her throat to her pelvis. She errantly plucked a pine needle from her palm, oblivious to the pain. She couldn't make sense of the scene before her and stared, slack-jawed. It felt like a dam had broken loose, and a river was flooding through her chest, but the only sound beyond the horses came from her shallow breaths.

Surely this is a trick of the spirits; I'm only seeing what I want to see.

She remained rooted in place by the scene before her. Miljin's words echoed in her mind. *Trust the spirits.*

She shook off the strange feeling that anchored her in place and committed to crawling forward into the clearing. That's when the man shouted, "Look out!"

Laryn recoiled back under the pine branches. Just feet away, a woman with jet-black hair stood in the clearing. From Laryn's hiding place, she spied the wriggling onyx sigil on the woman's forearm.

Abrogator? Dear spirits, to what have you delivered me?

The woman released a jet-black cord of power, and the man screamed in pain. Laryn lingered only a moment. She crawled closer to the abrogator and searched the ground. Her hand closed around a stout branch. She gripped the wood, reassured by the feeling of sap.

A rotten piece of wood wouldn't ooze sap, would it?

She lunged with all her weight and swung the branch at the abrogator's face just as she told someone else, "Tarkannen will want to see their heads."

The makeshift cudgel smashed into the woman's face, releasing a sound like a burst melon, and the abrogator dropped to the ground.

Laryn recovered her balance in time to see another abrogator standing by the two men.

Where did he come from?

The man coalesced a globe of black ether in his palm and hurled it at Laryn. She dodged to the side, and the orb smashed into a tree behind her. The black sphere erupted, showering onyx shards out in a radius. The surge of power made her stumble, and she fell forward onto her face as fragments of nadir pierced the back of her scalp, neck, shoulders, and legs.

She lay prone and stunned. Her breath returned, and she looked up to see the abrogator turning toward the younger man shuddering in agony on the ground. A thin blade appeared in the abrogator's hand, and he lifted his arm, preparing to scythe into the young man.

Chapter Forty-Six: Awakening

Kaellor wasted no time. Once the spasms of pain stopped, he rolled to the side and found his Logrend blade next to the litter. He turned to see the abrogator holding Bryndor immobilized on the ground. The man had crafted a long, curved black knife from nadir, and as he lifted the nadir blade in preparation for a strike, Kaellor lunged, pulling the sword in an awkward slice up from the ground.

The downward stroke of the abrogator stopped short as the Logrend sword sliced up through the air. The satisfying crunch and friction of metal cleaving through flesh vibrated down through the pommel.

The abrogator fell back, screaming in pain, his lifeless arm on the ground still clutching the strange black knife. Snakelike black sigils continued to writhe on the dismembered flesh. Without hesitation, Kaellor reversed his grip and sliced down, removing the abrogator's other arm just below the elbow.

The wounded man collapsed in apparent shock. Bright red blood stained the ground around him, pumping in rapid spurts.

"Mercy! Please," he whimpered, "you have no idea what he'll do to me, please."

"I have no mercy for the minions of Tarkannen. You cast your lot. Tell your master the Eidolon is coming, and I'm guarding his path." Kaellor swung the guardian sword and cleaved into the man's temple; the blade passed clean through, exiting by the ear. The top of the abrogator's head sailed off into the fog. His torso crumpled to the ground, and oily black tentacles erupted through the soil, ensnaring his corpse.

Kaellor watched in fascinated horror as the onyx coils penetrated the man's body, winding around and then through the corpse. In seconds, the body burst, dissolving into a pool of black liquid on the forest floor.

Kaellor turned back to his nephew but maintained a defensive posture. *The other abrogator might still be alive.* "Bryn, are you injured?"

Bryndor struggled to his knees, appearing exhausted from the long minutes of forced writhing and spasming. "I'm alright, just sore."

Kaellor stepped forward to assist the woman who had smashed the abrogator with the branch. She lay prone, and several wounds oozed blood from her scalp and back.

He placed a hand on her shoulder, relieved to see her draw breath. At his touch, she moaned and rolled over. He lifted his eyes to search through the mists for the other abrogator.

"I can't begin to thank you enough," he said.

The woman brushed a lock of white hair from her face to reveal cheeks painted with alluring and exotic designs. Something about her tear-filled slate grey eyes tickled at his memory.

A matter for another time.

He shook off the unsettled feeling and continued to search the clearing for the other abrogator. The woman cleared her throat, and he looked back again. She reached up and placed one hand on his chest and the other on his cheek. Her touch felt strangely intimate, and recognition shivered down his back and arms.

"Kaellor Baellentrell," the woman spoke with a firm, resonant voice, "my beloved, I release you."

Kaellor stumbled back as wave after wave of zenith coursed through his body. He could feel the burning ignition across the runes that flared to life, channeling zenith for the first time in years. In seconds, the symbols manifested and intertwined across his arms, traveling to his chest, face, and back.

He felt invigorated, sharp, and attentive. He felt . . . ready. He stepped forward to see—*Laryn? How is Laryn here on the ground?*

She inhaled a deep breath, then cried out as the runes of her birthright coalesced on her own body.

"I don't understand," he said, as much to himself as to her. "Laryn? How can this be? You're supposed to be dead."

Laryn propped herself up on her elbows and smiled. "I very nearly was," she replied.

Kaellor's arca prime erupted with light from under his collar, interrupting her response. Streams of zenith coursed along his runes and urged him to action. Without thinking, he lunged forward to a knee and drove the Logrend sword into the ground. He pulled in as much zenith as he could manage. The surging power coursed up his arms to the rune on his chest then erupted. A shimmering blue bubble surrounded them and extended back across Lluthean's litter in time to deflect two black spheres of nadir.

The female abrogator stood at the edge of the clearing with a mutilated and bloodied face. A large purple welt stained with blood completely deformed her cheek, nose, and one eye, causing her to cock her head unnaturally to the side. The balls of condensed nadir skittered off Kaellor's shielding into the fog, and the sound of the explosion and splintering trees echoed across the valley.

Kaellor felt the sword vibrate painfully in his hands, but the protective shield held. "Bryn, take Laryn and run. I'll buy you as much time as I can!"

Bryndor shot two arrows through the fog. They passed through the blue shielding, but the abrogator met them with what appeared to be a delicate web of nadir, and the missiles collapsed to the ground.

"I'm not leaving you here," said Bryndor. "Besides, there is no hope with Llu down."

The abrogator coughed, then blew clotted blood from one of her nostrils. She swore something guttural then murmured, and two thick streams of nadir surged forth, taking the shape of snakes. The onyx serpents coiled around the guardian shield and began to constrict.

Kaellor could feel the sword vibrate, causing a burning ache in his forearms. He struggled to maintain the shield, iridescent silver light flashing from under his collar. He chanced a glance at Laryn, who stood at his side. Her right eye blazed with the cerulean glow of her gift; her left burned like an ember from the moon of Lellen. He never realized how deeply he'd buried the memory of her within his heart. The sight of her alone made him incapable of any other thought or speech.

The glimmering bubble that shielded the group began to waver as the abrogator bent her will to their destruction. The snakes continued to constrict the bubble tighter and tighter. Laryn knelt next to him and wrapped her hands around his over the pommel of the Logrend sword.

"Two hearts are better than one, I think?" she asked.

The sword throbbed and burned in his hands, and he centered his focus. "If I do this, you have to release before it's too late."

She nodded once. "Do it."

"Eyes to the horizon then," Kaellor grunted. The veining and runes of Laryn's gift flared as she conveyed zenith. Kaellor felt his resolve strengthen. Currents of zenith channeled through her and along his runes. His gift flared, renewed, and a surge of power erupted from deep within his chest. His grip on the sword firmed. The power bubbled inside him with a warmth that became heat. He struggled to contain the new wave of energy for fear of losing control of the guardian shield.

The power continued to intensify, and at last, he cried out, "Now, let go!"

Laryn tumbled back, releasing his hands. The surging zenith reached a climax, and he threw it forward in ecstasy as a thunderous crack erupted. A shimmering blast wave decimated the inky black snakes constricting around the shield. The force threw the abrogator back into the fog, and as the guardian shield shattered, Kaellor collapsed in exhaustion.

He panted, overwhelmed from channeling so much zenith. Minutes passed, and he rose to his knees. From somewhere in the distance, he heard the abrogator swearing.

What does it take to kill her?

He rolled his shoulders and grabbed the Logrend blade, preparing to stalk into the fog after her. Something cool touched the top of his hand. He looked down to see the misty apparition of a small older woman. She stood only four feet tall and smiled at him with a kind face but shook her head as if to discourage his intent.

Laryn placed a hand on his shoulder before he could react. "It's alright. She brought me to you," she explained.

She turned to the ethereal spirit. "I need them all to come. Can you bring them all?"

The spirit looked past Laryn at Lluthean, Kaellor, and Bryndor. She waved them over to the litter, still hitched to Scout.

"Gather around the litter," said Laryn. Bryndor grabbed Boru while Kaellor retreated defensively to stand next to his youngest nephew. The spirit hovered above Lluthean. She began to move her hands in a welcoming motion, gathering up the clouds and mist.

Dense, cold swirls of cloud and fog swirled around the group. Kaellor gasped at the tickle in his belly when he felt the world fall away. In the distance, the explosions from nadir echoed across the mountainside.

The dense mists obscured even his hand in front of his face. He reached out and found a delicate but firm grip of reassurance. It was her hand.

My betrothed's hand.

For long minutes they drifted, and the only warmth he felt came from her grip. Just when he thought to ask where they were going or how they had escaped, warm breezes wafted past his face, and the distinctive aroma of flowers relaxed his apprehension. Through a strange gradual process, he felt his weight return. The mists retreated, and the world became visible around them. Kaellor found himself standing next to Bryndor, Laryn, and Scout. A group of short, painted, olive-skinned people surrounded them.

None of the small people carried weapons, and Kaellor looked again at Laryn. Their reunion felt nothing short of miraculous. He chanced a glance behind her to the litter. Neska fidgeted alone, whining and sniffing the air.

Kaellor staggered an uncertain step forward. He searched the clearing, attempting to quell the surging tide of desperation, but his gaze could not find what he searched for.

By the Giver, where is Lluthean?

Chapter Forty-seven: Epilogue

#

When the wild wolvryn scars the highborn one, the channelers of nadir will rise. The tethers that bind can leech or sustain. The chance for confluence emerges, but only from balance. The sundered bindings will unleash one who rules from the void. Seek the bearer who carries the burden, then look to reveal the Eidolon, but only after the sibling passes to the Drift. For a time shall come again when the forces of zenith and nadir are magnified into opposition. Here me then: channel zenith to save the world or nadir to destroy it. Channel confluence to become the Eidolon reborn.

— "The Abrogator Derivation," in *The Book of Seven Prophets*

ELDREK ELDREKSON SURRENDERED to exhaustion and took a knee on the top of a grassy hill. He tried to ignore the first stages of the draft, but the demand of channeling so much zenith for so long took its toll even from him. The charred smell of man and horse assaulted his senses, and the sounds of his troops regrouping behind him on the battlefront carried across the grasslands.

He looked east across the vast Plains of Jintha, across the sea of the countless dead. A flock of carrion crows swirled low on the horizon. They found no edible food source from the burned mounds of corpses in his immediate area, as all of his enemies had been devoured by rune fire.

How did it all come to this?

He knew now; he understood. Their leader, Kal'Malldra, had held herself up as the Eidolon. She fit the prophecy so well, from surviving the attack of a wolvryn right down to the death of her brother. She gathered them all here, all the zeniphiles. *She made us all believe that only through her could the balance be maintained. And we all believed her.*

Barl Fodensk had sailed his troops from the deep south, where they employed the currents of zenith to shape the wind and navigate the tides. The Shaman Queen, Maedra-ness, and her followers had left their wooded homes to join the war; they embedded with the other zeniphiles, providing mastery of the healing arts and creative use of the natural elements in combat. Winged animals, the beasts of the plains, and even the grasses underfoot moved to defend the troops.

Then the sisters fo'Vaeda and fo'Voshna had arrived with their armies from the west. Their subtle employment of zenith to forecast the movements of the abrogators had proved invaluable.

He sighed with self-recrimination. *I had to follow them all here from Aarindorn. I've lost my brother, and I still have no idea which sister I love more.*

That thought made him want to laugh. All this sacrifice, all this death, and he still had no idea which woman he loved more. He wouldn't even be here if he wasn't trying to protect them both.

They had all gathered in midsummer to support their leader, but the endless battles of the last three days proved that Kal'Malldra was not the Eidolon. She seemed no more able to establish a balance between the flows of zenith and nadir than the rest of them. In fact, if not for the warnings of Lutn Egaine, the only abrogator who seemed to understand the value of peace, Kal'Malldra's forces would have met their end on the first day.

He glanced at a blackened hillside to his right. Kal'Malldra and her most accomplished zeniphiles had staged their last stand against a tide of abrogators on the very spot just a few hours ago. His own brother, Borullean, had waded into the fray to save her. Borullean had unleashed torrential surges of rune fire, exhausting himself utterly only to succumb to the draft. In the end, the abrogators' coordinated use of nadir overwhelmed his defenses and Kal'Malldra's. All that remained of them now were massive shards of the strange onyx rock slick with the mercurial substance of the Drift.

Eldrek stared at the rocky barrow, willing the shale to scatter loose and reveal his brother pushing his way to the surface. Instead, Kelledar Lellendule appeared from behind the dark mound. The Aarindorian walked on wobbly legs and stumbled over the uneven, grassy ground. Soot darkened his upper lip and forehead, adding an ominous silhouette to sharp eyes that flared a deep ruby when he channeled. The blood of countless abrogators stained his blue uniform at the forearms so densely that it looked like he'd dipped them into a vat of red dye.

Kelledar dropped to both knees beside his friend. "That's a lot of crows, El. You were supposed to wait for me."

Eldrek grinned at his friend, but the smile felt half-hearted. The fatigue of the draft affected them both. For now, he needed to keep at least a portion of his focus directed internally or risk being overwhelmed by nausea. "By the looks of your uniform, you've seen your share of it up close and personal."

Kelledar shrugged. "It's not fair. You can call down rune fire and decimate entire hillsides of the abrogators. I'm left to summon blades of zenith and run through them in small numbers."

"Small numbers?" asked Eldrek. "I watched you extend your zenith blades well beyond ten feet. You single-handedly wiped out over a hundred, Kel. A hundred abrogators before you stopped channeling. That you managed to stumble over here without falling to the deeper stages of the draft is no small miracle."

Kelledar grunted, conceding the point. "You were right about the moons; somehow, they affect our ability to channel." He pointed at the horizon where two moons, one red, the other blue, hung evenly sized and low in the sky. "My strength wanes with the red moon while yours grows. It makes sense, I suppose, what with your eyes that intense blue."

Eldrek nodded. "None of that matters if we can't get Mogdurian to understand the threat he poses to all of Karsk."

A young officer approached and cleared her throat. They both turned to see the young zeniphile hop forward on crutches. Her right leg ended halfway past the knee in a smooth, rounded stump of blackened skin. Caused by a nadir blade, the wound healed quickly but had left a pain that would linger for years.

"Commanders," said the officer, "the abrogator is here and would have a word."

"Lutn Egaine? He's back?" asked Eldrek. "Send him up."

The officer waved downhill to the troops, and a lean man walked forward. Lutn Egaine attacked the hill with purposeful strides. He still wore the tan robes of a scholar, even here on the battlefield, and showed none of the signs of twitchy edginess typical of abrogators who channeled so much nadir that they developed the paranoia of the frenze.

"Egaine, it's good to see you alive. Have you had any luck persuading Mogdurian?" asked Eldrek. He considered standing, but fatigue pressed down on him more than the need for courtly decorum.

The scholar stood with his hands clasped behind his back and stared across the wasteland with a somber expression. Eventually, he turned to regard them both. "He doesn't believe the truth of my calculations. I can't even get him to concede that a disruption in the balance of zenith and nadir might tear a rift into the Drift."

Kelledar frowned, but Eldrek just nodded. "I didn't expect he would. People hear what they want to hear."

Kelledar pulled a fistful of grass in frustration. "Why can't he see reason? Is it the frenze?"

The scholar cocked his head to the side, considering the question. "I don't think so. He seems in control, and you must admit that his tactical moves follow logic and not emotion, at least as far as the battle is concerned. But, regarding the veil separating the Drift from our world, my arguments have yet to sway him."

This time Eldrek grunted. "Can't he feel it? I'm not an abrogator, and I can feel it; by the moons, we all can!"

Eldrek shivered, recalling the suffocating feeling they'd discovered when his forces first arrived on the plains. That first night, something from the Drift nearly pushed through. Every person, whether they commanded zenith or not, felt weighed down with oppressive fatigue. Then an unnatural frost had collected across the battlefield, accompanied by a rank putrescence of things rotten and moldering. The phenomenon lasted several hours and seemed to dissipate only after a battalion of zeniphiles surprised a flank of abrogators. As that first skirmish ended, the pervasive sense of dread, the eerie frost, and the otherworldly stench lifted.

He stared out to view the ocean of brown, dead grass in front of him. Behind him, the rolling hills appeared vibrant and green, but between the two forces, the ground remained a uniform sea of brown, dead grasses with islands of black where rune fire or the withering effects of abrogation had scarred the plains.

"Mogdurian stopped listening to me when he learned I was providing you with an equal measure of counsel," said Lutn. "He is driven by his belief that through abrogation, the world will remain ordered and controlled. He is a man who never steps off course once committed. I fear it would take an intervention far greater than us to redirect his—"

A roaring, tearing sound erupted across the plains. In the sky over the battlefield, a serrated black rupture appeared. Strands of hair gusted before Eldrek's vision as the wind shifted and rushed toward the unnatural rent on the horizon. He shivered not just from the immense size of the rift but also from the plummeting temperature. He wrinkled his nose as the aroma of corrupted, decayed flesh settled across the hillside. When he exhaled, his breath billowed out with steam.

Behind him, a clamor of startled voices rose as his troops experienced the otherworldly phenomenon. He pulled himself to his feet. Looking back, he could see signs of the strange taint from the Drift ripple across the camp. Men and women ran out of their tents with frightened and alarmed expressions. Most brandished weapons, and many worked to secure the clasps of their armor.

"El. What under the moons is that?" asked Kelledar.

For the first time all week, Eldrek felt the cold, iron grip of fear hold him immobile. The debilitating sensation came not from the rent in the sky but from the tenor of Kelledar's voice. Eldrek looked to his friend, who stood wide-eyed, pointing at the rift. Eldrek shook off the sensation and turned to face the enemy that had managed to strike terror into the bravest man he'd ever met.

Massive pincers, each the size of one of Foden's galleons, reached through the rift and pried it apart. More of the roaring, tearing noise echoed across the plains, and the serrated rent became a gaping hole. The head of an enormous beast pushed through the defect in the veil, followed by broad shoulders.

Black, chitinous plates ridged with horns covered the beast's shoulders and armored the creature down to its pincers. The dense carapace seemed to absorb sunlight—rivulets and ribbons of some mercurial substance undulated under the surface of its thick shell. Rows of eyes lined the side of its broad head, surrounding a burgundy valley of flesh. From the central, fleshy mass, thin tentacles writhed into the sky as if tasting the air.

The beast screeched, and something that sounded like a heavy metal chair being pulled across a stone floor made Eldrek's teeth vibrate.

"By the moons," said Lutn. "He's done it. That's a bosulk, a greater driftian. He sundered the veil."

With effort, Eldrek tore his gaze away from the massive beast as it tried to pull itself through the rift in the sky. A sallow color flavored Lutn's complexion, making the stoic scholar appear both abruptly ill and aged at the same time.

"Lutn," said Kelledar. "Lutn!" He shook the scholar by the shoulders. "How do we stop that thing? Can we stop that thing?"

"It is possible but not . . . possible," the abrogator mumbled, more to himself. "Only confluence can repair the damage done. Kal'Malldra was not the Eidolon, and even if she was, I don't know if even the Eidolon could stop that. By the moons, they're making it stronger! They bring death to the entire world."

Lutn pointed across the battlefield, where legions of abrogators had gathered in formation and were channeling dense currents of nadir. The ebony filaments merged into cords and ropes of power that plunged into one of the massive pincers of the bosulk. The carapace appeared to melt and smolder under the direct assault, but then the bosulk began absorbing the currents of nadir.

After a minute of the onslaught, the driftian shivered and rippled, then expanded. The damaged pincer fell to the ground in a burning heap. Cheers rose from across the battlefield as the abrogators continued their attack but stopped when a larger, fresh pincer erupted from the end of the creature's limb.

The bosulk turned its attention to the abrogators and pulled itself farther through the rift in the sky. A segmented, serpentine torso trailed back through the tear in the veil.

Where does the thing end?

Eldrek watched the driftian swing its massive claws into the front ranks of the abrogator host. Bodies flew through the air, scattered like sand in the wind, but the channeled ropes of nadir continued.

"If we commit everything right now, right here. If we channel zenith, will that have the same effect as confluence?" Eldrek asked.

The scholar stared at the beast with a vacant expression. Eldrek grasped him by the shoulders. "Egaine, will it have the same effect?"

Lutn turned to regard Eldrek, and some of the color returned to his complexion. The scholar looked past him to the troops of zeniphiles. "I don't know. Perhaps. But even if you gathered them all here, you've not trained like Mogdurian. His legions gather their focus and channel nadir with military precision. You can't hope to accomplish that with your different factions. Whether you stay or quit the battlefield, it matters not, that beast and the tear in the veil will mean the end for all of us."

Eldrek felt a vibration from his teeth down to his feet as the bosulk sheared the air with its screech. *Moons, that sounded like a cry of victory.*

"We're more organized than you know," he said. "Kelledar, fetch me a sender, one of the albino quints. We need to have the entire legion gather here."

Kelledar ran back down the hillside and returned in moments with a young woman. "El, this is Shaveen. One of her siblings is embedded next to the leaders of our forces."

Eldrek turned to study the young woman. Faint blue eyes stared past him through thick strands of white hair. Her mouth fell open when she gazed directly at the driftian.

Eldrek placed both hands on her shoulders to garner her full attention. "Shaveen, focus on me and listen. I need you to pass a message to the other generals. We have one chance to stop that thing, but only if everyone gathers on me immediately. I want everyone. Not just the fighters. I need the healers, provisioners, cooks, scribes, even the wounded. Tell them to leave weapons and armor behind, leave all equipment. Gather anyone who can channel zenith in any form here on me now."

Shaveen nodded once. The runes exposed at her neckline flared with delicate light, and her light blue eyes appeared more azure. After a few seconds, she released her gift and returned her attention to Eldrek. "Commander, it is done."

Eldrek looked back across his troops. At first, nothing changed. The masses of zeniphiles stood in fear or awe or both as they watched the bosulk lay waste to the abrogator forces. Then, like the ripple of a pebble cast into a pond, organized motion carried across their troops, and they began a fast march toward his hilltop.

In unison, two female voices said, "We are here, El." Usually, hearing the fo' sisters act in concert gave him cause for alarm. At this moment, he felt grateful for their presence.

Eldrek turned to fo'Vaeda and fo'Voshna, smiled, then sighed. In concert, the twins shook their heads to free the thick curls of kinky black hair from their azure blue eyes. They wore the light silks commonplace in their culture, but both crossed their arms to guard against the otherworldly chill air caused by the rift. The actions revealed goosebumps along their light brown skin.

"I shouldn't be surprised that you both knew of my intentions before I did. I don't suppose you can look far enough into the future to tell me how this will end?" he asked.

The two women shared a knowing glance. fo'Vaeda tilted her head. "You should know by now that we can sense intention, lover. But, no zeniphile can pierce beyond the present."

Eldrek nodded. "I know. If you both understand what I'm planning, then I'm glad the three of us are here at the end. Where did you send the children?"

"We decided to take you up on your offer and sent them all to Aarindorn to live with your sister," said fo'Voshna. "Sometimes, you have good ideas."

"What do you think of my intentions now?" he asked.

"Who can say what the light of the moons will reveal when the day is done?" fo'Vaeda began.

"But whatever steps from the shadows, it will be something we crafted together," fo'Voshna finished.

They stepped together in a circle and shared a long embrace. He grounded himself in their warmth, in the firm way they clung to one another and to him. In their arms, he understood the cost of what he intended, so he took a selfish moment to enjoy the subtle fragrance of their hair, the feel of them all breathing in time to one another, and their intimate connection.

He lifted his gaze to stare back down the hillside. An ocean of zeniphiles pressed in close. He loosened his embrace but did not let the fo' sisters step away.

"Shaveen, I have need of your gift once more," he said.

The sender stepped forward.

"Relay this message. We have one chance to repair the damage to the veil and repel the driftian, but it will require total commitment from each of us. I have long withheld my arca prime but will employ it now. It will only work if each person here willingly channels the full measure of their zenith into me. Have no fear; it will not harm me, but I am not sure it will be enough to destroy the beast unless everyone commits everything they have. I will channel rune fire once more as a signal. When you see and hear it erupt, touch the shoulder or hand of the person in front of you and send me everything you have."

He waited for the sender to finish his message, then watched as the signal passed through the troops. Within minutes the faces of children, men, and women stared back at him, expectant, fearful, and hopeful. They stood silent amid the clamor of the bosulk as it ravaged through the abrogator host.

"For those loyal to the fo' kingdoms of the east! For those who sailed with Foden from the seas! For the woodfolk under Maedra-ness and the followers of Kal'Malldra! For Aarindorn and the love of all those under the moons. For Karsk!" shouted Kelledar Lellendule.

The masses cheered, and Eldrek nodded his appreciation to his friend.

"For the love of us all," Eldrek said so that only the fo' sisters could hear him.

He turned to face the bosulk and channeled zenith, infusing the runes across his arms and shoulders. The currents raced along his gift, and he gave them shape but held back their release. He gathered, magnified, and intensified the flow until it coalesced from a small ember into an inferno, and at last, he surrendered. A brilliant gout of blue flame erupted along the flank of the driftian, incinerating one of its pincers and blasting a burn mark against the black carapace. The beast released a different screech, and Eldrek sensed an element of pain and alarm in the new sound.

Then the draft took its toll, and his legs buckled. He slumped, but the fo' sisters kept him propped up by each shoulder, and he felt Kelledar embrace him from behind. Together, they prevented him from slumping to the ground.

He swallowed back the acrid taste of vomit and tried to dismiss the overwhelming sense of vertigo. "Are they ready, brother?" he asked.

After a moment, Kelledar spoke softly in his ear. "We are all linked to you, El. If you can do it, it's time."

Eldrek allowed himself three deep breaths. On the first breath, he suppressed his nausea. On the second, he dismissed some of the dizzying effects of the draft. And on the third breath, he unshackled the filter he maintained over his arca prime.

He expected to funnel the combined power of the zeniphiles into a tight beam. At least, that's what he imagined his gift should allow him to accomplish. That kind of control required him to gather and concentrate all the streams of zenith. However, the devastating force that crashed into him propelled him along like a leaf in rapids. At the moment he allowed his arca prime to awaken, his senses became completely overwhelmed. He became dimly aware that zenith had flared out of him and scattered across the plains.

The uncoordinated release of power scattered across the battlefield and dissipated before the driftian. The creature rocked back once, like a moored ship rocking on a wave. Then the bosulk turned its full attention to the mass of zeniphiles. The hillside rumbled as a massive pincer dug into the ground to lever the creature forward.

The entire time the beast lumbered across the battlefield, Eldrek managed only occasional glimpses. His sense of balance and direction tumbled through the torrential onslaught of zenith pouring into him. He felt like a man drowning in a violent ocean. He glimpsed the beast rear back in preparation to swat them away like maggots gathered on a corpse.

"We give ourselves to you, Eldrek, do not waste it." The coordinated voice of the fu' sisters broke through his confusion and gave him focus as a dark shadow fell before him. He clawed to the top of the surging tidal wave of zenith and, with desperate purpose, gathered all the scattered power. For an instant, he prevented all the loose tendrils from escaping.

Violent rivers of zenith cascaded and surged across all of his runes. He felt the golden runes stretch and pull at his skin with searing pain. The magnitude of all that power, constrained to his purpose, pressed at the confines of his gift. He lingered in time for only a few seconds, but the agony felt much longer.

Just a bit longer.

He sensed the bosulk swing its massive pincer through the stilled air, then gave the ocean of power permission to use him.

A brilliant shaft of azure light erupted from the rune on his chest and split the darkness before them. The beam roared across the dead plains, sounding like a massive waterfall, and struck the bosulk on its segmented chest. The driftian staggered backward, but it appeared undamaged. Its pincer fell short in its swing and carved out a deep gash in the plains in front of them.

The voice of Lutn Egaine yelled in his ear, "Confluence, Eldrek! You must accomplish confluence! Wrap your zenith around Mogdurian's nadir!"

Eldrek strained to see past the immediate danger of the bosulk, now so close. The abrogators were concentrating a shaft of nadir into the side of the driftian's head. Eldrek strained and directed the zenith to the same location.

Instead of colliding, the two forces magnified into a roiling explosion. The blast cleaved directly sideways through the burgundy, fleshy head of the bosulk, incinerating the beast. The driftian rumbled a low-pitched screech and recoiled back once before its segmented body began buckling and collapsing under its own weight.

The ground trembled from the titanic weight of the bosulk flopping lifelessly from the rent in the veil, showering them all with stinging dust and debris. A part of his awareness recoiled from the humid stench of rotting flesh. He clenched his jaw tight and pinched his lips to keep from tasting the foul air.

Through the dust cloud, Eldrek continued targeting the current of nadir, following it back along the driftian's twisted body. Wherever the two forces gathered, the beast's carapace erupted in flame. Finally, the two shafts focused on the rift in the sky.

Several minutes passed as the entwined currents of zenith and nadir roiled in a storm around the rift. Silvery, thick clouds, appearing more as liquid than air, churned across the breach. Erratic flashes of zenith flared across the rent in the sky like blue lightning.

Eldrek sensed the strain on his gift wane and felt the contribution to his source dwindle.

How many have we lost already, then? How many gave themselves entirely to this task, and how many more will be required?

He allowed his gaze to focus on the rift but made sure to target the nadir to maintain confluence. The serrated breach began to collapse as the intensity of the zenith ray dimmed from azure to blue, then pale blue. The strain on his gift dwindled further.

A moment later, he sensed cold air breathe against his shoulders, where the fo' sisters stood. From the corner of his vision, he saw their withered bodies collapse to the hillside next to him.

"Nooooo!" he screamed the word until his voice burned, and his breath left. He tried to reach for each of them, but something held him firmly under his armpits.

"I'm with you, El. They gave you everything, and so will I, but it means nothing, nothing if you don't finish it," The voice of Kelledar growled in his ear.

Eldrek wanted to push his grief to the side, to cleave it away and become cold, clinical. Instead, he used the strength of his loss to fuel one last blast of zenith into the breach. The serrated rift sealed with a sucking sound just as he depleted the last of the zenith.

He fell back, staring at the sky, barely aware that his head was resting on Kelledar's thigh. With the breach closed, the moons of Baellen and Lellen appeared brilliant on the horizon, casting a mixture of red and blue hues across the sky.

A familiar hissing sound caused him to lift his head in curiosity. He stared to the east, to the abrogator forces. In the distance, black tentacles ranged forward, searching and hungry.

"By the moons, can't we just be done?" said Eldrek to nobody in particular.

"We very nearly are, my friend," said Lutn Egaine. The scholar sat down cross-legged next to him.

"You can go, Lutn; you don't need to stay. If Mogdurian finds you here, there will be no mercy," said Eldrek.

"There will be no mercy for any of us on this plain, my friend. But thanks to your sacrifice, Karsk and the rest of its inhabitants will persist." Lutn spoke the words in that strange emotionless tone and seemed more aware of the wrinkles of his robes as they gathered around his knees than of any approaching danger.

"Is everyone gone then? Did I—did I spend them all?" he asked.

"You did what needed to be done," answered Lutn with a tone of respect. "But whether we are discovered by Mogdurian matters not. Can't you feel it? The world shudders from all that Mogdurian set in motion. May you find peace in the Drift, Eldrek."

He did feel it. Something rumbled and vibrated deep underground. The slow rocking increased to a rumble and then a violent shake. Eldrek felt too exhausted to do anything further. He reached an open hand to Lutn, who grasped it in turn.

Despite the scholar's presence, something inside Eldrek shuddered with the emptiness of facing death without those he loved the most. He blinked away tears to gaze once again at the fo' sisters. They had collapsed in awkward positions next to him, and he couldn't discern which sister was which, even at the end. He craned his neck to look one final time on the face of his friend, Kelledar. The warrior stared to the sky, flickers of zenith reflecting in his empty eyes.

A vision, something of the possible future, appeared and melted the icy core of fear that had begun to overwhelm him.

"Ahh, I see," said Eldrek. "Thank you for showing me. Thank you for being here. May we both . . . find the same peace Lu—" His words broke apart as did the Plains of Jintha. Violent streaks of wild zenith surged down in flashes of lightning from the sky. Wherever the zenith strikes landed, ridges of rock and soil rippled then erupted into the air. Rivaling streams of nadir lashed about in a similar chaotic fashion, causing the newly formed pillars of rock to collapse. Eldrek watched a writhing tentacle of nadir flail about and then collapse directly on his hillside. The world fell away and swallowed them all in darkness.

Glossary of names, places, and terms

Aarindorn (AIR-in-dorn)—a kingdom in the Northlands, surrounded by the Great Crown Mountains.

Abrogator (AB-roh-gate-or)—a term used to describe one who wields the reductive force of nadir.

Amniah (am-NIGH-yuh)—a young female Outrider gifted with the ability to gust (shape wind) who hails from Stellance. A member Karragin's quad.

Arca prime—the central rune of a zeniphile located on the center of the chest and determining the zeniphiles strongest affinity or ability.

Baellentrell (BAE-len-trell)—the last name of the current ruling family in Aarindorn.

- Bierden (BEER-den)—Kaellor's grandfather, capable of summoning rune fire.
- Bryndor (BRIN-dur)—oldest of two nephews to Kaellor. Older brother to Lluthean.
- Eldrek (EL-drek)—founder of the Baes line and first king of Aarindorn.
- Japheth (JAY-feth)—king of Aarindorn during the Abrogator's War. Father to Bryndor and Lluthean, brother to Kaellor.
- Kaellex (KAY-lex)—father to Kaellor and Japheth, grandfather to Bryndor and Lluthean.
- Kaellor (KAY-lore)—uncle to Bryndor and Lluthean.
- Lluthean (LOO-thee-in)—youngest of two nephews to Kaellor. Younger brother to Bryndor.
- Nebrine (neh-BREEN)—mother to Bryndor and Lluthean, wife to Japheth.

- Phethnem (FETH-nem)—mother to Kaellor and Japheth, wife to Kaellex.

Balladuren (bal-uh-DOO-ren)—family in Aarindorn famed for breeding Aarindin.

Barl Fodensk—this zeniphile led his forces from the deep south by ship to fight against the abrogators in the Great War. His forces were gifted in controlling the forces of wind and water.

Bashing Ram—a tavern and inn at Journey's Bend.

Beclure (beh-KLURE)—a duchy in west Aarindorn.

Benyon Garr (BEN-yun)—a wizened trainer of the gifted in Aarindorn, member of the Aarindorian military, and adviser to the Outriders.

Bosulk (BO-sulk)—a.k.a. a greater driftian, a massive creature from the Drift.

Borsec (BORE-sek)—ruling monarch over the northwest region of the Southlands, including Riverton and Journey's Bend.

Braveska (bra-VES-kuh)—the royal family in Hammond and Malvress in the Southlands

- Leland (LEE-land)—duke in Malvress and youngest brother to Vendal.
- Lesand (leh-SAND)—niece to the king of Hammond and daughter to Duke Leland in Malvress.
- Shelland (SHELL-and)—queen in Hammond.
- Vendal (VEN-dull)—king in Hammond.

Callinora (cal-in-NORE-uh)—a city in northwest Aarindorn composed of erudites, scholars, and healers. The formal educational training of medics, healers, alchemists, and related fields takes place here. The city is a protectorate of Stone's Grasp with no specific familial loyalties but rather loyal to the welfare of Aarindorn. The kingdom's Sanitorium is located here.

Callish (CAL-ish)—port city along the northeast coast of the Southlands.

Cataclysm—the Great War in which the forces of abrogation caused a rent in the barrier between the world of the living and the Drift. The death toll was estimated at well over thirty thousand and led to the separation of Karsk into the Northlands and the Southlands. The timing of this event is used as the source of the dating system on Karsk, with dates being either before cataclysm (bc) or post cataclysm (pc).

Cloud Walkers—a tribe native to the valley deep in the center of the Korjinth Mountains. Formally called the Damadibo (dahm-uh-DEE-boe), meaning "the people."

Crush—a herd of six to ten grondle.

Damadibo (dahm-uh-DEE-boe)—the Cloud Walkers, the term means "the people."

Della—the proprietor at the Bashing Ram of Journey's Bend. She manages and owns the tavern with her brother Ingram.

Drexn (DREK-sen)—the name for the sun god in the Southlands.

Dulesque (doo-LESK)—a duchy in west Aarindorn.

Eidolon—prophesized in *The Book of Seven Prophets* as a person capable of wielding both zenith and nadir, and someone required to save the world.

Elcid—a bandit in Hammond.

Ellisina (el-eh-SEE-nuh)—a Cloud Walker child.

Endule (en-DUEL)—a family of nobles in Aarindorn related to and branching from the Lellendules. Currently ruling the duchies of Dulesque and Beclure in Aarindorn.

- Alvric (ALV-rick)—former Outrider recruited into the city watch in Stone's Grasp.
- Berling (BURR-ling)—a young man gifted in the healing arts and a medic in the Outriders.
- family and assumed the Endule name.
- Dexxin (DEX-in)—an Outrider, sender, and triplet to Craxton and Mullayne.
- Endcra (en-DEER-uh)—the duchess of Beclure, mother to Velda.
- Phelond (feh-LOND)—the duchess of Dulesque, married to

Bexter, mother to Berling.

- Velda (VEL-duh)—an Outrider skilled in archery. Daughter to Endera, from Beclure.

Exemplar Gre'Kanth (greh-KANTH)—the holy leader of the Immaculine, a sect founded in Caskayah in the deep south of the Southlands.

Festian Planes (FES-tee-un)—prairie and plains south of Callish in the Southlands.

Feth—a stableboy who works with his father, Steckle, at the Bashing Ram.

Firth—a name utilized by Lluthean while traveling anonymously.

fo'Vaeda and fo'Voshna—zeniphile sisters gifted in prophecy and prediction, both involved in a tangled relationship with Eldrek in the times of the Cataclysm.

Foden (FOE-den)—Southlander name for the god of the seas and wind.

Gavid Strictor (GAV-id STRIK-turr)—an official of the Immaculine.

Geddins (GEDD-ins)—a high family in Aarindorn.

- Ashrof (ASH-rof)—the oldest son gifted with the ability to survey and measure distances.
- Marsona (mar-SAW-nuh)—younger sister to Ashrof.

Griggs—a guard at the southern gate to Aarindorn. He is a sifter.

Grotvonen (GROT-voh-nen)—The "grot" are humanoid creatures who live in clans underground. Their senses evolved to survive in that environment. They possess only vestigial lips and utilize a language of nasal snorts, clicks, and a guttural speech pattern.

Guster—a zeniphile who controls and manipulates winds or air.

Gwillion (GWILL-ee-un)—the former alchemy master in Aarindorn, disgraced by his addiction to vivith.

Hawklin—a family in Journey's Bend.

- Bruug (Broog)—the oldest brother.
- Heff—the middle brother.

- Rusn—the youngest brother.
- Gruus—the father of the Hawklin family.

Hillen—a deceased Cloud Walker. When he died, a pregnant wolvryn bonded to him became feral and slipped from the misted valley, later to become the mother to Boru and Neska.

Homnibus—the lead rector or abbot in service at the Abbey on the Mount in the Southlands.

Immaculine, the (im-MAC-u-you-leen)—a religious sect from Caskayah. They hunt and kill abrogators and zeniphiles alike.

Ingram—the proprietor and co-owner with sister Della of the Bashing Ram of Journey's Bend.

Journey's Bend—a rural Southland town not far from Riverton, childhood home to the "Scrivson boys," Bryndor and Lluthean.

Kal'maldra—a zeniphile who rose in power and assumed the title of the Eidolon in the time before the Cataclysm.

Kaldera (kal-DEER-uh)—Overwarden in the Outriders, he serves at the pleasure of the regent and sets strategy for the group.

Karsk—the continent of the Northlands and Southlands, used interchangeably by the people there to describe the world.

Kemp—an alias name used by Bryndor during anonymous travel.

Korjinth Mountains (CORE-jinth)—the mountainous peaks of this range erupted, and the central valley was formed, after the Great War when Eldrek Baellentrell marshaled the zeniphiles to wield their collective zenith in tandem with Mogdurian's abrogators. The colossal release of force, poorly synthesized, resulted in the formation of this range on the Plains of Jintha, and divided all of Karsk. Currently, warring currents of zenith and nadir make crossing the summit nearly impossible.

Krestus (CREST-us)—a fallen knight from Malvress.

Lacuna (luh-COO-nuh)—a secret sect in Aarindorn.

Lawn Whirik—constable in Journey's Bend.

Lefledge (leh-FLEJ)—a high family in Aarindorn

- Karragin (CARE-uh-gin)—an Outrider, sister to Nolan, daughter to Therek.

- Nolan (NO-lun)—an Outrider, son to Therek, brother to Karragin.
- Therek (THARE-ik)—the regent in Aarindorn.

Lellendule (lell-en-DOOL)—a noble family in Aarindorn

- Chancle (CHANS-ul)—the vice regent in Aarindorn, brother to Hestian, cousin to Laryn. He is a trusted friend to the regent and has helped stabilize Aarindorn after the Abrogator's War.

- Charlest (char-LEST)—the last ruling Lellendule queen in Aarindorn and mother to Tarkannen.
- Hestian (HES-tee-en)—older brother to Chancle. He is a trusted friend to the regent.
- Kelledar (KELL-eh-dahr)—one of the first Lellendules, loyal friend to Eldrek Baellentrell.
- Laryn (LARE-in)—a healer trained in Callinora, she married Kaellor in a secret ceremony and returns to Aarindorn as his wife and a prominent member of the Lellendule family.
- Tarkannen (tar-CAN-en)—the Usurper who reintroduced the utilization of nadir over zenith and resurrected the abrogators. In real life, the author's daughters argue about the best pronunciation. Some prefer "TARK-anon," others "tar-CANN-on." The author is perfectly content to let the reader decide which pronunciation suits their worldview for Karsk.
- Volencia—born gifted as a zeniphile but embraced the path of the abrogator.

Lemm Sogle—a drunkard from Journey's Bend
Lentrell (LEN-trell)—minor nobles in Aarindorn related by blood to the Baellentrells.

- Elbiona (el-bee-YOH-nuh)—an Outrider warden in Aarindorn. She is rumored to be exceptional with a bow.

Leveck—titled Commissioner Leveck, an officer of the court in Beclure in the employment of house Endule.

Lutn Egaine—an abrogator and famed mathmetician and tactitician who sought a neutral relationship between zeniphiles and abrogators. Because he was seen by some as playing both sides, he was later remembered as the trickster and in the Southlands incorporated into the pantheon.

Lutney (LUT-nee)—Southland god of luck, tricks, and the unseen.

Maedra (MAY-druh)—Southland god of nature and healing.

Maedraness—in the time of the cataclysm, this zeniphile, known as the Shaman Queen, joined Eldrek and the other zeniphiles. Their natural talents lay in the healing arts and communicating and controlling plants and animals.

Mahkeel (mah-KEEL)—the wolvryn handler of the Cloud Walker tribe.

Malldra (MAHL-druh)—Southland term for the mother of the pantheon of gods, thought to have died birthing the other gods.

Margrave Rolsh—the ruler in Riverton and by default the territories in Journey's Bend, loyal to King Borsec.

Miljin (MILL-jin)—an elder shaman among the Cloud Walkers.

Mogdure (mog-DURE)—the Southland god of death, darkness, and illness.

Mogdurian—in the time of the Great War, he led all the abrogators in his quest to bring order to Karsk.

Monk—affectionately, a Man of No Knowledge.

Moorlok (MORE-lock)—a vast and ancient tract of timber in the Southlands bordering Journey's Bend.

Oren (ORE-en)—the captain of the city watch in Stone's Grasp.

Ranika (RAN-ih-kuh)—aka Nika, a waif who befriended Reddevek in Callish.

Reddevek (RED-eh-vek)—a warden in the Outriders. One of the few gifted with tracking. He rarely uses his last name, Tain.

Riverton—a city adjacent to Journey's Bend in the Southlands.

Rolsh—the margrave in Riverton.

Rona (ROE-nuh) Scrivson—the aunt to Bryndor and Lluthean in the Southlands.

Runefather/mother—an adult zeniphile in Aarindorn who assumes a semi-formal relationship with a gifted child to uphold the cultural norms of society. This person is often involved in training and the rituals such as the Rite of Revealing.

Runeling—the gifted child who is the recipient of the mentoring relationship with a runefather/mother.

Sadeen Tunkle (suh-DEEN TUN-kull)—a townswoman in Journey's Bend.

Sender—a zeniphile who can telepathically communicate with another sender. In the entire history of Aarindorn, senders have always been born as twins, triplets, etc. As such they are rare.

Shass—the former servant to the Volencia and Mallic at their estate in Callish.

Shaveen (shah-VEEN)—one of a set of five albino quintuplet zeniphile senders who lived in the time of the Cataclysm. Their arca prime gifts them with the ability to telepathically communicate with each other over any distance.

Shelwyn River (SHELL-win)—a river in the Southlands.

Sheshla (SHESH-luh)—a butterfly named in the Valley of the Cloud Walkers.

Sifter—a zeniphile who can recall people or events with an identic memory.

Steckle (STEK-ul)—hired hand and handyman at the Bashing Ram in Journey's Bend.

Stone's Grasp—the castle and capital city of Aarindorn.

Tellend (TELL-end)—a family of farmers in Journey's Bend.

- Emile (eh-MEEL)—wise matron of the family.
- Harland—son to Emile and Markum.
- Markum—Emile's husband.

Timson (TIM-son)—a stable boy at the Abbey on the Mount.

Tomlek (TOM-lek)—a rector in Journey's Bend.

Tovnik (TAHV-nik)—a medic among the Outriders.

Umbral—a.k.a. shadowmen, creatures wandering the Drift and wielders of nadir ruled by the forces there. Their origins are poorly understood, but they are likely abrogators who died while steeped in the frenze and are now enslaved by forces in the Drift.

Vaeda (VAY-duh)—Southland name for the goddess embodied as the red moon.

Vardell Becks—an assassin hired by the Lacuna from Aarindorn. He is gifted with gusting.

Vesta—servant to Mallic and Volencia in their estate in Callish.

Voshna (VOSH-nuh)—Southland name of the goddess embodied as the blue moon.

The Animals, Elements, and Plants of Karsk

Aarindin (AIR-in-din)—a prized stock of horses bred for their combination of stamina, speed, and intelligence and preserved for use by the Outriders, a branch of the Aarindorian military and elite classes. The breed standard are a jet black or ebony color. They can use zenith to grip a chosen or preferred rider and are most often ridden bareback for this reason.

- Zippy—Reddevek's loyal steed.

Bandle root (BAND-ul)—a.k.a. stilben root in the Southlands or dreamsong among the Cloud Walkers. The herb can be steeped into tea or ingested raw. Low doses cause sedation, while concentrated dosing leads to dissociation or temporary paralysis and numbness. The herb smells and tastes like anise or black licorice.

Bear claw leaf—used to treat minor pain and fever.

Billow tree—a common tree along riverbanks in the Southlands. The tree produces seed pods with a woody outer husk of smooth, marbled brown. After a time, once exposed to water, the husk splits to release wispy seeds of white fluff, which billow into the air.

Blue trumpet—a vine that grows in the Borderlands and can be used to aid breathing/wheezing.

Broga's beard—a flowering plant that lives on its ability to absorb concentrated strands of zenith. Broga was a fabled mountain god from the Cloud Walkers, the native region of this plant.

Darksun—a flowering plant that grows wild in the Borderlands and can treat the flux.

Embertang—referred to as embertang in the Northlands and devil's tail in the Southlands, an antiseptic, hemostatic oil that, especially if undiluted, causes severe caustic pain even to casual skin contact. The less potent devil's tail is found as more of an oily resin.

Gellseed root—given with blackberry tincture to treat diarrhea.

Heh-gava—a powder used to treat a cough or wheezing.

Kaliphora—antiemetic.

Kevash—a juicy, tangy fruit that grows all year in the Valley of the Cloud Walkers.

Maedra's pitchers—a plant that blooms south of the Korjinth Mountains and can be steeped into a tea that dulls pain and improves healing. Scholars suspect that the tea somehow enhances a body's ability to absorb zenith.

Nettle tea—a diuretic.

Resco—a distillate of wine akin to whiskey.

Vivith—an illegal stimulant. Brewed as a tea or smoked, it is highly addictive and often leads to paranoia. The smoke smells like pine resin.

Weeping bark—used to treat minor pain and fever.

Wolvryn—creatures related to wolves but much larger, far more intelligent.

- Boru (bo-ROO)—male companion to Bryndor.
- Ghetti—matriarch of the pack in the Valley of the Cloud Walkers.
- Neska (NES-kuh)—crafty female companion to Lluthean.

Don't miss out!

Visit the website below and you can sign up to receive emails whenever Lance VanGundy publishes a new book. There's no charge and no obligation.

https://books2read.com/r/B-A-LQHL-AOZTB

BOOKS 2 READ

Connecting independent readers to independent writers.

Did you love *Awakened Runes*? Then you should read *Runes of the Prime*[1] by Lance VanGundy!

[2]

"What kind of home are we returning to that a man has to be able to defend himself with the sword?" These heavy thoughts preoccupy Bryndor, who is trapped in the Valley of the Cloud Walkers. Violent supernatural storms devastate the summit of the Korjinth Mountains, insulating and isolating any in the valley. He uses the time to train with the sword, to understand his wolvryn companion and something of his place in the world.

In Aarindorn, Karragin leads Outriders on missions against grotvonen. But something else lurks among the hordes under the mountains, something that hints at the resurgence of an evil thought long ago vanquished.

---

1. https://books2read.com/u/baDzkq

2. https://books2read.com/u/baDzkq

Not all challenges rise from the arcane. The regent of Aarindorn struggles to hold together a kingdom threatened by dark forces without and the Lacuna within. His scribe, Ksenia, bears witness to the growing tide of unrest. Despite her desire to remain above the politics in Stone's Grasp, she finds herself steeped in its controversies.

When all of these forces collide, who will survive the devastation? Can the runes of the prime channel enough zenith to shape the future of Karsk?

Read more at https://www.lancevangundy.com/.

Also by Lance VanGundy

The Rune Fire Cycle
Awakened Runes
Runes of the Prime

Watch for more at https://www.lancevangundy.com/.

About the Author

Lance grew up in central Iowa, the product of public education and good parents. He attended Cornell College in Mount Vernon, Iowa where he obtained a Bachelor of Special Studies with anthropology and biology majors. Then he attended medical school at the University of Iowa. He has lived in central Iowa with his wife of more than thirty years where they raised three daughters. There he continues to practice emergency medicine and the whimsical art of escapism with all things Scifi and fantasy for as much as his wife can tolerate... that is significant... He is, after all, a very lucky man.

Read more at https://www.lancevangundy.com/.